Thank You
...for buying this book.

There are many people who've helped me get this far on my journey as an author. Please read the acknowledgments section at the end of this book.

I'm already working on my second book. I'd love you to read that too. If you would like to join my valued team of ARC reviewers and get an opportunity to read and review the next book before it is published please get in touch via the contact page on my website.

www.armstrong-taylor.co.uk

First published in 2023 by Tim Armstrong Taylor.

British Library Cataloguing in Publication Data.

A catalogue record for this book is available from the British Library.

ISBN: 978-1-7393076-7-7 (hardback)
ISBN: 978-1-7393076-8-4 (paperback)
ISBN: 978-1-7393076-9-1 (ebook)

Typeset in Minion

Editor: Bryony Sutherland

Cover design and typesetting: Jamie Keenan

www.armstrong-taylor.co.uk

An URN for the WORSE

TIM ARMSTRONG TAYLOR

An URN
for the WORSE

PROLOGUE

Tuesday 8th July, 1986

IT WAS THE INFINITE calmness of the beach that struck him. Below the bank of flinty pebbles lay the most serene, geometrically flat surface in the world. No matter how many families dug trenches, built sandcastles or sculpted mermaids with seaweed hair interrupting the purity of its sublime flatness, the sea would always wash back up upon the shore, an immense watery blanket erasing all evidence of sandy construction and gifting a flawless blank canvas to the next group of creators.

Nick loved being the first person to leave footprints across the sand. It gave him the same pleasure as taking that first spoonful of a newly set raspberry jelly or that first dive into a jar of midnight-black Marmite. He relished the way his feet sank, encouraging water to seep into his footprints, the sun sparkling on the wetness of the sand around them. He imagined that people had done this for millennia, enjoying the same degree of satisfaction, though not quite so long for jelly and Marmite.

He found the perfect spot for his sandcastle and knelt down to begin. It was far enough away from other families arriving to claim their section of beach and wasn't in any immediate or obvious path to the beach, and it was too near the breakwater for swimmers to venture. The only risk would be from dogs. It was early in the day and locals were already walking dogs on the beach, but they were some way off.

It didn't take Nick long to build the most elaborate sandcastle he'd ever imagined. He loved building sandcastles and had spent some of his pocket money on a sturdy bucket and spade and a few paper flags. His father had promised to help but had instead stayed at the guest house to look through some business papers, even though it was his father's birthday. He'd said he'd be down as soon as he could. Nick hoped he would be in time to see it and add some finishing touches. He'd love to share this moment with his dad.

Nick's castle had castellated walls, a motte and bailey, a bridge at the entrance and high towers at each corner. It was surrounded by a deep moat and a long trench ran out towards the sea. From certain angles the trench looked like it stretched to infinity. He imagined that the castle would be inhabited by a splendid royal family, who protected their subjects against invasion. Their army would sally forth across the drawbridge and see off any threat.

To his horror, he realised that any tiny army emerging from the castle would be no match for the approaching peril of an enormous golden beast, bent on destruction. A large playful Labrador pursued an errant tennis ball, which had just bounced and narrowly missed his castle's keep, taking a small section of wall with it. He turned to see that the projectile had been thrown by his mischievous older sister,

Tracey. She stood with her hands raised in a gesture of denial, even though she was the only other person on their section of the beach.

Fudge bounded forward at great speed but then stopped dead, just short of the castle, and began barking. She had been in the sea and was still waterlogged. The air was warm but the sea still cold, and Nick didn't fancy a freezing shower.

'No, Fudgie,' he screamed as she began to shake, head to tail.

Sparkling droplets of water flew through the air, narrowly missing Nick and landing on his sandcastle where they glistened like jewels, just for an instant, before dissolving.

Despite this moment of chaos Nick felt blissfully happy. Being on the beach in Frinton, with his annoying sister, his dog and his mum watching from the promenade was his happy place. If only his dad had been there too, it would have been perfect.

1

Thirty-six years later
Wednesday 15th June

CONSCIOUSNESS CREPT UPON Nick Swift like a slug with ME. Barry was barking downstairs and probably needed to go out before he woke all the dogs on the west side of Welwyn Garden City. Nick would be the one who would have to get up to let him out. The kids would sleep through a jumbo jet landing on the roof; Barry's barking wouldn't come close to disturbing their impenetrable teen slumber. His wife Louise lay next to him, snoring inoffensively, unshifted by the hollow, yet strangely penetrating ancient woofs emanating from Barry's fourteen-year-old vocal cords.

If Nick didn't get up within the next thirty seconds, Barry might just lay a poo trail through the hallway. Or he'd do what he'd done a few mornings before: take a dump impossibly close to the kitchen door. When Nick opened it to enter the kitchen, the spoils of Barry's defecation jammed in the gap between the bottom of the door and the floor, painting the flagstones with an earthy-coloured stainbow. This was followed by Barry's pensively laboured footprints through the foul stripes and into the hallway carpet with four-point monotonic pointillism from each paw. The memory was incentive enough for Nick to overcome his forty-nine-year-old body's insistence that it wasn't time to get up yet, and he made it to his feet, to a chorus of clicking from his joints reminiscent of the street fight from *West Side Story*.

Nick's day wasn't due to start for another fifteen minutes. Six a.m., when the first of his human alarms went off, was when the burden of his responsibilities hit him hardest. He didn't want to have to get up and deal with domestics; he wanted to get up and go straight to work. He had a company to save, his company, and whilst he kidded himself that things were fine and going according to plan, the knot in his stomach didn't agree with him. He checked his emails on his phone.

Oh God. Where to start?

Barry's barking summoned him once more. At times like this, Nick entertained dark thoughts about the ageing hound who had recently turned from a Labrador into a liability. Smelly, deaf and blind with little left to offer the world, Barry had taken on many of the qualities of Nick's father, Charlie. Each time Barry barked, Nick forced himself to remember the happy times; halcyon days in sepia playback. Nick didn't have many happy memories of his father, and neither would the staff in the care home where Charlie now lived. They would therefore not have the same patience with Charlie as Nick had with Barry. Nick knew the barks were a warning Barry was about to mess himself if he didn't get someone's attention promptly, something which, no doubt, would soon come to Nick's dad.

Nick eased himself down the stairs like a new knight in his first suit of unoiled armour, his tendons and muscles not yet as awake as his brain. Or, for that matter, his ears, which were receiving an aural assault increasing in intensity the closer he got to Barry.

He took great care not to step on the second from bottom stair as it creaked more loudly than his joints and had the power to wake next door's identically vociferous genetic mix of a bullmastiff and toy poodle, which his neighbours said was a mastidoodle and, to their constant annoyance and his constant amusement, he called a masiff-poo. Barry's barking burgeoned with enthusiasm until the shadowy intruder in his hallway came close enough to identify himself with a familiar smell; that of his old master. Now Barry's woofs ceased and his tail swept left and right, expressing his unbridled joy at seeing his favourite person in the world and realising that all he wanted was company and not a poo.

In an instant Nick's bad temper evaporated, as he was assaulted with affection from Barry. The sheer volume of love that the old dog was capable of expressing wrapped him in a high-TOG duvet of emotion, and Nick found himself sitting on the floor hugging man's best friend and feeling guilty about the dark fantasy of the final trip to the vets he'd been planning only moments earlier. Barry's advancing years required him to crouch next to his master in the manner of an elephant trying to perch on a dozen eggs without breaking them. With a warm and heavily dog breath-scented exhalation, Barry settled down and the house fell into a blissful silence.

Lying across his master's lap whilst having his ears stroked, Barry adjusted his position, forcing his master to lean backwards onto the trigger stair, which dutifully creaked, setting off the neighbour's massif-poos and catalytically drawing all the neighbouring dogs in Attimore Road, Elmwood and Handside Lane into a canine dawn chorus.

2

ANTHONY DYEMA WAS DRESSED in his finest suit; a new, crisp starched pink shirt; the Windsor knot in his old club tie a little tighter than usual; his favourite cufflinks holding his double cuffs together; pressed trousers with a strong crease, just how he liked them; and a waistcoat which had always been a little too snug, but not today. His jacket, which completed the heavy wool mix trio, draped rather more loosely over his body than it had for most of his life. The three-piece suit was far too heavy for the current weather, but Tony didn't mind.

His socks were made of bamboo, a new fabric he'd embraced later in life for the freshness and softness it afforded him, having spent so much time on his feet in his Hatton Garden shop. There he'd worked for many more years than he needed to, refusing to retire, being a celebrated member of the jewellery community and a highly respected authority on diamonds, rubies and sapphires.

Tony Dyema was a man of few words and today even fewer. Though he could wax lyrical for hours about the beauty of gemstones, today he said nothing, and not by choice.

Tony Dyema, currently lying peacefully in his mid-priced coffin in an undertaker's parlour in the centre of Hatfield, would never again speak of the wonders of diamonds, the only gemstones made of a single element, being 99.95% carbon, formed at immense pressure 100 miles below the surface of the earth, as he liked to remind his customers, though most of them were only interested in price and how well their diamonds caught the light. There were of course the young men buying rings for their prospective brides, full of hope as he had once been and, more recently, same sex couples. The more the merrier as far as Tony was concerned. But whilst he loved diamonds, he wondered why people weren't more captivated by rubies and sapphires, his true passion.

Tony's wife Valerie had been looking forward to another diamond for their sixtieth wedding anniversary. Considering her husband's profession, she had been displeased with the engagement stone he'd picked out for her. This, coupled with the disappointment of no honeymoon in Florence, which he'd alluded to and never delivered on, meant that their marriage had started off on the wrong foot and never really recovered. Valerie could have been happy. Instead, she ended every day in an alcohol-induced haze of anaesthesia.

All the other jewellers she'd met seemed happier with their more affluent lifestyles. Valerie did own one of the only swimming pools in the Woodhall area of Welwyn Garden City, but that was already installed in the garden when they bought the house. Having had no children themselves, and since that unfortunate incident involving their nephew, Ray, it had not seen much use.

Few people appreciated diamonds the way Tony did, and that was why, along with countless rubies and sapphires, all the high-quality jewels he'd acquired over the years had never been sold. Unknown to Valerie, he'd kept them instead, sewing them into little pouches that he hid, not in a safe, but in the lining of his favourite three-piece suit, which normally hung in his wardrobe. He removed the pouches on the rare occasions that he had the suit cleaned. He would then revel in their beauty before returning them to the security of his suit lining. The suit he had chosen to be buried in.

Tony had ensured that his prized jewels would remain with him in the ground, long after his flesh and bones had turned to dust. In the highly unlikely event that anyone ever found them, then good luck to them. Whoever did could keep them all. All £5 million worth of them. His will said so; he'd wished he could be present at its reading, just to see Valerie and Ray's faces.

After Tony died, Valerie decided she would have a new ring after all. Something to mark her new life and sixty years since her wedding. To save money, she'd sold her husband's burial plot for rather more money than she'd hoped. He would be cremated instead. Together with Tony's life insurance policy, Valerie had enough for a decent ring and two weeks of luxury in Florence. She would have her Roman Holiday at last.

3

'FOR FUCK'S SAKE. IT'S like a bloody war zone in here.' Chaos reigned in the kitchen and Nick was hit by a wall of sound blasting from the TV in the snug, just off the dining area. Something had been spilt on the hob and the ensuing streaming cloud had created a smokescreen worthy of a battlefield and had set the fire alarm off.

'Is no one else bothered by this irritating noise?'

'There's an irritating noise in the kitchen now,' Louise muttered under her breath.

There were more people present than Nick anticipated. Was that his daughter's boyfriend popping in early? He had better not have spent the night. Nick stretched up with an accompanying dad grunt and silenced the smoke alarm to a deafening reset bleep.

'Jesus, that's loud.'

He had just under ten minutes to cook himself a decent breakfast, as no one else would because they all liked to cook different things for themselves. The disorder before him was painful to behold. There was a mountain of dishes next to the sink. Hopefully, in there somewhere was a semi-clean saucepan, as he had a taste for some quick, creamy scrambled eggs. He salivated at the thought. He'd spotted the last piece of sourdough at the back of the cupboard last night and was looking forward to it. Toasted to perfection with a golden crust and white fluffy centre, covered in melting butter. Surely, as it required someone to search for more than a couple of seconds, the bread would still be there. There was no simplicity at mealtimes, no let's-all-eat-the-same-thing to save on food, washing up, water and power. No. His seventeen-year-old daughter Charlotte was going through yet another vegan phase, which meant she had to cook her breakfast in a pan that had never seen any meat products. Nick was certain she'd come home from a night out two days ago having eaten a guilty bacon cheeseburger, but her part-time activist diet couldn't be debated without a massive drama and accusations of his inherent fascism due to his age and unenlightened politics. What this meant for breakfast was that everyone would cook for themselves that morning and would make a mess and not bloody clean it up, and he would have to just deal with it.

'Is it too much to hope that anyone knows the whereabouts of a clean saucepan?'

Silence. No one seemed to hear or see him. Had he stepped into a new Netflix drama where he lived in one reality and everyone else in another?

Louise sat at the breakfast bar, eating an elaborate concoction of eggs, smoked salmon and avocado all nestled on sourdough toast.

'Was that the last slice?'

No answer. It clearly was. Bugger. He'd have to have some plastic toast surviving from last week's shop, irradiated to last until doomsday. At least he could bury it in eggs. Unless…

'I sincerely hope there are some eggs left.'

No one responded. Barry lumbered past and peered up at him with pitying eyes. Could Barry see him through his cloudy cataracts? Barry's interaction at least confirmed to Nick that he was part of this reality and not in another dimension. Or was Barry a conduit, able to see into Nick's dimension? No one else at that moment seemed able to. Louise hadn't yet looked up from her breakfast as she was busy comparing what one of her Instagram friends had had for their breakfast. She decided that her breakfast was superior, and once she'd sprinkled some cracked black pepper on it, she photographed and uploaded her winning entry, until seconds later when another friend posted something even more spectacular. Jesus, even breakfast was now a socially competitive event.

Nick opened the fridge, avoiding touching the part of the handle that had been smeared in ketchup some days ago. He found an egg.

'There's only one egg! One fucking egg. There were at least half a dozen yesterday.'

His wife had clearly had two and Charlotte was eating some sort of muesli-cum-porridge concoction, which meant that there should be four eggs left.

'Even without the help of a spreadsheet, I know that six eggs minus Mum's two is four but all I see here is one fucking egg. Where are the other three?'

He managed to get Charlotte's attention.

'Have you had them?'

'I'm a vegan. Go figure.'

'Today you might be a vegan—'

'What did you say?' She fixed him with a stare worthy of

the Queen of Narnia and for a moment he turned to stone; the ubiquitous rhetorical question posed before an outbreak of violence.

'Nothing. I didn't say nothing. Er, anything, I mean. I couldn't hear you over the television.' His excuse was pathetic but after an uncomfortable pause she showed him mercy on this occasion and turned to sit next to her brother and watch whatever garbage it was that passed for morning entertainment. Nick weaved his way across the kitchen floor avoiding sports bags, three pairs of shoes, one welly boot, a water bottle and a patch of something sticky and unidentifiable before finally arriving at the dishwasher. He had decided to drop the recent conflict's negative energy and think positively about his next task. Through the power of this positive thought he would find a clean saucepan inside the dishwasher in which to boil his egg.

He prised open the dishwasher door only to discover it was mid-cycle and it showered him in hot, chemically-infused water.

'Oh, for fuck's sake.'

No saucepan. He slammed the door shut and the dishwasher returned to its business, ignoring him, much like his disinterested family.

'Please. Stop. Shouting.' Louise had at last put down her phone and recognised his existence in her dimension. 'Don't forget that it's Harry's twelfth birthday tomorrow and you promised to come to his party at Laser Kombat in Stevenage. Don't let him down.'

'Of course I haven't forgotten about the party. Why would I forget my own son's birthday party?'

'Yeah, and don't forget you've promised to help me out with my fundraiser for St Francis,' Charlotte called out from the snug. She was being nice to him now that she wanted something.

'I will try and help,' he said, 'but don't forget I'm a busy man with a business to run and a family to support.'

'Your mum keeps calling too,' Louise reminded him. 'She says you haven't been to see your father in hospital, and he's been in almost a week this time.'

Fuck. Twin pangs of guilt lurched through Nick's stomach like a pair of fighting eels. This in turn annoyed him. His mum was playing games with his head again. Trying to make him feel guilty.

His father never called him, never bothered about him. Was not interested in the kids and how they were doing. The last call he'd had from his dad had been before he'd gone into his care home. He'd needed help with something to do with his broadband speed. He only ever called Nick when he had a tech query or to let him know that Tracey required help with something.

The noise from the TV was getting too much. Nick asked what an earth they were watching and to his horror saw that he recognised the man on the YouTube channel, which Charlotte had cast from her iPhone to their smart TV. The children never watched terrestrial channels now. The screen in the snug was now an Orwellian violation, probably watching them through the camera the kids had insisted he buy on Amazon, as everyone else had one so they couldn't possibly live without one either.

'That's your Uncle Keith, isn't it, Dad?' asked Harry.

'Yes. Yes, it is,' he confessed. 'Your great-uncle. All six foot of him.'

'Grandad is tall too. You're only five foot ten and a half, aren't you, Dad?'

'I'm five foot eleven.'

'Maybe you'd look a bit taller if you were fit, like Uncle Keith.'

'He's got over 984k subscribers.' Charlotte was impressed. 'Why don't we ever see him?'

'Yeah. I'd love to meet him,' Harry continued. 'Mum says he only lives in Redbourn.'

'Well, it's complicated. Grandad and Uncle Keith have never really got along. They're like chalk and cheese. Uncle Keith is a free spirit and never wanted to be tied down, I guess. Your grandad, on the other hand, is the opposite. He always liked certainty and security. He worked long hours, often evenings and weekends. Grandma always said he was married to his work. He never had any spare time for friends or family.'

Charlotte and Harry gave him both the same knowing look.

'He's well famous,' a deep alien voice interrupted from behind Nick. 'And he looks after himself, he's in good shape. He must work out.' Charlotte's nameless boyfriend had resurfaced from somewhere with six pieces of toast and three eggs in three egg cups. The mystery of the missing eggs cracked. Nick was now feeding a third bloody child and this one was a man-child with the appetite of Godzilla.

'Once he hits one million subscribers something will happen,' Godzilla said.

'Lots more people will get to enjoy his pearls of wisdom,' Charlotte exclaimed. 'This is brilliant, Dad, you should watch it. On Great Uncle Keith's channel—'

'*Karmic Keith's Motorcycle Mantras*,' Harry shouted.

'—he reviews motorcycles, paraphernalia and popular motorcycle touring routes whilst dispensing Buddhist-like advice on how to live your life. He's becoming a legend and nearly one million people are benefiting from his deep insight into life.'

Nick snorted. 'You mean one million people will be bored by his platitudes.'

'His what?' Godzilla didn't understand. He thought a platitude was an amphibious creature. He then proceeded to consume another egg, slightly troubled by the fact that platitudes laid eggs too.

Nick reached for the remote control to silence Uncle Keith. Charlotte stopped him. 'No, Dad. Not yet. He's about to sign off with his catchphrase. His catchphrase is sick.'

With a dramatic flick of his long silver ponytail, Keith turned to the camera, as Clint Eastwood turned to his defeated criminals in the *Dirty Harry* movies, and in an impossibly low and gravelly voice intoned, 'Remember. It's the ride that matters. Not the destination.'

Charlotte and Harry echoed the sentiment joyfully and were joined nanoseconds later by Godzilla. The room resounded with the mantra. Uncle Keith disappeared from the screen and was replaced by an advert for erectile dysfunction medication.

4

'HOW MUCH? FOR FUCK'S SAKE.'

You had to take out a small mortgage to park at a hospital now. Did the price of each parking space go up the fewer that were available? Nick had searched for a whole five minutes in the multistorey car park at the Lister Hospital in Stevenage, before squeezing his beloved Tango-Red Audi Q2 in between two other SUV tanks. Surely the money wasn't going to the hospital; it was going into the pocket of some unscrupulous investors as part of a bloody Blairite PFI scheme, when it should be going to buy new scanners and train new medical staff. Nick could hear the words in his head as clearly as if Charlotte was saying them.

He had to admit that he wished he'd been part of one of those schemes, working in banking and finance, rather than risking his entire future developing SwifTech (UK) Data Solutions Ltd, his integrated web-based software service for small businesses. He should've thought bigger. But his degree in computer science and subsequent two-year MBA could well mean that he would reach his goal of selling his business to a much bigger corporation, like PlanIT-UK, owned by the permanently tanned, chiselled and fragranced Jeff Silverman, whose ego was almost as big as his LinkedIn profile.

Jeff Silverman, ex-marine, former-Olympic swimmer and bronze medallist, motivational coach, entrepreneur of the year and owner of one of the fastest-growing tech companies in the UK, had the audacity that morning to get his PA to call Nick to postpone their meeting to the following day. Jeff allegedly apologised but had decided to stay on another day at his Florida home to play golf before hurricane season started. Nick would understand, surely? Priorities, yeah?

Fuck his priorities, thought Nick. He *probably needs to polish his little bronze medal to match his tan. Shouldn't take him too long. They don't take as long to polish as gold ones.* He took a deep breath. Not the best state of mind in which to see his father.

Ignoring the sinking feeling in his stomach, Nick took the chip coin from the machine at the barrier and pocketed it. He'd try not to stay too long at the hospital. He needed to get Silverman, or should that be Bronzeman, to buy his company. How was Nick going to afford to take a year's sabbatical before starting his next venture if Silverman didn't buy him out? If Silverman didn't buy his company soon, he might not have a company to sell. He'd spent too long concentrating on product development and not enough time on what it was all costing. Brian Matthews had a different view. He could hear boring Brian's nasal monotone echoing around his head: 'It's quite simple, Nick. What comes in needs to be bigger than what goes out.' It reminded him of the platitudes delivered by his uncle, Karmic Keith.

Nick knew he should listen to what Brian had to say. Nick had worked with Brian for some years now. Brian was an experienced Chief Financial Officer, offering his services to a number of companies like Nick's on a freelance basis. He'd seen the potential in Nick's business and had invested in it in its early days, receiving a ten per cent stake. He occasionally checked to see if his investment was doing well. But some personal issues and other commitments had meant Nick hadn't seen much of Brian over the last couple of years, until recently when they'd discussed the preparation of the business for sale.

Which ward was Dad in? He hadn't been to this hospital recently and had no idea how to find his way around. He checked his phone and saw a message from his mum.

ABOUT TIME. HURRY AS DOCTORS WILL BE HERE SOON. BLACKBERRY WARD. LEVEL SIX. FOLLOW PURPLE LINES.

It annoyed him that she always typed in capitals as if she were shouting at him. He'd better get a move on.

If he hadn't had such a distant relationship with his father, Nick might almost feel sorry for him. After all, he'd put up with his mum for long enough. He'd worked hard all his life and for what? To repeatedly bail Nick's sister out for the last eight years until he'd almost run out of money.

Nick foolishly thought his mum might be pleased to see him, as he'd responded to her request to visit in record time. She didn't need to know that he was only there because Silverman had postponed their meeting.

Nick dashed into a WHSmith, conveniently located on the ground floor of the hospital, grabbed a paper for his father and can of Coke for himself, and followed the faded pinkish-purple line. He was on track to get in and out quickly now, what could possibly go wrong?

After fifteen minutes of wandering around the hospital, with two unplanned return trips to Smiths, it took Nick a further five minutes of explaining to convince the two psychiatric nurses, one of whom was very big and had an extremely strong grip, that the line he'd followed was more purple than pink and that he wasn't there for a self-referral, he was trying to find his father who was in BLACKBERRY WARD on the sixth floor.

No need to shout the ward's name, they told him. After Nick calmed down, they pointed him in the right direction. He was to focus on his breath, taking slow steps and not veering from the mauve line. There was no purple line. He'd been following the magenta line which had, they had to admit, a hue of purple.

Once they were satisfied that Nick posed no threat, he was buzzed through the sliding door where the mauve line ended abruptly. He stepped into the dim, silent corridor and breathed in the smell of antiseptic, his footsteps echoing off the polished floors and dark hardwood 1960s doors. There seemed to be more doors than it was possible there were rooms or cupboards behind them, and none of them had any indication as to what might lurk within. He kept walking until he reached a T junction. Only two choices here and one direction was labelled Bluebell. The other had a missing sign. It had to be Blackberry.

He approached the nurses' station in the hope of attracting someone's attention. After all, he'd just been buzzed in, and they would no doubt direct him to the right place. No one looked at him for what seemed like an eternity, then his mum appeared from a bay on the left. Behind her thick glasses she looked worried.

'Here I am, Mum, where's Dad?'

'I can see you're here. He's in there. You've got about forty-five minutes until the doctors come and see him on their rounds,' said Barbara.

They stood for a moment, staring at each other. Nick felt deeply uncomfortable. The truth was that he hadn't spent much time with his mum in the last few years either. But that was the way it was for everyone, wasn't it? You grew up, left home and had a family of your own. Except for Tracey, who still spent long periods of time living at home and was back again after her sixth relationship had broken down. Mum said that everyone was worried about Dad as he hadn't spoken all day. He'd been improving the last day or so but now seemed to be taking a dip again. 'Your dad's covered in tubes,' she explained. 'Quite a sight. He's on oxygen and has a saline drip to rehydrate him. The home obviously wasn't making him drink enough and he got a bladder infection. He looks like he's given up. Now he's got pneumonia. They say…' She stopped, choked up, unable to continue.

Nick froze. He didn't know what to do. His mum was clearly in pain, and it disturbed him to see it. He hated to see anyone in that kind of pain. But this was his mother and there seemed to be a gulf between them, one he felt unable to cross. He was about to try when, to his great relief, Tracey made an appearance from the family room. She was looking unusually well and holding two cups of coffee. She had kind eyes, and despite the difficult life she'd led, didn't have a bad bone in her body. She acknowledged Nick with a brief warm smile and then invited Barbara back into the family room, as it was now free again. The family that had been there had wished her luck before leaving, hugging each other, and sobbing for their loss. This unnecessarily detailed explanation of why the room was empty seemed to upset Nick's mum even further but she was happy to accept Tracey's comforting embrace, taking care to avoid the two flimsy paper cups of steaming hot coffee. Tracey suggested that Nick go and sit with Dad whilst she and Mum had a coffee. Mum and Tracey entered the family room, arm in arm. Apparently, it had an amazing view over the A1M.

Nick stepped into the bay from which his mother had appeared but couldn't see his father. He returned to the nurses' station and this time was greeted by a larger-than-life nurse by the name of Malika.

'Hello, you must be Nick. Charlie was hoping you would come. I'm delighted to see you here. Your mother said you would not come at all,' she sang cheerily in a resonant Somalian contralto.

His mother's comments weren't surprising but what his father had said astonished him.

Malika came and took his arm. 'Come with me, young man. I will take you to see him. He has something he needs to tell you.'

In an instant Nick transformed into a little boy. The illusion was aided by the fact that Malika had far more presence than him, both physically and energy-wise. He willingly followed her into the bay where his father was sleeping.

'There he is, my darling. Go and give him a little kiss and tell him you love him.'

Two things Nick had no memory of ever having done and certainly not since he learned to tie his own shoes.

Nick had not recognised Charlie when he'd first looked into the room. Now he saw that the man before him was indeed a version of his father and, although he didn't resemble the image of the near-death trauma victim his mother had painted, it took some moments for Nick to place his father in the shrunken person who now sat propped up before him. How long had it been since he'd last seen him?

He'd lost so much weight. His normally rotund physique had wilted, his once chubby cheeks were hollowed out and his shoulders and arms bore no muscle. It looked as if all his bulk had slipped and he now resembled a shrink-wrapped pear.

'It's okay,' said Malika. 'You can sit with him.'

Charlie was starting to slump to one side of his pillows. Malika helped him sit up again. His breath was laboured, and Nick could hear the rattle of pneumonia from deep within his lungs. He had a tube attached to his nose to give him oxygen and he was hooked up to a drip, as was everyone else in this ward of four, with one recently vacated bed now being prepared for its next transitory occupant.

Nick sat down on the high-backed easy-clean armchair next to his father and tried to make himself comfortable. The chair clearly wasn't designed for this purpose.

Without looking he sensed that Malika had spirited silently back to her station, leaving him alone with his father.

Charlie had always been a proud man but now, dressed in a hospital gown which offered little in the way of comfort or style, he just about managed to maintain his dignity. Not that it looked like he cared. Wisps of beard had been missed in his recent shave and his nails were vampire long.

Nick leant forward and whispered hello to his father.

'Is she gone?' Charlie's words were barely audible, his tone extremely breathy. But he had spoken.

'You can talk!' Nick was startled by his father's waking. 'I thought you were asleep. Mum says you haven't spoken at all for a couple of days.'

'She just keeps talking about God.'

Charlie's breathing was laboured but he didn't appear to be as close to death's door as Barbara seemed to think. Not that Nick knew anything about death, unless he had died and was living in purgatory. The way things were going with his business, it felt like it.

'Your mother's rather upset, but I needed a bit of peace. She just sits there and sobs, asking me not to leave her at the same time as saying that Jesus will be waiting for me with open arms.' Charlie coughed, unable to clear his lungs. 'I was confused by this at first as Jesus is one of the South American orderlies here. He brings me my meals sometimes. It was bread and fish last night. No wine, sadly. She keeps asking me to say hello to her mum and dad when I get up *there*. If there is anything after this, they are the last two people I want to see.' He started to laugh but was cut short with another unsatisfactory and arresting cough.

He seemed so weak. Mucus was gathering in the corners of his mouth, and it needed to be dealt with. Nick looked around for help. He spotted a small kit of sugar cube-sized sponges on sticks whose purpose was clear. Nick picked up a sponge and started to wipe the corners of his father's mouth. His father had clearly had this done a number of times as no objection to the indignity was raised. The act was intimate and uncomfortable in equal measure, as Nick was caring for his father in a way that his father had never cared for him.

'I'm sorry,' Charlie said.

'It's okay, Dad, don't apologise.'

'No, not this. This can't be helped. I'm sorry I've not been there for you. I never have.'

What? Could Nick get that in writing?

Nick hadn't known what to expect when he came in, but this certainly was not it. He was hoping for a perfunctory visit of mild pleasantries. When he'd heard that his father wasn't talking, he'd been relieved. He'd planned to sit here, do his duty as quickly as possible and leave. So far this had been the longest conversation he'd had with his father in years and they were only a few sentences in. His father had never been one for apologies and self-analysis. Was this his death-bed moment? Had his body been taken over by a woke angel, intent on giving Nick the father-son experience he ought to have?

'Where did it all go?' Charlie whispered.

'Where did what go?'

'The time, the years. I need help. To make amends, to do the things I should have done. I want your help.'

What the fuck? This was an alien. 'With what, Dad?'

'I want to write a list.'

23

'Oh no, not a bucket list, surely?'

'Yes and no.'

'But isn't it a bit late for that?'

'It may be. All the same, I want you to help me write one.'

Nick scratched his head in dismay. 'Bucket lists are nonsense. I can't see you swimming with dolphins. You've seen the pyramids and been in a hot air balloon, you must remember that? Mum jarred her back and had to stay in bed for a week. What else is there to do?'

'I want you to write down a list, please.'

'Look, I'll happily write down a list, but I can't really—'

'Just oblige me. Please.'

Nick searched in the drawer and cupboard but found nothing to write on or with. When Nick suggested he create a Google Document on his phone his father objected and consequently, for the third time that day, Nick took another trip to the ground floor to WHSmith. On his way out of the ward his mum accosted him and asked him how his father was.

'He's fine. He's still sleeping peacefully.' Nick didn't feel the need to tell her that he could talk and in doing so felt complicit in his father's deception. When he explained he was going to get a proper cup of coffee on the ground floor before coming to sit a while longer with Dad, Tracey decided it was a good time to take Mum home for a rest. Dad wasn't going to die today. He'd better not, as Barbara would never forgive him if Charlie died without her present. She'd probably accuse Nick of killing him.

When Nick returned to his father's bed, he found him

propped up in a much more comfortable position. He seemed ready to engage in conversation and the compiling of his bucket list. Progress was understandably slow but within half an hour they had discussed the merits of a number of activities. Whale watching was ruled out on the grounds that you'd probably spend many hours getting cold and wet and not seeing anything anyway. They agreed that swimming with dolphins didn't actually mean that you would spontaneously find a pod of dolphins, happy to oblige out in the open sea; it would more likely mean going to Florida to swim with an incarcerated and depressed dolphin having to jump through hoops (quite literally) to pay its board and lodging, when it would rather be free. Nick's father revealed that he'd often felt like that.

What surprised Nick was not so much what didn't make the list as what did. Nick's dad had always wanted to learn to dance properly, so he wouldn't embarrass himself or Barbara at weddings and events. He also wanted to learn to meditate properly, to remove stress from his life. He wished he'd done it years ago, as his mind was always full of work. Even now, some years after retiring, he'd spent way too much time worrying about all things financial. He regretted not having learned cardiopulmonary resuscitation, as he'd not been able to save someone once. Nick could see this was painful for him to talk about and decided not to press him for more information.

'What about cage diving?' Nick suggested.

'Why on earth would I want to do that?' Nick's dad was horrified.

'I thought Mum said you wanted to do that?'

'No, she wanted to do it. With sharks, so she could get close and look 'em in the eye. I said I thought it would be cruel.'

'How can that be cruel?'

A slow smile spread across Charlie's face. 'Your mother would terrify the sharks.' He winked, before his bony frame was racked by another bout of coughing. 'For heaven's sake, don't encourage your mother to try anything dangerous for a while after I'm gone. If there is anything after this world, I'd like a few months' peace up there.'

Nick couldn't help but smile back. 'Dad, you're going to be around awhile longer.'

'This is my third time here, Nick. I can't keep coming back. It has to stop at some point.'

Nick's phone bleeped with a message from Brian Matthews.

'Art. I've always wanted to be able to draw and paint, especially life art models.'

'Really? A bucket list is meant to be about experiences you can brag about, isn't it? Stuff you can stick on social media. Not about how to draw the saggy bits of old exhibitionists.' Nick looked at the message from Brian. 'I'm sorry, Dad. I've got to go.'

'Can't you stay a little longer?'

'I can't. Something has come up at work that requires my attention.' Nick hesitated. He really wanted to hear what was on the rest of his father's list, but he would surely understand. When you ran your own business, it came first. His father had spent his life living by that maxim, so why shouldn't Nick? 'I'll leave the list here and we'll carry on with it next time. I promise. But I need to go now.'

At that moment Malika wafted into the room with two doctors on their rounds. 'See you again soon, Nick,' she said in the manner of a statement rather than a question.

5

IN THE NARROW KITCHEN of her garden flat in the Haldens area of Welwyn Garden City, voluptuously proportioned Amira Hariq emptied the sixth and final packet of luxury cat food into a little pink bowl next to six other little pink bowls, all lined up ready to lower to the floor to feed her six best friends in the world. An extra bowl, for now though, would remain empty. Not in memory of a missing moggy but in anticipation of her dream and seventh cat, an Ashera. A cat so rare it had so far eluded her ownership. She still had some way to go to save up and her current job was not well paid.

Amira adored feeding her cats. She loved to make a fuss of them, sometimes preparing elaborate banquets from fresh and cooked food, though she knew that some preferred it raw. Despite the way she had trained their palates, they still insisted on bringing her gifts of dead birds and rodents, which she understood to be a great honour.

She loved cooking human food too, but not to share with humans. She'd never met the right ones and she didn't count her family, especially not her mother, with whom she often ate, most recently at Amira's birthday tea, in Amira's flat. with all six cats present.

Yes, she loved to cook but hated baking, recently having had a disaster whilst trying to bake herself a cake for her thirty-second birthday party with Mum and the cats. Her father refused to come because he had an allergy to cats which left his eyes streaming and his temper flaring. But her cats were hypo-allergenic, she had explained. She'd done everything she could to ensure her father's experience with her cats was as painless as possible. She regularly groomed them (as well as herself) and her flat was immaculately clean with an air filter to remove allergens. Still, he would not come. There is no such thing as a hypoallergenic cat; all cats, even her ugly hairless one, spread dander, he had corrected her. It was no wonder that she had not attracted a husband when the poor man would have to fight his way past baldy and the five hair-shedding guardians of her bedroom, her father had observed.

Amira didn't care about having a husband. She neither wanted nor needed one. Whilst her mother was the only other human that ever came in and out of her front door, someone did, however, enter through another. Giuseppe always came in around the back through the garden and in through the French windows, which she would leave unlocked on Sundays, Tuesdays, Thursdays and Fridays. Sometimes she would hear the doors rattling on a Monday, Wednesday and a Saturday, but she let them rattle. She needed to make sure that Giuseppe stayed keen. Plus she needed nights on her own, with the cats.

Giuseppe didn't have a problem getting past her cats. He had plenty of his own hair too, all over his body, which he had shed in a great number of places around Amira's flat.

Amira knelt down, lowering herself to the floor in the most elegant way her generous physique would allow, as if performing a yogic salutation. It wasn't a long way down, as Amira was not blessed with great height. She appeared wider than she was tall, but she was perfectly proportioned with the firmest, smoothest, velvetiest skin and she was surprisingly flexible according to Giuseppe, a Krav Maga self-defence instructor, who kept coming, time and time again and consequently so did she. Whenever he could get in through the French windows, that was. As well as hair, Giuseppe was blessed with an overabundance of muscle, but not brain cells, which meant that he continued to try to gain his amorous access every Monday, Wednesday and Saturday without success and never progressed along the learning curve. In her new position below the kitchen worktops Amira greeted each of her beauties with their supper: Carmen the Siberian, Tatyana the Russian Blue, Tosca the Bengal, Dido the Burmese, Brünnhilde the Sphynx and her favourite (although she told none of the others), Musetta, a British Short-Haired. She longed for the day when she would welcome her Ashera, which she planned on calling The Countess because it would be the most regal of the bunch, certainly in terms of its cost.

She stayed to watch them eat and after they had finished, she dutifully returned their bowls, each with their names on, to the worktop by the sink so that she could clean them. They all had their own bowls; she had to be careful to put the right food in each. Being pedigree cats, they had different dietary needs and if they got the wrong food they might suffer. They had to have exactly the right amount of the right thing, which presented Amira with a challenge, as she had a tendency to get things mixed up, especially when not bothering to wear her glasses. Brunhilda had been unwell on one occasion when Amira had given her Carmen's food by mistake. She now labelled all their food packets as well as their bowls. Here in the kitchen a mistake could become a life-and-death situation. She had enough death in her life already. She was surrounded by it at work.

As she turned to raise herself up, she came face to face with her oven and noticed it needed a thorough cleaning following her earlier baking disaster. She would have to put it on its pyrolytic self-clean setting and then would scrape the ashes out and dispose of them. She'd resisted completing this task to date, as it was reminiscent of her current employment as a crematorium technician. She never brought her work home with her and she didn't intend to start now. Well, only a little of it when she ran out of cat litter. She made a mental note to add that to her shopping list.

6

THIS WAS THE THIRD door Ray Dyema had knocked on that morning with no reply. The houses became increasingly ramshackle as he advanced up the street in the small village just outside Luton. Gardens long ago cared for now resembled mini municipal recycling centres. Even the sunshine breaking through the clouds could do nothing to brighten the scene before him. The rays had the effect of a forensic investigator's torch shedding light on the evidence of criminal activity rather than cheering up the day.

Ray was reminded of the times he'd shone a torch through a Swarovski crystal as a child. He was fascinated by the infinite number of tiny rainbows he could see within the glass. They were so pure. So perfect. Ray had anisocoria, a condition brought on by trauma to his left eye that meant the pupil was permanently dilated, giving his eyes the appearance of being different colours, much like the singer, David Bowie. When he looked closely at objects, he would close his left eye as the vision in it was slightly blurred. This didn't stop him falling in love with his nan's collection of figurines. He would visit her on the way home from school and spend hours playing with them, handling them with the greatest care. When she died he was devastated: not only had he lost his lovely nan, but he lost access to her Aladdin's cave of sparkling figurines.

Adult Ray had his eye on the Swarovski Bell Jar Pine

Tree and Stag figurine, which currently had £20 off online. He wanted it so badly but didn't have the £380 he needed to buy it outright, and as tempting as the zero per cent finance and payments of £14.26 a month were to him, he knew that taking such a loan was a slippery slope. It was too easy to borrow and then borrow some more until you couldn't pay, something Ray knew well in his line of work as a debt collector and bailiff.

Besides, Ray had his eye on a bigger prize.

He was convinced that his late Uncle Tony had left him something in his will, or rather that his Auntie Val would give him something so he could reconsider his career choice. Uncle Tony had been a Hatton Garden jeweller and was worth millions. He had no children of his own to leave anything to, just Auntie Val, who, although she didn't seem to have many jewels of her own, had possession of his nan's collection of Swarovski crystals. Uncle Tony and Auntie Val had shot round to Nan's council flat as soon as she'd died and cleared it out of anything of value. They were incensed to discover that the tiny 1976 silver crystal mouse was missing. It was highly collectible, being the very first *objet d'art* produced by Swarovski. Nan had let him look after it when she went into the local authority nursing home, where she died in her sleep three weeks later. He checked the lining of his heavy leather jacket. The mouse was there, safe in a duvet of bubble-wrap and sealed in a Jiffy bag.

That was one thing he had learned from his Uncle Tony. Although Tony had employed the latest high-tech security systems and triple-locking safes at work, one should always keep what's of value in plain sight. Criminals always went for the safe first, before trying everywhere else, but they wouldn't hang around if disturbed. At a family birthday party Uncle Tony had once drunkenly shown a five-year-old Ray where he kept his most precious jewels. He showed Ray to his wardrobe and took out his favourite three-piece suit, laying it on his super-king double bed. Carefully, he unpicked a corner of the waistcoat's lining, which revealed a number of small flat pouches; he delicately unpicked one from the heavy fabric and opened the pouch. After asking Ray to check that no one was coming up the stairs, he emptied the contents of the pouch onto the deep blue velvet bedspread. Diamonds, rubies and sapphires had spilled onto the fabric, creating a perfect starry sky. It looked like the picture Uncle Tony had hanging in his hallway downstairs. Ray instantly fell in love with their sparkle and their purity, but knew even then such riches would be forever beyond his grasp.

Swarovski crystal was the next best thing.

Uncle Tony and Auntie Val had been burgled many times and although their humble house had been trashed, the thieves had never found Tony's treasures. Still, the jewels would no doubt now be in the possession of Auntie Val, who seemed to be keeping quiet about it.

Auntie Val would surely share some of her wealth with him now that Uncle Tony had died. Hopefully, she'd forgiven Ray for losing his temper when, as an unstoppable sixteen-year-old, already over six feet in height and, despite his sinewy frame, disproportionately strong, he had lashed out. In a blind fit of rage, Ray had smashed one of Nan's Swarovski crystal glass star candle holders when Uncle Tony had refused to let him inherit any of Nan's figurines.

Ray had never had control of his temper. Even as a little boy his tantrums had a supernatural power that had earned him the nickname of 'The Hulk'. This was reinforced by the fact that afterwards, he couldn't remember what had happened during the episodes of rage. Events came back to him in dribs and drabs. It wasn't something he'd thought to mention in his army application when he signed up, a few months after smashing the candle holder.

Uncle Tony had never forgiven him for this outburst, and he had never forgiven himself; not for upsetting Uncle Tony but for the wanton destruction of such a beautiful object. Not only had Uncle Tony refused to let him have any figurines, he'd accused him of stealing the tiny crystal mouse; an accusation which, although accurate, was not supported with any evidence or proof, and which further fuelled Ray's rage.

Auntie Val had always been a little more generous. She assured him that the breakage didn't matter and that people were more important than things. But despite the words of consolation, his outburst had deeply troubled her and terrified Ray's parents. It was at that point that Ray had gained their consent to sign up. No one knew what else to do with him. They thought the army would sort him out, which it had for a while until the incident with the crystal mouse in the barracks in Helmand Province.

Ray shook his head, dispersing the memory. Most cars parked in the street in the small village just outside Luton showed evidence of having once been prestige cars, apart from one shiny and pimped-up yellow Vauxhall Corsa with an unfeasibly large exhaust and blacked-out windows, which sported an optimistic *For Sale* sign. The chrome on the bumper gleamed with a sparkle that could only have come from a specialised car-valeting product. Ray loved sparkles.

It was hard to tell if anyone was home at number seventeen, as they weren't answering. There wasn't much he could do about it, unless they let him in, which would mean they were either desperate, stupid or uninformed. Like a vampire, Ray wasn't allowed in unless invited. Getting them to invite you in, or to leave the door open, was the trick.

This particular debtor wasn't wanted for anything criminal like non-payment of parking fines, so he couldn't have any fun here with no right to force an entry. This was just another muppet who'd defaulted on payments, buying something they didn't really need with money belonging to someone else, and was now unable to make the payments. He was pretty sure the lady was in but couldn't be certain. She may have gone off on foot. If she went out the back door, his associate, Kevlar Kevin, would get her. Kevin had earned his nickname from his time in the army, as he'd been shot three times and stubbornly refused to die on each occasion. He was now twice the size he'd been in the army and not very fit. He was often used as a human barricade, which was why he always went around the back.

It had been easier to determine that the debtor was in the last time they'd called, as her car was parked in front of her house, where the yellow Corsa now resided. Thanks to him and Kevin, her car was currently at an auction house, ready to be sold to help pay off part of her debt.

Ray knocked again, much louder this time. 'Mrs Boswell, I need you to answer the door. I know you're in.'

A moment later, Ray's pocket vibrated. He reached in and pulled out his iPhone in its sparkling Swarovski case and answered it.

'She's done a fuckin' runner,' spurted Kevin, breathlessly. 'She's stashed some stuff in a rucksack, whacked me in the nads and disappeared through a hole in the fuckin' 'edge.'

'Get after 'er then, you lazy twat.'

'I can't. Can't get through the gap.'

'You fat twat.'

Ray ran around the back of the house to find Kevin bent double and making a noise like a constipated rhino. 'Right in me crown jewels,' he managed to squeeze out between laboured breaths.

'Well, she struck lucky. The chances of whacking you in the nuts would get really good odds at the bookies.'

This comment was met with a string of expletives from Kevin.

'No point in trying to chase her now,' concluded Ray.

'No, she's built like a whippet with the punch of a March Hare. She'll be long gone. Look though, she's left the door open.'

'Well spotted. Our invitation awaits.'

Mrs Boswell had been foolish enough to leave her back door wide open, which meant they could simply walk in and, once they'd established there were no minors or vulnerable people present, retrieve whatever they could, according to the guidelines. They had to leave behind essential items such as clothes, fridges and cooking appliances, but pretty much everything else was fair game.

And there was plenty of it. Even before they entered they could see that Mrs Boswell's abode resembled an Amazon warehouse, if you ignored the squalor and broken items everywhere.

After satisfying himself that no one was home, Ray strode through the kitchen and into the tiny living room. There he came to an abrupt stop, his advance arrested by the most appalling sight he'd ever seen.

7

Thursday 16th June

'ALTHOUGH I'M PLEASED WITH the presentation so far, I'm afraid I still haven't received the audited accounts back from Gill Bland,' Brian admitted.

'Why has there been a delay?' Nick asked, his eyes narrowing.

'Apparently, Josh Wedgwood hadn't sent her all the information she needed. She says she has it now.'

'Good, I'm glad Josh got on the case.'

'He didn't, Nick. I did.' Brian gripped his stapler tightly. 'I have never been happy with his appointment, he shouldn't have been put in charge of overseeing the day-to-day finances. You know that, Nick.'

'Yes, you have mentioned it a few times but you've been busy with other things, so I had to get someone in for that stuff,' said Nick on a long out-breath. 'When will we have the audited accounts? They need to be ready for the 8th July meeting.'

'She's promised she'll have them to me this morning. I'll call you when I get them. Hopefully everything will be in order, and then we can finalise the proposal.'

Satisfied that he'd done all he could for now, Nick said he'd see Brian later and headed to his car. He had just enough time to check on his dad at the Lister Hospital in Stevenage before heading back to his office in St Albans.

Oh, and then Harry's Laser Kombat party, in Stevenage. He couldn't miss that. Traffic was favourable and Nick made his way to Blackberry Ward without incident. Despite the early hour, it seemed busier than the day before. The well-oiled machine was turning, cleaners were sweeping and mopping, orderlies were serving breakfast, the smell of which hit him as he entered the ward, taking him right back to primary school. It never failed to amaze him how a smell could transport you to a moment in time or to spark a deep-rooted emotion, or both at once.

The uplifting sound of Malika's laugh infected the ward with happiness and optimism, alleviating people's pain with her unique brand of medicine. Nick couldn't stop a big smile spreading across his face. His decision to come here had been worth it if only to hear her voice. She was clearly someone with a purpose in life, an angel if you believed in that kind of thing.

As Nick turned to enter his father's bay, the smile vanished from his face at the same speed that his stomach fell from his body with the brutality of a medieval execution. He stared in disbelief at the scene before him. His father had gone. He had been there and now he was not. There was just an empty bed and an empty chair. No Dad. Charlie's bed was now being made, ready for the next patient.

For a moment he couldn't move. He couldn't believe that his dad had died and yet, here before his eyes was the evidence. His father was gone. No one had called him or asked him to come into the hospital. His mother and sister must know; bloody typical that they hadn't told him. Why weren't they here?

Or had it only just happened? Would he have to tell his mother that Dad had died? How do you do that? Could he do it by text? Facebook post, with Mum and Tracey tagged? WhatsApp video call? No, he'd have to go and see her in person. The thoughts whizzed through his mind at a million miles an hour.

An orderly turned to Nick and, seeing his expression, asked him if he was okay.

Nick stared at him, unsure of the answer. A plethora of emotions presented themselves to him like a tailor asking him to try on different suits. *Try this one on, sir. How does Deep Sadness and Regret feel? What about Wretched Guilt of the Uncaring Son? That seems to suit you quite well, sir. We might need to let it out a little.*

'When did he go?' Nick surprised himself with the unusually high pitch of his voice.

'They wheeled him out about ten minutes ago. You only just missed him.'

What? Was this person not trained in bedside manners? Did he miss that part of the course or opt instead for the Sadistic Training Module? How quickly did they need the bed; did they stop caring once the patient had died?

Why hadn't anyone called to let him know Charlie was dying?

Nick was about to say a few things that he would no doubt regret for a long time afterwards when a warm hand materialised on his elbow, and he was embraced by a magical calming aura.

'Hello, Mr Swift.' The comforting treacle voice was

unmistakably that of Malika. 'It's okay. We're moving your father as he took a turn for the worse in the night. We would have called but he stabilised and we didn't want to bother anyone. But we think it best that he now has a room of his own. He has been asking for you. Give us ten minutes to settle him in and then I'll come and fetch you. Wait in the family room, help yourself to coffee.'

Malika's instructions were clear and not to be questioned. Nick was glad that he didn't have to make any decisions for himself for the next ten minutes. Malika had done that for him.

Nick went and got himself a coffee. His father had died and been brought back to life within the space of fifty-five seconds and he had been on a rollercoaster of emotions, unable to process any of them. Exhausted, he didn't know what he felt or was meant to feel. He checked his watch. Shit, he wouldn't be able to stay long. He would have to get back to the office soon. He had so much to do. Being here was ridiculous; his father had never shown him this much attention during his whole lifetime. Was Nick here for his father or for himself? What was he thinking? He didn't know. He probably wasn't thinking.

He checked his phone. Jesus, how could that many new emails have been sent in the time since he'd last checked at 4.45 a.m.? Didn't people have lives? The office was already firing on all cylinders and he should be there. If he was going to properly prepare his business for sale he couldn't let this get in the way. He took another sip of lukewarm coffee and poured the rest down the sink. He'd pop back and see his dad later if he had time.

'Mr Swift, you can see your father now. And he is not in that direction, his room is this way.' Malika arrested Nick's progress towards the exit, scuppering his plans.

He could pretend he could not hear her and keep walking towards the exit. But he was unable to refuse her commands. She held a power over him he was defenceless against. He stopped, took a breath and turned around. He could be out of here in five minutes if he needed to be. He would wait until Malika had gone and then make good his escape.

Alone in the room and tucked up in bed, Charlie looked even smaller and more fragile than he had just yesterday. A light next to his bed illuminated the surroundings in a cosy way, giving it a more homely feel. This room was a much better place for him to be in than the four-bed ward. His dad looked comfortable and appeared to be sleeping. Nick sat down next to his bed. He wouldn't wake his father, just let him rest. He would leave soon and get back to work. This whole business had already taken up too much time.

'Nick? Is that you?' Charlie stirred and opened his eyes. A smile spread across his face like a tortoise being given a fresh lettuce leaf. If a tortoise could smile, that was, maybe they only did that in cartoons. The smile took a while to take possession of his face but when it did it was like a rainbow emerging from the clouds. It might not be there for long, but while it lasted it gave Nick a sense of peace and happiness, something he'd not felt in the company of his father for years, if ever.

Nick now noted how much Charlie resembled a tortoise, what with his loss of hair, the last of which had given up the futile battle for residency upon his head some years ago, and his neck, longer than ever and jowly. Yes, his father had morphed into Master Oogway but without the staff, or the ability to perform Kung Fu on a large group of villains.

'The list… '

'What?'

'Get the list from my drawer.'

Nick had to lean in really close to hear his father.

'We don't have long before they come round with that slop they call breakfast.'

Nick took out the notepad and clicked the pen so that the nib appeared, ready to write.

'Where are we?' his father asked.

'In the hospital, Dad.'

'No, with the list. I'm not senile yet.'

Nick smiled. 'Well, so far it's not too exciting. We've ruled out swimming with dolphins and sharks and whale watching and we've got learning to draw – especially a life class, learning how to give CPR, how to meditate and how to dance. Is there any order in which you'd like to do these things? Remember you've done the Pyramids and a hot-air balloon, but not skydiving.'

'Skydiving. That would be good.'

Nick could see that Charlie was struggling to breathe. His chest sounded much worse today than it had yesterday. He wondered if he should call someone.

'Skydiving is definitely a more traditional bucket list activity, Dad. What about another?'

'Life-saving … swimming. Stop someone drowning.'

Nick was beginning to wonder what had happened to his father. Had he once seen someone drown and been unable to help? Was he thinking about himself now, drowning in his own body?

'We'll put that one on the list too.' *I should call someone.*

'Motorcycle riding. Like your Uncle Keith.' Charlie coughed feebly, unable to clear his chest.

'I'm going to get someone.' Nick stood up.

'No … I'm fine. Keep writing.'

Nick was beginning to wish he hadn't come. Why had he put himself in this position? Here he was with a dying father he hardly knew, writing down a bucket list his father would never accomplish. He wasn't ready to deal with this now. He needed to get out.

'Escapology … like Houdini.'

Was his father reading his mind? Nick certainly wanted to escape from this situation. He added it to the list.

'Self-defence … the Israeli type.'

'You mean Krav Maga?'

The list was becoming more and more bizarre. What did his father know about Israeli special forces self-defence techniques? Must have come from a book he'd read or a film he'd watched.

'Tightrope walking and climbing.'

Nick wrote them down too.

'Volunteering … at a soup kitchen.'

What? Did those things still exist still? What had happened to his father? This was a bizarre and eclectic list of things to do before dying. If by some divine miracle his father made a full recovery, he would become a benevolent

James Bond figure, falling from the sky to serve homeless people soup, entertaining them with his circus skills and dancing before rendering them in watercolour, rescuing and resuscitating those unfortunates who'd lost the will to live and tried to drown themselves. Clearly his mind had gone.

'Have you got that all down?' Charlie coughed again. It sounded painful. 'How is Louise?'

'She's fine.'

'And Charlotte and Hugo?'

'It's Harry, Dad.'

'That's what I said. I haven't seen them in ages.' He sounded breathless.

'No. I know.' Nick realised he hadn't seen them either for two days. He'd been too busy.

His phone vibrated in his pocket. He checked it. Brian again. He could hear his voice as he read the text. Brian had a way of making things sound extremely urgent and phenomenally dull at the same time.

'I need to go, Dad, sorry.'

'You're a good father, Nick.'

'I have to go to work.'

'I'm not. I haven't been.' Charlie coughed again.

'Sorry, Dad. I'll pop back again soon, I promise. I'll send the nurse in to check on you.'

'The list … it's not finished.'

'We'll finish it next time. I promise.'

'No, Nick, you can't go yet.' The smile dropped from his father's face, and he held up a shaking hand. Charlie attempted to take Nick's wrist but didn't have the strength to do so. His words were so breathy and his voice so hoarse that Nick had trouble hearing him.

'Dad, I have to go.'

'The list… '

'Yes, we'll finish it next time.'

'It's not for me to do.'

'What do you mean?'

'It's for you. I want you to complete the list for me.'

'But it's your list, Dad.'

'No, it's our list, son. It's all the things I would have liked to have done with you and haven't. I haven't got time now and I certainly don't have the ability.' A smile returned to his cracked lips. 'I'm so sorry, son. I haven't been a good father to you.'

Nick sat down. The hospital room swam before his eyes. His phone vibrated again. Brian's name appeared on the screen along with his profile photo; a shiny bald head and an inappropriate moustache. He resembled what Nick imagined a 1970s porn star might look like. He really needed to go. He glanced up and noticed that his father had closed his eyes and was lying back on his pillow. He looked drained and even paler than before.

'I'll be back again soon, Dad. Dad?'

His father didn't answer. He'd fallen into a deep sleep and was snoring heavily. After a quick word with Malika, who informed Nick that she would see him again soon and that she would look after his father in the meantime, Nick hurried back to his car.

8

RAY HAD A BANGING headache. He sat bolt upright, wiped his face with the back of his hand and took a sharp intake of breath. He had no idea how he had got back to his flat in the centre of Hatfield last night. He had no memory of climbing the thirteen stories to his floor. He hadn't been drinking; there was no evidence of it around the room. He'd slept on the sofa in his T-shirt and boxers.

He stood up and stretched. The sofa wasn't an ideal place to sleep and his back ached royally. He was beginning to get an idea what had happened when he heard his phone ping with a message alert. A text from Kevlar Kevin confirmed it: he'd had a blackout episode. The debtor who'd escaped them yesterday had trashed her flat, either taking or destroying anything of value. Kevin had joked that the debtor had seen Ray's David Bowie eyes through the spyhole in her front door, freaked out and run off in a panic. When Ray entered her sitting room, he'd seen what she'd done to a large collection of Swarovski crystal figurines. She too, had evidently been a collector, but she'd smashed them all, including a Swarovski Bell Jar Pine Tree and Stag figurine, the piece he'd had his eye on. This had clearly been the trigger for his blackout.

Ray's stomach turned over. Last time he'd had such an episode he'd ended up in serious trouble. He called Kevin, who explained that he'd not done anything bad and certainly nothing he needed to worry about. He'd become comatose for about five minutes, staring at the mess and had then carefully picked up all the pieces of broken crystal he could find, wrapped them in kitchen towel and put them in a carrier bag. He had walked, zombie-like, back to his van and had driven home. Kevin had followed him back to make sure he was okay, but had been unable to get a word out of him. Back at the flat, Ray had suddenly turned and threatened him. Kevin had seen that look before and knew to leave him alone.

Relieved, Ray spotted a Lidl carrier bag on the table. He couldn't believe the amount of carnage it contained, but not all of it was unsalvageable. A little rubbing down of the edges with fine-grit sandpaper before gluing the pieces back together with E6000 and then buffing them with a lint-free cloth and most of it would look, to the untrained eye, as good as new. Some pieces were irreparable and had no intrinsic value. They were expertly cut glass, not precious stones. Not like the stones his Uncle Tony had dealt in. If Ray possessed only a few of the special stones that his uncle had secreted away, he would never have to work again.

He laid out the pieces of broken crystal and tried to group them together. It looked like most of the pieces were there. He was confident that he would have them restored soon, just as he'd repaired and restored his precious crystal mouse. If he'd known that the Swarovski Crystal was repairable, the chain of events leading to a violent attack and Ray's discharge from the army might never have occurred, but it was all too late to worry about now. The guy should never have taunted him. The mouse was his pride and joy and the only connection he had to his nan. You could just about see the faint crack in the mouse's head following its repair. The crack in the head of Private Warner had taken a little longer to repair and had earned Ray an immediate discharge and the end of a promising career. His best mate Ross had stepped up to defend Ray, but by the time the hearing came around, Ross had been killed by an IED. Ray had never forgiven himself for not being on patrol with him at the time. His blackout and subsequent attack on Colin Warner had put him in the glasshouse pending the inquiry.

Ray covered the pieces with a cloth. He couldn't bring himself to start the repairs now and the memories were becoming too painful. He pulled back the rug in front of his sofa and unscrewed a floorboard. Carefully, he removed a robust plastic bag and put it aside, before replacing the floorboard and rug.

Ray set to work, cleaning his Glock 17 Gen 4 pistol. Removing numerous pieces of metal and plastic, he began a meticulous process of cleaning he learned in the army, making sure that the gun was in good working order, before lovingly wrapping it up and concealing it once more beneath the floorboards. After his Swarovski Crystals, the contraband Glock was his most prized possession. Once belonging to a fallen comrade, he'd managed to get it smuggled back from Afghanistan by a mate, another weapon that had been 'lost' in battle. Ray's attention was drawn to an old framed photo on his bookcase of three smiling soldiers, in full combat attire. Ross's bright blue eyes stood out, following Ray around the room wherever he went.

The light reflecting from the crystals on the frame

returned Ray's thoughts to his uncle and the fortune he must have left behind. Maybe he should pay his Auntie Val a visit soon. He hadn't seen her since he was sixteen. The Christmas before he joined the army.

9

'NICK, WHERE THE HELL are you?'

Brian no longer sounded like Brian. Nick had to check his phone to see if it was actually Brian's caller ID on the display. Brian's tone had switched from a nasal monotonic robot to that of an angry parent chastising a drunken teenager.

'I've been trying to reach you for the last two hours.'

'I'm at the hospital. Keep your—'

'Nick, *please*.' It was as if Brian had been swapped with another Brian from a parallel universe; a blip in the fabric of the space-time continuum, to use Brian's language, had occurred. Something was seriously wrong. 'The audit has come back from Gill Bland. I need to see you now to discuss the figures. I'm afraid we have a bit of a situation, putting it mildly.'

'What are you talking about? I thought Josh had been through everything with a fine-toothed comb before sending the accounts off? You assured me everything was fine.'

'I thought it was, Nicholas.'

Nicholas?

Brian was now morphing into an angry version of Nick's mother. Nick started to feel sick with anxiety. He had never heard him like this before. Brian was unemotional, dull and thoroughly comfortable. He was the human personification of a beige sofa. Brian was normal. Ordinary. The centre of the spectrum. He was dependable, and although you wouldn't want to go on holiday with him or get sat next to him at the Christmas party, he was someone you wanted on your team. If Brian had been the captain of the Titanic it wouldn't have sunk. But now, judging by the tone of Brian's voice, he fully expected his next sentence to be '*Women and children first. Set out the deckchairs and get the string quartet to play "Nearer, my God, to Thee"*.'

'You need to come into the office now, Nick, this is serious.'

∗   ∗   ∗

Nick's journey to the office in Beaconsfield Road was a complete blank. He had no memory of it except for narrowly missing a motorcyclist as he pulled out of a junction. The motorcyclist calmly gave him the middle finger as he sped away, becoming an animated spec in Nick's rear-view mirror. The experience had shaken Nick out of his stupor temporarily, but he soon drowned in it again.

Nick parked his beloved new Audi, hurriedly grabbed his briefcase from the back seat and locked the car. He ran-walked into the shared office building, ignoring the jovial greeting of the too-glamorous-for-her-uniform receptionist-cum-security guard.

'How rude,' the guard muttered under her breath through a broad ventriloquist's grin.

Nick offered up his security pass to allow himself access to the stairwell and leapt his way to the first floor, missing every other step. He tripped on the top step and almost fell over, narrowly avoiding someone coming through the door to the first-floor offices.

'Woops-a-daisy,' cried Shirley Hopkins, in her sing-song-voice. Shirley's purple rinse became a deeper shade of lavender the closer she got to retirement, like a working-life-span litmus test. Judging by its current hue, Nick's office manager was planning to stop work in the next few weeks. 'Someone's in a hurry,' she uttered melodiously from behind a large coffee mug confirming her status as the world's best grandmother.

'Yes, good morning, Shirley.' Nick's clipped manner barely disguised his mood and embarrassment.

'Someone got out of bed on the wrong side this morning.'

Nick wished her hair would soon become a deep shade of purple, with no hint of grey.

'Shall I hold the door open for you, love?'

'That would be kind of you, thanks.'

'What will you do without me?' She waited for a reply that never came. 'Shall I add holding the door open for the boss to my job description?'

Nick ignored the last comment and was carried through the open doorway by a mixture of anxiety and annoyance. Although Shirley had been an amazing office manager over the years, she had slowed down since her retirement date had been agreed. She now spent most of her time unapologetically making coffee and browsing the internet. Her replacement had not yet been sourced, as her job description, which seemed to be as thick as the bible, had not yet been completed.

'You look stressed, young man,' she remarked. 'You should meditate, learn to slow down a bit. There's a wonderful YouTube channel of a handsome old boy who rides a motorbike and says Zen-type things. You should watch it.'

Realising she was referring to his bloody uncle's channel, Nick's annoyance grew.

'About time,' Brian called, seeing Nick from outside his corner office, before hurrying back in. Nick looked around to judge the reaction of everyone present. How dare Brian speak to him like this? Everyone had the good sense to keep their heads down and get on with their work, though the place was unusually quiet. Nick followed Brian into the corner office.

'You had better close the door, Nick.' Brian seemed marginally calmer now. A heavy sense of expectation filled the room. 'It seems I was right to be concerned about your appointment of Josh Wedgwood.'

'Where is he?' Nick's stomach lurched.

'He left his resignation letter on your desk after I went through the audited accounts with him this morning. He fucked up, Nick. Said not to worry about paying him this month, apologised, cried a bit and then left. I think he may be having personal problems.' Brian pronounced the word 'fucked' like a non-native English speaker trying it out for the first time. It sounded almost comical, but this was no moment for humour.

'What's going on, Brian?'

'What's going on? What's going on?' Brian was barely able to contain his obvious frustration. 'That muppet you hired has been beyond incompetent, fucking up our plans to sell—'

'*Shh.*' Nick tried desperately to silence Brian. Only he, Brian, Gill Bland and the AWOL Josh knew about his plans to sell the business. He didn't want a panic setting in and everyone finding new jobs before the deal was sealed.

'That fuckwit,' Brian continued at a lower volume, 'has made a number of errors of omission. If I didn't know better, I'd think they were not unintentional.'

Nick thought he understood Brian's use of the double negative.

'Your speedy engagement of his services, which for the record I said at the time I wasn't comfortable with, has resulted in a considerable VAT liability.'

'We can adjust on the next return, can't we?'

'It's a considerable liability and not just the last quarter, Nick,' Brian stared at him incredulously. 'The errors are in the last five returns.'

'Oh dear. Is that all?' Nick couldn't help the flippant comment that nervously escaped his lips.

'Don't be a dick, Nick.'

Nick was clearly in an alternate reality. His universe upset, flipped on its head. Brian had called him a dick. He'd been away from the office twice, the business had seemingly fallen apart and Brian had been replaced with his evil doppelganger. His thoughts drifted to his father and the list. He should have been here, not wasting time with a dad he'd never really known.

'Please calm down, Brian. You're not yourself.'

Brian stared at Nick for an eternally long ten seconds

without saying a thing. He took off and polished his glasses and then replaced them, the nervous tremble in his hand amplified by the arm of his glasses. 'I am now calm.' The nasal monotone had returned. 'I am annoyed with you for employing Josh, which I've said before, however, I am most annoyed with myself for not keeping a closer eye on what the fuckwit muppet was doing. I have let you and the business down. I should've come in more often, but I thought you had it under control, Nick.'

'I'm sure it's not that bad,' Nick replied in as positive a tone as he could manage. 'Tell me it is redeemable.'

Brian made him wait a painfully long time, whilst he tapped away on his keyboard. He stopped abruptly, turning to Nick with a fatalistic look. Nick expected him to say '*Computer says no*'. He resisted the urge to share this thought with Brian.

'To be clear, the errors Josh has made could be down to incompetence and laziness. They are so bad they look intentional. The problem is that unless we can tidy this mess up, we're not going to be able to sell the business. As well as a plethora of minor inaccuracies, the omissions he has made, fortunately spotted and triple-checked by Gill Bland, mean that we fed the wrong figures to HMRC for the last year and a quarter.'

'How much do we owe them?' asked Nick pathetically, the lurching in his stomach now a full-on spin cycle.

'We probably owe in the region of a quarter of a million.'

'What the fuck? There must be something we can do to the figures?' Nick had already mortgaged his house and there was no way he would be able to find that kind of money. He sat down, the room now spinning to match his stomach.

'I have a few ideas, but I'm afraid that it will only buy us a little time,' Brian continued. 'I would suggest rescheduling today's meeting so we can tidy the proposal up a bit. We need to work out where we are going to find that money. We'll have no choice but to pay it and that's going to make a massive difference to our projection for next year.'

'Jesus. Where do we start?' asked Nick, wishing the ground would swallow him up.

'We'll need to make some immediate savings. I know how much you love your new car, but it will have to go back. We'll need a new internal accountant, maybe I'll take that on for now. But we'll have to cut other costs, look at streamlining things. I'm not sure what half the people in the office do.'

Despite the awful news, Nick felt comforted by Brian's return to normality. If Brian were to release a music album now it would be entitled *Back to Beige*.

'Nick, this is serious. Whilst we may be able to mitigate the damage here, and a potential buyer could build in the liability to the purchase by adjusting the price, it makes it look like we're incompetent and that will put them off. If you can't sell the business, we're royally fucked. We could ask for investment but we'd both agreed a sale was best.' There it was again. Brian's unsettling use of profanity underpinned the seriousness of the situation. 'We need to cancel the visit from PlanIT-UK today and sort this mess out.'

'Silverman could've stayed in Florida longer. He won't be happy. What reason will I give for cancelling?' asked Nick, at a loss.

Brian leant forward and looked at him over the top of his glasses. 'I'm sure you'll come up with something, but it will have to be good at such short notice. Tell them there's been a death in the family or something. That should do it. There's some other bad news, I'm afraid.'

What now? What could be worse?

'Dave Dolon has been talking to Jeff Silverman too.'

'What? Oh fuck,' said Nick in a low, slow whisper.

'Oh fuck indeed,' echoed Brian. 'Yes, your old partner and unethical contact book thief is trying to sell his carbon copy business to Jeff Silverman.'

'How do you know?'

'My friend at the golf club overheard them. It's not great news, is it? We stood to make an absolute fortune from the sale of the business. Because we're not ready right now, we may lose out completely or have to sell at a much-reduced price. If Silverman has a choice, they'll knock more than £250,000 off the price.'

Nick suspected that his old nemesis Dave Dolon had been brought in by Silverman to help him lower his offer. Things were heading south in a hurry.

Brian reminded Nick that he had never trusted Dolon either.

'Yes, Brian, you were right about that too,' Nick said humbly.

'I think we need to stay calm and behave professionally. We need to present a confident face to the world and keep a low profile. The company, with you as the CEO, needs to look in complete control. I'd suggest you switch off your phone, put all calls on hold and sit with me in here until we've ironed out the worst of these errors.'

Da da-da da da … da da. Shirley's jovial signature knock resounded on the office door.

'Not now, Shirley, please,' Nick barked.

'Ooh,' Shirley vocally sine-waved her reaction to Nick's outburst, covering at least two octaves. 'I thought you'd like to know that I've just seen you on YouTube, boss.'

'Yes, Shirley, the company has lots of clips on YouTube.'

'Not like this one. It's a video of you practically knocking Karmic Keith off his motorcycle as you swerve off down the road at great speed, almost hitting an old lady and her little fluffy dog. I have to say that Karmic Keith deals with the situation in a most philosophical way. That is your new bright red car caught on his helmet camera, isn't it?' She held up her oversized smartphone to show them both. It was indeed Nick's car in the video entitled 'Lessons to be learned from a rude and out-of-control middle-aged male motorist in a bright red penis-compensation mobile.'

Fuck.

'It's already had over thirteen thousand views and hundreds of comments. Luckily, your smoked windows hide your identity reasonably well, but the number plate is clear. I'd get a new car pretty soon, if I were you.'

10

AMIRA WOKE TO A cacophony of mewing coming from the other side of her bedroom door. What was wrong with her darlings? She turned over to check the time. She was aware of Giuseppe's cologne clinging to her bedsheets as she rolled over the spot where he'd dozed off post-coitally. A tickle on her lips prompted her to remove a number of Giuseppe's testosterone-rich hairs, which covered her face with one glued stubbornly to her cheek. Her little pink cat alarm clock revealed that it was ten-twenty in the morning.

Shit! She'd overslept and her alarm hadn't gone off. Either that or she'd not heard it. Normally, if her alarm failed the cats would come and wake her. Musetta had an appetite to match her size and never ceased to remind her of her duties as keeper of the pride. Giuseppe must have forgotten to leave the door open when he left. He was not allowed to stay the night and always had to enter and leave under the cover of darkness. Occasionally, she would make him wear a cloak and a mask and enact a fantasy. He would be Don Giovanni while she played a helpless lady, Donna Elvira or Donna Anna, or the peasant girl, Zerlina. He would enter her chamber, enter her, exit her and then the chamber. She insisted he learn to sing the canzonetta from Act 2 of Mozart's opera. His voice was sweet and naturally his Italian was perfect, but his intonation was poor and he always hurried the second verse, by which time he was ready but she wasn't, and then he'd run out of breath.

Last night he had turned into what he referred to as *uno stallone purosangue*. Judging by his whinnying and his insistence that she remain on all fours throughout the exhausting session, she deduced it had something to do with horses.

She looked at the clock: only thirty minutes to drive to work in North Watford. She would never manage it in time. She would have to get a move on. She needed to wash off the evidence of her night of animal passion. The mewing would have to continue a little longer, she decided as she cantered to the shower.

Remarkably, Amira was only ten minutes late for work that morning despite a long queue at Park Street roundabout. She would have been on time had she not stopped to say goodbye individually to each of her cats in turn. She even took a moment to say goodbye to The Countess's bowl in the absence of the new cat itself. She looked forward to a time when she could do that.

'You're late.' As Amira walked into the locker room to change, her supervisor stood with her hands on her hips, her body language giving off vibes of a disappointed sports coach. 'You know we've got a busy day today and I'm rather disappointed that you're not on time.'

'I'm really sorry, Lauren. I've suffered a sports injury and it's taken me longer than usual to get ready.'

'I didn't know you did sports.' Lauren's tone implied she didn't believe that Amira looked the type. 'What sports?'

'Equestrian,' Amira answered.

Lauren looked confused, a scowl spreading across her face.

'You know, horses. I ride.'

'Really. Did you fall off?'

'Oh, no. I think I may have pulled something though.'

Amira put on her overalls and boots and took a new pair of latex gloves from the pack on the wall. The smell reminded her of the previous night.

'You don't need to wear all that kit, you know. Jeans and a T-shirt is fine. You will need a mask today, though. We've got a reeker.'

Lauren referred to partially decomposed bodies as 'reekers'. She always went into far too much detail about the state of each body's condition.

'The coroner reckons this one had been dead for a month before the neighbours reported the stench. It's a right honker – made me gag and that's saying something. I'd appreciate it if you could put her to the front of the queue ahead of the medical cadaver. I don't suppose he'll mind now, he's already in pieces.' Lauren chuckled. Her sense of humour was beyond dark and she always found herself more amusing than Amira did. 'He's preserved too, so he'll keep a bit longer. Just make sure you put all the pieces in together at the same time this time. It's not cheap firing up the ovens, you know.'

'Will you give me a hand with the first one please?' Amira asked. 'I may have trouble lifting her.'

'Nah, you won't have any trouble. She's *dead* light. I think most of her is still stuck to the chair she was in. She was sitting in front of a heater so most of her has gone. I'm amazed the neighbours didn't catch a whiff sooner. No one's come to claim her, sad really. I've taken off her jewellery. She was wearing a diamond necklace and a diamond ring.'

'But won't her jewellery stay with her?'

'No. For two reasons.' The look on Lauren's face suggested she was about to launch into a lengthy explanation. 'One, believe it or not, diamonds will vaporise in a cremator once it hits 760 degrees. There won't actually be much left of them once it reaches 600 – another interesting fact you can say you've learned when you have your six-month appraisal next week with the boss.'

Amira grunted. She had been considering mentioning Lauren's inappropriate and disrespectful comments at the appraisal, provided Lauren wouldn't be sitting in on it.

'Two, she had no family, no friends and no will, so the state gets to keep her assets. If her will or family had said she wanted to be cremated wearing her finest, then of course we'd honour that, but in reality there would be nothing left of the diamonds after the cremation. In this case there is no will and she was Norma-no-mates, so the jewellery has been removed. Actually, her name was Margaret – don't get her mixed up with the other Margaret, who has a service this afternoon. You must label the urns carefully. Remember, if we label them left to right on the shelf, according to the time of each cremation, we can be sure there are no mix-ups.'

Amira put in her EarPods as a signal to Lauren that she was no longer interested in what she was saying and wished to get on with her work. She scrolled through Spotify until she found a recording of Tosca with her favourite tenor, Franco Corelli, singing the role of Cavaradossi. His voice thrilled her from head to toe and everywhere in between. Her favourite was a 1967 live recording, but the quality wasn't great, so she settled on the 1978 version. She skipped straight to 'Recondita Armonia' and bathed in the majesty of Corelli's stentorian tones.

To say Amira wasn't drawn to Lauren was putting it mildly. At first, she had liked her supervisor but Lauren's own growing ease with Amira meant that she made increasingly inappropriate and disrespectful comments, which in turn made Amira deeply uncomfortable. Amira decided she would have to wait and see the outcome of her appraisal and probationary review. Once she felt safe in her position she could then challenge Lauren, either directly or via Lauren's superior, Ms Fiona Perkins. Amira didn't want to lose her job. Although the pay wasn't great, it offered secure employment and it gave her a strange sense of wellbeing. Having a regular reminder of her own mortality made her appreciate her own life so much more, as well as that of her cats and even Giuseppe.

Perhaps next week she'd make him play Cavaradossi to her Tosca. She had a way of helping him hit the high notes.

11

NICK AND BRIAN HAD spent all day going through the figures. Despite how annoying he could be, today Brian's accountancy superpowers had been a reminder to Nick of why he had asked him to come on board initially. It was a shame they were in this situation now. If Brian had been more present over the last couple of years, they might not be. Brian, if he chose to, would be able to retire if the deal went through, so it was no surprise that he had been so irate when he discovered all the errors in the financial report to be presented to PlanIT-UK. Nick realised that most of Brian's frustration, though expressed outwardly, was with himself. He couldn't believe that he'd missed so many errors in Wedgwood's accounting. The more they went through the financial report, the more errors they discovered.

Nick's day had been a white-knuckle ride, and he didn't calm down until he had called Jeff Silverman's office to cancel their meeting. He felt a quiet discomfort having used his father's situation as his get-out-of-jail-free card. His father was unwell but, as far as Nick could tell and contrary to his mother's insistence, he wasn't about to die anytime soon. Although he could imagine all too well his mother's pleasure at proving Nick wrong, the way she always did.

Nick finished his seventh cup of coffee and looked over at Brian. They had told their colleagues they were only to be disturbed in the case of a natural disaster, terrorist attack or a death. No other disturbances. Zip. No matter who was on the phone. The office was quiet now and the sun was beginning to cast long shadows outside.

He and Brian, but mostly Brian, had managed to rectify the errors in the accounts and consequently the financial report. The company looked, on paper at least, like it was a good proposition for a buyer, despite the VAT liability. However, they knew that, if they weren't able to sell, their impressive growth would be for nothing and their cash flow would not sustain the growth. For now, though, Nick felt calmer. He could relax for a moment. With a start, he realised that he had really enjoyed the day. It felt like the early days of the business, rolling up his sleeves and getting stuck in. He and Brian had performed nothing short of a miracle, thanks to Brian's ability to plug himself into the system, as if he were a human-cyborg interface. Half-man, half-spreadsheet.

'Right.' Brian rolled his sleeves back down and fastened his cuffs. 'Time to get back home to Elizabeth. She'll be wondering where I am.'

'I didn't know you had a new partner?' Nick realised he knew very little about Brian beyond their working relationship. Always curious about his work colleagues' private lives, Nick had never managed to deeply engage Brian, who rarely attended social events. Brian had attended the odd conference and one corporate golf day, which he'd committed to in a concerningly competitive manner, missing the point of chatting to clients and tacitly rejoicing in their defeat. Beyond that, Brian remained an enigma.

'Elizabeth,' Brian said, 'is my pet tarantula. No one will ever replace Jane.'

'No, of course not.'

'Well, goodnight, Nick. Onwards and upwards.'

As he reached the stairs, Brian turned to look back at Nick for a moment before giving a brief nod of his head. The door closed behind him, and Nick was left alone. Nick turned back to his corner office and noticed a large number of neatly arranged Post-it notes stuck to the outside of his office door. They were written in Shirley's unmistakable handwriting, decorated with flowers and the i's were dotted with perfect circles instead of normal black dots. The embellishments became less prolific with later notes. The notes were perfectly aligned in a column from top to bottom; the first and most decorated note, which used multiple colours, was at the top, marked 3.30 pm.

Your wife called. Please call her back immediately.

The lowest and final note was written in plain black capitals and simply read:

DON'T BOTHER CALLING NOW!

The final note had been placed on the door at 5.34 p.m. No doubt Shirley would be claiming for overtime.

Nick wished he'd been a bit more specific in his instructions to Shirley. Did she not realise that he wouldn't want to miss his son's birthday party? Maybe Louise hadn't told him. Maybe he was being set up for a fall. Either way, he'd promised he'd be there and he'd missed it.

Nick switched on his phone. He had nine missed calls from Louise and three from his mother; the increasingly irate messages from Louise confirmed that he had missed the party. Initially, he felt terrible and then his emotions turned to anger. It wasn't his fault he had missed the party, it was Josh Wedgwood's. If he hadn't messed up so catastrophically, Nick wouldn't have had to work late again. Shirley was also to blame. If she had had the sense to properly filter his calls, none of this would have happened.

At the end of the day, he was doing all this for his family, not himself. Harry wouldn't be able to have a Laser Kombat party with all his friends and a brand new PlayStation 5 if Nick wasn't dedicated to bringing home the bacon. He wouldn't be able to have Papa John's delivered to the house and a movie and games night on their home cinema system with surround sound. Louise had a right to be disappointed, but not a right to be angry. Surely Harry would understand. He looked at his watch: 7.45 p.m. If he hurried, he might be in time to get home for the cake cutting and pizza before the movie started.

Nick tried to call Louise several times from his car, but she didn't pick up. She was clearly livid and now airing him. Harry didn't pick up either, so he tried Charlotte. She answered monosyllabically, explaining that Mum wasn't happy and Harry was busy. The pizza had arrived, and they were soon going to cut the cake. She didn't ask why he wasn't there.

Nick got home in record time, despite having had to slightly reduce his speed after a motorcyclist waved at him to stop and then gave him the middle finger, revving his throttle and accelerating off after turning left up Oaklands Lane. He thought this odd but thought no more of it until a further two bikers and an old lady walking her dog did something similar as he bounced over the irritating speedbumps going through Hatfield Garden Village.

Then he remembered.

Uncle Keith's YouTube channel. They must have recognised his car. Despite his rush, Nick decided it was vital to park in the garage, rather than risk any passers-by recognising his car and giving it any unwanted attention.

As Nick walked into the kitchen, he heard the final phrase of an untuneful 'Happy Birthday' being sung in three different keys simultaneously by his family and seven of Harry's friends, with no one able to reach the high note. A cry of applause and three cheers for the birthday boy. He kicked himself. If he hadn't worried about parking in the garage, he would have made it in time to raise the roof with everyone else.

The look on Louise's face said it all: a picture of relief followed by a mixture of disappointment and seething anger. She swiftly turned her back on him and handed her parents, both of whom looked embarrassed and awkward at seeing him, a glass of champagne each. There wasn't one poured for Nick as she had not expected to see him. He could pour his own.

Charlotte leant against the kitchen island. Raising her head a fraction of a degree, she regarded him with complete indifference whilst twirling her hair and posting pictures of Harry's birthday cake on Instagram and TikTok simultaneously.

'Made it,' Nick announced as he approached the revellers. 'Happy birthday, son! I'm sorry I didn't make the laser tag.'

'It's okay, Dad,' Harry lied. 'I wasn't expecting you to.'

Ouch.

'Grandad filled in for you and he was epic.'
Double ouch.

'We were a brilliant team, weren't we, Harry?' cried Louise's father Paul in a voice rather too loud for the moment.

'Who wants a slice of cake?' Louise's mum Judi was brilliant at distraction. She started handing slices to the gannet-like nest of hungry boys.

'Let's go and kill some terrorists,' Harry screamed, holding his new PS5 game and controller aloft for all to see. A great sugar-fuelled cheer went up, with arguments about who would be allowed to play first, as there were only four controllers and eight boys. The boys disappeared into the living room and with them the mood in the kitchen went from happy to hideous.

'Nice to see you, Nick,' Louise seethed. 'Yet again you've missed a family event that you'd promised to be at.' She wasn't pulling any punches and didn't care that her parents were present.

'Another glass of champagne, anyone?' Judi stepped forward in another attempt to distract. 'Paul, you must need one after all that running around in the dark, shooting people.'

'I had to work.' Nick felt his phone buzz in his jacket pocket. Better not answer it right now.

'Then you must need a drink too,' said Judi, passing him a glass.

'I tried to call you on your mobile,' said Louise, 'then I called the office and was told you weren't to be disturbed. That you would return calls immediately after you were out of your very important meeting. It's your son's birthday party, Nick! You'd promised Harry you would be there.'

'Nibbles anyone?' Judi offered.

Nick's phone buzzed a second time.

'I am here. No thanks, Judi.' Nick turned back to Louise. 'And he doesn't look too bothered that I missed the laser tag.'

'He was really upset.' Louise was getting exasperated now. 'Not surprised a bit, but really upset and did a great job of hiding it. It was the fact that you didn't call and let us know, and we couldn't get hold of you. You haven't been in touch all day.'

His phone rang a third time. Who the hell was it calling so many times?

'Oh look, the tide's out.' Judi had drained her glass. 'Is there another bottle in the fridge, I wonder?'

'You could at least have called him and wished him a happy birthday.' Louise sounded so angry now that Charlotte's attention was drawn away from her phone.

'Oh, come on, I said I was sorry. I had to work, something came up.' As the words tumbled out, Nick realised they sounded like a cliché.

Their home phone rang.

Everyone was taken by surprise as it never rang, and its tone was unfamiliar. It was probably a telemarketer or an ambulance-chasing firm of solicitors.

After the briefest pause, Nick continued. 'I don't work for fun, you know. I do it so he can have parties like this and nice presents. I missed the laser tag, but I'm here now. It's not like anyone has died.'

'It's Nanna,' said Charlotte, handing Nick the phone.

12

NICK SNATCHED THE PHONE from Charlotte and spoke to his mum. Her tone of voice told him the news before her choice of words was able to.

'Your Dad's gone, son.'

He could hear the frog in her throat. It was a moment before she continued.

'He died peacefully about an hour ago. I loved him so much…' She couldn't continue.

Tracey took the phone. 'Hello Nick.' She sounded a little more composed than his mum had, though was barely audible. 'We tried to reach you a few times. We couldn't get hold of you.'

'I was in a … it doesn't matter. Where are you now?'

'We're still at the Lister. Can you come?'

'Where's Dad?'

'He's … in heaven with the angels.' She started to cry and set her mother off. Nick could hear her wailing dramatically in the background. When she let rip, she really went for it. Public displays of emotion made him squirm.

'No, I mean have they moved him yet?'

'No … sorry.'

'It's okay, Tracey.'

'Malika is giving him a wash now and says you will be here soon to say goodbye to him. We were with him when he went.'

'That's … that's good.'

'Before he fell asleep, he asked when you were coming again. Come soon, Nick.'

'I will.' He waited for her to speak, unable to find any words himself.

'Love you, Nick.' Tracey said.

Nick paused, trying unsuccessfully to form the same words on his lips. 'I'll be there as soon as I can.'

Nick had been given another get-out-of-jail-free card. He knew that his father's death meant his row with Louise would now have to wait. Her anger and frustration subsiding, Louise gave Nick a gentle hug and Charlotte joined in. It was decided that now wasn't the right time to tell Harry the news and that it could wait until after his party. If Nick wasn't back in time from the hospital, Louise would tell him.

As Nick left, the heavy silence in the kitchen was broken by the sound of prepubescent battle cries from the living room, as more terrorists were eradicated with unfeasibly heavy ordnance in a virtual arena of death.

The garage door opened respectfully at a funereal pace. Nick's bright red Audi seemed absurd. It was as if the car itself were now sticking up a middle finger at him. Through new eyes it looked less like a smart executive vehicle and more like Daddy Pig's car from *Peppa Pig*. He returned to the kitchen to get the keys to Louise's Mini Cooper. It would be a safer bet and he didn't want to draw attention to himself right now.

13

RAY HAD DECIDED NOW would be a good time to visit his Auntie Val. It was getting late, and she'd probably be into her third or fourth gin and tonic.

Auntie Val lived in a modest house in the leafy suburb of Woodhall on the east side of Welwyn Garden City. Ray's uncle had bought the house before Ray was born, and it had a swimming pool in the back garden, which was hardly ever used. There was about as much point in having an outdoor pool in Welwyn Garden City as there was in having a convertible car, which Auntie Val had always wanted but had never been allowed, though some people on the west side had them. Of course they did.

It was because of that swimming pool that Ray harboured a life-long fear of water. One summer's day after school he had rushed round to see Auntie Val so he could use the pool. She, Ray now realised, had been sunbathing and had consumed more gin than a child carer could responsibly manage at so early a point in the day. She hadn't taken the cover off the pool and Ray had thought it a good idea to jump onto it right in the middle. The insulating cover had wrapped itself right around Ray like a giant squid, dragging him down to the bottom of the pool. If it hadn't been for the fast-moving neighbour peering admiringly over the fence at Val's tanned form, Ray would have drowned. He felt sick thinking about it even now. It took a lot to get Ray anywhere near water.

Ray squeezed his van in behind Auntie Val's Qashqai on her narrow drive. Just like her small front garden, the old Qashqai was immaculately maintained. Everything about their home had been immaculate, not overly ostentatious as despite the wealth they must have accrued over the years, they never seemed to spend any of it. They never bought anything cheap, but they never wasted money on things for the sake of it. Their car had been the biggest extravagance they'd allowed themselves in years.

He locked his van and, once satisfied by the comforting bleep of its alarm, he rang Val's doorbell. He heard the familiar sound from inside of the old tubular chimes, reminiscent of a 1970s sitcom. Ray's mum had always called his uncle and auntie 'Terry and June', which hadn't meant much to Ray but always amused his father.

The light came on in the hallway and through the frosted glass panels Ray could see the diminutive silhouette of Auntie Val staggering down the hallway towards the door.

'What time do you call this? Whatever you're selling I'm not interested. Can't you see my no cold callers sign?' Her words were unmistakeably slurred.

'Auntie Val, it's me, Ray.'

Although she could just about make out familiar faces through the frosted glass, Valerie had insisted on having a spyhole fitted in the front door, low down to suit her height. She pressed her face against the door and looked through it, getting a clear view of the Fred Perry logo on Ray's jacket. He bent down, leant back a little and waved at her through the spyhole so that she could see it was him. Startled, she took a step backwards. Val hadn't seen Ray in years but he still had a distinctive French crop, an acne-scarred face and a gold chain. But it was his David Bowie eyes which left her in no doubt as to his identity. She expected his appearance was to do with Tony's death.

She spent the next minute fiddling with the security chain before opening the door and looking him up and down warily.

'You haven't changed that much, though I don't remember you being quite so tall, Ray. You'd better come in.'

As she ushered him into the hallway, Ray became immediately aware of the plug-in air fresheners, which had recently emitted another dose of toxic lavender-scented faux cleanliness into the air.

'I hope you'll oblige me by taking your shoes off. There's a spare pair of slippers should fit you there.'

The mules had no doubt belonged to Uncle Tony. Ray put them on whilst Val watched.

'There, they fit you just fine. Why don't you come through to the kitchen.'

Ray noticed a number of backlit figurines on a recessed shelf in the hallway that winked at him provocatively as he walked past.

'Can I get you anything? Now you're here, I think I'll have a little gin. I don't like to drink alone,' she lied.

'Just a cup of tea, please. Milk and two sugars. I'm driving. But don't let me stop you.'

'Don't mind if I do.' Val led him through to the kitchen where there was a wilting bouquet of flowers. 'Your mother sent me those. Lovely, aren't they? And they've lasted really well. She sent them the day he died.' Ray had to admit that they were remarkably well preserved, a bit like his Auntie Val.

'I'm sorry about Uncle Tony.' Ray shuffled his feet.

'Don't be. I'm not. Oh, did I say that out loud?' Val started to giggle and then poured herself a large gin and drank half of it in one go. She stuck a finger in the air to demonstrate that she had not forgotten his tea. 'Milk and two sugars?'

'Thanks.'

'I've hardly noticed he's not here, to be frank. He wasn't around much anyway, always working even at his age. I thought he might retire soon and we could travel a bit, but no. I'm meeting the solicitor to go through his will tomorrow. Is that why you're here? Did your mother send you?'

Ray felt a shock of cold. Auntie Val had seen straight through him and in that moment, he felt completely transparent, as if she knew everything he was thinking.

'No,' he lied. 'Mum texted me. We don't speak much and I haven't seen her and Dad since they moved to Canada. I was wondering when the funeral is. Mum said I should come as they won't be able to. I've never been to a burial.'

Val scoffed. 'The funeral's been a bit delayed due to some administrative stuff and he's not going to be buried now. He'll be cremated. He wanted to be buried, I don't want him to be. I want him cremated and gone. I spent my entire life tending to his needs and from what I can gather, he hasn't left me much, so I don't see why I should spend the rest of my life tending his grave. He's had the best of me already. It's my time now.'

She passed him a cup of tea. It was too hot and strong, and she'd only put one sugar in it. Surely Uncle Tony had left some money. He must have kept an account somewhere, maybe offshore or in Switzerland. Ray didn't know about these things.

'I can't believe he didn't keep a large stock at his shop,' Val wondered out loud. 'His safe at work was practically empty. There were a few jewels and gemstones, but they all belonged to clients and were awaiting setting. He'd taken to doing repairs and resizing in the last few years, like he knew he was winding down. If he ever had a massive stash of stones, they must be hidden somewhere very safe.'

Then Ray remembered. A flashback from his youth. His brain lit up like the Swarovski Clear Crystal Star Christmas Ornament his nan always put on her artificial Christmas tree. He knew where his uncle kept his stash of diamonds, rubies and sapphires: in the lining of his suit.

He just needed to get hold of it.

14

IT WAS NEARLY 9 P.M. by the time Nick arrived at the Lister, and the sun was beginning to drop. The sky was beautifully clear with a few long clouds blanketing the horizon. Nick parked up without any drama and with no thought given on this occasion to the cost of his parking. He made his way to the ward and found Tracey waiting to let him in at the sliding door. He pressed the button and the door slid open in a noisy manner with no empathy for the occasion.

Tracey was alone and clutching a traumatised tissue. Nick could see she had been crying. She said nothing, opening her long arms to embrace him. She was statuesque, Amazonian in appearance. He'd never won any of their childhood fights, as she'd always given far more than she'd got. It had taken Nick years to learn that despite him being a boy and only a couple of years younger than her, she was tough, physically at least. Mentally, she was a wreck, unable to hold down a relationship and now, in her own amusingly self-deprecating words, between husbands.

During their uncomfortably long embrace Tracey went from the role of comforter to comforted, starting to sob into his shoulder. Nick realised he hadn't done much hugging lately; it felt alien to him. He wanted to enjoy the embrace and give his sister what she needed, but found himself breaking away as soon as he could.

'I'm sorry,' Tracey said softly.

'Don't apologise, it's okay,' Nick said awkwardly.

'No. I've left a bit of snot on your jacket.' Tracey's laugh broke the tension as she wiped it off with the last remaining clean section of her tissue.

'Where's Mum?'

'She's with Dad. Do you want to come and see him?'

Oh God. I've got to go and see the body of my dad. Of course I have. That's why I'm here.

Nick had never seen a dead person before. What would it be like? What would his father look like dead? What if he had one of those after-death exhalations of air or spasms? Didn't dead people smell really bad too?

'This way.' Tracey led him along the corridor by his hand. The intimacy felt uncomfortable. He wanted to be left alone. He wanted to be able to go in and see his dad without having to talk to anyone, without having to ask anyone how they were coping and without having to answer sympathetic questions about how he was feeling. He didn't know how he felt. If he felt anything at all in that moment, it was nothing. Emptiness. A vacuum for a new emotion to be learnt.

The ward was peaceful. The business of the day was over and many of the patients were already asleep. Blinds had been pulled down to shade them from the setting sun. As they approached his father's room, Malika appeared from within, closing the door gently behind her. The internal blind over the door's window had been drawn for the family's privacy and his dad's dignity.

On seeing Nick, Malika gave him the most perfect look of empathy. Her eyes were warm and full of understanding, her look not in any way overly sympathetic. It was the perfect greeting from someone who genuinely cared for their work, their patients and the families who came and went. His body flooded itself with endorphins and in that moment, unable to control himself, hot tears flooded down his cheeks. A lump the size of a cricket ball appeared in his throat and he was unable to speak. He fought this emotional assault on his body as hard as he could, but failed to halt its flow.

Tracey looked at him, wanting to help but felt a resistance from him. Malika stepped in and offered him a handy box of tissues, asking him to follow her into the family room for a moment, which mercifully was unoccupied.

Nick walked to the window in the corner of the room and saw that the sun was setting in an epically biblical way. He half expected a throng of angels to appear. Then Malika spoke; her voice was pure aural analgesia. Nick felt completely calm and comfortable with her. She seemed to have the perfect approach to every situation.

'You can see him when you're ready, Nick, or not at all if you wish.' She waited patiently for a reply which didn't come. 'Would you like a cup of tea?'

Nick turned and nodded his acceptance. He was still unsure if his voice would work without betraying his current state of emotion.

'Your mother is in with your father at the moment. She said you could go in and join them when you arrived. But it may be something you wish to do alone.'

Yes. It was. Malika had hit the nail on the head again. Nick felt a palpable sense of relief. A great weight lifted from him; an immense catharsis. He didn't want anyone else in there when he saw his father. He had no idea how he would feel. He didn't want either his mum or Tracey to gauge his reaction or to monopolise the moment, making it about them and not his dad.

Malika passed him a cup of tea and he took a sip. It tasted delicious. He looked at Malika and had thoughts of wanting to bottle her essence. If only he had his own Malika on tap for every tricky situation.

'I would like to see him alone. I'll wait as long as I have to.'

'I'll leave you to drink your tea. I'll be back soon.'

Nick turned to enjoy the sunset and sipped his tea. This was the calmest he'd felt all day. Moments later the door opened and Nick's mum's presence entered the room. Her body would take longer.

'Come here, son.' Barbara opened her arms and waited for Nick to join her where she blocked the open doorway. Tracey was trying unsuccessfully to get past her. Nick would rather have hugged his mum in a more private space but realised that to fuss over the location of their hug might open a can of worms, so he embraced his mother where she stood. Where everyone in the corridor could see them.

'I'm sorry, Mum.' By this Nick meant he was sorry that Dad had died and he was sorry for her loss.

'That's okay, son. I know you were busy working and couldn't be here when he died.'

There was the guilt trip he'd been expecting.

'You can go and see him now. I'm sure he's looking down on us all. I won't come in with you, neither will Tracey.'

Malika had obviously given them subliminally incontestable instructions.

'Unless you'd like us to be there?'

'No. It's fine ... thanks. I'll go in. Alone.' Nick managed to break away from his mum's bear-like grip and took a step back to allow her to enter the room. She didn't move.

'There's a beautiful sunset,' Malika said from behind Tracey. 'It would be a shame to miss it.'

His mum and Tracey walked over to the window in the corner of the room to see the last of the sunset. Nick slipped past them and made his way to see his dad, for the very last time.

The moment Nick entered his father's room he could sense the absence of any life force other than his own. Despite the presence of his father's body, he knew that his father's essence had gone. Charlie looked completely at peace. Nick had always heard that dead people look like they are sleeping, but it simply wasn't true. That was a romanticised notion. No one sleeps in such an uncomfortable position. His father was definitely dead. All that remained was a pale white shell. An abandoned home, never again to be occupied.

Nick was overcome with a sense of relief for his father, a sense of something totally natural having occurred. In a way it was like witnessing something beautiful like a magnificent mountain view, or an infinite ocean scene; it had the same magnitude as witnessing the birth of a child. All feelings of regret, blame, remorse and confusion left him, swept away by a tidal wave of love filling every fibre of his body. The love he felt for his father at that moment was so great that there wasn't the vaguest possibility of there being any space for other thoughts or emotions. For the first time in his living memory he stopped thinking and started feeling. His father had gone. To where – who knows? Probably nowhere, but equally, possibly, somewhere. This was an ending and there is always comfort in endings. The sentiment surprised him as he'd had so little contact with his father, and not much that he could remember from his childhood.

Nick stroked his father's head and told him he loved him. He was so glad to be there alone with him; this wasn't a moment he wanted to share with anyone else and he was grateful that Malika had deftly engineered it for him and his dad.

Nick spent a while sitting with his father, thinking over their last conversations together and the creation of his father's bucket list. His father had said it was *their* list, the things he'd have liked to have done with him. He looked around his father's bed and to his relief, he couldn't see it. It had must have been thrown away. He'd not agreed to anything, so it would remain a secret, just between them. It was a crazy idea. Why on earth would he want to complete a list of tasks to please his dad? It meant nothing now. He had far more important things to get on with. The list was gone, along with his dad.

Nick realised he'd lost all sense of the time and became aware that his mum and Tracey might want to come back in to spend more time with his dad. He didn't want to be there to witness their intimacy and the performance his mum might put on if she felt so inspired. He appreciated that they would come in together as they were close, much closer to each other than he to either of them, and that was fine. The years had passed, and they had fashioned their own lives, sometimes losing touch. His focus was on providing for his family; he, like his father, had been busy trying to forge a better life for the kids. That was the right thing to do, though right now he'd have liked to have known his father a bit better. Or, in fact, at all.

Nick left the room, having said a final goodbye. He would of course say goodbye at the funeral too, but he wasn't comfortable with public displays of emotion and found funerals so impersonal and claustrophobic. So many people would attend to show their respects when they didn't want to be there, having lost touch years before. People even older than his dad would be there to show that they'd won that particular race. The family would put on brave faces and stiff upper lips and listen to an uninspired eulogy by a vicar who 'knew the deceased' and struggled to make the afterlife sound convincing or even attractive. Nick had said goodbye to his father on his terms and that was it. He could lock the emotions that had just violated him back in their cupboard and get on with his life. Didn't he have something important to do? The sale of his business. Oh, and getting back to his son's birthday party.

Tracey was waiting outside the door to their father's room as Nick left. She said nothing but moved in for a hug before he found the space or time to out-manoeuvre her advance. Nick explained that he needed to go but Tracey held him a little longer. Their sumo match was broken up with the approach of his mum and Malika.

'I have something here for you from your father,' said Malika.

Tracey released Nick and turned to Malika, thinking

she was addressing her.

'It is for Nick,' continued Malika. He could see the little notebook in her hand and his stomach dropped.

Oh fuck.

'What is it?' his mum cut in.

'It's nothing,' said Nick in a defensive manner. *Damn, that came out badly.*

'No, come on, share it,' said Tracey.

'Really, it's just something Dad wanted me to have. It's of no importance.'

Malika went to hand the notebook to Nick but it was snatched from her hand at the last minute by Barbara. For the first time in the short time Nick had known her, Malika looked surprised and annoyed. 'Mrs Swift,' she said in the voice of a benevolent school teacher, 'your husband asked me to give this to Nick personally.'

'I'm sure he would have wanted me to see it. We never had any secrets,' Barbara threw back. She opened the notebook and flicked through the pages. 'What is this? It looks like a bucket list.'

'That's exactly what it is, Mum,' Nick said, taking the book from her. She let it go without a struggle. 'He asked me to write down a list of things he would have liked to have done. We didn't get to finish it.'

A brief and awkward silence followed, interrupted by Malika a moment later. 'Your father woke just after you'd gone and asked me to write something else in it.'

'But he was hardly talking,' his mother erupted.

'You're right, Mrs Swift, he wasn't speaking much, but he dictated to me before he passed and I wrote his words down as he wished,' Malika assured her in a healing tone.

'What? What did he say?'

'Read it, Nick,' Malika instructed.

'I … I can't. Will you please read it, Malika?'

'Okay.' She took the book from Nick, turned to the last page and began to read aloud.

My dearest Nick,

Although I have loved your mother and Tracey immeasurably all my life and will always do so, I have not given you, my son, the time you deserved. Yet these last few days with you have been among the happiest of my life. Forgive me for not being the father I should have been, and realise now I wish I had been.

My final wish is for you to take my ashes on a journey of discovery. I might not be able to be with you in person, but I can be in spirit, if you'll allow my urn to accompany you. As you complete my post-bucket list, know I will be with you. As you paint, as you dance, as you walk a tightrope and as you leap from a plane, know that I will be with you.

One more thing I ask of you, my final wish. When our journey is at its end, scatter my ashes at Frinton beach where we had so many happy holidays. The tide will come and take me away, but not the memory of me. Do this on my next birthday, and think of me, knowing I love you and will always be with you.

My son, do this for me and for yourself. Allow me to be a proper father to you and then go and be a proper father to your children.

All my love,
Dad

Malika fell silent. Nick looked around. Barbara and Tracey had dissolved into a heap of tears, clutching each other for comfort. He looked at Malika.

'He went to sleep after that,' she said.

'Never to wake again,' Tracey added, unnecessarily, setting her mother off again.

So that was it. Charlie's dying wish had been that Nick take his ashes on a demented virtual road trip to fulfil an odyssey of guilt alleviation. Great. And now his mother and sister knew about it. How could he explain to them that he was too busy and the whole thing was utterly pointless?

15

'ACTUALLY, I WILL HAVE a drink, if I may. Can I get you another?' Ray lifted Auntie Val's empty glass from the coffee table in front of her. She was clearly very relaxed now and had put on a Michael Bublé CD.

'I shouldn't. I'm feeling a bit tipsy, I'm not used to it. I don't drink much these days and neither did your uncle, so we haven't got much in. But please, do help yourself. There are Stellas, Becks and Asahi in the fridge, also Stella Cidre, Strongbow blackcurrant cider and Thatcher's cloudy Haze. If it's ale you're after, there's Proper Job, Black Sheep, Camden, Marston's, Old Crafty Hen and a lovely bottle or two of Timothy Taylor. If you want some wine or rosé, check the wine fridge. It keeps it all at the exact temperature, you know, an unusually extravagant purchase for your uncle, but necessary. There's a Merlot already open on the side and more reds on the rack. Feel free to open a fresh bottle. If you fancy something a bit stiffer there are nine different flavours of gin, as well as the more traditional ones. I like a Gordon's, a Bombay Sapphire or a Tanqueray. There's flavoured vodka in the freezer, tequila in the cupboard under the cooker and mixers in the fridge and larder. Ah, I do like Michael Bublé, don't you, Ray? He's almost as good as Barry Manilow. Oh, and there's some whisky too if you want some, and some sherry—'

'I'm sure I'll find something, Auntie Val,' Ray reassured her and agreed that Michael Bublé wasn't too unpleasant.

'I will have another drink, thanks Ray. You've twisted my arm. Go on. I'll have a rhubarb gin with Fever Tree Mediterranean mixer please. Ice and a slice. Make it a long one. I like a long one.' Val giggled loudly as she attempted to stand, steadying herself on the back of the sofa before wandering across the room to peruse her collection of CDs. 'I'm in a Manilow mood now. The Copacabana!' She easily found the CD in her alphabetically arranged collection and started to hum, free from the constraints of any tune.

'Back in a minute, Auntie.'

Ray mixed Val's drink according to her wishes, giving her enough gin to anaesthetise an elephant. He couldn't believe her diminutive form could take so much alcohol and still be standing. He searched the drawers for a bottle opener to take the top off his beer and spotted a spare front door key, which he pocketed.

Auntie Val joined in as Barry Manilow sang about a showgirl named Lola. Her banshee-like wailing made Ray hurry up fixing the drinks. It was painful to listen to; she didn't have the benefit of Michael Bublé's Auto-Tuning. Manilow sang in tune without any help, Ray mused, which made it even more apparent how much Val disagreed with his tuning. He needed to get more gin down her and quickly – to hopefully knock her out. Ray grabbed a Stella from the fridge.

'Here we are,' Ray announced triumphantly as he handed Val her drink.

'I asked for a long one,' she protested in a mock-hysterical manner, laughing again at her own humour. 'No, that's lovely love. Perfick!' She had to raise her voice over the now much louder Manilow filling her living room.

Auntie Val segued seamlessly into the second verse and started singing about someone called Rico who wore a diamond. The key of her rendition was now locked in a disharmonious battle with the original; she was showing no signs of flagging. Ray even thought that Manilow might eventually have to bend to her will.

Rico's diamond reminded him of why he was there, reinforcing his need to find the treasure he believed was upstairs. A jolt of excitement shot through him. He could be rich if he found it. When the fuck would she get tired?

Auntie Val got to the point in the song where blood was spilled in a single gunshot. A single gunshot would solve all his problems right now. Auntie Val carried on wailing about the Copacabana. He could wait no longer.

'I need the loo, Auntie,' Ray announced in a barely audible voice.

She gave him the thumbs up as she carried on singing and dancing, slopping her gin in the process, forcing her to drain a little more from the long glass. Quite a lot more in fact.

Ray headed in the direction of the downstairs loo. He noticed that it was being decorated again. Although with a careful aim he could manage, he decided out of respect that he would go to the upstairs bathroom. A remarkable stroke of luck.

Ray made his way up the plushily carpeted staircase to the darkness of the upstairs landing. The landing was of a generous size with five doors opening onto it. He could just about make out which was the master bedroom and he went in. Once inside he closed the door and turned on the light, which illuminated a crystal chandelier hanging from the high ceiling above the bed. He turned the dimmer down to low, and although it did nothing to make him anymore hidden, it offered a false sense of security. He immediately set about searching the wardrobes. One whole wall of the room was lined with sliding mirror doors. Everything within was pristinely clean and organised in a fashion that would have thrilled his old Sergeant Major. Dresses, skirts and blouses hung from the rails. There were drawers full of immaculately folded shirts, tights, underwear and on the shelves were neatly stacked shoeboxes.

At the other end of the wardrobe, he found what he was looking for. His uncle's clothes, taking up less than a quarter of the width of the wall-long wardrobe, had not yet been cleared out. A strong scent of Floris awoke the memory of Uncle Tony. Ray felt like Indiana Jones at the opening of a cave, ready to take on whatever challenges were needed to procure the treasure, now surely within his grasp.

He could still hear his auntie singing along to the song. How much longer would she be distracted? A moment later another song started and with it his auntie's Foster-Jenkins accompaniment.

He started to sort through the suits, trying to find the heavy three-piece he'd not seen for over twenty-five years. His uncle's favourite. He couldn't see it. He started frantically feeling the linings of suits at random, discovering no bulges or anomalies in any of them. They all seemed perfectly lined and unaltered. It must be there.

He turned the lights up higher, having first made sure

the curtains were drawn so none of the neighbours would see him at work. He took out all the suits and laid them on the bed. One by one he patted them down, searching for clues as to the whereabouts of his treasure.

Soon he started to take less care with them and became frustrated, throwing jackets and trousers into a heap on the floor once he was satisfied that they contained no hidden secrets. In his frenzy he hadn't noticed that Barry Manilow was now singing alone, a sad song about not being able to smile without someone. Ray had his arm stuck halfway down one of his uncle's jacket sleeves when he was interrupted by his auntie, standing in the doorway.

'You only had to ask if you wanted to have any of his clothes. But I don't think any of them will fit you, love, you've grown so tall and your uncle wasn't very big, in any way whatsoever.'

Ray slowly extracted his arm from the jacket sleeve, pulling it inside out in the process.

'Is there anything in particular you fancy?'

'I remember he had a lovely three-piece suit.'

'Oh, that old thing.'

Had she thrown it away? Ray felt suddenly sick. Feeling the blood rushing away from his head, he sat down on the edge of the bed, atop a tired-looking deep blue velvet bedspread.

'I'm not keeping that one.'

Oh fuck. It had gone. His treasure, lost.

'He wanted to keep it, though,' she continued. 'He's wearing it now. It was his favourite and he wanted to be buried in it.' She stopped abruptly to mark the silence as Barry Manilow stopped singing briefly before starting a new middle-of-the-road emotion. 'Oh, I love this one!' Auntie Val began her banshee-like humming again, vaguely in time with Manilow.

'But he's being cremated, isn't he?' Ray cried.

'Indeed, he is. On Friday June 24th at 3 p.m. at Pinewood Crematorium. So, if it was his favourite suit you wanted to keep, I'm afraid you're well and truly out of luck.' Seamlessly she segued from humming to singing the chorus of a lesser-known Manilow song in her gin-enthused broken soprano, something about the one that got away.

Only for now, Ray thought. If his uncle was being cremated, the stones would surely survive the heat of the oven. Diamonds are forever, right? As well as rubies and sapphires. Maybe he should Google it, just to be sure, then it was just a case of getting hold of the urn before anyone else did. Unless of course, he could get to the body before its cremation.

* * *

Back at home, Ray booted up his laptop and waited for it to decide that it had run all the updates it insisted on doing before he was able to start his search. After two frustrating hours of searching, entering numerous questions into just about every forum on jewels he could find and ascertaining the heat needed to cremate a body, he came upon the one answer he didn't want: diamonds aren't forever. Rubies and sapphires are. If he wanted to fully cash in on his uncle's fortune, he would have to get to his uncle's body before one third of the jewels went up in smoke.

16

NICK WANTED OUT OF the hospital and quickly. He had to get home as soon as possible; he was exhausted, and he needed to be away from his mum and sister.

'I'm really sorry, Mum, Tracey. I need to go. It's Harry's birthday today and I need to get back to the party.' That should do the trick.

'Yes, you go. We'll be fine,' Tracey said.

'Yes, you get off. If you must,' said Barbara. 'I've sent Harry a text to wish him a happy birthday from me. I forgot to call earlier with everything that was going on.'

'That's okay, I'm sure he'll understand.'

Tracey had texted Harry too. She always did, as she was always late with birthday cards and promises of presents that never materialised. Harry had calculated that she owed him £175 in undelivered promises.

'I wished him happy birthday from your dad too,' Barbara said.

'Oh, that's lovely,' said Tracey.

'From heaven.' Barbara sobbed into her hanky.

Nick's stomach sank. Again. 'Oh. We hadn't told him yet, Mum. We were going to tell him in the morning, after his party.' He wondered whether Harry had seen the text yet. There was a chance he hadn't. Nick wasn't sure how upset he'd be. He hoped that Harry's birthday date wouldn't morph into 'the day Grandad died'.

There was a disapproving silence from his mother at the idea that the news wasn't important enough to interrupt a birthday party.

'I'll call you in the morning and come over and help,' Nick blustered. 'I'm sure there's a lot that needs sorting, but you won't want to think about any of that now.'

'Mum's already called the undertaker,' Tracey said.

'But Dad only died earlier today.' Nick was dumbfounded.

'Well, you know what she's like. No point in hanging around and she wanted to busy herself. The funeral is going to be held at Pinewood Crematorium.'

'Friday June the 24th at 3 p.m.,' his mother confirmed. *Dad is still warm(ish) on his deathbed and he's already been processed. Jesus.* 'Don't we need to let people know? Aren't there people we need to check with to see if they can come?' Nick thought about saying that it might have been nice if they'd checked with him and his family, but didn't quite dare.

'Everyone that needs to know knows,' explained Tracey. 'I set up a mailing list.'

'What, this afternoon?'

'Mum asked me to do it two weeks ago so we were ready when the moment came. We knew it would be too painful for us to think about it then. So, I created a template ready for the moment. It's even got an embedded link.'

'She's so clever,' Barbara chimed in. 'I don't even know what an in-bed-link is.'

'Stop it, Mum,' Tracey continued. 'Dad didn't have many close friends so there aren't that many people to inform.

Family knows. Uncle Keith knows and Auntie … can't remember which one he's on now. I could look at YouTube, I suppose. You should get an email too, Nick, as I set it up to go about now.'

Nick heard a ping and looked at his phone. Sure enough, he'd received an email from Barbara and Tracey, his name noticeably absent.

It is with great sadness that we inform you of the passing of beloved husband, father and grandfather Charles 'Charlie' Swift, who died peacefully in his sleep on [INSERT DATE HERE]. *The funeral will be held at Pinewood Crematorium at* [INSERT TIME HERE] *on the* [INSERT DATE HERE]. *No flowers, please. Please send donations instead to* [BENEFICIARY TBC]. *Please join us for a reception afterwards at our humble home.* CLICK HERE *for directions.'*

Nick quietly informed Tracey that she might want to think about re-sending the email.

17

Friday 17th June

AUNTIE VALERIE HAD ASKED Ray to be at the solicitor's office in the centre of Welwyn Garden City for 9.45 a.m. exactly. They had a meeting with his uncle's solicitor at 10 a.m. and she didn't want him to be late. They were the only people who'd been invited to hear his will read.

The solicitor's office was hidden amongst the multitude of eateries and charity shops on Fretherne Road, accessed through a door at ground level that led up to the first floor. The brass plaque was barely readable and hadn't been polished in years, but it dimly confirmed that *Gerald Jones, Solicitor* could be found there. His door was wedged between a greasy spoon cafe and an Indian restaurant. The individual smells of stale cooking oil, bacon and exotic spices fought for attention and turned his stomach. Auntie Val didn't comment on it; she probably couldn't smell it as she seemed to have fallen in a vat of perfume that morning and had narrowly missed drowning. She, once again, was probably masking the alcohol that exuded from every pore of her body.

They buzzed the office to be ungraciously told they were early and would have to wait five minutes whilst Gerald Jones, Solicitor finished with another client, as he didn't have a waiting room for them to sit in. Ray wondered whether the smell upstairs in the office was worse than the odour on the pavement, where they would have to wait. He hoped this whole experience would be over soon; he'd taken the morning off work especially. He wondered for a moment whether his uncle had taken the jewels he'd kept hidden in his suit and deposited them somewhere safe, now to announce that he'd left them all to Ray and nothing to Auntie Val. Had he hated his wife so much that he had relished in the idea of her pain at hearing such news? It was a ridiculous fantasy, a fantasy worthy of those who continue to play the lottery even though the odds are appalling.

Auntie Val moved closer to Ray and overpowered him with her scent. His stomach swam in another direction. She leant in close to him, beckoning him with her finger. 'There won't be anything for you, Ray.' She was clearly still drunk from the day before. 'He's left nothing for me, and I doubt there will be anything for you. I can't imagine why you need to be here.'

Ray backed away from his aunt's potent breath. 'Let's just get it over with as soon as possible.'

Neither of them spoke for a while after that. They had nothing to say, both wondering why they were there and both hoping there might be a surprise in the will.

The door buzzed and clicked open, inviting them into a stairwell which started almost immediately behind the opened door. Val pushed through first, only to have to step back out onto the pavement, as a very large couple took an inordinate amount of time to come down the dark, narrow staircase. The man came first, followed by his wife, who made no efforts to cover her tears. She sobbed heavily into a handkerchief and stopped at the threshold to noisily blow her nose. Ray took a step back to avoid being sprayed by the droplets her insignificant handkerchief failed to catch.

Once the doorway was clear Val led the way up the creaky staircase, the walls of which were decorated sporadically with fading prints of imagined landscapes interspersed with small posters advertising services at rates available on request.

The battle between spice and stale oil was finally decided by the time Ray reached the first floor, the winner a new entry to the contest. The victor appeared in the form of Gerald Jones, Solicitor. Gerald had obviously found his own way of dealing with the combatant smells attacking his office from below and had decided to cloak them in his own aroma, a particularly pungent scent of body odour that thrived in his tiny unventilated room. Ray wasn't sure he would make it through the hearing without vomiting and adding yet another aspect to the room's miasma of fetid fragrances.

Gerald invited them both to sit and gave them a perfunctory welcome. Another weapon he clearly used in an attempt to dull his senses was a smoking habit. Although there was no evidence to support this other than that offered to Ray's olfactory senses.

'This won't take long.'

Gerald was as accurate in that statement as he was in all his communications. Tony Dyema had ensured that his wife would be fine and accommodated for until her death. She would now be the sole beneficiary of the pension he had set up for them both. She had the house and the car, and could afford a reasonable standard of living. She couldn't afford the foreign holidays she wanted each year, but the sale of his burial plot had seen to that for this year, at least.

As she had expected, Val had been left with no large sum of money or collection of jewels to sell. Gerald covered the fact that although Tony had wished to be buried in his favourite suit, it was not binding as the request had been on a codicil, which had not been signed. To further annoy his wife, Tony had left his collection of Swarovski figurines to the Hospice charity shop. Ray too was annoyed by this, but it meant he might be able to acquire the collection if he explained the situation. However, that spark of excitement died away as soon as it appeared. He wanted the jewels.

It was the next section of the will that shocked Valerie and confirmed Ray's suspicions. Tony had left a fortune in diamonds, rubies and sapphires. At the last estimate they were said to be worth nearly £5 million. The only problem was that the whereabouts of the jewels was unknown. Gerald Jones, Solicitor, took great amusement in this fact and coughed his way through the final sentence.

I leave my fortune in jewels to the first person that finds them, whether that be a family member, acquaintance or a complete stranger. I have secreted them so that one day someone may find them. I leave no clues as to their whereabouts other than the fact that they will not be in my house. A public announcement should be made in the Welwyn Hatfield Times *to this effect in the first publication after my funeral.*

Gerald's eyes lit up at the idea of finding them himself. Ray could see the cogs whirring away underneath his untended eyebrows.

On hearing this news, Valerie's face grew ashen, blending in with the decor of the small office. But Ray knew where the jewels were and once he had them in his possession, they would legally be his. There would be no need for him to steal them and then illicitly sell them at a low rate to a dodgy dealer. The best part was that Auntie Val had no idea where they were and neither did anyone else.

Back outside in the less challenging air, Ray turned to his aunt. 'Let me know if there's anything I can do between now and the funeral, otherwise I'll see you on the day.'

'I don't need any help thank you,' she sobbed.

'Just out of interest, are you using Morton and Sons undertakers?'

'No, Kerton's are the funeral directors. Morton's were too pricey. Why do you ask?'

'Will he be laying in a chapel of rest there?' Ray persisted.

'No. No one needs to see him. You don't, do you?'

'I would like to say goodbye,' he lied.

'Well, you can do that at the funeral. You can ride with me in the car. I'll get them to pick you up. But now I need to get home.'

'Would you like me to come with you?'

'That won't be necessary. I have a lot to do. Some things to sort out.'

Ray expected that she did. But she wouldn't find the jewels. He would. He would have to get them before the cremation and then make up a story about where he found them. He would think of something. His pulse raced at the thought. He too had some things to sort out and a little more Googling to do.

18

AT JUST AFTER 3 A.M. at his Hatfield Branch in the centre of the town, funeral director and business owner Graham Kerton opened the back of his private ambulance and pulled out a removal shell containing the body of Doris Phillips, long-retired gymnast, who'd died peacefully at home after a lengthy illness. Her husband Lionel had called the doctor first, and then Kerton's. He apologised for the lateness of his call but respectfully wanted the matter dealt with before the morning. The transportation coffin's wheels opened underneath it as Graham slid it out.

'Can you close that for me please, Stu?'

'No probs,' said Stu.

Stu pulled the ambulance's hatch door closed, and took his place at the end of the trolley. He began to push it across the forecourt towards the loading bay, past Graham's pride and joy: an enormous BMW R1200RT motorcycle. The type of bike used by the British police, Graham had told him on numerous occasions. Graham headed towards the loading bay roller door and knelt down to put a key into the heavy padlock securing the door to the ground.

'For fuck's sake,' he said, mindful of the fact he had to keep his voice down, it being the middle of the night.

'What's up?' whispered Stu.

'Someone's tried to force the fucking lock. Look at it.'

Stu came over and knelt down to get a closer look. As they did so, they heard a loud noise from behind them as a wheelie bin was pushed over and a tall, lanky man in a balaclava and dark clothes darted out from the shadows and made a dash for the open gates. Graham spun around and leapt to his feet.

'Oi, you! Stop!' shouted Graham as he sprinted towards the escapee. Stu too, got up to pursue him through the yard. At this point the burglar was parallel with the removal shell, which he forcefully pushed over. To Graham and Stu's horror the shell smashed down, and the lid came off, giving elderly Doris her very last opportunity to somersault through the air and roll across the ground to her penultimate resting place. The tall, lanky burglar vanished swiftly into the night, no longer pursued by the two undertakers who were frantically dealing with a new undertaking.

19

Friday 24th June

THE STRANGEST THING HAPPENED that morning. Nick slept in. It had been just over a week since his father's death, and he had been phenomenally busy at work. He had told Brian that he probably wouldn't be in the office on the day of his father's funeral. When the heavily perfumed Shirley heard that he was even considering coming in she gave him a shocked look and told him that he must do no such thing – 'How could you even consider it, young man?' – he should take the whole day off and spend time with his family. The truth was Nick did want to spend the day with his family, but only particular members, and at forty-nine he didn't consider himself a young man. He hated anyone telling him what to do, especially Shirley, who had become so much bolder with every passing recolouring of her hair. Brian showed little sympathy, but wished him luck with the day's events and mentioned that he could always catch up on the preparation work the next day.

From Nick's comfortable spot in bed, he could hear that the rest of the household had awoken and the ground floor of his home was buzzing with activity. It was a school day, but the kids were both off for the funeral and were up much earlier than usual. From the relative tranquillity of his room, he was aware of numerous electrical devices competing for attention: an Alexa with a notification in one room trying to be heard over Siri and OK Google in another, TikTok blaring out on Charlotte's phone and Spotify on another device somewhere. If the machines were preparing to take over the world, they were starting with his home. He could also hear the rumble of a distant motorbike accompanied by Zen-like spa music and then a heavy power chord or two. He recognised it as his Uncle Keith's YouTube channel jingle.

'Oh, for fuck's sake,' Nick uttered aloud to no one in particular.

'I'm having trouble understanding you,' Alexa replied. She had heard, which meant many others may have too and possibly a hacker, or several, somewhere across Eastern Europe.

Nick dragged his permanently unrefreshed body out from underneath his duvet and sat on the edge of the bed. He waited for the familiar ache in his lower back to subside before leaning forward and pushing down into his feet, as gravity assisted his forward swing into a standing position. Various other habits kicked in here: a hawk to clear his throat, an automatic testicular scratch and a vague attempt at stretching, first his arms then his back and finally his legs. He knew he really ought to exercise. The fact that when he stood naked and looked down he was unable to see the end of his old chap without the aid of a mirror was a catalyst to weight loss. Nick went through all his other morning routines mostly involving preparing his ageing body for the day, before dressing. He thought of his father, now unable to do any of the things Nick had just done, and felt simultaneously sad, depressed at the inevitability of ageing and grateful for still being in the game.

In the kitchen the atmosphere felt more like Christmas day than the day of a funeral. The children were excited and Louise looked stressed; just like Christmas morning at about this time, the only real difference being that no turkey was being prepared, no one had an alcoholic drink in front of them and the dog wasn't wearing tinsel.

Barry, having been the only one to notice Nick's presence, greeted him with a sloppy lick of the hand. The expression on Barry's face gave away his desperate need for breakfast, which Nick provided, only to find out that Barry had already been fed and had just pulled a fast one on him; a genetic trait inherent in all Labradors.

Louise started to relax once she had a coffee in her hand. Nick stopped to notice that she looked incredibly elegant, dressed all in black, in two-inch heels. She was stunning. He was a lucky man.

Meanwhile, both Charlotte and Harry were beside themselves with excitement, watching the smart TV in the snug, which was blaring out *Karmic Keith's Motorcycle Mantras.*

'I can't believe we're going to get to meet him today,' Charlotte said between mouthfuls of cereal.

'Me too,' said Harry, without bothering to wait until his mouth was empty. Even Barry looked excited, and he wasn't going to get to meet Great-Uncle Keith. Godzilla sat with Charlotte, sharing what looked like a mixing bowl into which they'd emptied an entire packet of Shreddies.

'I'm looking forward to meeting him too,' said Louise. 'He's handsome, in a rugged kind of way. Like one of the

Hairy Bikers but younger looking, almost sexy.'

'Ew, that's so gross,' sneered Charlotte.

'I'm gonna blow chunks of Marmite toast,' warned Harry.

'He's old enough to be your father, Louise.' Nick joined in the protest.

Louise smiled. 'He's younger than your dad, though.'

'Yes, by eight years. He's sixty-nine, I think.'

'His girlfriend is younger than you, Mum,' Charlotte said. 'She looks it anyway, see?' She indicated a svelte female riding pillion on Keith's latest motorbike. 'She's incredibly fit. She appears with him a lot, doing yoga and stuff.'

'He can obviously keep her well satisfied!'

The reason the room fell silent at this point, apart from the voice of Karmic Keith demonstrating an 'Om' technique, was that the last statement came from twelve-year-old Harry.

'Oh my god, you're such a dick, Harry, that's vile,' said Charlotte. 'And totally offensive to women.'

'How do you know that it's not her keeping him satisfied?' Louise said.

'Ew, Mum, that's gross,' Charlotte protested.

Harry retaliated inappropriately and within seconds the room returned to its normal state of cacophony and conflict with every person, animal and device contributing to the chaos.

Nick's phone vibrated in his pocket. Damn. He'd meant to put it on Do Not Disturb.

He put down the spoon he'd absentmindedly been trying to butter his toast with, pulled his phone from his pocket and saw it was Brian.

What now? He shouldn't be calling me today. It's either a butt-dial or serious.

Nick took the phone into the study. It wasn't a butt-dial. It wasn't that serious, but Brian seemed to think it was and was beginning to have another meltdown. The calm captain of the Titanic seemed to be seeing an increasing number of hungry polar bears on top of approaching icebergs lately.

'Jeff Silverman's team have just sent us through another due diligence request. Well, a few actually.'

'Can't this wait until tomorrow?'

'Technically, yes. But they will keep doing this and if we don't look at each request immediately, they will all mount up. They sent in a load more yesterday. They want to verify that the company has title to the assets on the balance sheet; property, patents, goodwill, intellectual property rights, trade debtors etcetera.'

'You didn't mention that—'

'They came in by post, would you believe.'

'By post?'

'Yes. Shirley didn't put them on my desk until the end of the day. She forgot.'

'Oh, for fuck's sake.'

'My sentiments exactly.'

'I only need twenty minutes of your time, Nick. I hate to ask.'

Nick looked at his watch. He had plenty of time. Although his office was in the opposite direction from the crematorium, he could easily get there in time. Nick felt a sense of dread at the flack he was about to receive, but he wouldn't be able to focus at all today if he didn't pop into the office to help Brian.

'I'll be back soon, I promise,' he said, before pouring himself a small coffee and chugging it down.

'What? No!' said Louise. 'You're not going to the office today.'

'I have to, briefly. I'll be back before you know it.'

'*Nick.*' Louise sounded serious now. 'Can't you Zoom?'

'No, it's a paper thing.'

'Paper? If you aren't back in time, we'll have to go without you.'

'See you later, kids. I have to pop to work for a bit.' Nick grabbed his jacket and patted Barry, who had reset once more and was hoping for a third helping of breakfast. 'You kids, I don't know. It's your grandad's funeral today and you seem more excited about meeting Uncle Keith.'

'Of course we are,' said Charlotte. 'I'm sorry, but we hardly knew Grandad. He was always at work.'

'Just like you, Dad,' said Harry without looking around.

20

AMIRA WASN'T IN A great mood today. She'd received a call asking her to come into work when she'd booked a day off to contact breeders in her quest for an as yet elusive Ashera cat. Lauren had called in sick, claiming that she was developing asthma. This came as no surprise to Amira, as Lauren never practised what she preached. She often scraped out the ovens without putting on a face mask. Asthma could be the least of her problems; the carcinogens left after the burning process were probably many and to risk inhaling them was foolish, but Lauren always knew best.

Amira arrived only five minutes late, which considering the notice she'd been given was pretty good. Yesterday had been a Giuseppe-free day so Amira had been able to make her bed without the usual hair-removal delay. Tomorrow morning would be an altogether different matter.

Today was going to be busy, and there should have ideally been two technicians on duty but Lauren had insisted she could cover it. When she called in sick, that left Amira on her own, not an ideal situation but one she was confident she could handle despite being relatively new on the job. This was her chance to prove herself – to prove that she could manage everything according to the protocols. With no one constantly watching over her shoulder, she might even be able to relax and start to enjoy herself.

As she walked into the committal room with the two

cremators, she made a mental note to talk to Mr McFall in maintenance about a loose window that had the habit of blowing open in a strong wind. It was beginning to rattle a little today, but fortunately it wasn't swinging open. With one of the cremators open it could cause quite a draft.

At first Amira felt nervous, a sensation in her tummy of butterflies, not altogether unpleasant. She couldn't decide whether the feeling was one of excitement or of mild anxiety so she decided not to worry and, being the optimist she was, she decided it was excitement at being in charge. She enjoyed her brief engagements with the undertakers; normally Lauren dealt with them, but today was her opportunity to make a good impression.

All the urns needed for today's cremations were on the shelf and Lauren had laid out their identification labels nearby, ready to be stuck on. Things were going well. She'd dressed in her overalls and boots, pulling on her hood and donning her mask. She stepped forward to get a closer look at herself in the mirror and noticed that her outline was a little fuzzy. It was at that moment that the butterflies in her stomach flew into a frenzy, as if someone nearby had just turned on an extraction fan and they were being sucked into the blades. Her outline was fuzzy because, in the rush to get to work, she'd forgotten to put her contact lenses in. She had no spare glasses with her; she'd taken her work pair home because her others had been broken during role playing with an overenthusiastic Giuseppe one week earlier. Amira's long-sightedness meant she'd been fine driving to work, but would have to get by with a lot of squinting for the rest of the day. She would just have to remember the instructions without referring to the manual. She had done it enough times now. It would be fine.

Amira reminded herself of the process after the cremation itself: the ashes, once cooled on the cooling tray, would be treated, meaning that metal would be removed by a magnet and then the ashes would be put through a grinder. The remains would be decanted into a robust polythene bag, which itself would be stored in a cardboard urn unless otherwise instructed. This would be labelled with the date and name of the deceased, and put in temporary storage, before being given to either the undertaker or directly to a family member, usually within the week. If the urn wasn't collected within a month, the family would be charged storage. Even the dead had to pay rent, she reflected. She would have to trust that Lauren, who was normally very efficient, had put the labels in order from left to right according to the time of the cremation. She could check all the finer details tomorrow once she had her eyes back in; who would collect and when, whether the ashes were to be interred at the crematorium or scattered in the garden of remembrance. She didn't need to worry about any of that today.

With a little time before the first of today's ten cremations, Amira decided to get ahead of herself, so she started to attach the labels to the urns. After mindlessly attaching the eighth label she became aware of the silence in the room, normally filled with Lauren's eclectic playlist ranging from Coldplay to Alanis Morissette. Today Amira could call the shots. She connected her phone to the Bluetooth speaker and peered at the screen; she could just about make out the image of her playlist if she held her hand at the right distance from her face. She pressed play and Verdi's *Il Trovatore* blared out; the stentorian tones of the tenor Franco Corelli singing the exciting aria, 'Di Quella Pira'.

As she returned to the shelf to affix the final two labels to their urns, she noticed that the door to one of the cremators was ajar. She decided to check that it had been properly cleaned at the last cremation. As she leaned over and pulled open the cremator door, she felt a substantial draught rush past her into the cremator and up the chimney. The faulty window high up behind her rattled and banged. It stopped immediately when she closed the door to the cremator.

Amira turned to finish her earlier task and noticed that the two labels for the day's final cremations were no longer on the shelf by their plastic containers. She froze in horror, the intense drama she felt within equally matched by Corelli's impossibly long and ringing high C. Frantically, she searched the room. To her great relief she found both labels lying by the door to the committal room. She picked them up and went to affix them to their containers, then stopped. Which label went with which container? She could not read the labels no matter how hard she squinted, and she didn't want to go and ask for help, especially as her all-in-one overalls did her voluptuous figure no justice. She'd labelled eight urns correctly and the odds that the last two were correct were 50:50. Odds she was prepared to live with today.

No one would ever know the difference and really, what harm could it cause?

21

'YOUR MOTHER IS ON line two.'

Shirley had tried to get Nick's attention through the viewing pane of his office door but had given up and decided to go in, even though he'd asked not to be disturbed. He'd mentioned something about 12.30 p.m., but she'd had trouble hearing the exact details over the expensive coffee machine, which she was making the most of in her remaining time at the company. Nick's head had been down all morning and he'd managed to get several issues ironed out for the proposal. But it was a struggle; every time he thought he'd solved an issue another appeared in its place.

Shirley stood directly in front of his desk and cleared her throat. '*I said*, your mother is on line two, Mr Swift.' She always used his surname when she was irritated with him, which these days was often.

'Yes, thank you, Shirley. I can see a number of missed calls on my mobile, but I said I didn't want to be disturbed until 12.30 at the earliest.'

'Yes, I think you may have said that.'

'Then, with respect, why the interruption?'

'Because it is now 1.15 and I believe you have a commitment this afternoon.'

'What? Oh Jesus. Why didn't you tell me what the time was? I need to go,' said Nick, desperate to blame someone else.

'Your mother is still on line two, Mr Swift,' Shirley

retorted. 'Shall I tell her you'll call her back *after* the funeral?'

'No, I'll take the call. Thank you.' Flustered, Nick reached for his mobile and noticed he'd left it on Do Not Disturb, which had silenced the alarm he'd set himself and had blocked incoming calls. Three from his mother and two from Louise. He dialled his mother. Needless to say she sounded stressed. In fact she choked up and passed the phone to Tracey.

'Are you joining us in the family car? The funeral director will be here in twenty minutes.'

Oh fuck. He wouldn't make it. He'd have to see them there. He desperately tried to think of an excuse as to why he wouldn't be there on time.

Tracey saved him having to find one. 'You're at work, aren't you?'

'I … yes. Yes, I am. Issues here.'

He could hear his mum saying something in the background.

'Mum says you're just like your father,' Tracey repeated.

Nick felt a deep annoyance as well as a sudden hollowness. He hated being compared to his father and he hated the way that Tracey was so often a vacuous conduit for his mother's thoughts, repeating without giving any consideration to their meaning. Maybe Tracey had the same thoughts. Maybe Tracey didn't have any at that time. But if she agreed with her mother on this occasion, then he had to confess that he agreed with them. This was just the sort of thing his father would have done.

'I'll see you at the crematorium.'

There was silence at the end of the line.

'Tracey?'

She had hung up. He tried to call her back but it went to voicemail, so Nick left a message and texted her to say he'd see them there.

Brian told him that he would carry on answering the queries and that Nick really ought to get going. He wished him luck and apologised for putting pressure on him to come in. There it was again, Brian acting in a very un-Brian way.

Nick laid his jacket on the back seat of his Audi so that it remained crease-free for the funeral. He sat in the driver's seat and closed the door. He entered the address of the crematorium into the satnav. It didn't take long to offer him a route. But even the best option was not what he was expecting. Fuck, it was going to be tight. But why? It was mid-afternoon before the school run when the lanes would be chock-a-block with Chelsea Tractors and over-sized SUVs driven by people who never went anywhere near a green lane. Had there been an accident? If so, it wasn't showing on the satnav. Fuck. Fuck. Triple fuck.

He backed out of the parking space and left the car park, following the quickest route offered to him. He had two choices now: he could resign himself to his fate and try to remain calm, trusting that to rush rarely expedited one's journey; or he could panic and drive like a lunatic in the hope of getting there in time. He chose the latter.

Nick managed to pass a number of cars and buses before running into a short queue for a junction; there was no way he was able to over-take at this point, and he started to feel a rising hysteria in his chest. He simply could not miss the funeral. He could see a learner driver up ahead trying to turn right.

'For fuck's sake, turn left,' Nick shouted obsolescently. He couldn't bear it anymore. He checked his mirror and then signalled to pull out. As he did so, a motorcycle appeared from nowhere and came alongside his car. Nick had to slam on his brakes. The motorcyclist seemed to anticipate this and managed to stop just in time. He turned to look at Nick and lifted up the flip-front of his helmet to reveal his face, though he still had his sun-visor down, resembling some sort of Terminator. Nick was expecting a diatribe of abuse and fumbled for the window control to close the window, missing it and closing the passenger window instead. The Terminator simply looked at Nick, surveyed his car and then slowly raised his left hand and gave Nick a middle finger. He did all this without any expression of emotion. He then revved his engine with a deafening roar before pulling away and carefully negotiating the junction ahead, filtering through the cars and turning left, in the same direction Nick was headed.

*   *   *

'Where are you, Nick?' Louise sounded stressed. 'I'm at the crematorium and your mother and sister have just arrived but you weren't in the car with them. You said you'd be there in time. I don't suppose I really need to ask why, do I?'

'Look, I will be there soon. I'm stuck in traffic.'

'You shouldn't have gone into work, should you?' Louise

was trying to keep her frustration under control but failing. 'You should be here with us and your mum and sister right now.'

'I had to go in. The world doesn't stop when someone dies. If it wasn't for the fucking traffic, I'd be there. Has there been a crash or something?'

Louise didn't feel like telling him why there was a long queue up to the crematorium. She could see that another service was about to take place in the second chapel which was causing a little more traffic, but not much. She'd watched as an extremely short, well-preserved and deeply fake-tanned woman had stepped out of a funeral director's car, accompanied by a tall young man with bad skin; there were a few in their party, but not many.

After checking the signs to see where they should be going, they walked towards the other chapel. They hadn't gone in yet and were waiting for their hearse, which had been delayed for the same reason Nick was sitting in traffic. There were far more people at Nick's father's funeral than expected, all there to show their respect. But not for Nick's father. No, Nick could wait and find that out himself. Louise was so annoyed with him currently that the thought of this revelation amused her and she found some comfort in it. It was a spectacle she and her children were enjoying, along with tens of thousands on YouTube.

* * *

Motorbikes! What looked like fucking hundreds of them were lining the open road on both sides, all the way up to the crematorium. Was it a biker's funeral? Had an ageing heavy metal star died?

Then the penny dropped. The biker with the middle finger at the T-junction was a disciple of Karmic Keith. They were all here to support him. Had he invited them? Nick's annoyance at his uncle increased exponentially with every motorcycle he passed. There were bikes and riders of all shapes and sizes, all standing to attention by their parked motorbikes. Some were chatting, others were polishing their mirrors and some were filming each other. One spotted Nick's bright red Audi and filmed him riding past. Was everything a spectacle these days? All moments seemed to be public, nothing was private.

Nick carried on up the road, giving the bikers a wide berth. He looked at the time; he hoped he could park easily, otherwise his day was going to get a lot worse.

∗   ∗   ∗

Both hearses had arrived, and the undertakers solemnly ushered the families into the two chapels. No bikers had made their way into either chapel, with the exception of Keith and his partner Sunflower, who looked more beautiful in the flesh than on the YouTube channel. She resembled an Elven Princess, like Galadriel in *Lord of the Rings*. She was tall and balletic, with flowers in her hair and a gentle smile. Uncle Keith, meanwhile, seemed to have an extraordinary, rugged quality which attracted people – not just bikers but everyone in search of some sort of truth, whether they knew it or not.

Louise had spent some time now watching his YouTube channel and knew that there would be a two-wheeled cortège today. She'd intended to warn Nick but got annoyed when he didn't pick up. The kids had been beside themselves to meet their great-uncle Keith. Harry had been delighted at being able to wear Keith's *Easy Rider* American flag helmet and sit on the Harley-Davidson he was road-testing. It was possibly the noisiest motorbike Louise had ever heard, but she had to admit it looked pretty cool. She herself felt secretly thrilled at being able to meet Uncle Keith at last, although he had rather hijacked his own brother's funeral.

Remarkably, Nick found a space between two-oversized motorbikes and parked. He pulled his jacket from the back seat and put it on whilst he ran towards the chapel buildings. There were several bikers loitering around a large motorbike with a bright stars and stripes helmet hanging from the handlebar.

Nick stopped in his tracks. Which chapel was it? Should he go left or right? He had seconds to decide. One of the anonymous bikers raised his hand. Nick expected the customary middle finger, but instead the biker pointed, indicating the way. Nick thanked him and hurried into the chapel on the left.

He snuck in through the door to the chapel and was surprised to hear a poorly amplified recording of Shirley Bassey belting out 'Diamonds Are Forever'. Inside the chapel there were less people than he'd expected and he couldn't see anyone he recognised. Most people were located in the front couple of rows, and he couldn't make out his mother, sister or anyone in fact. Nick took a seat in the back row.

The music died down and a tired-looking vicar welcomed the congregation.

'Today we are here to celebrate the life of Anthony Dyema. Known to his friends and family as Tony...'

Wrong chapel, wrong cremation service. *Fuck*. This was all Nick needed. He stood up and snuck back out of the chapel. Once in the open air he ran back towards the other chapel. The biker who'd pointed him in the wrong direction was sharing a cigarette with another biker; they graciously waited until Nick had passed them before bursting into unsuppressed laughter.

By some stroke of luck, the doors to the other chapel were still open and the service had not yet started. A few people were still filing in. The room was awash with dark clothes and the outlines of individuals seemed to blur into one dark mass, with the exception of two people in the front row in full motorcycle leathers complete with reflective strips. On the back of each jacket, spelt out in metal studs, was the message *It's the ride that matters ... not the destination*. The first part of the message was on one jacket, with the sentence completing on the next.

When Uncle Keith turned to look at Nick and smiled, the perfect smile for the occasion, Nick had to admit he had a certain charm. Keith beckoned him over and shook his hand, not saying anything. He looked remarkably like a younger and more enigmatic version of Nick's father. He was tall, standing at just over six feet in his boots. He appeared well built and filled out his jacket. A slight paunch reminded Nick of Charlie's own habit of over-indulgence.

Keith ushered him between Tracey and Louise. His mum was seated to the right. She didn't look at him. Her eyes full of tears, Tracey took his hand and wouldn't let go until the end of the service.

The brief service was punctuated by two of the most depressing pieces of music ever written: 'Abide With Me' and 'The Lord's My Shepherd'. The packed congregation made a valiant attempt at both, Uncle Keith's resonant baritone leading the charge.

After a perfunctorily delivered eulogy by the Rent-a-Vicar, Uncle Keith was invited to come forward to say a few words. Nick had not been asked to say anything and Tracey had had the good sense to refuse her mother's request.

Keith's motorcycle leathers creakily accompanied his short walk to the front of the chapel, where he stood with his legs unnaturally far apart in a pose that required an electric guitar to make it complete. For one horrible moment, as Keith drew breath, Nick thought he was going to sing.

'My brother, your husband, your father, your grandfather...'

Oh God, thought Nick, is *Uncle Keith going to mention every possible relationship to everyone here?*

'... your work colleague, your associate and your friend ...' He paused for effect. 'Has reached the end of his ride.'

Nick felt his stomach tighten with embarrassment for his uncle. What 'wisdom' was Uncle Keith about to dispense from his *Ladybird Guide to Enlightenment?* He looked around and saw that Keith had everyone's undivided attention. No one else was feeling any degree of embarrassment; they all wanted to know what he was going to say next. Unbelievably, they were hanging on his every word.

'When I say he has come to the end of his ride, I mean that he has reached his destination. We all have a destination, a destiny, over which we have no real control. Control is an illusion. It is attachment. Attachment is pain. Charlie and I weren't close, not because we didn't wish to be, but because he was so goal-focussed. Whatever games we played he was more interested in who won than in the playing. When we rode our bicycles, he would always want to race, to see who could get home first. Well, Charlie, you won this race. We talked about this recently when I visited him in hospital. He had a number of regrets that he wanted me to share with you and a few things he wanted to say, but never stopped long enough by the roadside to acquire the vocabulary.

'Charles "Charlie" Swift was Swift by name and swift by nature. Always in a hurry. I have him to thank for my juxtaposed outlook and I told him so. I spent so much time watching him grow physically but not spiritually. He wouldn't listen, not until the end. Now, I don't want to put a downer on all this because what was then was then and what is now is now.'

What the ...?

'The truth is that Charlie loved his family. He was besotted with Barbara from the moment he set eyes on her at Bognor Butlins, and who can blame him? She was a catch, and she still is.'

Nick's mum smiled and cried simultaneously.

'Charlie was beside himself with joy when Tracey was born. Tracey was a difficult birth, if I remember rightly. And there have been difficult times.'

You don't say. Nick shifted in his seat. What was his agenda?

'But Charlie doted on Tracey until the day his ride ended, last week.'

Tracey joined her mother in a pool of tears at this point and grasped his hand even more tightly.

'He wanted you both to know how much he loved you, which was … unquantifiable. Know this, and keep it next to your heart always.'

More tears.

What was this? The fucking Uncle Keith Show? Give him a few bright lights, a bit of make-up, a low stage and a couple of small, comfortable sofas, and he might as well be bloody Oprah.

Keith continued to gaze over at Tracey and Barbara for what seemed like an eternity, then slowly cast his gaze over Nick.

'Now I come to Charlie's other pride and joy. His beloved son, Nick.'

At this, Nick felt ice run through his veins as if he was being pumped full of a lethal injection of toxic chemicals. If only that were the case at that moment. Where was this going? It didn't feel right.

'Nick visited his father in hospital on his deathbed, as any good son would.'

Nick wanted to run screaming from the chapel. He could feel all eyes on him now and, no doubt, a couple of secreted smartphones streaming this live on *Karmic Keith's Motorcycle Mantras*.

'Nick helped his father to write a list, which I have here.' With a flourish, he produced a piece of paper from his pocket, reminiscent of Chamberlain's list of promises from Hitler.

Nick had the same intentions as Hitler when it came to honouring the promises on his list.

'This is a bucket list, well more of an "urn list" actually, as Charlie will be in an urn when he and his beloved son complete all the tasks, sorry, as they share all the experiences on the list. Thanks to the help of one of the NHS's angels, Malika, who is with us here today on one of her few days off, Charlie was able to finish his list before he closed his eyes for the final time and his life force left his husk. Nick and Charlie will spend time together doing all the things that fathers and sons should do together, and I'm not talking about lap-dancing clubs. Charlie added one more wish to his list, which we have here thanks to Malika, I will read you Charlie's final note, which he dictated to her.

'My dearest Nick...'

As Keith began to read out Charlie's letter, Nick wished the ground would swallow him whole. Not just because these words were personal, too personal for a public occasion, but because now there would be no way out.

'Forgive me for not being the father I should have been, and realise now I wish I had been.' Keith stared into the middle distance as he spoke, his deep baritone voice caressing the ears and tugging at the hearts of all present. 'As you complete my post-bucket list, know I will be with you. As you paint, as you dance, as you walk a tightrope and as you leap from a plane, know that I will be with you.'

Despite his abject horror, even Nick began to get sucked in.

Keith took a long, deep breath and continued. 'One more thing I ask of you, my final wish. When our journey is at its end, scatter my ashes on Frinton beach where we had so many happy holidays. The tide will come and take me away, but not the memory of me. Do this on my next birthday, and think of me, knowing I love you and will always be with you.' Keith paused, thankfully omitting Charlie's last words.

His timing was perfect. He looked around at everyone in the chapel who would meet his eye and gave them a slow nod of compassion as if he knew what they were all thinking. Even rent-a-vicar's eyes welled up. Enough tissues were produced to fell a small woodland area.

Nick suppressed a small cough.

'Beautiful words, I'm sure you'll agree. And an honourable journey for Nick to take. I am so proud of them both.'

The cough threatened to turn into a small fit, and Nick wanted to vomit.

'But today isn't about me, Karmic Keith dot com, for those of you who'd like to discover my website as well as my YouTube channel. It's about my brother, your husband—'

For fuck's sake.

'—your father, your grandfather, your work colleague, your associate and your friend … Charlie.'

The tiny chapel erupted into applause. Nick tried to stand, but his knees buckled under him and he sat down again. What the fuck was happening?

22

THE DAY HAD GONE remarkably smoothly for Amira. The first eight cremations, including her very first solo cremation, had run like clockwork.

Knowing that Amira was alone, the crematorium manager had come in to check that everything was on course. Ms Perkins always dressed in black, with her long black hair tied up in a large bun, which sat right on the very top of her perfectly round head. Her slim, boyish figure, together with the large bun on her head had the effect of making her look like an inverted human exclamation mark. She complimented Amira on her professionalism, admiring the way Amira had already lined up and labelled all the urns, although she observed that one label was upside down. Amira had no idea which one as she couldn't read any of them, but she thanked Ms Perkins for her support.

Ms Perkins noted the way Amira wheeled the coffins into the committal room and slid the coffins into the cremator with the greatest respect, the way she fired them up, the way she emptied the cremator afterwards and then the way she lovingly spread the ashes onto the cooling rack. She then complimented Amira on the way she carried off her one-piece overall with hood, observing that the facemask highlighted her eyes before she left to return to her administrative duties.

Amira had rather enjoyed the company of Ms Perkins

during the time she had spent with her that afternoon, but was under no illusions as to her motive for being there. Ms Perkins was mentally executing a workplace assessment that would no doubt be written up the moment she got back to her desk. Amira was confident that she had convincingly acted out the reading of notes and labels, as she was unable to see anything in detail without her lenses in.

Amira sat out of sight of the mourners during her late lunch break, hidden from view by a large ornamental shrub. As she reflected on the morning's success and the efficient cremation of eight correctly labelled departed loved ones so far, a low thunderous roar interrupted her peace. At first, she thought a storm was coming but the sky was an azure blue and there was no wind. She looked around for an aeroplane but saw nothing close enough to be making such a sound. Her curiosity got the better of her and she snuck around the corner in her conspicuous white overalls to see a ground-based ride of the Valkyries approaching in the form of what looked like hundreds of motorbikes progressing up the drive, sending vibrations up through the ground and her entire body. She began to hear Brünnhilde in her head, along with the rest of Wagner's Valkyries crying 'Hojotoho! Hojotoho! Heiaha! Heiaha!' The sight was a truly magnificent one, the motorcycle Valkyries throwing up a massive trail of dust behind them on the hot day.

Amira made a mental note to dust off her Brünnhilde costume and get Giuseppe to polish his chest plate and sword so that he could become her Siegfried once more. The thought of Giuseppe attempting to sing in German with his thickly layered Italian accent made her laugh and broke her from her reverie, as did the appearance of Ms Perkins, who politely suggested that she remove herself from view even though the view was very pleasant.

The small funeral party that had turned up around the same time had their service delayed as their hearse took some time to make its way through the fleet of motorbikes, each biker removing her or his helmet – it was difficult in some cases to know which – as the hearse went past.

Amira followed all protocols and procedures as she remembered them, faked the reading of labels and paperwork in case Ms Perkins happened to pop in for another spontaneous assessment and respectfully dealt with each of the two remaining departed, from arrival in the committal room through to ashes grinding and urn filling. She filled the two remaining plastic urns and put them on the shelf. She felt a pang of dissatisfaction in the final act as she didn't know, and no one ever would, whether the ashes in the final two cremations were in the correct urns and would end up reunited with the correct family. Tomorrow morning, with her lenses in or glasses on, she would read all the labels and check the notes to see what was to be done with each of the urns.

One tall and slim anxious-looking young man with different coloured eyes had turned up, asking when his uncle's ashes would be ready for collection. Amira offered her condolences, saying it would be best if he called back in the morning when someone would be able to give him an answer. She had to ask him to repeat himself as the ill-fitting window was banging away whilst she stood with the door open. He commented on it, and she apologised, explaining it was broken and wouldn't close properly.

Amira smiled to herself. She had enjoyed her day alone and in charge. With any luck tomorrow Lauren would still be unwell, and Amira would work alone again, free of disturbances and hopefully not too many workplace observations.

23

NICK KNEW THE BEST place to hide was in plain sight. He needed to escape not only from all the distant and ancient relatives who'd made an appearance from the past, but also all the disciples of Karmic Keith that his mother had invited back to her home on the Lower Luton Road just outside of Wheathampstead, who seemed to be filming everything they could on their smartphones. The weather was perfect, without a cloud in the sky and a gentle breeze blowing across the enormous garden and infecting everyone with a sense of excitement at a party about to begin. When Barbara asked for a volunteer to go and fire up the barbecue, Nick grasped the opportunity to escape by jumping up and down enthusiastically and shouting, 'I'll do it! I'll do it!'

People were spilling out of the house into the garden, but the kitchen seemed to be where most of the action was; the whole event had a carnival atmosphere.

Outside the kitchen door Nick's mother had been trapped by a group of male bikers. 'It's a beautiful house you have here, Barbara,' Nigel, who'd ridden all the way from Milton Keynes observed.

'I couldn't agree more,' agreed Ken, who'd ridden from Weedon, near Aylesbury, 'and you really have looked after your garden well. I was just discussing the condition of your clematis with Terry here.'

'Indeed he was. A lovely clematis it is,' confirmed

Terry, who'd ridden all the way from Frampton, where he spent most of his time birdwatching at Frampton Marsh. 'Clematis tri-colour,' continued Terry, 'is ideal to plant if you wish to attract butterflies, insects and bees.'

The words seemed incongruous coming from the lips of a man who looked like he would be equally at home discussing how best to attack someone with a Viking's axe. 'But should you wish to attract birds to your hedgerow, I would recommend firethorn pyracantha.'

'I wouldn't argue with that,' said Ken.

'Barbara, you have obviously used the correct mixture of compost in that pot to produce such a lovely clematis. I would say you have used a soil-based potting compost with a fifty per cent peat-free compost. Doing that creates a much healthier root system,' said Terry.

'Never use peat-based compost, Barbara,' warned Nigel, 'it's unsustainable. Bad for the environment.'

Terry, Ken and Nigel unconsciously stood to attention as Keith turned his attention from another group of people to them.

'I always like to attract birds to my garden, so I will discuss the procurement of a firethorn pyracantha with Sunflower,' he announced. 'Birdwatching is an intense form of meditation. It can really clear your head. It's at times like these when we need to find that peace; that space and calm that exists in every moment always, no matter how fraught.'

'I love what you say about how motorcycle riding is also a form of meditation,' remarked Nigel.

Keith nodded, sage-like. 'Indeed it is, Nigel. When riding we have to be fully present, in the moment with heightened awareness, otherwise we are not safe and neither are those around us.' He had said this countless times on his channel.

'Yes, it's not us, is it? It's all those other fuckers,' said Terry.

'Right, well, if you don't mind, I'll go and see who else needs tea.' After an awkward hiatus, Barbara excused herself and went into the kitchen.

Nick asked a distant, ancient relative to tend the barbecue for him whilst he went to the kitchen to find more meat to undercook. He saw Uncle Keith go into the kitchen and get greeted by just about everyone in there. Harry shot out from the throng and bear-hugged Uncle Keith with a squeal of delight. Nick felt a pang of jealousy which he quickly suppressed. He was about to enter the kitchen when his mum appeared from nowhere and pulled him to one side.

'I think it's great that you have agreed to do your father's list with him,' she said.

'What do you mean?'

'The urn list. Your dad's final wishes. I'm proud of you, son.'

'Mum, much as I'd love to do it, I haven't actually said that I will.'

'Yes, you have.'

'No, I haven't agreed to it. And if I did, I'd be doing it on my own. Even if I had Dad's ashes with me, it's not the same as if I'd done it with Dad, and it's too late for that.'

'No, it's not. Keith says we're all made of energy and that energy vibrates and transcends time. By engaging with this quest, for want of a better word, you will be accompanied not only by your father's remains but by his energy. Energy can neither be created nor destroyed.'

'It's matter that can't be created or destroyed, not energy, Mum.'

'Whatever it is. We're all full of energy, Keith says. He's full of it.'

'He's certainly full of something,' said Nick.

'And your father was full of energy. It wasn't always directed well, but it was there. That energy has now left his body and is in the ether, ready for you to harness. These list experiences are a chance for you to do that.'

'I thought Dad was in heaven with the angels?' Tracey had joined them and looked confused.

'How much time have you spent with Uncle Keith, Mum? It's as if he is speaking through you.'

'It's not him. I've always thought these things, but your father was never interested in discussing what wouldn't fit on a spreadsheet.'

'Look, I'm sorry but I can't possibly find the time to go on a trip with Dad's remains. I'm at a critical stage with my business and need to focus on that.'

'Then why did you agree to it?' she persisted.

Had his mother become senile all of a sudden? She was normally as sharp as a tack.

'Look, maybe when the dust has settled we can discuss it again. But can we please put a lid on it for now? Karmic Keith has had his moment in the chapel. Tomorrow he'll be gone, and we can get on with our lives. People will forget about the list. People are probably already forgetting about it and about me doing it. So, let's calm down and grieve privately. Our lives don't need to be made into some ghastly third-rate reality TV show.'

Barbara said nothing. She regarded Nick with an air of well-practised disappointment, pursed her lips and headed back into the kitchen with Tracey.

As Nick followed them in, a spontaneous burst of applause erupted as everyone turned to face him, whooping and cheering and patting him on the back. He looked behind him to see if the adulation was being misdirected. There was nobody there. People were holding their smartphones aloft, filming him. Keith stood in the middle of the kitchen, beaming with a set of teeth the Bee Gees would have been proud of.

A chorus of 'For He's a Jolly Good Fellow' followed, as Tracey made her way towards him through the throng. 'Well done, Nick,' she said, giving him a hug.

'What for? What have I done?'

'You agreed to carry out Dad's final wishes.'

'But I—'

'Dad, you're famous!' Harry was jumping with delight in front of Nick.

'Yeah, Dad,' Charlotte cut in, 'over sixty thousand views in the last half hour. It must be a record. Go Dad!'

'What has got so many views?'

'The video of you agreeing to do Grandad's bucket list. Look.' Charlotte was surrounded by people grinning inanely as if some sort of happy gas had been released into the air. 'It's on YouTube, TikTok, Instagram and is even making news websites. It's gone viral.'

Nick looked at Charlotte's ridiculously oversized iPhone where he could clearly see a subtitled video on Uncle

Keith's channel saying, 'This is the reaction when Karmic Keith's nephew Nick was asked if he would honour his father's dying wishes.' The video seamlessly cut to a clip of Nick jumping up and down enthusiastically and shouting 'I'll do it! I'll do it!'

24

Saturday 25th June

NICK FAILED TO EAT his breakfast; his stomach simply would not contemplate even the blandest food. Although Barry had already been out several times, his senility caused him to continue to bark for no apparent reason. His barks were all the more painful because they were accompanied by an orchestral bass drum whacking the inside of Nick's head as if trying to escape. With each bang of the drum he was presented with a flashing memory of the day before and the realisation that he was screwed. Hundreds of thousands of people had now seen the faked video of him 'agreeing' to carry out his father's dying wishes.

Nick let Barry out again into the garden and headed straight for the medicine shelf in the kitchen cupboard. The ibuprofen was nowhere to be seen and the paracetamol had been raided, leaving only one tablet. It had been a heavy night for both him and Louise. Visions came back to him of bikers who'd decided to stay the night at his mother's and tequila that had appeared from nowhere. Louise had joined in the fun, listening to multitudinous stories from rich lives and learning a lot about British flora and fauna. In the absence of enough painkillers to touch the sides Nick was forced to drink almost half a bottle of ancient sickly-sweet strawberry-flavoured children's pain medicine, in the hope of getting a large enough dose.

Barry came back inside and curled up next to Nick on the sofa in the snug. Nick had mixed himself a non-alcoholic recovery cocktail to bring him back down to earth. He was due at work in half an hour. *Fuck.* He wasn't even sober enough to drive and knew from Brian that most drink-drive tragedies happened the following morning.

Nick couldn't remember exactly what had been said the previous evening. Events swam around in jigsaw pieces in his mind and he slowly started to piece them together.

Feeling manipulated, Nick had accused Uncle Keith of being duplicitous. What could have been an angry scene was diffused by Keith's calm confession that someone else, not him, had posted the film. He would take it down if Nick really didn't want to carry out the tasks on the list, but maybe he should think about it because by that time the damage had been done. Keith explained that fate sometimes played an important part in people's personal development and the path of non-resistance to its ways was a path to peace. For fuck's sake. If everyone felt like that, nothing would ever get done. It was people like him, the innovators and entrepreneurs, that made the world spin.

Barry's paw appeared on Nick's thigh, and he looked into the old dog's eyes, holding a gaze of adoration for some time. Barry snuggled in closer to Nick and let out a long and happy sigh. Barry experienced many moments of bliss, it seemed.

Nick spent the next ten minutes throwing ideas around and Barry listened attentively. They agreed that it would be difficult for him not to at least attempt the list now it had been made so public.

With the help of his team at the office, he could organise the logistics of most of the tasks in no time. On the other hand, if he didn't get all the tasks done it wouldn't matter anyway. No one was going to be watching and no one would know. He'd would 'try' of course, but he'd have to stay connected to his office and check in constantly. He'd take his laptop and connect to the office via a VPN through his phone or public Wi-Fi access points. So long as he scattered his dad's ashes on his dad's birthday, when no doubt someone would be watching, everything would be fine; people would forgive him for not completing all the tasks. How would they know – was his mother going to send an invigilator?

Nick had a mission in life and it took priority over everything: he wanted to prove to himself and everyone that he could be a success. That had nothing to do with this list. He had to focus on his business and its sale. If he didn't, he might lose everything. Once it was sold, he could start a new project and move on.

People didn't get rewarded without taking risks and Nick was prepared to take many. Brian had been impressed with Nick's continuing commitment to the business when Nick had proved it once again by mortgaging his house to help with the business's cash flow. This wasn't something that Brian would have done, but Nick had. One rather major issue was that Louise didn't know he'd done it. Nick convinced himself that she didn't need to as his plan would work, and she need never be troubled by it. What Brian and Louise also didn't know was that Nick had received a final demand from the bank. If he didn't make his next payment, things could get tricky.

Nick dismissed the thought. He'd make the sale. He had to.

He would go and see his mum and sister and tell them he would take on the list and complete it in time to scatter the ashes early on the morning of his father's birthday, before his big presentation in the afternoon. Then everyone would think him a good son and a great businessman. But first he had work to do. He called Brian at the office, saying he'd be working remotely this morning and had a few things to sort post-funeral before he came into the office.

25

WHEN NICK ARRIVED AT his mum's house there was still evidence of the excesses of the previous day's wake. He found his mother on the driveway in her gardening clothes, with the deluxe litter picker she had picked up from the central aisle at Lidl for a steal and had finally found a use for. She looked suitably pleased with herself. Tracey was standing nearby, also looking pleased with her ability to multitask as she drank from a cup of coffee whilst holding open a robust-looking garden rubbish sack, into which Barbara dropped what looked like the remains of a barbecued sausage. They looked round at his car quizzically.

'Where is your bright red penis-extension-mobile?' Tracey enquired as Nick climbed out.

'Ah, yes. I've decided to get rid of it, this is Charlotte's car. I don't want to risk anything happening to the Audi now it's going,' Nick replied.

'I thought you loved your new car?' asked his mum.

'I do but I have to redirect my finances elsewhere.'

'Why?' Tracey looked even more confused than usual.

'It's costing a fortune and I can't justify the expense.'

'Are you in trouble, son?' Barbara asked with genuine concern. 'Do you need some cash? There's quite a bit now that your dad's … I could lend you a few thousand pounds.'

A few hundred thousand might help for a while. And

'lend'? Why couldn't she give him money if she was going to offer to help? Tracey had had enough fucking handouts. He was sure she was wearing a new dress and shoes …

'No thanks, Mum, I'm good. Very kind of you but everything is fine.'

Barbara looked unconvinced. When Nick was a boy, she could see right through him the moment he felt miserable or down about anything, and he'd always feel so much better getting things off his chest. If only life were that simple now.

Thanks Mum, actually I need a few hundred thousand pounds to tide me over. I've mortgaged my house without Louise's knowledge and unless I can sell my business soon, I'm fucked. I'm so glad I told you, Mum, I feel so much better now. Can I have a hot chocolate, a Hobnob and a cuddle?

He noticed that his mum looked refreshed. She seemed reenergized somehow. Perhaps now the funeral was out of the way she was starting to move on. Hopefully, his news would cheer her up.

'Mum, I've decided that I will do Dad's list.'

'I knew you would, son.'

No, you didn't. I hadn't agreed to it.

She walked over to embrace him. With her deluxe litter picker held in front of her perpendicular to the ground and the sun behind her she resembled an attacking dalek with arthritis.

'I just need you to understand that I will try my best to get all the tasks done, but I still have a business to run.'

'I'm sure you'll manage one way or another. Your father would have been proud of you for trying. Plus, you won't be on your own.'

145

Was she referring to the ashes or the spirit of his father? Nick had a vision of his father standing at the open stable door to the kitchen. A place he would stand with a cup of tea to watch Nick kicking a ball around or running away from Tracey after kicking the ball at her. He remembered the few times his father would join in. The vivid memory promised to start a cycle of emotions within him he wasn't prepared or equipped to engage with at that moment.

'You won't be on your own,' his mum repeated, 'you'll be with your Uncle Keith.'

What?

'He's kindly volunteered to accompany you in all the tasks. I thought you'd like the company.'

'He's not doing it to check up on you and report back or anything,' Tracey said, giving the game away.

The low rumble of an approaching motorbike interrupted Nick's horror and he turned to see Uncle Keith arrive on an old-looking motorbike. He was wearing full protective gear despite the warm weather and had a number of cameras attached to himself and the bike.

He pulled up in front of them, put down his side stand, switched off his engine and dismounted. Lifting the front of his flip-helmet, he carried on speaking into a microphone with a foam wind cover that was affixed to his helmet.

'So that, viewers, was my first ride on the Royal Enfield Himalayan 2021 version, the update of the bike ridden by our lovely Dutch friend Noraly, otherwise known as Itchy Boots. I think you'll agree it's a fun ride and great through the twisties. I'll give it the full walkaround later. Right now, I have more important things to attend to. Family matters.

And indeed, they do.'

He said all of this without breaking his stride and whilst looking directly at Nick, which Nick found disconcerting.

'So, tune in again soon when I'll give you the full spec and discuss how it compares with the original model. For now, stay safe and remember what Karmic Keith always says … it's the ride that matters, not the destination.'

Once again, Nick had been manipulated against his will. The ride certainly did matter, and the emotional rollercoaster Nick had just taken in the last five minutes left his head spinning. This was all turning out to be extremely annoying and inconvenient. Would Keith be willing to help him lightly shirk some of the tasks? He thought not. How much fucking worse could the situation get?

'Good to see you again, Nick. It's going to be great getting to know you properly whilst we undertake all these tasks together.'

Was he still filming? He had the air of a TV presenter. Ben Fogle sprang to mind, only Uncle Keith looked more like an old wizard.

'I know that all my viewers are going to love getting to know you too.'

A million fucks! The situation just got worse.

'I've set up a new stream called *Love isn't always easy … sometimes you have to urn it.* What do you think?' Keith didn't wait for an answer. 'It's had thirteen thousand likes already, another record. Your story really seems to have connected with my subscribers. It's going to be epic. I might even write a book about it. You'll get royalties, of course. I'm not a mercenary. Some of my cut will go to a bereavement charity.'

For fuck's sake, not only would he be chaperoned by an old Buddhist hippie on a motorbike, but tens, possibly hundreds of thousands of people were going to be following his whole journey. How would it look if his clients and his potential buyer tuned in to the ludicrous circus? Things surely couldn't get any worse.

'With my team of tech-savvy support staff, we have linked to all the SwifTech social media channels,' Keith continued.

It just got worse.

'So, thanks to Shirley and your IT guys, your company website has a link, as does your YouTube channel, Facebook page, Instagram, LinkedIn – Charlotte knew the password for that one – and not forgetting your Twitter. I can't believe you don't have TikTok, you should get that too. I don't think I've forgotten anything … My last tweet just got retweeted seven thousand times. It's going to drive heaps of traffic to your website.' This time he waited for a response. When none was forthcoming, he said in a cheery voice, 'You're welcome! Your kids will be so proud of you too, Nick. They are amazing. They were telling me yesterday about their bring-and-buy to save the local animal shelter. I think it's great that you're going to be helping them on the day of the fundraiser.'

Oh fuck, Nick had forgotten about that – how could he possibly fit that in too? Everyone would see that he was spending time away from his company, with his hand off the tiller. What kind of message would that send to people? He couldn't get out of this now, even if he wanted to. He was committed to his own personal hellish odyssey.

26

DESPITE THE TIME OF year, the morning was unusually chilly and a mist clung stubbornly to the streets, too early for the sun yet to have burnt it off. Nick had borrowed Louise's car and had driven to the Welwyn Garden City branch of Kerton's Funeral Directors, which was sandwiched between a greengrocer and a hair salon in a long parade of shops in the Woodhall area, not an area that Nick knew well. He knocked on the door but got no answer and then noticed that it wasn't open until nine-thirty and it was now only six in the morning. The area was pretty sleepy at this time; a few zombified commuters were making their way to work and the local bakery's scent wafted tantalisingly through the air, enticing people in with the comforting smell of fresh bread and pastries. A dedicated runner ran past the newsagent just as it was opening up, uninterested in the news. Nick felt uncomfortable standing outside the undertaker's and after ten minutes he decided to call Uncle Keith, who explained that they were meeting at the Hatfield branch, and texted him the address.

Ten minutes later Nick arrived in Hatfield's town centre and parked on the street outside the undertaker's. He found himself wondering why on earth Uncle Keith had insisted they meet so early. The mist seemed thicker here, and the air felt cooler. Through the mist Nick spotted a light behind the large black iron gates and two shadowy figures. Their silhouettes were magnified by the light behind them, and Nick saw that one had to be Uncle Keith. The other had a tall top hat on and towered above Uncle Keith's six feet; it looked like a scene from a Jack the Ripper movie. A chill ran down Nick's spine.

He locked the car and approached the figures, who came into increasing focus with every step he took. Nick recognised Graham Kerton, the undertaker from the crematorium service.

'Good morning, Mr Swift,' said Graham, 'I'm so sorry to have got you out of bed so early. I still don't quite understand why we had to meet so early and why your uncle insisted I wear my mourning dress and top hat.'

'The light is rather spectacular at this time of day, don't you think?' Uncle Keith asked rhetorically.

He was filming and Nick realised it was part of the drama of the story. He wondered how many people were tuning into his live feed at this time of day.

'This is one of my favourite times of day,' the undertaker said, addressing Keith's camera. 'I've actually been up a while as an elderly gentleman passed away in the night and I've just been to collect him from his wife. I didn't dress like this, though. This is for services only, normally. But, as I said, Keith insisted I wear it.'

'Because you look great in it. Our thoughts, of course, are with his family at this time,' Keith stated.

Sweet Jesus. Was every minute of their day going to be filmed?

'We're leaving the live feed now, viewers, but will be back later with edited highlights of the coming day.' Keith went on to sign off in his usual manner.

'Right,' said Nick. 'Can we get on with this, please?' He felt annoyed at the situation and didn't care if it showed.

'Oh, good thing we aren't on a live feed. We'll edit that out,' said Keith.

'If you'd like to come this way, Mr Swift, we'll go and collect your father's urn.'

After Graham had entered a security code into a pad on the door, installed very recently as they'd had an attempted break in, Nick followed him into a dimly lit storage room with a low ceiling. It felt oppressive, and Nick wanted to leave as soon as he entered. Against two walls were racks filled with coffins of different styles. He recognised the style that his father had been in. There was a trolley with a utilitarian-looking coffin on it called a removal shell. This was a coffin in which bodies were collected. He commented that the current incumbent would need to be moved into one of the large chillers, which occupied another wall. Graham walked up to one of the units and opened it, commenting that it was full and making a mental note to put the body in the other fridge.

Nick followed him into another room. Behind Nick he could feel the uncomfortable gaze of Keith's webcam. In the next room were more shelves, a little smaller than in the previous room. Upon these shelves sat a number of urns. Some urns were made of robust plastic and had not yet been transferred into the urns he saw on another shelf, which all varied in shape, size and decoration.

'This is the room where we store the ashes once we receive them from the crematorium,' Graham said, stating the obvious.

'There's quite a variety of urns to choose from there and scattering tubes,' Keith said, inviting further information.

'Yes indeed and, although urns can be expensive, we always do the very best we can for our customers, pricewise. We offer special rates to bikers who join our funeral plan. You may know that I myself am a biker, which is why we have a special motorbike and sidecar hearse available.'

This was turning into a surreal infomercial.

'Which one contains my dad?' Nick curtly interrupted.

'Well,' said the undertaker, 'knowing that you are undertaking – oh, pardon the pun, it was unintentional—'

'I'm definitely keeping that in. Pure gold that was, Graham.' Keith looked delighted.

A smile came to Graham's face for the first time, lighting up his professionally emotionless face. 'Knowing that you are *undertaking* a wonderful journey with the ashes of your dear father, Charlie Swift, we'd requested that the crematorium put his ashes in a robust plastic urn or Polytainer. Considering that you'll be taking the urn with you to the bucket list experiences we thought it best that it was unbreakable. I understand that there are a number of tasks that involve some degree of physical exertion. We have discretely Gaffa-taped the lid on, so it does not come off easily.'

Graham took the urn from the shelf, remarking that it was one of three he'd had the honour of dealing with on the same day at the crematorium. He handed it to Nick slowly and with great respect. As Nick held out his hands to receive the urn, the gravity of the situation hit him. He now held in his hands all that remained of his dad. The urn was heavier than he'd expected.

'This feels quite heavy,' Nick commented.

'Yes, I thought that too, but it's not unusual,' Graham replied.

'Charlie must have had dense bones,' Keith commented. 'Our mum always joked that he was big-boned, may she rest in—' Keith stopped mid-sentence, at a rare loss for words.

Nick expected him to say something profound, but he said nothing at all, as he was clearly choked-up. Keith looked at Nick with watery eyes and tenderly patted the top of the urn in Nick's hands. 'Take care of your dad, Nick. Your adventure is about to begin.'

27

NOW THAT NICK HAD his dad's urn, he could get on with the business of completing the list of experiences they would 'share' together. He could get this out of the way and get on with his life.

He'd already had one call from Brian at a ridiculously early hour, needing assurance on an IPR matter. Nick told Brian he would pop into the office but couldn't stay long as today he had to attend to the first task on the list, a meditation morning at the Buddhist temple just outside Hemel Hempstead. He would have to navigate the Magic Roundabout at Hemel, which he hated. It was a large roundabout made up of six mini roundabouts giving drivers way too many options. Keith had heard rumours that once some people got onto the roundabout system they were never seen or heard of again. He suspected that it was designed by town planners who wanted people to hang around longer in Hemel as so many seemed to just pass through. The stress levels the roundabout produced in drivers were probably the reason why a monastery was needed nearby. They needed a meditation experience after tackling it, if they were lucky enough to take the correct exit.

Nick had agreed to meet Keith there. His uncle had offered him a ride on the back of the Kawasaki Versys 650 he was riding that day, telling him he had a spare helmet in the top box if Nick fancied feeling more in touch with the road and the present moment at the same time. He also had spare boots, jacket and trousers. Nick politely refused, saying that he preferred the isolation of Louise's Mini Cooper. Keith had raised a Spock-like eyebrow, observing that Nick's isolation was self-imposed and he was at liberty to free himself from his spiritual and psychological incarceration of his four wheels at any time. Nick just liked to feel safe, listen to music and take business calls; he wouldn't be able to do that on a bike. Keith pointed out that, even with hands-free calling, the brain, according to studies, could not multi-task, and speaking on the phone whilst driving was irresponsible and a danger not only to himself but others. He recommended he listen to a podcast by Derren Brown on the subject, but not whilst driving. Nick had to agree that the next week was going to be painful; maybe meditative techniques were what was required. Had his father chosen meditation as the first task in order to prepare him? Had his father wished that he himself had meditated more?

The Amaravati Temple was a welcome sight after Nick had negotiated the roundabout from hell. As he pulled into the car park, he could see Keith chatting with a number of people, none of whom particularly cared about their appearance. Amongst them were a couple of bikers and a monk, and they were all smiling and laughing, turning to greet Nick as he approached. Keith introduced them as the people who would be meditating with them and then introduced Toshin, a mini-monk who would be leading the session.

'It is a pleasure to meet you, Nick. I understand you are on a very important journey.' Toshin spoke incredibly slowly, his unerring gaze penetrating Nick's eyes. His deep voice was far too voluminous for his frame and reminiscent of George Takei. 'I have known your uncle for some time now. He is a wise man. If you have a small percentage of his wisdom you are blessed.'

Was Keith's life one big ego-gratifying trip? Had he paid people off for his channel? Were these people actors in a hidden-camera show? Although Keith's camera was not in any way concealed: he was openly filming the whole thing.

'I sense that you have forgotten something, though,' continued Toshin. 'You were not destined to be here alone today. I understood that you were to bring your father. You are to connect with your memories of him through meditation. To share experiences. Where is he?'

'Well, he's dead … did Keith not—'

'Yes. But you do have his ashes?'

'Yes, over there, in the boot of the car.'

'Then please go and fetch him.'

'Really?'

Surely the point was to go through the list of tasks to 'honour' his father. He didn't actually need to be holding his father's ashes, did he? What new-age nonsense.

'Yes,' confirmed Keith. 'This won't work without Charlie's ashes with us.'

'They're only in the car over there. That's close enough, isn't it?'

'I see that there is work to be done,' Toshin said, now transforming into a hybrid of George Takei and Yoda with Uncle Keith as the spirit of Sir Alec Guinness's Obi-Wan.

'Yes, the road is long,' said Keith.

Nick expected him to start singing about winding turns at that point, just to confirm the absurdity of the situation. Forgetting that he was being watched by thousands, Nick let out a big petulant sigh, shrugged his shoulders and returned to the car to fetch the ashes whilst checking his email. Who said he couldn't multitask?

Next, the group welcomed Charlie to their meditation circle. Toshin said that what Nick held within the urn had more value than he could possibly imagine. Nick did well to not roll his eyes. They were just ashes for heaven's sake. It wasn't his dad.

Toshin asked Nick for his phone, saying that he wouldn't need it during the session and that phones were not allowed in the monastery. He could leave it in the car or one of the other monks would look after it for him. He opted for the latter.

The group walked in silence past the main temple and the courtyard, in which people were walking in silence, like zombies between meals. He recognised one of the walking meditators from the day of the funeral. It was one of the bikers that he'd stood chatting to, he was showing great interest in a large plant that Nick didn't know the name of but was sure that Terry would. Terry who, despite his contemplative meditative state still looked like he could flip at a moment's notice into a Viking berserker and slaughter all the other people in his meditation class.

Terry glanced up and, seeing Nick holding his father's urn, gave him a warm, easy smile and gentle nod of approval. Nick stopped for a moment, unsure how to react, settled for an awkward nod of the head and walked briskly on to catch up with his party.

Toshin led them all to an outbuilding away from the main temple. They entered a room where they were able to leave any jackets, shoes and, in the case of Keith and the two bikers, a lot of kit and heavy boots. Toshin assured them that all their things would be safe and invited them into the main room, which was laid out with a number of cushions on the floor facing a large Buddha surrounded with a bright display of flowers. The silence and calm were palpable but did little to combat Nick's anxiety at being cut off from the world by not having his phone. How on earth was he going to survive a three-hour meditation session?

Toshin invited them all to sit, or kneel, whatever was comfortable, but with a straight back. Nick spent some time trying to find a position that didn't make his feet go numb. In the end he sat with his legs crossed in front of him in an attempt at the lotus position, his father's urn in his lap. Toshin gave simple instructions to focus only on his outbreath and not to worry if his mind wandered. If his mind did wander, which it was certain to, he was to simply acknowledge it and return his attention to his outbreath. He did as directed and within moments his eyelids started to feel heavy and drifted shut.

Nick could still hear the sound of Toshin's voice but began not to hear what he was saying. The next thing he was aware of was an image of his father on his hospital bed, lying with his eyes closed. Nick wasn't sure whether he was asleep or dead, but he looked at peace. Nick felt a warmth gently caress his body and then he was on a beach. Before him was the most elaborate sandcastle, with a thousand turrets and numerous drawbridges. Numerous tiny flags danced in the wind and he looked up and saw his father there, bucket and spade in hand, kneeling next to him and smiling broadly, the sun lighting up his face and warming them both. A deep sense of bliss washed over him which, all too soon, was interrupted by a tap on his shoulder.

'Nick? Nick, it's time to go now. The session is over. The three hours have passed.'

Nick's sense of deep peace vanished the moment his phone was returned to him and he checked his emails. He would have to go into the office to deal with a few issues at lunchtime before meeting with Uncle Keith again for another task in the afternoon. If he had time. As he hurried back to the car he could hear Keith expounding the benefits of meditation and the monastery to his followers and signing off with his usual catchphrase, adding that as destinations went, the Amaravati Temple was worth a stop on your ride through life. As Nick left the carpark he couldn't get the image of the beach and his father out of his head.

28

RAY HAD RANG THE doorbell at least four times without an answer. He was sure Auntie Val was in as her car was parked on her drive and she famously never walked anywhere. He went round to the back of the house to see if she was sunning herself by the pool, but there was no sign of her there either. The garden was a mess, with stepping stones lifted up and random holes dug in the lawn. The pool still had its cover on and the sight of it brought back the shocking memory of his near-death experience as a boy. He tried the back door, but it was locked. He peered in through the kitchen window and saw chaos abounded. The cupboard doors were open, the drawers hanging out. The worktops and kitchen table were covered in the contents of the cupboards and drawers. He banged on the back door. Still no answer, so he went back around the front of the house, took out the stolen front door key and let himself in.

The house was an absolute wreck. His immediate thought was that she had been burgled but the state of the garden suggested otherwise. He called out but there was still no answer. He'd seen plenty of trashed houses in his time and this one would definitely make the nominee list for the-most-trashed-house award. He called again, making his way along the hallway. The door to the cupboard under the stairs was open and bags and boxes of papers, cleaning products, shoes and coats were scattered everywhere. The house looked like a couple of thieves high on crack had been carrying out a frenzied search to find something to sell to procure their next fix.

The trail of devastation led directly to the living room, where he found Auntie Val passed out on the sofa, evidence of her drinking surrounding her. He tried to wake her but failed. She was too far gone and would have the mother of all hangovers if she didn't choke on her own vomit before then. Ray suspected that she got into this state quite often. The rest of the house was in the same state and she'd been in the loft too. It was amazing she hadn't fallen and broken her neck.

Val had been looking for the jewels but had failed to find them. Despite the will saying that the jewels could not be found in the house, she hadn't wanted to risk them not being there. Tony might not have had the opportunity to hide them before his death, but Ray suspected not. Ray had missed his best chance to get the jewels at the funeral directors in Hatfield and now, following the cremation, only two thirds would remain. The diamonds would have melted, leaving only the sapphires and the rubies intact within the ashes. Ray hadn't been able to go back after they'd fitted a state-of-the-art security system. Perhaps he should have waited as just retrieving the urn from Val would be easier. The worry was that she might look in it at any time, and then it would be game over. The state of the house wasn't going to make it easy to find. He had another really good look in the living room, safe in the knowledge his rooting around wouldn't wake Val up.

He spent two hours searching but couldn't find it

anywhere. He wasn't exactly sure what he was looking for either, which didn't help. Something urn shaped. He took out his phone to Google urns, only to find they could be any shape. He thought it unlikely that Auntie Val had opted for anything fancy or unusual, so stuck with his original plan of something traditionally urn shaped or a simple cardboard box urn. Perhaps she'd buried it in the garden, hence all the holes. His thinking started to become desperate. He had to find it.

He was just about to give up when he saw Auntie Val's car keys. Maybe she hadn't bothered to bring the urn in from the car, having picked it up at the undertaker's. He knew she'd picked it up as he'd been back to the crematorium and spoken again to the office there, who'd said that although they still had some ashes there from that day, his uncle's had gone to the undertaker's and his aunt could pick them up there. He called the undertaker to find out that she'd already collected them. They'd had three cremations that day and still had the ashes of two of them, but his uncle's ashes had definitely gone.

He took the key and checking that she was still out for the count he went and opened her car. There it was! In the boot, resting on a box of car-cleaning products. Ray took it out and went to his van and opened the rear doors. The shade of the house, in a dark corner by the garage, helped to conceal what he was doing in case there were any particularly nosy neighbours, which he guessed, in a dull area like this, there probably were.

Ray had come prepared. He had a sturdy plastic container into which, his hands shaking with excitement, he emptied the contents of the urn. His heart raced in his chest. His van's interior light wasn't working and it was too dark in the shade of the high hedge to see the rubies and sapphires amongst the ashes, but he was confident they were there and even with the diamonds having gone, he was still quids in. He took a bag of ash he'd scooped up from a bonfire he'd found in the garden of a debtor and emptied its contents into his uncle's empty urn; he spilled some in his van, but it didn't matter. There was nothing of value there. He put his uncle's urn back in his aunt's car, locked the car and returned the keys to the house.

He checked that his aunt was still alive before heading off to celebrate. She had vomited over herself but had not choked and was breathing. She was such a pathetic sight, he almost felt sorry for her.

29

NICK'S HEAD WAS ABOUT to explode. He'd spent the last twenty minutes driving up and down a country lane searching fruitlessly for a large Edwardian house hidden behind some high hedges. Allegedly, it had a swimming pool in its garden where he was to learn life-saving techniques, including how to rescue a drowning person and how to resuscitate them afterwards if necessary.

The lane into the small village of Kimpton was a rat run between the village and nearby Harpenden. Nick had already had to pull over for a number of oversized Volvos and Range Rover Evoques, as well as having to back up for an enormous timber merchant's lorry loaded with felled trees.

An eclectic collection of homes lined the narrow lane on either side, occasionally visible from behind the wild hedgerows. Some of the homes were humble ex-tied cottages whilst others had enormous gates, behind which ostentatious displays of wealth had led to houses Kevin McLeod would thrill at being built. One house rather bizarrely had two concrete cows on its drive.

Nick's phone rang. It was Uncle Keith. Nick was in the right place, but had to go further up the lane where he would find the large Edwardian house, which Keith said looked like something out of an episode of Poirot.

When Nick arrived at long last, he realised he had

driven past it earlier but had been distracted by having a standoff with a cantankerous old man driving a Land Rover who'd refused to back up in the lane, resulting in Nick having to reverse about ten metres, scratching the rear wing of Louise's car. She wouldn't be best pleased. Nick spotted Keith's bright green Kawasaki parked outside of the house, known locally as Lido Mansion. Next to Keith's motorbike was another, larger bike covered in panniers and fairings and towing a small trailer.

'I hope you brought your Speedos, I've got mine,' chuckled Uncle Keith as Nick got out of his car.

Nick hoped he was joking. The idea of Uncle Keith in Speedos turned his stomach.

Keith introduced Nick to the owner of the house, one Mrs Lillian Anderson, and to a tall, broad-shouldered young biker called Marnie, a good friend of Sunflower, who was to be their instructor. She had piercing eyes, shining red hair and was enigmatically attractive, handsome even, and in her robust leather armour, she wouldn't have looked out of place in an episode of *Game of Thrones*. She introduced herself in a strong Australian accent, explaining that teaching lifesaving was just one of the many things she did, including photography, writing and life modelling for art classes. As she delivered a potted version of her resume, she commented on how hot it was, unzipping the front of her motorcycle jacket to reveal nothing but a bikini top beneath it.

Nick almost dropped his dad's urn and being completely wrong-footed, introduced himself in a clumsy manner, hoping she hadn't noticed him looking at her breasts. He was sure they had held his attention for two nanoseconds, which was far too long to be polite, but he couldn't be sure. Marnie smiled at Nick, who felt a flush of embarrassment wash over his face. She broke the awkward moment by asking him to help carry 'Bob' up to the pool. Bob was a resuscitation mannequin she kept in her trailer. Bob was just a head and torso, designed to float if he fell in the pool.

Lillian led them all around the side of the house and up the garden to the pool. She busied herself offering them soft drinks whilst trying to distract them all from a couple of empty bottles of champagne, five empty glasses and a pile of discarded clothes and underwear strewn on and around a nearby set of tables and chairs. She indicated a pretty little chalet painted in white and azure blue behind the pool with three doors, where they could get changed. She then excused herself, saying she would be back with some refreshments.

Once by the pool, Uncle Keith removed his helmet, gloves and jacket and went to change in the left-hand room of the chalet. Nick reluctantly followed him in. The changing room was small and they changed back to back, Nick desperately trying not to bump bare bottoms with his uncle. He failed and felt himself brushed by a very hairy bum cheek. Keith announced that he was ready and marched boldly out into the sunshine. He wasn't kidding about the Speedos, which were branded. On the back Nick could see the end of Uncle Keith's catchphrase: '… not the destination.' He knew what was written on the front and didn't want to look.

Keith stood proud before Marnie, telling her he was

ready. She gave him a slow visual inspection and announced that he certainly was. Having read the first part of his catchphrase, she asked him to spin around, and he was only too happy to oblige.

Nick emerged from the changing room in his swimming shorts, which had a Bermuda theme, his skin colour pasty in stark contrast to Marnie and Lillian's expensive-looking tans. Uncle Keith had a dad tan, which produced a panda-like effect.

To Nick's relief Marnie produced a long-sleeved rash vest and pulled it over her head. Nick tried not to look again as she raised both arms above her head to slip it on. Once she was covered up, he relaxed and prepared himself for the task ahead. With his father's urn safely sat upon a tabletop in good view of the pool, they could begin the lessons.

'Everyone in for a few lengths,' commanded Marnie, diving in and reaching the end of the fifteen-metre pool before he'd processed her instruction. Uncle Keith jumped in, creating a small tsunami and showering Nick with ice-cold droplets.

As Nick dived in he realised why the droplets felt ice-cold. The pool wasn't heated and as the breath rushed out of his lungs, he sank like a brick to the bottom of the pool, where his testicles sounded the retreat, leaving his scrotum feeling like a sun-dried fig. He panicked and started to gasp for air. Before he had a chance to calculate which way was up, he was swept from the bottom of the pool and, with a hand under his chin to hold his head out of the water, pulled to the side of the pool.

'You okay, mate?' Marnie asked.

Nick was starting to recover by that point and grabbed onto the side of the pool, heaving up water onto the side of the flagstones. He was relieved that neither Marnie nor Uncle Keith would have to give him the kiss of life. The horrific image of the latter soon passed as he coughed up more water and his lungs and throat began to burn.

Keith came over and helped to pull him out of the pool. After a few moments of recovery, Marnie congratulated Nick on taking the lesson so seriously and playing the role of a helpless swimmer in trouble so convincingly. Nick wasn't sure whether her words were genuine, but it alleviated his embarrassment. She later explained that it had been going from the hot air into a freezing cold pool that had caused Nick to go into a brief state of shock.

The rest of the afternoon went well, with each of them taking turns to rescue the other. Uncle Keith seemed to need more practice and insisted on rescuing Marnie several times to demonstrate his understanding.

Bob the resus-man, as Marnie called him, got a good pounding and Marnie congratulated Nick on passing the course. He was now ready to save lives, provided that if he ever got into a situation where cold water was involved, he should take a few breaths and mentally prepare himself, getting into the water slowly.

Uncle Keith was uncharacteristically quiet. Marnie, noticing this, asked him if he was okay.

'I'm fine thanks, Marnie,' he said with a sad smile before turning to Nick. 'Nick, you may be wondering why your dad put this lifesaving course on the bucket list for you to complete.'

'I've been wondering about most of it, actually,' Nick said.

'Well, you may or may not know that Charlie and I used to love swimming when we were boys, but we stopped after a tragedy one summer when I was just eight years old. Your dad would have been sixteen. We were swimming in a disused gravel pit. We'd been told not to swim there but everyone did, and we all ignored the signs. We went down there with our cousin, Davina. She reckoned she was a strong swimmer, but she got in trouble, and we all panicked.' His voice started to crack. 'She ... she went under and didn't come up. Sucked down by some sort of current produced by the difference in temperature of the really deep water or something. We got her out eventually and tried to give her the kiss of life, but had no idea what we were doing. Your dad never forgave himself. I didn't blame him, and Davina was old enough to make her own mind up. Fucking tragedy. I guess Charlie wanted to lay this to rest and putting it on the list, knowing you might one day save someone, made him feel a bit less guilty.' He stopped, wiping the back of his hand across his eyes.

'Thanks for sharing, Keith. That can't have been easy,' said Marnie.

'It is always good to share a burden with friends,' said Keith in his TV voice. 'When we share our feelings and worries it may not make them go away, but it lightens the load.' Keith had turned his head to the camera he'd left on the table, almost obscured by the urn. Nick had completely forgotten about it and hoped it hadn't got a shot of him panicking after the shock of the cold water – he wouldn't want that on the internet. One thing he could be grateful for was that he wasn't in Speedos. The water was way too cold for that.

A long overdue Lillian appeared with a tray of lemonade and, having given Uncle Keith the onceover, carefully reading the first half of his catchphrase on his Speedos, announced that he was welcome to join her at her pool party that evening.

30

IT HAD BEEN A long day, Nick reflected as he turned the corner into Attimore Road. Pulling into his driveway, he had to brake suddenly as a small recovery truck emerged with his Tango-Red Audi on the back. Nick had forgotten they were coming to fetch it, and hoped they hadn't told anyone why they were collecting it. The motor dealer who'd arranged the pick-up of the Audi had mentioned his son was selling a car at a bargain price and, keen to not have the hassle of looking for a new car, Nick had accepted his offer to try the new car out, especially as he was going to drop it off at the same time as collecting the Audi. He would have some explaining to do when he got in the house. It would be difficult to convince Louise that he preferred an eleven-year-old Vauxhall Corsa over his departing Audi, but he'd think of something.

As Nick walked into the kitchen, he expected a heavy silence from Louise, but she was laughing with Charlotte at something on Charlotte's phone.

'Dad,' cried Charlotte, 'your TikTok' has over forty-three thousand views and rising.'

'What TikTok?' said Nick defensively. 'I don't do TikTok.'

'No, but Great-Uncle Keith has posted it on his channel,' said Harry. 'It's really embarrassing, Dad. Everyone at school will make me suffer for this. Why can't you do something cool on there? Look at it. You're on a loop, puking up water by the side of a swimming pool.'

It was indeed horrific, but people seemed to glean great enjoyment of a man's near-death experience and consequent humiliation. Especially Charlotte and Louise.

'Oh, come on,' said Louise. 'You've got to admit it's amusing. And the edit is very clever.'

'Yes,' agreed Charlotte. 'And I love Karmic Keith's Kaption: "Like all of life's problems; it's better out than in." People have started making memes, Dad. Your journey is producing a lot of traction.'

Nick was mortified. This wasn't working out as he'd planned, but at least this little stunt had distracted everyone from Cargate. He picked up his laptop and had started to walk towards his office when Harry called to him.

'Dad, why has someone towed away your tomato mobile and left you with a crap car?'

'Don't be rude,' said Louise. 'I'm sure your father has a perfectly good reason for wanting a bright yellow Corsa. Don't you, Nick?'

'That's right,' stumbled Nick. 'I've decided that the Audi is too ostentatious and sends out the wrong message. So, I've opted for something a little more humble and less conspicuous. I want to send out an image to my clients of someone who spends frugally and not extravagantly. Someone who is happy in an inconspicuous car.'

'So you haven't seen your replacement car yet?' questioned Charlotte.

Nick had to admit that he hadn't.

'It looks like an aspirational boy racer's car. One who

has career designs on becoming a pimp. It's got alloy wheels, a lowered suspension and a massive exhaust pipe.'

'Yeah, Dad. If you park it down Montgomery Drive, people will come and try to buy drugs from you.' Harry's statement drew several raised eyebrows. 'It's got tinted windows and a bass bin in the back. It's sick.'

'It's sick in more than one sense,' Louise cut in. 'You can't drive it. You'll have to drive Charlotte's car. I need mine back. She can have the *Breaking Bad* Mobile.'

'The what?' Charlotte said incredulously.

'Never mind,' said Louise. 'Why have you really got rid of your Audi, Nick? I thought you loved it.'

Nick's phone rang, saving him from having to answer Louise. It was a private number, which he wouldn't normally pick up, but the occasion warranted it.

'Hello, Nick Swift speaking—'

'Swifty boy!' The coarse tones at the other end of the line were instantly recognisable. It was Dave Dolon, his old business partner. 'How's it all going, my old mate?'

'Yeah, fine thanks, Dave. All good. How can I help you?' Nick replied dryly.

'No need to be so formal, Swifty. I'm ringing from Paris, where I spend a fair bit of time these days, to see how things are going for you. They must be going pretty well,' Dave Dolon shouted down the phone, as if he needed everyone at both ends of the line to hear him. His accent was a broad cockney; he wouldn't stand out in one of Guy Ritchie's gangster movies, Nick thought.

'They are going really well, thanks. Business is booming.'

'Well, it must be if you've got time for a new career as a TikTok star!'

Oh Jesus, if he's seen it, it must be everywhere.

'I was sorry to hear about your old dad. But you weren't that close, were you?'

Dave had a talent for asking inappropriate questions. Nick decided not to answer and let a Louis Theroux silence hang in the air.

'Anyway, I just wanted to touch base and find out how things were going for you and the business since I left to set up on my own.'

Silence.

'Are you still there, Nick?'

'Things have never been better, thanks.' Nick was beginning to struggle to cover up the annoyance in his voice.

'Good, that's good.'

Another silence.

'They are going really well for me too, thanks for asking,' Dave continued. 'In fact, I'm just about to do a massive deal. Humongous. Monstrous. Gargantuan. Well big.'

'That's great, Dave, and I'd love to hear all about it, but I have to go into a meeting now. We'll have to catch up another time.'

'Yeah. We must do that drink we've been talking about having.'

Never gonna happen. 'Yes, we must. Take care, Dave. Must dash.' Nick hung up without waiting for a response from Dolon. *What a twat.*

'Who was that on the phone?' Louise enquired.

'Oh, it was Brian. I need to go in.'

'It didn't sound like Brian. Do you have to go now?'

'You said you'd watch *Spider-Man 3* with me, Dad,' complained Harry.

'I'm sorry but I have to pop to the office. It's important.'

'You can't have my car Dad – you'll have to take the Pineapple Express. I'm not driving that. I'll get too much attention at school.'

* * *

Nick called Brian on the way into the office to tell him he was going in. Brian was already there, fretting. When Nick arrived, he found that his route through the office to his room had been decorated with printouts of memes from his day's activities with captions including 'Nick is sick', 'Better out than in' and 'Baywatch audition mega-fail'.

As he opened the door, he found Brian looking nervously out of the window into the car park.

'I think someone's using our car park to sell drugs. Should I call the police?'

31

RAY DROVE BACK TO his flat with 'Diamonds Are Forever' blaring out on his sound system.

No they fuckin' aren't, he thought, *rubies and sapphires are.* Bassey needed a new song.

Ray had turned up the music so loud that people stared at him at traffic lights, but he didn't care, he just waved and smiled and sang along with Bassey, replacing the word 'are' with the word 'aren't' each time it came up in the song.

He felt like he'd won the lottery. He'd still have at least £3 million in stones, if not more. He imagined himself a pirate who'd just discovered a shipwreck and had single-handedly recovered the riches, having beaten all sorts of other challengers to get it. He knew that the stones would legitimately be his. His uncle's will explicitly stated that whoever discovered them could keep them. It hadn't mentioned any specifics about where they might be at the time. That meant his aunt couldn't prove anything, as she didn't even know they were in the urn, otherwise she would have taken them out and her house wouldn't have been in such a state, and neither would she.

Ray felt a sense of elation, the extent of which he'd never felt before, maybe with the exception of when his nan had first given him the crystal mouse. He was still miffed at the fact that Auntie Val and Uncle Tony had taken all her other Swarovski collectables, which would now end up in a charity shop. But he didn't need them now. He could buy an entire collection with the money he'd get from selling the jewels. He might keep one stone or two to remind him of his success and would probably get one set into one of his teeth. He couldn't decide whether that should be a ruby or a sapphire.

As he drove down the road, Ray felt not just happy but ecstatic. It was like he was high on something, he felt truly in love with the world. From now on everything would be great, all his problems would be solved. He couldn't wait to get home and sort through the ashes.

Ray parked his van outside his block of flats, took the ashes out of the back, and locked it. He looked around to check that no opportunist muggers were hanging around and made his way into the lobby. There was no working lift so he sweated his way up to the thirteenth floor and turned left to enter his flat. It was getting later now and the sun lit the stairwell with an intense glow. He stopped for a moment, the golden aura making him reflect on his riches, which within minutes he would have laid out before him.

He went inside his flat and locked the door behind him. Picking up a free newspaper from the doormat, he went through to the lounge, where he pushed aside his coffee table and spread out sheets of paper on the floor.

Ray returned to his kitchenette to get some masking tape from under the sink, then taped the pages of the newspaper together so that he had one large sheet across the floor. He fetched a bottle of beer from the fridge to crack open in celebration once the jewels were sorted from the ash.

Back in the lounge, Ray knelt down and pulled the lid off the Polytainer urn. Carefully, he spread its entire contents across the newspaper.

Something wasn't right.

Nothing shiny appeared in the ashes. Ray couldn't see anything vaguely resembling a ruby or a sapphire.

A white-hot sickness possessed him and, if he hadn't been kneeling down, his legs would have given way beneath him. No fucking jewels! Perhaps they had been blackened in the cremation? He started frantically picking out anything that vaguely resembled a jewel shape and anything that might have been an uncut stone. He took a handful of pieces to the kitchen and, grabbing a fine sieve, he washed the stones under the tap. Nothing. It was just ash, just ground-up bones.

There was nothing there. There had never been any jewels in his uncle's ashes. They must be somewhere else. Or his aunt was lying, and he hadn't been cremated in his favourite suit.

A rage rose within him as powerful as the elation he'd experienced only an hour ago. He picked up his bottle of celebratory beer and threw it at the mirror above his sofa; both smashed. Beer ran down the broken glass and dripped onto the sofa.

32

RAY WAITED UNTIL IT was getting dark before driving from Hatfield back towards Auntie Val's house in Welwyn Garden City. He decided to park in the street around the corner from her house, walking the rest of the way so as not to alert her of his arrival in case she had anything to hide, which he suspected she might. She also might not, but he was desperate for anything now, having had his dreams ripped from his hands.

The road was eerily silent. There was very little traffic sound now and only the rumble of a distant aeroplane high above gave away evidence of human life. Ray turned his head away each time he passed the Ring doorbells and overly sensitive security lights that now peppered every suburban street. Auntie Val, however, still had her antique two-tone seventies sit-com doorbell.

Val's car was where he expected it to be. If she'd been able to get into it she would have driven straight into a lamp post, the state she was in. Ray squinted through the living room window. Val had moved from her last spot. Maybe she had managed to drag herself upstairs to bed. The hall light was on and beyond it the kitchen light; she could still be up, looking for another drink or something to dull the inevitable pain she would feel in the morning.

Ray snuck around the back of the house to see if she was in the kitchen. He couldn't see her anywhere on the ground floor and, after having tried the back door and finding it locked, he went back to the front door and quietly let himself in.

In the time since he'd left she'd roused herself and made some attempt, albeit a perfunctory one, to clear up. The sink was filled with glasses and plates, and the recycling bin was overflowing with bottles. There was still plenty of evidence of her earlier search strewn around.

Ray turned out each of the lights as he passed through the ground floor. He checked the larder and the downstairs bathroom in case Val had passed out in either. Satisfying himself she was not downstairs he started to climb the stairs. He froze when he heard footfall above him and saw the bathroom light come on.

He heard Auntie Val sit on the toilet, urinate and then flush, all the time humming an unidentifiable tune. The next thing he heard was the sound of an electric toothbrush. The humming continued alongside the buzz of the brush. She had no idea he was in her house. He carried on up the stairs and stopped on the landing as he heard her finish cleaning her teeth, but sadly not her song.

She turned the light out and came out onto the landing, walking straight into him in the dark and reeling back. She screamed like a demented banshee. Instinctively, Ray grabbed her around the neck, pulled her about and put his hand over her mouth to stop the awful wailing. She lashed out, kicking him in the shins. It didn't hurt; she was as harmless and defenceless as a featherless bird fallen from its nest. In her fake silk and feather nightgown she came close to resembling one, with her scrawny neck sticking out of the top of it.

'For fuck's sake it's only me, Auntie,' Ray whispered hoarsely. He released his grip on her and she lurched towards the stairs. She reached for the light switch and a low energy bulb struggled to illuminate the dull landing along with a portrait of a sad-looking clown.

'What the ... what ... what on earth are you doing here? How did you get in?'

'You left the back door open,' he improvised.

'What do you want?'

'I want what you want, Auntie.'

'What are you talking about?'

'You know what I'm talking about. The jewels.' There was no point in messing around now. He needed to know where they were.

'They aren't here. I've looked everywhere. And anyway, you've no right to them. They're mine.'

'They should've been in his ashes, Auntie Val. You told me he was cremated in his favourite suit. The three-piece suit he wore on special occasions.'

'He was,' she slurred. 'I took it round to the undertaker's and they put it on him while I waited. He had his favourite shirt, tie and shoes on, too. Oh, and his favourite socks. And his paisley boxers.' She had started to babble when the penny finally dropped. 'Do you mean to tell me that the jewels were in his suit?'

'Full marks. Yes, I am telling you that, because he showed me once, years ago when I was a little boy. It was at a party here one Christmas and you were drunk. Again.'

'I am not an alcoholic,' she slurred whilst righteously wagging her finger at him.

'I worked out where his jewels were so when I find them, they are mine, legally. Not yours. But they aren't in his fucking ashes, so they can't have been in his suit, which means you must have taken them out.'

'I didn't and I don't have them. Do you think I've turned my house and garden upside down for fun?' She paused, a look of horror spreading across her face. 'Have you been through his ashes? How dare you! You evil child.'

'Well, if they aren't in his ashes, where the fuck are they?'

'Maybe you've got the wrong ashes, you greedy little shit.'

He hadn't thought of that.

'What if the undertaker took the jewels out of the suit's lining?' Ray growled.

'I was with him when Tony was dressed. I said goodbye to Tony and the undertaker closed the coffin. He would have had no idea that there were any jewels in the lining of the suit and neither did I.' Val was getting angry now. 'Tomorrow I will go to the undertaker's and see if he's given me the wrong ashes. Mistakes can happen and there were a few cremations that day. Then I will collect *my* beloved Tony's ashes and get *my* jewels and you, you thieving, good-for-nothing odd-eyed freak, can fuck off!' She started to cackle and wagged her finger at him. 'Now get the fuck out of my house.'

Val had a lot of gumption for such a defenceless person. Ray felt like he was being evicted from the Vic in *EastEnders*.

'Go on, fuck off!'

Ray's blood boiled. The jewels would be his and his

alone. He strode forwards, forcing her to back away. She started to hit him repeatedly on his chest. All it took was a gentle shove with a light pressure to her sternum and she toppled over backwards down the stairs, missing the first four steps; the first and last flight of a cawing, flightless bird. He heard the snap of her scrawny neck as she landed in an unnatural crumpled heap.

Suddenly, there was a blissful silence.

33

Tuesday 28th June

AMIRA HAD ENJOYED HER Monday back at work after a peaceful weekend and was looking forward to preparing for Tuesday's cremations. As a special treat, she had seen Giuseppe outside of their normal agreed times the evening before, but she had told him that it would not set a precedent. He'd been excited about a new client, a YouTube influencer, who wanted a special Krav Maga self-defence session. Amira had never heard of him until Giuseppe played a short film of him reviewing a motorbike.

Amira had a warm feeling inside. Lauren was still unwell and had been temporarily replaced by a retired technician who came in occasionally to cover when they needed it. George Jackson was a quiet man. He rarely spoke, only occasionally uttering biblical references and prayers for those that had died and their families, whether they wanted it or not and irrespective of their religion or absence of one. He didn't bother Amira and made no objection to the increasing number of cat photos that started to adorn the walls of the staffroom. With each new photograph she posted he would simply say, 'Bless you.'

Despite George Jackson's years of experience, he was happy to let Amira manage him, which she did in a gentle way. He'd done everything she'd asked on the previous Friday when he had started, and she'd been grateful of the little company he offered as she had no visits from Ms Perkins that day. Ms Perkins didn't work on Fridays; it was the day she attended an art class, apparently. On Monday, George helped her organise all the urns from the previous Thursday when she'd had her little mishap with the labelling. He didn't know that she'd had a mishap and it would remain that way. Because of the relatively low number of cremations that Thursday, it was straightforward enough. Of the ten cremations that had taken place, one undertaker had already been back and collected three urns on Friday, one widow and one widower had collected theirs early on Monday, and another undertaker had taken two late Monday afternoon, one of which was headed straight to a gentleman in the local Shady Cedar Trees Care home. Apparently, he liked cats too, and been allowed to take in his wife Joan's cat, Toffee when she died. This meant that there were only three more urns to be collected. Once they were gone there would be no chance of anyone finding out her little mix-up and she could relax. She was already beginning to do so, in fact.

Friday and Monday had been much busier days and she'd remembered her glasses and brought in a spare pair to keep in her locker, which she kept in a furry pink kitty case. She had made a mistake, but her mother always said that mistakes were good, you learnt from them. Amira's mother loved dispensing wisdom to her only child.

Amira breathed a satisfied sigh of relief as she pulled into her parking spot in the staff car park. Yes, today would be a good day too. No Lauren, just Mr Jackson, as he liked to be addressed, and probably occasional visits from Ms

Perkins, who had now taken to inspecting power sockets on a regular basis.

Amira's day was playing out like her own Disney movie in which she was the princess, right up until the moment that she walked into Ms Perkins. Ms Perkins was in a considerable state of alarm. Amira wondered if she had found a socket which wasn't working properly, which would be surprising after how many times she had checked them on the previous few days she'd been in. Ms Perkins led her into the storage room where she was greeted with the sight of Mr Jackson on his hands and knees with a dustpan and brush, surrounded by empty urns and ash. Not only had the contents of the three remaining urns from the previous Thursday been scattered across the floor, but so had a number of others.

'A most unholy thing has happened here,' said George, as he stood up with a creak. 'Whoever did this is deeply disturbed.'

'I think it might have been a wild animal.' Ms Perkins was almost in tears. 'It must have come in through that window up there. It doesn't close properly and there are muddy marks around it.'

Amira comforted her with a hug, which seemed to help greatly, but each time Amira tried to break away, Ms Perkins cried again and had to be comforted again.

'I don't think it was an animal. They wouldn't have been able to get the lids off the urns or open the plastic bags so easily. These bags have been opened with a knife,' said Mr Jackson. 'The ceramic urns aren't smashed, either. An animal would have knocked them off the shelves. These were opened and emptied. This was a person. Probably a misguided teenager playing a prank or carrying out a dare.' He observed that time was moving on and they really ought to find a solution, as they would soon need to fire up the cremator.

The ashes had been spread right across the room, covering every inch of the floor space and were irrevocably mixed together. It was impossible to know which ashes were which, so it was decided that they would be swept into one pile and divided equally between the empty urns. That way the odds were fair that at least some of the right ash went into the right urn. Mr Jackson would get on with preparing for today's cremations, whilst Ms Perkins helped Amira to clean up the mess on hands and knees. Finding some purpose in this task seemed to cheer Ms Perkins up, although she occasionally stopped to sob, and needed hugging again to alleviate her sadness. Mr Jackson came back into the room to find Ms Perkins seeking further consolation from Amira and blessed them both.

34

'THANKS FOR HELPING ME out last night, Kevin.'

Ray took another sip of his Coke and surveyed the street ahead of them. They had already made one visit today and had two more to go. One car repossession and whatever they could pick up of value if they could gain access to the final defaulter's home. They sat in Kevin's car, parked on the eastern side of Luton with the windows down. It was a warm day but not too hot yet. Another jet from a budget airline roared by overhead, temporarily halting their conversation.

'Happy to help, especially for thirty per cent of your booty.'

'Twenty-five per cent, Kevin. How many fuckin' times do I have to tell you?'

'Just jerkin' your chain. What do you reckon the whole lot will be worth?'

Ray was beginning to wish that he had never asked for Kevin's help; he was showing almost as much interest in the money as he was in the packet of chocolate biscuits he was demolishing. But Ray couldn't have gained access to the undertaker's or the crematorium office without Kevin's experience and equipment, and there was no way he would now have the names and addresses of all the people who'd been cremated that day. Sure, he could break doors down, but subtlety was what was needed to get in and get out without raising the alarm.

Ray was exhausted. He hadn't slept last night but the

adrenaline had pushed him through. It had brought back memories of his time in Afghanistan, the times he and Kevlar Kevin had been on patrol. The night before had been a rollercoaster of elation and disappointment. But his frustration at not yet finding the jewels was eating him up and driving him on.

'I have no idea what the whole lot will be worth, but I reckon, even without the diamonds, you could be looking at a three-quarters of a mil for your cut.'

'That means you get two and a quarter mil,' calculated Kevin.

There it was again. Kevin's unhealthy interest in Ray's cut. Why couldn't he just be grateful for what he was going to get?

'We'll never have to work these shitty jobs again,' said Kevin. *Well*, he thought, *three quarters of a million doesn't go that far these days. But my cut will.*

'As soon as we're done here today, we'll visit the first one on our list,' Ray announced.

'Are we going to break into their homes and simply nick the ashes?'

'No, we aren't. Supposing they've already scattered or interned their ashes?'

'Good point. We need to question them. I can do that.'

'I'm not sure your methods of questioning will work, Kevin. It needs to be subtle and undetectable. We can't be found out. The police will be on our case if we start roughing people up. We need to box clever. They may already be suspicious after last night.'

'No, we were careful last night at both the crem and the undertaker's.'

'I hardly think emptying all the contents of those urns over the floor of the crem was subtle.'

'They'll think it was an animal.'

'It was, it was you.' Ray laughed and Kevin joined him through a mouthful of chocolate Hobnobs. 'I've got a plan. We'll disguise ourselves as undertakers and visit each of the people on the list with the "correct" urn. Apologise for the mix-up and take theirs away.'

'Genius!'

'I know,' agreed Ray, patting himself on the back. 'We'll be methodical. Starting at the top of the list and working our way down just like we do as bailiffs.' Ray referred to the list in front of him and pulled a pen out of his pocket. 'We can cross off my uncle and cross these three off too, as three of their urns were still at the crem and one was still at the undertaker's we visited. It's only the families of these remaining six we need to visit: Joan McCormick, Thomas Turner, Bernard Wyles, Lily Brooks, Jacqui Young and Charles 'Charlie' Swift.'

'It's gonna be like taking candy from a baby,' said Kevin gleefully but almost inaudibly through his mouthful of biscuit.

Yes indeed, thought Ray. *And then I will take it all from you.*

35

BRIAN HAD RUNG NICK that morning with a rare inspired idea relating to marketing rather than anything mundane. Could Nick please use the opportunity of being viewed by tens of thousands of people to promote SwifTok, their time-management module, the newest part of their small-business management pack? The new module linked with a smartphone app to demonstrate how people could find a work/life balance. This might bring people to understand why Nick was spending an inconveniently inordinate amount of time away from the office when he should be trying to prepare the business for its sale – though he wasn't to mention that part, as they were still keeping quiet about it so as not to panic the staff and cause an exodus. Nick asked Brian if there was something he wanted to tell him. Brian said that there wasn't, but could he pop in at the end of the afternoon for a catch up.

Nick sat in his car outside Hertfordshire Sports Village. The facility before him housed a climbing wall of some twelve metres, complete with 'dramatic overhang, vertical and slab surfaces'. Nick didn't really care about the overhang or the surfaces; he hated heights and that was all that mattered at this moment. He didn't remember his father ever wanting to rock climb or do any outdoor pursuits other than playing golf, which Nick hated. Why did people feel the need to dress like that to hit a little ball with a stick? What was the attraction? They didn't even have little windmills to hit the balls through. His dad had once shown him his golf clubs, but had never offered to take him to his club to play.

Nick sighed and checked the small backpack he had brought with him containing his father's urn. It was pretty light so hopefully wouldn't present any challenge if he wore it climbing.

Uncle Keith appeared on a bright orange motorcycle which was evident as soon as it entered the car park. He had a matching bright orange helmet and jacket with the large letters 'KTM' emblazoned on the back. He was either reviewing a new motorcycle brand or had taken a job as a courier.

A sharp tap at Nick's window made him jump out of his thoughts. A nervous-looking young man with challenging skin wearing a lilac Nike hoodie with Bugs Bunny playing basketball on it was trying to get his attention. His outfit got Nick's attention before the young man did. Nick dismissed the notion that this young man was trying to mug him and unwound his window just enough to hear what he was whispering to him from beneath the lilac hood.

'Got any gear, bro?' the hoodie asked, almost inaudibly.

Nick leant in closer to the window. 'Sorry, say again?'

'Do you got any gear?' The hoodie said it slowly, as if Nick was old or foreign or both. Which right now he felt.

'No gear, no. I expect you can hire it inside.'

'Don't mess with me, bro,' the young man said nervously.

'What do you mean? What do you want?' Nick hadn't caught on.

'Have you got any cheddar?'

'What?'

'You know … *haze*,' the young man continued in a voice incongruent with his ethnicity. 'Come on, bro. You know, dank, grade, trees, flowers…'

'What are you talking about?'

'Peng, piff, gwarn, buds, lethal grizzle … do I have to spell it out more clearly, bro? Smoke, bags, skunk, wacky backy, blow, weed, hash, ganja, dope—'

'Oh Jesus.'

'Have you got any marijuana for sale, bro? Cannabis, bro!'

'I don't have any drugs for sale. I am not a drug dealer … bro.'

The young man in lilac stepped back in a dramatic fashion. Nick assumed he was already pretty high on what he'd managed to previously procure so early in the day or maybe the night before.

'You tell me you is not pushing? In a set of wheels like that, bro? I'm not gonna lie, man, but who is you kiddin'?' He started laughing raucously and walked off in a practised fashion, swinging his arms and his very bendy knees towards the entrance, his bright lilac leisure attire complemented with unnaturally glowing white trainers.

Grateful that he had not been mugged, Nick grabbed the small backpack containing his father's urn from the passenger seat, exited and locked the now aptly named Pineapple Express, which made a ridiculously conspicuous pimped-up bleep as the security system cut in. He caught up with Uncle Keith by the front door.

'Not too keen on heights, you know.' Keith looked uncharacteristically ill at ease. 'As a boy I once fell off a climbing frame in the days before padded flooring and wrapping kids in cotton wool. It taught me a lesson.'

'What was that?'

'That concrete hurts when you hit it head first.'

'Deep,' said Nick. 'Why do you think this one was on my dad's list?'

Keith had no idea but assured Nick that plenty of lessons could be learned from climbing and that inspiration would come if they allowed space for it. He filmed himself whilst he was saying this. He then gave a monologue to the camera explaining today's task. With every sentence Nick became more nervous and then remembered what Brian had asked him to do.

'Yes indeed, Karmic Keith,' Nick cut in, as if they were both sitting on a comfortable sofa in a daytime TV studio, 'and the only reason I have time to be here today is because I manage it so well with SwifTok, the new time-management app from SwifTech.'

'The good thing here, Nick, is that there is plenty of room for development in your presentation skills,' said Keith with a wry smile. 'Shall we enter?'

'Let me hold the door for you, bro,' said a young man in a lilac tracksuit.

'That's very kind of you, young man,' said Keith.

'I know you, bro. You're that old hippie dude on a motorbike who is well wise. Welcome.' He swept his arm in a grand gesture, beckoning Keith through the door like a royal servant.

'Thank you ... ?'

'Benedict.' The young lilac man answered, his voice slipping into his chest with a tone of received pronunciation betraying his attempt to cover up an expensive education and his true socio-demographic standing. 'My friends call me Cucumber Patch, after the actor. You can just call me Patch, as in nicotine. I'm your instructor for the day.'

Great, thought Nick, *a stoned climbing instructor, in an environment where safety is paramount.* He wondered whether he should refuse to continue, or tell Keith that the boy had tried to score drugs from him in the car park. Either option looked like he would be trying to get out of the day's task and that he was too scared. Given that Keith already seemed nervous, Nick didn't want to scare him anymore. He decided on a direct question.

'Excuse me ... Patch. For reasons of safety, do you have to take a drug test before climbing the wall?'

'No, bro. You're good. But if you have taken anything you really shouldn't have driven here.'

'I haven't taken anything,' said Nick defensively.

'I'm joking, bro. I can see you're not the type.' Patch spoke with such authority and clarity that Nick began to feel a lot calmer about his potential level of intoxication. Maybe he'd misread him. What a ridiculous idea that a climbing instructor would be high.

As the morning went on, Patch's street voice slowly toned down and he began to return to his authentic self with occasional slips between accents, depending on whom he was speaking with. It didn't seem to bother him; he was comfortable with both identities.

Nick and Keith signed the insurance disclaimers and commenced the basic training lesson. They were introduced to all the kit they would need, which wasn't much. A harness each, a belay and a locking carabiner. As Nick's footwear was not appropriate he had to borrow a pair of trainers, which were slightly snugger than he'd have liked. The trainers were a spare pair belonging to Patch and were overly decorated with shiny bits.

The wall was busy for a Tuesday morning due to a school outing and a small party of disabled young adults who were already doing a much better job of scaling the wall than Nick knew he would. Keith had already been over and interviewed a number of them, asking for tips. One of them had told him to 'own his fear', which he liked very much, and another had said 'It's about the climb, not the summit', which delighted Keith immensely. Keith asked if he could quote them all and they excitedly agreed. Like him, they all appeared to be filming everything. Brian would be pleased with the traction that this might get, but Nick suspected that the group weren't particularly interested in time management.

Keith went up the wall first, attached to Nick at the bottom. He let out a holler of delight when he reached the top and appeared to be giving a running commentary into his helmet camera, which was mounted on an arm so it could take in his reactions along the way.

Patch coached Nick through the role of a belayer and Keith descended slowly, not slipping once. The closer Keith got to the ground, the more Nick's sense of impending doom grew. If Keith hated heights, he hadn't shown it. Nick had done a good job of keeping Keith safe, but he wasn't sure he'd be able to trust Keith to do the same for him.

Nick assured himself that the wall, despite being twelve metres tall, did not actually look that high. He would be up and down in no time.

Keith abseiled the last few metres smoothly before landing with a soft bounce next to Nick. 'Wow,' he said, 'it looks a lot higher when you're up there than it looks from down here.'

That was not what Nick wanted to hear.

'Okay, Nick, it's your turn now. Are you ready?' asked Patch. 'Remember. Three points of contact at all times and if you get stuck and want to come down, Keith here has got your back.'

'That was awesome, Nick. You'll love it. Own your fear – you'll be fine,' Keith assured him.

'Any last-minute words of wisdom?' Nick asked Patch nervously.

'Nope. Just go for it,' said Patch, 'but without the backpack. You can't wear that. It will have to stay at the bottom.'

Nick walked over to the wall, put the bag down and clipped himself to the rope. Keith took up the slack. Nick blew on his hands and rubbed them together. *Three points of contact.* He started to climb, point by point, looking around him for the next handhold or foothold. He was doing well. *Own your fear.* He felt in control. He was conquering his fear. He felt like a little boy again and wanted to share the moment. He wanted to be praised for his achievement. He really must bring Harry here sometime.

Nick couldn't help himself. 'Look at me, Uncle Keith, I'm doing it,' he cried. He must have been at least ten metres up the wall now. The encouragement from below spurred him on, no one telling him he was only actually three metres up, a way to fall but not much of a climb.

Nick kept going. He kept looking straight ahead, not down. The top of the wall would appear soon, and he could start going back down. Surely he was nearly there? He could hear Keith below reminding him that it was about the climb and not the summit, and it was at that moment that he couldn't see where to put his hand next. There didn't appear to be a visible handhold, just a couple of protuberances the size of a complimentary bar of soap, upon which he couldn't get a proper grip. He then spotted a larger handhold, just as the wall started to lean away from him. He stretched towards it but couldn't quite reach. All at once, the strength left his legs and his muscles started to shake.

One last effort.

He reached out and pushed up, his thighs screaming in complaint. He would have to break the three-points-of-contact rule to reach the handhold. He had no choice. He went for it, managing to reach it and swinging his left leg to join his right on the foothold below. To his horror the foothold wasn't wide enough, and both his legs gave way.

Nick lost his handhold and fell.

He seemed to fall for ages, but in truth it was only a couple of metres before Uncle Keith took up the slack and locked him in place. He swung in and banged against the wall a couple of times, injuring his pride more than his body. He clung onto the wall, his muscles trembling with fatigue. He only had a few metres to go to reach the top, but he didn't care. He just wanted to go down now, he had had enough. He froze where he was, unable to move.

A second later Patch appeared from nowhere, next to him, without a harness. He had sprung up the wall like a mountain goat on acid. Which he probably was.

'You've got this, Nick,' he said. 'I'll be your guide from here to the summit, and Keith has got your back. We're a team. No one can achieve greatness without the help of others.' Had Keith told him to say that? 'You need to show the little ash-man in the bag down there that you can do this.'

Nick looked out from the wall directly in front of his face towards Patch, who was grinning inanely, and felt a sudden wash of inspiration. This may not be Everest or K2 but it was Hertfordshire Sports Village's twelve-metre challenge and, with the help of Keith and Patch, he would conquer it.

One hold at a time, he inched up the wall until he reached the top, to the applause of all the school children and the party of disabled climbers below. All he had to do now was get back down.

Patch suggested he should abseil as he was fatigued and climbing down was not necessary to fulfil Charlie's task. As Nick approached the bottom of the wall, he could hear Uncle Keith telling his followers that life was full of ups and downs, and what was important was sharing those moments and having your friends there to help you through.

That may be true, Nick reflected, but it was he that had kept going to the top. No one else. He had to do the same with his business, admittedly with Brian's support. He picked up the *little ash-man's* bag and headed straight back to the office to get his head down.

36

SEAN PRESSED HIS HANDS into the arms of his chair and leant forward to give himself a better chance at standing in one go, with the help of a bit of kinetic momentum. He was still in pretty good shape for a ninety-three-year-old, physically that was, but he knew his mind was going because his daughter kept reminding him that that was the reason he'd recently had to move to a new home. He didn't know what was wrong with his old home in Ayot Green, just a stone's throw from the A1M and his favourite local, a good old-fashioned English pub run by a Frenchman. He and Joan had been very happy living in Ayot Green since their marriage in 1949. They'd raised their four children there and had many happy years together, which he now struggled to remember along with the names of their many pets.

Sean now lived in a nearby care home on the opposite side of the A1M from the pub. He was intrigued by a strange vase that had mysteriously appeared on the mantelpiece in his living room. Toffee, his cat, who had been allowed to move to the home with him, had paid it some initial interest and then ignored it. He had a habit of doing this with everything, including humans. The vase had a lid and no flowers in it. It was bloody ugly and utilitarian looking. Joan would know what it was. He called out, but she didn't answer. He called again and then started to become angry that she wasn't answering him. He looked around the living room. Why was there a bed in it? He called again but there was still no answer from Joan. She must be in the garden. He looked out of the window. There were strangers sitting in his garden. He suddenly felt very worried. He called for Joan again.

'It's okay, Mr McCormick, it's okay.'

Sean looked round to see a stranger in his room. Shocked and frightened, he asked her who she was and what she was doing in his room. But as she got closer to him, he recognised her. He didn't know from where, but his fear dissipated, and he started to feel calmer.

'Do you remember where you are, Sean? Mr McCormick? This is your home now. This is where you live, you and Toffee. This is your own special room.' Ekemma started to stroke his hand to help calm him down. 'Let's get you back in your chair, Sean, you shouldn't have got up without calling me. You might have fallen over. You are a naughty boy!'

'I'm fine. I don't need help,' he replied gruffly.

'I'm sure you don't, but I like to help you,' Ekemma assured him.

'What's that?' he said, pointing at the urn.

'What's what?'

'That thing, that ugly vase on my mantelpiece. Will you get rid of it please?'

Ekemma took a gentle breath and began to explain again to Sean that it wasn't a vase. It was an urn. She was about to say what had happened and why he was there when he remembered.

'It's Joan, isn't it? That's why she didn't answer me. She died.' He looked over at the photo of his beautiful wife next to the urn on his mantelpiece.

Ekemma sat down on his bed next to him and continued stroking his hand. 'Yes Sean, your wife Joan passed away recently, which is why you are now living here with us. Your lovely daughters and son come to visit you here.' *Some more than others*, she thought. She was about to continue explaining when the home manager appeared in the doorway.

'Ekemma, can I have a word?'

Ekemma assured Mr McCormick that she would soon be back, and he should sit tight until she returned, when they would play a game of cards.

Out in the hallway Mrs Shaw explained to Ekemma that there were two gentlemen in reception from the undertakers who had Joan's ashes and the ashes in Mr McCormick's room actually belonged to someone else and they needed to swap them over. Mrs Shaw held up a new urn, altogether different from the one sitting on top of Mr McCormick's mantelpiece and suggested that Ekemma simply swap it when Mr McCormick wasn't looking.

Ekemma told Mrs Shaw that swapping over the urns now would cause even more distress to Mr McCormick and it might be better to leave him with the wrong ashes. They were after all, just ashes, and no one need know, least of all Mr McCormick.

Mrs Shaw explained that the gentlemen from the undertaker's were very insistent and having two men in funeral attire, standing in the reception area in full view of the communal television lounge, was making all the residents deeply uncomfortable.

A crash and the sound of cracking glass from Mr McCormick's room interrupted their discussion. Sean had evidently decided he hated the new vase with a lid and had thrown it out through the open window. It had bounced off the windowpane, cracking it on its way down to the ground below, where it shattered, spreading his wife's ashes all over the residents' patio.

When this news was relayed to the two gentlemen from the undertakers in reception, they disappeared outside at a speed totally incongruous and inappropriate to their profession, falling over each other to get out of the door first.

Back in Mr McCormick's room, Sean asked Ekemma why there were two men dressed in black on their hands and knees, frantically sweeping up dirt on the patio below. Were they new gardeners from a formal contract company? Ekemma said not to concern himself and whilst he was distracted, she put the new urn at the back of the high shelf inside Mr McCormick's wardrobe, where he and Toffee were unlikely to find it.

37

Wednesday 29th June

NICK HOPED THAT HIS father's interest in escapology had reflected his interest in such people as Houdini and David Blaine and not in something darker. The very idea had brought up memories of his father's engagement with Saturday night television. Watching Saturday night TV was one of the things they occasionally did as a family, when his father wasn't out with friends or business contacts or both, as in most cases, they were one and the same.

Uncle Keith seemed particularly excited by today's bucket list experience. Nick wondered what it was they were going to be learning to escape from. Keith had taken it upon himself to organise this particular task and, through his network of followers, had come across a relatively local escapologist, illusionist and magician who'd enjoyed some success online and had even made a daytime television appearance or two. The escapologist lived in the unusually named Hertford suburb of Bengeo, in a quiet cul-de-sac in his deceased parents' house, from which it appeared, judging by the average age of the residents who came out to see why a noisy motorcycle and a drug dealer's car had invaded their quiet close, there was no escape.

Keith deftly dismounted his Honda NC750X DCT and put his helmet in the top box. He greeted his virtual followers, making a comment that whilst he loved the comfort of his latest ride and acknowledged that it would be perfect for some riders, he felt the automatic gear change wasn't his cup of tea. 'In life we need to change our own gears, not allow a computer to do it for us. Especially when cornering or going around a bend.'

Keith had been going round the bend for some time, Nick concluded.

Keith signed off with his viewers, promising to check in later and explaining he had to sign a non-disclosure agreement, giving away the magician's secrets upon pain of death. The last bit wasn't strictly true, but it added a bit of drama to this suburban setting, in which it looked as if nothing ever happened other than a sex scandal or serial killer's rampage. It was always the most unassuming places that held the biggest secrets. So, Keith would not be filming this morning, which was a relief for Nick. He could relax and enjoy being tied up or whatever it was the escapologist had in store for them.

Nick grabbed the urn, noisily locked his car, making one of the neighbour's curtains twitch, and walked up the crazy paving towards the Magnificent Mysterioso's double front door in translucent frosted glass. Uncle Keith was already standing there, ready to press the doorbell, which he did as Nick arrived. It had an unusual ring, a loud 'Ta-da'; amusingly appropriate for the Magnificent Mysterioso, also known as Gary Parkes. There was no answer from the front door when suddenly a voice said, 'He doesn't appear to be in.'

The voice came not from Keith or Nick but from a man who had inexplicably appeared between them, possibly at the very moment of the 'Ta-da'. The proximity of the caped man in the top hat and the cutting edge of his voice made them both jump out of their skins. It was at once impressive and terrifying.

With a flourish, Gary introduced himself and welcomed them to his home of mystery. He held both arms out before him and mimed straining to push the front door open from a distance. The latch clicked and the door swung open, revealing a dark, empty hallway. Keith appeared excited at this magic, but Nick felt a knot in his stomach, as if he were about to become part of a news report appealing for witnesses of missing persons later discovered in the dungeon of a disillusioned illusionist.

'Walk this way,' said the Magnificent Mysterioso, as he adopted a very strange walk into his hallway, as if he were gliding on tracks, a forward moonwalk. If David Walliams were to play Willy Wonka, he would come close to the Magnificent Mysterioso. Nick felt the hair on the back of his head stand up and noticed that he had goosebumps on his arms. He already wanted to escape and, on the upside, soon he would learn the skills to do so. Uncle Keith followed on, rubbing his hands with glee. The front door swung shut behind them with a bang. Nick jolted at the sound and held his breath for a moment.

The Magnificent Mysterioso took off his top hat and held it high above his head where it magically hung, suspended in the air with no obvious signs of support. Nick suspected fishing lines and magnets might be involved. What it did was draw Keith's attention to a large hook on the ceiling. This, they discovered, was where the

Magnificent Mysterioso hung when practising one of his routines. The floor above had been specially strengthened to accommodate his size and his swinging around to free himself from a straitjacket and chains.

'Do you have a romantic partner, Gary?' Keith enquired.

'They come and they go,' came the reply. Apparently, Gary was dating an erotic cabaret dancer who was famous for her eleven-foot python and the fact that ninety-four per cent of her body was covered in tattoos.

Nick didn't ask which six per cent wasn't covered but secretly wanted to.

The Magnificent Mysterioso's hallway was decorated with framed photographs of himself on stage, interspersed with photos of other historical artists with their names under each of their photographs: Madame DeLinsky, Charles Rowan, Janaka Basnayake, Dr Vivian Hensley, Gilbert Genesta and others. He was horrified to hear that Nick had never heard of any of them but was happy to explain that they all died performing a magic trick or stunt, some more horribly than others, and that escapology in particular had inherent risks. Dicing with death, the Magnificent Mysterioso reflected, made one appreciate the gift of life more. Nick could see Uncle Keith making a mental note of that in the absence of any digital video recording equipment.

'I see that you are close to death,' said Gary, staring at Nick and holding his gaze silently for at least five seconds until Nick was able to look away.

Nick asked him what Gary meant by it.

'You are holding an urn.' The Magnificent Mysterioso

roared theatrically at his own joke.

Nick and Keith did not.

Gary seemed excited by the idea that they would be in the presence of death whilst he taught them some of his death-defying skills. 'Come this way,' he sang as he led them into his kitchen. 'This kitchen is unchanged since the 1960s. I wish I could say the same about myself.' He roared again at his own humour. 'Can I offer you a caffeine-free tea or coffee, or simply a glass of water? No artificial stimulants will be needed as your pulses will be racing quickly enough. You will need to remain as calm as possible once you have entered the Domestic Dungeon of D-e-a-t-h!' He strung out the last word as long as his breath would allow. 'Come and sit at my original, genuine Formica kitchen table where two disclaimers are laid out ready for you to sign. Please. Oblige me.'

Nick felt a wave of nausea, or was it fear, sweep over him. He couldn't tell. The fact that they had to sign the papers with a large purple and black quill added to the drama of the moment. He imagined that he was about to sell his soul in a Faustian pact.

Following an un-calming chamomile tea served in a 1960s green utility crockery teacup, the Magnificent Mysterioso led them into his dining room.

'Behold,' he cried. 'The Domestic Dungeon of D-e-a-t-h.'

The dining table and chairs were pushed to one side and the blackout curtains were drawn. In the middle of the room, illuminated by a single bare hanging bulb, was a high-backed wooden chair covered in straps. Nick was relieved to see it wasn't plugged into the mains. Draped across another smaller chair was a large black satin cloth and a smaller black satin bag. The bag would go over his head and the cloth over his entire body. To demonstrate this escape required removing most of Gary's clothes, down to a pair of ill-fitting black leather shorts. Magic was all about misdirection and distraction and the Magnificent Mysterioso's body was certainly a distraction, one Nick couldn't look at. Gary needed to look after himself a bit better and didn't much resemble the photos of himself in his hallway in his heyday.

'Gentlemen,' said Gary in the manner of a Victorian Master of Ceremonies, 'I invite you both to strap me to this firm and sturdy chair, put the hood upon my head so that I cannot see and cover me up in the black satin cloth.'

Nick and Keith both did as directed, Keith eagerly pulling on the straps.

'Nice and tight,' Gary enthused. 'Well, someone is a little nervous. Your hands are trembling, Nick. Don't worry, I can't hurt you.'

Nick realised his hands were shaking; in fact his body temperature seemed to have dropped. 'It's cold in here,' he said.

'Ah, that may be a presence from the other side,' Gary offered.

Nick didn't believe in any of that nonsense normally, but his body appeared to disagree with him. At least it was light in the room and this trick would soon be over.

'Now,' bellowed Gary in a commanding voice, 'close the door, turn out the light and make your way to your seats using the wall to guide you.'

Keith skipped over to the door and shut it, as Nick

walked towards the wall so that he would not lose his way to his seat and end up sitting on Gary's lap. Keith then switched off the light and they were plunged into absolute blackness.

After an eternity of listening to the Magnificent Mysterioso's deep breathing, the silence was broken.

'Alexa,' Gary ordered, 'play "Also Sprach Zarathustra" on Spotify.'

Nick hadn't noticed a speaker in the room, but then a circle of blue light spun around, temporarily illuminating the room, and casting an eerie light on the black-clad Gary Parkes, strapped to his chair.

'I'm sorry, I don't know that one,' Alexa apologised.

'Alexa,' Gary repeated in a commanding voice, 'play "Also Sprach Zarathustra" by Richard Strauss on Spotify.'

'I'm sorry, I'm having trouble understanding you.'

'Alexa! Play "Also Sprach Zarathustra" by Richard Strauss.'

'Playing "Also Sprach Zarathustra" by Richard Strauss on Amazon Music.'

Gary let out an audible sigh of relief as the music began.

On the final timpani note of the first phrase of music, the room was rudely illuminated by the single bulb, revealing an empty chair with discarded hood, cloth and straps. Sitting next to them in another chair they hadn't before noticed was the Magnificent Mysterioso in nothing but a pair of leather shorts and now a top hat.

Keith leapt to his feet in a fit of applause. Nick sat staring, unable to believe his eyes. Keith couldn't wait to have a go, but was disappointed to learn that he wouldn't get to learn the whole trick, that there were no spare leather shorts in his size and the top hat was unnaturally small for a man of Gary's size.

'There are a number of ways of escaping from bonds, straitjackets and chains involving trickery I am not allowed to share with my followers,' Gary told Keith. 'But there are a number of other common-sense techniques one could employ if one ever found oneself being tied up for whatever reason, and let's face it, these days anything is possible.' He went on to explain that you could breathe in deeply to expand your chest and girth for instance, meaning that your body would expand, and the bonds would not be so tight when you exhaled. Simultaneously, you could tense your muscles, pumping them up so that their size would decrease when relaxed.

Keith impressed the Magnificent Mysterioso greatly when he managed to step through his hands, which had been handcuffed behind his back, and bring them in front of him. Keith explained he was able to do this because of his years of yoga and his need to keep his flexibility up not only for health but to meet Sunflower's demands.

Nick allowed himself to be strapped to the chair, and following all Gary's guidance, managed to extricate himself in about ten minutes. Uncle Keith had managed it in an impressive one minute and twenty-seven seconds. Whilst tied up, Nick's mind began to wander. Why did his father want this on the list? It seemed really odd. In fact, the whole list was odd and was beginning to feel extremely inconvenient. This particular experience hadn't been much fun. He felt like he'd been invited on the world's worst stag weekend as the designated driver. He couldn't wait to escape from the escapologist.

Once the ordeal was finished, Nick and Keith thanked the Magnificent Mysterioso and returned to their respective vehicles. Keith caught up with Nick by his car and asked him if he wouldn't mind saying a couple of things to camera before he drove off, as they'd not been able to stream any of the experience. Nick agreed.

'So, Nick, what was a highlight for you today? What did you learn?'

'To be honest, I'm not really sure. What's clear is that things are not always what they seem to be. It's a mystery why my late dad wanted this experience on the list. I suppose I've learned that I don't much like being tied up by a man in nothing but leather shorts and top hat, but I think I probably knew that already.'

Keith laughed and then turned the camera on himself, thanking Nick. 'So, what have I learned today? I guess that Charlie felt a need to escape from something and wanted his son to understand that. We all need to escape now and again, and it's not the nature of the escape that matters, it's having the courage to do it in the first place. Nick had the courage to try it today. If Nick escaped from nothing else today, he escaped from his fear. Well done, Nick. I'll see you on our next adventure. For now, I need to escape from here before that storm comes in. I don't want to be riding in the rain.'

Later that day when Keith watched the film back, he was stunned to see a pot-bellied man wearing only a cape, a top hat and leather shorts had photobombed his video blog without either him or Nick noticing. No matter how many times Keith played back the footage at a slow speed he couldn't see where the Magnificent Mysterioso had appeared from or where he disappeared to afterwards.

38

'WHAT'S THE PLAN WITH today's acquisition, Ray?' Kevin took a bite out of his enormous bacon sandwich, the grease and tomato ketchup mix dribbling down his chin onto his crotch and narrowly missing the front seat of Ray's van.

'The plan is that we get the fuckin' stones,' said Ray. 'It's only a matter of time before someone else discovers them and then what?'

'Then we're fucked. Royally. But they might not discover them if they don't know to look. Only you and your auntie know or, in her case, knew.'

'True, but someone might discover them by chance, so let's get on with this. And will you please stop making a fuckin' mess by eating in my van. There are crumbs everywhere. You could do with losing a few pounds, too.'

Kevin didn't much enjoy that last comment, but Ray was right. He could lose a few pounds. Ray was still a dick for saying it though and he needed to mind his manners.

The morning had been bright but the storm that had come in an hour ago meant they could barely see the small group huddled together under their umbrellas at the interment of their mother's ashes at a church opposite the tradesman's entrance to Brocket Hall. No one else was foolish enough to be out in this weather. Through the downpour they could just about make out the outlines of a few mourners and the windswept vicar, whose umbrella did little to keep the weather off his robes.

Today Ray and Kevin weren't disguised as undertakers but as workmen, cemetery inspectors if asked. Their story was that they'd been sent by the local council to test the integrity of the gravestones and graves in the area for health and safety reasons. They would have to make sure that no graves would give way underfoot and that no gravestones would fall on any unsuspecting mourners.

It was the responsibility of the local authority to maintain the graveyards and keep those within it safe, the ones that were still alive, that was. Those that weren't didn't matter, but the council didn't want them injuring anyone living. Kevin wasn't to phrase it like that, though.

Ray's van was parked just inside the cemetery gates with a good view of the memorial corner where most ashes were buried. They sat side by side in the van, which now contained a number of valuable appliances and possessions that had until recently belonged to the unfortunate debtors they'd visited that morning. Kevin had stuck a couple of false license plates on Ray's van in case anyone decided to make a note of their presence. Why two cemetery inspectors had the need of two bicycles, an iMac, a fifty-two-inch flat screen and a chiminea to do their job was anyone's guess, but it was unlikely that anyone would be looking. To be safe, Kevin pulled a tarp over the lot.

They hadn't bothered to visit Jacqui Young's relatives before today as they'd seen on the paperwork they'd taken from the crematorium that she was to be interred today and it would be far easier to simply come and dig up her ashes, swap them with the last lot, take them away and check them for the treasure back at Ray's flat. Not that there were much of the ashes from the last lot left. The moment they arrived below the window of Sean McCormick's room at the care home to collect his wife's ashes they'd seen there were no jewels there. The ashes were spread thinly right across the patio and covered the table and chairs and part of the barbecue. They'd done their best to maintain the illusion that they were undertakers so as not to blow their cover, and had graciously swept up the mess as quickly as possible, borrowing a handy dustpan and brush from the cupboard underneath the nearby barbecue. They'd swept up in a hurry, not bothering to be particular about what went into a carboard box they procured from the home. Back at Ray's flat Kevin was horrified to discover that amongst Mrs McCormick's ashes was a charred finger, which was still largely intact. Ray assured Kevin that no finger could survive the cremation process and that it was almost certainly the remains of a charcoaled barbecue sausage, which he swiftly disposed of.

Ray sat with Mrs McCormick on his lap and patted the lid of the new urn she'd been rehomed in. It was the most attention she'd had in years and, despite now being mixed with the remains of the last weekend's lunch at Shady Cedar Trees Care Home, she would have really enjoyed the attention and the adventure now awaiting her.

The weather died away and with it the mourners. One person hung back longer than the others and laid a small bouquet of summer flowers on the spot where the ashes had been interred.

Good, thought Ray. That would leave them in no doubt as to where to dig.

39

Thursday 30th June

UNCLE KEITH JUST WOULDN'T stand still. Every punch and kick that Nick threw or swung at him he deftly avoided, ducking and dodging like a professional boxer, his ponytail swishing from side to side. For someone of sixty-nine years Keith was in exceptional shape, which, he kept reminding Nick, he put down to daily yoga practice and having to keep up with Sunflower. Recently, though, he'd spent a lot of time answering calls from Marnie, who had joined them today to film the session at the Gosling Sports Park. Apparently, Marnie was going through a tough time with her boyfriend and needed considerable reassurance, meditation, chamomile tea and shoulder massages.

'Excellent, Keith,' said Giuseppe the instructor. 'The best form of self-defence is to get out of the way of trouble, although Nick here poses you no threat whatsoever.'

Nick frowned and attempted to pose a bit more of a threat, but soon realised that Uncle Keith was not going to allow any of his attacks to make contact with the pads he was holding to protect himself.

'And relax,' said Giuseppe. 'Now, Keith, it is your turn to attack Nick. Please give the pads to him and put on the boxing gloves.'

Noting he had broken quite a sweat, Nick passed a pair of slippery gloves to Keith. The pads Keith passed back to

Nick were bone dry.

'Remember to use your height to your advantage, Keith. Okay, ready? Begin!' Giuseppe waved an extraordinarily hairy forearm just inches from Nick's face.

One second later a whirlwind of a sexagenarian crossed the considerable gulf between himself and his sparring partner in a rainbow-tie-dyed blur of brightness. Before he knew what was happening, Nick was flat on his back on the crash mat. Keith had assimilated all the information that Giuseppe had given him in their brief instruction session on using one's body weight as one's greatest asset, and consequently directed all his eighty-four kilos into a flying roundhouse kick, hitting both of Nick's pads simultaneously and knocking him to the floor.

'Fantastic!' cried Giuseppe. 'Down like a sack of potatoes.' Giuseppe would have said a sack of pasta but didn't want to reinforce any racially stereotypical images anyone might have of him. His Italian side was far easier to detect than his father's Israeli birth, hence Giuseppe's interest in Krav Maga, which his father had taught him.

Keith went over to Nick to ask if he was okay.

'Yes, yes, yes. Please don't fuss. I am perfectly fine.' Nick scrambled to his feet, his tone giving away that nothing had been injured more than his pride.

Marnie caught this all on camera, adding to Nick's humiliation. Perhaps he could prove himself to be more capable on the next task.

'Pretty good for an old man, eh?' said Keith.

Giuseppe said he couldn't believe how old Keith was considering the shape he was in. He then went on to say that in Tiana, the Sardinian village where he was born, that Keith would be considered a young man and his level of fitness would not be unusual, but here in the UK he was exceptional, as most people were unfit like Nick.

Having looked forward to this particular task on Charlie's list, Nick decided he was not enjoying it as much as anticipated. Being beaten up by your uncle was not only painful but annoying, and being humiliated by the instructor was not enhancing the experience. He wouldn't like to come across his uncle in a real fight, but couldn't imagine Keith would ever hurt anyone. Although maybe Keith had a dark side. If Darth Vader could turn good in the end, maybe Karmic Keith could flip the other way.

He grabbed a drink and sat for a moment next to his father's urn. Today he found its presence irritating. He wished his father were there in person. If for no other reason than he could watch Uncle Keith showing him a thing or two.

'Okay, so now we work with some weapons,' said Giuseppe.

'Weapons? Grrrrrreat,' cried Keith, morphing into the Frosties Tiger and rubbing his hands together gleefully, taking an incremental step towards the dark side.

Giuseppe produced a large rubber knife and held it out before himself, slashing it backwards and forwards like a demented musketeer. 'What do you think you should do if someone comes at you like this?' Giuseppe lunged at Nick and then at Marnie's camera, which she found very amusing. 'What would you do, Keith?' Giuseppe waved his rubber weapon at Nick, who deftly avoided every feigned attack.

'Actually, I'd run away,' answered Keith.

'Is the right answer,' said Giuseppe. 'Run away. Your chances of defending yourself against a knife attack are negligible. I once heard a wise person say that disarming someone with a knife without getting hurt is like trying to take a marker pen from a defiant child without getting any of it on you. Just run away.' He paused for dramatic effect, looking into the camera. 'I am serious. Just run.' He put the knife back in his kit bag. 'Running away is the most effective form of self-defence. We should never be ashamed to run away.'

Nick reflected that this was sensible advice indeed but was distracted by the amount of hair poking out the top of Giuseppe's T-shirt.

'The only time you should not run away is if someone is pointing one of these at you.' From nowhere, Giuseppe produced a rubber handgun. 'This is a replica of a semi-automatic pistol,' he said, brandishing the weapon like a gangster. 'This is the exact shape and weight of a Glock 17 Gen 4 pistol as used by the British Army.'

Too much information, thought Nick. *It's a rubber gun.* 'Why would I not try to run away from that? It's far more dangerous than a knife.'

'Try to run away now,' answered Giuseppe.

'What, right n—'

'BANG,' shouted Giuseppe, interrupting Nick and miming shooting him. 'You see? You are dead. No time to run.'

Behind Nick, Marnie started to convulse with laughter. She stifled it when Nick looked round at her, apologising and saying she promised to take things more seriously. Nick could see Keith biting his lip with a sparkle in his eyes.

'A knife is more deadly than a gun because your assailant is more likely to cut or slash you. Psychologically, it is very difficult for someone to pull a trigger unless they are a psychopath. You see, trigger-pulling means you die, in most cases. I slash you a bit with a knife, nasty, but you might live. Or that is what the attacker may believe. I stab you, you possibly die, but the gun – bang – you are dead.'

Nick wondered where Giuseppe did his research, but it sounded logical.

'So, if someone points a gun at you, you have a chance of disarming them. Nick, take this gun and point it at me as if you are wanting to rob me.'

Giuseppe handed the gun to Nick, which felt surprisingly heavy in his hand. Nick held the gun out in front of him and decided he would commit himself to playing the role of an armed mugger with glee. He would show Giuseppe.

'Gimme your money, you motherfu—'

In less than a second Giuseppe seized Nick's wrist, jerking him forward and off balance with one hand whilst grabbing the top of the pistol with the other. With a simple inward twist, he skilfully removed the weapon from his hand, back stepping several metres away from Nick and pointing the gun at him. Nick tried his utmost not to let go, but Giuseppe made it impossible. It was impressive.

'You see, now I have the gun and I am far enough away from you that you will not be able to do the same to me if you do...'

'Bang,' said Uncle Keith.

'Unless, of course, you are not going to pull the trigger because psychologically most people are unable to do so?' said Nick, feeling slightly smug.

'Yes, but you don't know that because you are a motherfucker,' said Giuseppe. 'Don't take that personally.'

Nick wasn't warming to Giuseppe. Keith could see this and moved things along, saying that Nick should go first in learning how to disarm Giuseppe.

Nick found it surprisingly easy to get to grips with the gun technique and they spent the next twenty minutes practising it. Giuseppe was impressed and Keith thought Nick was a natural. Nick started to relax and enjoy the session. Giuseppe introduced them to other techniques layered upon the basic one. One technique involved getting in close to your assailant whilst unarming him and then swinging your elbow into his face to put him down. Nick was particularly good at this and received praise from all around.

Nick noticed that, apart from the beard, the tied-back hair and the general lithe muscular build, Uncle Keith looked quite like his father once had. But the interest and enthusiasm he showed Nick would have been alien to his father.

After a short break for refreshments, they practised again and again until the moves became instinctive. Keith went over to Marnie and did a piece to camera, something about awareness and preparedness for all situations, but always avoiding trouble if you could.

Nick was lost in thought when Giuseppe produced

another prop from his kit bag. It was a large chainsaw, which he noisily fired up.

'Only joking,' he cried. 'I am also a tree surgeon.'

40

'OH YEAH, THAT'S GOOD, *molto bene, molto bene*, that's so good, touch me, touch me there, touch me there again. *Toccami lì!*'

Giuseppe felt Amira's hot breath on his ear and obligingly did as he was asked, though he struggled a little with his hands cuffed together. He'd spent weeks getting Amira to agree to this particular al-fresco fantasy and to stop worrying about her bloody cats. He assured her that it would be a beautiful night.

'*E lucevan le stelle,*' he whispered, and the stars were indeed shining brightly, high above. The night air was cool, but they had agreed that their *passione* would keep them warm.

Amira looked resplendent in her red empire line dress fashioned in the style of Maria Callas's 1949 *Tosca* costume. Her tiara sparkled in the moonlight and her thick eyeliner enhanced her already beautiful eyes.

They lay in a clearing in a small copse in the Dunstable Downs, away from the hill's edge, where dog walkers enjoyed the magnificent views, families flew kites and where widows and widowers sat on memorial benches toasting their departed whilst drinking overpriced coffee from the artisanal van which did its business in the layby nearby, except in inclement weather.

Giuseppe couldn't believe his luck. *Oh fortuna!* The

weather had changed for the better; the previous day's storm, which had threatened to cancel or at least postpone this moment, had blown over and the sun had appeared, warming his world once again and baking the earth dry. He had taken the precaution of bringing a large blanket with him, which he had gamely sported as a cloak before removing it and shackling himself to a tree post in the middle of the small clearing; it would become his cell in the Castel Sant'Angelo for the night. He knew this location well as his tree-surgery business had tidied up the area only three weeks before for a very reasonable price, which had helped him to identify the perfect spot for this Act Three scene in which Tosca found her beloved Cavaradossi easily in the dark, albeit with the help of a small battery-operated candle. Things were going well for Cavaradossi so far.

'*Ed olezzava la terra,*' he continued, wishing he could get out of his handcuffs as things might go even better, but hey, one step at a time.

Amira pulled up her dress a little further to aid his progress, and then grabbed him around the collar of his authentic loose-fitting, unbleached nineteenth-century-style linen shirt, before pushing him further down her crushed velvet, applying a gentle pressure on his shoulders. He did not resist.

'*Stridea l'uscio dell'orto…*'

'Si Cavaradossi, the garden gate…'

'…e un passo sfiorava la rena… ' Giuseppe was ready now, and pulled unsuccessfully at his rough britches.

'Oh! I hear footsteps. I hear footsteps,' whispered Amira passionately.

'*Si, e un passo sfiorava la rena* … and a footstep grazed the sand. Don't break the mood, darling.' Pianissimo, he continued the aria: '*Entrava ella fragrante, mi cadea fra le braccia—*'

Amira gently but firmly placed a hand over his lips. 'No, no, no. Shh, I can hear someone.'

At that moment they both became aware of voices just outside of the copse. The outline of two men appeared, one tall and slim and the other much shorter but built like an ox, scanning the ground of the hillside with bright LED torches.

'There is fuckin' nothing here! Are you sure he said she had been scattered here?' The tall one was trying to keep his voice down but the anger in it made it carry all the way into the copse.

'Yes,' said the ox. 'Her husband said up here, near the benches was her favourite spot. She loved to sit here after walking her dog. If we were going to find them, we'd see them glittering in our torchlights. There is nothing here. Let's move on.'

After a few more minutes of scanning and expletives they walked off in the opposite direction.

Giuseppe's spirit felt a little deflated, which couldn't be said for the rest of him. They lay in silence for a moment, Giuseppe fully expecting Amira to call the whole thing off when she began softly whispering again.

'*O dolci baci, o languide carezze, mentr'io fremente le belle forme disciogliea dai veli!*'

And with that she indeed covered him in sweet kisses and, trembling with excitement, stripped his beautiful form of its veils.

41

Friday 1st July

THE WINDOWS WERE WIDE open in the high-ceilinged room, but this did nothing to help with the humidity. The pint-sized art teacher, Ms Oceane Bartell RA, had done well to pull the blinds down, which she thought would help to create some interesting light in the room, but the gesture hadn't helped to manage the stifling heat. The temperature was oppressive, and Nick was already sweating profusely. He was glad of his loose-fitting *It's the ride that matters* T-shirt his uncle had given him. There was a tangible buzz in the room, which was packed with nearly every easel taken.

Knowing that Keith's friend Marnie was going to be modelling for the life class in St Albans today had made Nick feel quite uncomfortable following the CPR incident, when she'd caught him unconsciously looking at her breasts. He'd opted for an easel as far back in the room as was possible. He couldn't see Uncle Keith anywhere yet and so he sat at an empty easel next to a tall, slim young woman dressed in black with a large black bun of hair sitting on top of her head. She looked like she'd stepped out of a nineteenth-century period drama.

The class should have started ten minutes earlier, but Keith and Marnie had yet to turn up, so Nick had ventured in alone. The Friday morning class of mostly retired students was becoming restless. Knowing Marnie was coming today had effected a full turn out amongst most of the older men in the class; the women seemed keen too as Marnie was a popular model, judging by the different images of her on the walls in mixed media.

Looking around the room at some of the other more interesting model options made a little of Nick's discomfort fade away. He could have spent the day painting someone altogether different, so Marnie would be a welcome relief in that sense, especially when compared with some of the male nudes that had been painted. What kind of man would want to expose himself in front of a room full of strangers? Nick certainly wouldn't do it. It would have to be an egotistical exhibitionist.

Nick couldn't help thinking that Keith had found it all so amusing and had enjoyed watching him squirm yesterday when Marnie had mentioned that she would be modelling for today's class after their Krav Maga session. She modelled most Friday mornings when she didn't have a photo shoot or a life-saving session, which paid much more.

Nick introduced himself to the lady in black, who must have felt even hotter than he did, but didn't show it. She shyly made his acquaintance, introducing herself as Fiona. He expected to see her horse and trap tied up under a tree outside. He took his dad's urn out of his knapsack and placed it underneath the easel. Fiona looked over at it and then glanced up at him. Nick said he hoped that the urn didn't make her uncomfortable and she explained that it did not; in fact she was quite used to them as she worked in the funeral industry. Looking at her, he believed it.

'While we wait for our model to arrive, let's remind ourselves of a few things. When you are painting, look for light and shade always. Think about what is causing the light, think about its source. Maybe it is being reflected from somewhere else.' The diminutive art teacher's accent revealed that she was from the west coast of the USA. She spoke with confidence, as if she was the director addressing a room of federal agents in a multiple murder case. 'Focus on the neutral spaces, get those shapes right and everything else will fall into place. We've been looking at the great Renaissance artists this term, in particular the works of Sandro Botticelli.'

Oceane walked over to her cluttered desk and produced a large bottle of water, which she nearly emptied, jangling her numerous bracelets as she did so.

'Last term was the Primavera semester.' She wiped her lips, pausing before continuing, 'This semester we've looked at other Renaissance works and the more observant of you will have noticed the large polystyrene oyster shell I've borrowed from the drama department's production of *The Little Mermaid* ... who can guess which iconic painting we are going to be reconstructing today?'

A number of hands shot up around the room, some more eagerly than others.

'Yes, Susan?' Oceane pointed at a colourfully dressed mature student in the middle of the room.

'The birth of Venus,' Susan called out enthusiastically, looking around for recognition, which she received from her supportive classmates. All apart from one older man sitting right behind her who seemed annoyed with her and, judging by the way Nick had heard Susan speaking to him earlier, was probably her husband.

'Yes! Arguably Botticelli's greatest work. I even have this long auburn Renaissance-style wig for Marnie to wear that I also borrowed from the production of *The Little Mermaid*.' Oceane stopped to look at her watch. 'So, for today we will not worry about the figures to the left and the right of the painting – anyone know what they are, incidentally?'

Susan knew that the winged wind god Zephyr and his female peer were to the left of the painting and the figure to the right holding the cloak represented the embodiment of one of the three Horae, a minor Greek Goddess of the seasons. She elaborated that the floral decoration of her dress suggested that she was the Hora of Spring, or Primavera, which they had studied the previous term.

'Well done, Susan. Would you like to come and take the class for me?' Oceane said dryly. It was a compliment, but to anyone that didn't know her it might come across as deeply insulting.

Judging by Susan's beaming grin she had opted for the former.

'Some people believe that Botticelli's painting of the naked goddess Venus emerging from her shell gave people new hope, embodying the rebirth of civilization following on from the chaos of the Middle Ages. We could do with some of that now, couldn't we? When you paint, draw or charcoal sketch Marnie, I want you to think about what Botticelli was intending to achieve with his painting.'

Nick would try very hard to focus on that thought as Marnie emerged from her shell.

Oceane was about to continue when someone knocked at the classroom door and beckoned her over. She turned to the class. 'Excuse me for a moment, please. Discuss amongst yourselves what you would like to portray in your version of the birth of Venus. I won't be long.' She closed the door behind her which had its internal blind pulled down to make the nude model, when she arrived, more comfortable.

Fiona turned to Nick and asked him which media he would be working with.

'I'll be using pencil as I've never painted before and I suspect I will struggle with anything else,' he admitted. 'And you?'

'Although I usually use charcoal, I like its natural burnt feel and the fact that you can blur the edges to cover up any inaccuracies,' Fiona replied. 'I am going to start using acrylics with plenty of colour today. In my painting I want to represent having recently fallen deeply in love and, a bit like Venus I am experiencing a rebirth, my own renaissance!' She whispered this with the greatest enthusiasm her quiet voice would allow, and went on to explain that she would be painting the love of her life from memory, using the model as a guide.

'Wow,' said Nick. 'Can I ask what his name is?'

'Her name,' Fiona corrected him, 'is Amira.'

'Sorry, I shouldn't have assumed. How long have you been together?'

'We're not, yet. She doesn't know how I feel about her.'

As she said this a look of melancholy descended upon her and she started to weep gently. Nick was about to attempt to console her when the door to the classroom swung open and Ms Oceane Bartell RA marched back in, leaving the door open behind her. To Nick's relief it looked like the class was about to be cancelled. He wasn't sure he could manage three hours in here in the sweltering heat, next to a tragic Victorian heroine he had somehow managed to upset, and trying to not look at the model he was meant to be drawing. And where on earth were Keith and Marnie?

'Some good news and some bad news, people,' said Oceane, waving her bangles in the air. 'Marnie can't be with us today, but she has asked a rather well-known friend to step in for her and … *he* has boldly agreed!'

Oh no. Please God, no.

42

'IT'S FUCKING COLD IN here, even with this kit on.' Kevin was not happy about having to be the one swimming around the perimeter of the boating lake at Stanborough Park, looking for jewels in the silt, but Ray had refused. 'I don't see why you can't be the one doing this – it's not exactly deep. You aren't going to drown in it,' he complained.

'You can drown in a teacup full of water. I fucking hate water. I told you that already. Now, get your head back down and keep looking.'

'I don't know how much longer I can tolerate this, Ray. It's like looking for a needle in a haystack. This wetsuit is crushing my vitals and the flippers are two sizes too small. I have no feeling left in my feet and my nads have retreated north like a sumo wrestler's.'

Ray had to admit, this wasn't a great plan and he was pissed off with himself for not putting Thomas Turner's ashes higher up their list. A phone call to his widow Jeanette had been answered by her daughter, who'd apologised that her mother wasn't in and no, she didn't have a mobile phone number she was prepared to share. She went on to say that she was pretty sure her mother had already scattered her no-good father's ashes at the boating lake and didn't care that the undertaker had given her mother the wrong ashes and that she might have scattered the remains of someone that people actually gave a shit about.

Luckily, there was only one old boy sailing a model boat today. He'd been keen to explain to Ray and Kevin that his pride and joy, *Ellen*, was a sixteen-inch Kingfisher pond yacht and had a beautifully hand-carved hull made from a lightweight African hardwood, sustainably resourced of course. His particular model was fitted with traditional cambric cotton sails. Kevin replied that it looked very nice, but would he please move on before he felt the need to scupper it. The gentleman obliged, murmuring something about boat enthusiasts not being the same as they had once been, and that he hoped they didn't find the motor that had dropped off their remote-control power boat as they were nasty, noisy things that spoiled the pond for the real men who relied on mastery of the wind and not batteries for their enjoyment.

Kevin continued for another fifteen metres around the perimeter of the pond before standing up once more and angrily pulling off his mask and snorkel.

Ray was about to run across to him when he became aware of an old lady carrying a large tote bag, approaching him from the left.

'What on earth is that man doing swimming in the boating pond?' she asked.

Ray explained what had happened with their fictional remote-control speed boat and the lady seemed impressed that they were bothering to look for it. It must have been expensive, she concluded. She asked him if he often came to the boating pond. He said that he did not.

'Then you won't know my husband,' she said.

'Probably not.' Ray was distracted by Kevin, who was

now sitting on the edge of the pond while trying to remove one of his flippers. 'What's his name?'

Kevin's flipper got the better of him and, as he pulled violently at it, it pinged off in one direction, sending him toppling backwards in the other, straight into the pond, creating a wake big enough to capsize the passing *Ellen*. Ray saw that he was in trouble and needed help, judging by all the splashing around with no visible sign of Kevin's head above the water.

'My husband's name is, or rather was, Thomas Turner. I've brought his ashes here to scatter them.' She produced an urn from her tote bag and put it on the wall of the pond.

'Help!' cried Kevin between mouthfuls of boating pond water and silt.

Ray could see *Ellen's* owner running towards Kevin, not to help him, he suspected.

'Don't you think you think you should go and help your friend?' said Mrs Turner.

Ray was torn. He could see that Kevin was in trouble and had managed to pull up copious weeds from the bottom of the pond and was now entangled in them. He fought valiantly with the slimy green strands that seemed to have taken on a life of their own. Ray was now witnessing a scene from a B-movie in which a monster from the deep devoured an unfit, greedy treasure hunter with an eye on the booty and not on his own safety.

'I did know your husband,' improvised Ray.

'Your friend—'

'I suppose he was a friend—'

'No, not my husband. Your friend in the wetsuit. He's

drowning! You should go and save him.'

At this point the elderly gentleman had grabbed a lifesaving ring from nearby and threw it into the water towards Kevin. It hit Kevin on the head, sending him under again.

'Oh fuck. Let's all go and save him, come on,' Ray said to Mrs Turner, grabbing the urn from the wall and running off in Kevin's direction.

Mrs Turner seemed quite unfazed by this and followed him and Thomas as quickly as she could.

After the drama of rescuing a cursing Kevin from the pond, Ray introduced him to Mrs Turner and her husband's urn and suggested they all warm up with a nice cup of tea at the park's tea shop.

'Thank you for the kind offer, but I will decline,' Mrs Turner said. 'I have come to scatter my husband's ashes and must do so.'

'Are you going to be scattering them alone or will your daughter be joining you?' Ray enquired.

'How do you know I have a daughter?'

'Your husband told me. Why don't you allow me to join you in scattering your husband and my friend Thomas into his beloved boating pond after we've had some tea?'

'Yes. Very well. That's a lovely idea.'

As they waited for their tea and cakes, Jeanette said how delighted she was that Thomas had made a friend at last, as he didn't have any and that she was equally delighted that he'd mentioned his daughter to him. 'My daughter refused to speak to her father for years. She only came home again after his death,' she explained.

They sat and chatted for some time, drinking several pots of tea until Jeanette needed to visit the little girls' room. When she came back out again, Thomas's new friends, whose names she hadn't caught, had gone, taking Thomas with them but leaving her with the bill.

43

Saturday 2nd July

Nick's morning had been frenetic, as he tried to get Harry out of bed before 11 a.m. and into the kitchen without a three-hour delay involving a virtual online deathmatch on his PlayStation with four of his friends and thirty-plus strangers, which could include any number of anonymous sexual deviants and terrorists. Nick was determined Harry would do something constructive with his day now that all Saturday morning sports fixtures had finished for the summer.

Charlotte hadn't yet appeared from her room, having been brought back from a party by an Uber in the early hours. To say that Louise wasn't happy with her was an understatement; Charlotte would find that out later. The state of the kids' bathroom and raided medicine cupboard left some evidence that the previous night's party hadn't ended well for Charlotte, and she would probably spend most of the day recovering.

Nick had been up early with Barry who, having emptied and filled his tanks, had eaten his breakfast and curled up on his favourite sofa spot for the day. Nick wished he could do the same.

He checked his email. There was still a huge amount to do in preparation for the business sale as well as its day-to-day running. Nick had managed to hide another notice from the bank that he didn't want Louise to see. If she found out there would quite rightly be hell to pay. He knew he was risking everything now he had remortgaged his home to solve the business's cash-flow problems. Whilst he was confident it was the right thing to do, Louise wouldn't see it that way. He had to admit that every time he thought of what he'd risked to stop his business going under, he felt sick to his core. Today's symptom was bile rising in his throat and stinging the back of his mouth. But it would all be fine. Wouldn't it?

He thought of all those times his father had ignored problems, burying them deep in his consciousness and advising Nick to do the same. But he'd always helped Tracey with her problems, stepping in emotionally and financially. Nick was a boy and boys had to get up after a fall, brush themselves down and carry on as if nothing had ever happened.

Louise stood by the breakfast bar drinking coffee and checking her many social media channels. This prompted Nick to check his phone; he had a text from Uncle Keith reminding him when and where to be today. He didn't need a reminder from Keith as SwifTok had reminded him several times. There were still too many tasks to complete before 8th July, the anniversary of his father's birthday, and the day he had to scatter the ashes.

Today he would be learning to cook, or rather cater on a large scale. They were going to help out at a soup kitchen. Nick wondered about his father's assignment of helping the homeless. Was this another death-bed regret for his father, assuaging his guilt for something he had not done? The irony that Nick was risking the roof over his own head to further his business and life dream was not lost on him, but his father wouldn't have known quite how ambitious Nick was.

Or had he known? Had his father assumed Nick was the same as he had been? Were they cut from the same cloth? Nick considered all these things whilst giving his urn a clean. It still had some paint and charcoal on it from the art class and looked a bit tatty from the trip it had been on so far. A spot of paint wouldn't come off the urn and started to irritate him, so he went into the utility room to search for a more abrasive cloth.

The utility room was chaotic. Already filled with overflowing boxes from the garage, it was now filled with even more boxes that needed sorting from well-meaning donors. Charlotte and Harry's plan to save St Francis Animal Sanctuary by organising a bring-and-buy sale had started to take over their lives.

He found a cloth in the cupboard above the worktop on which he'd left the drawing of Uncle Keith as Venus. The sight of it reminded him of the trauma he'd experienced the previous day. He really ought to throw it away before one of the kids became equally traumatised. Looking at it, Nick realised he had surprised himself. Apart from having to draw his naked uncle, he'd enjoyed the rest of the experience. He'd hated art at school and couldn't remember much about it. It was one of those things that you could either do or you couldn't, but this art class had been different. He had started to see things in a different way. He'd started in pencil but found it limiting and, after a brief experiment with charcoal, had opted for coloured acrylics. Oceane had taught him more in half a day than he'd learned at school in years. He now saw shapes and spaces and became aware of how light created shade and changed colours. Oceane had been particularly pleased with how he'd managed to recreate the sparkle of the shell Uncle Keith had been standing in. He'd had to focus on that and tried to avoid painting his uncle's genitals, which Oceane had insisted he do. He hadn't been able to bring himself to admit to her that Keith was his uncle; it just seemed too weird.

Nick took the cloth and returned to the kitchen where he almost bumped into Charlotte who materialised before him like a gothic apparition. She wore her hangover like a hooded winter coat. Seeing her state reminded him of all the times it had taken him to learn not to party so hard. In truth he still managed to forget, but not so often these days.

'Have you seen my Jack Wills hoodie?' Charlotte asked no one in particular.

'It's in the laundry,' Louise replied.

Nick returned to the urn and started to rub off the paint. The new cloth worked well. A scream of laughter from the laundry room interrupted his work. Charlotte reappeared, holding the picture.

'Where did this drawing of a Trans-Venus come from? Why has it got such a massive dong?'

'Your father drew it yesterday. It's your Uncle Keith.'

'Ew,' cried Charlotte, mock gagging.

'Your dad said he had to tone it down. It's actually bigger than that.'

'My God, that's so gross. But Dad, good drawing, really. You have a gift.'

Nick had no words.

'Don't forget you promised to help me organise all the boxes on Tuesday,' said Charlotte. 'You promised to take the day off work.'

She disappeared back into the laundry room with Uncle Keith's portrait as Nick experienced simultaneous feelings of horror and pride. His daughter had praised him, which rarely occurred. It was just a shame this memory would be forever associated with an image of his naked uncle in an auburn wig.

44

'THIS HAS GOT TO be the one,' Kevin said between slurps of his fourth can of Coke. 'If it isn't, I'm going to start worrying that something's happened to those jewels.'

'I've got a good feeling about this one, Kevin. I reckon it will be it.' Ray's pulse was racing; he felt like a greyhound waiting for the release of the hare. This had to be the one. Although technically it was still a fifty-fifty chance. The flip of a coin. The odds were increasingly in his favour with every urn. Within ten minutes he could be super rich. What was super rich these days? Jeff Bezos, Elon Musk or Bruce Springsteen? Okay, not super rich. Pretty rich like David Beckham or Elton John. No, not that rich either. Gordon Ramsey? Gary Lineker? Ray actually had no idea what rich meant or what rich people had. So, he eventually concluded that within moments he could be financially comfortable depending on the standard of living he chose or how he invested his bounty. But he couldn't help thinking that, without Kevin, he might be a little bit richer.

Kevin was having similar thoughts, but his internal monologue wasn't processing it in quite the same way. Kevin's formula for his projected wealth was simpler: Lots of jewels minus Ray equals more jewels plus more money for Kevin.

'Let's stick to the plan. Do you remember the plan, Kevin?'

'Yes, Ray, you keep repeating it. If I didn't know any

better, I'd think that you think I'm thick. The plan is that you go to the door and say you're from the undertaker's, that you're checking everything is okay and that they were satisfied with the service. I will wait here in the van.'

'And?'

'And once you get access to the house and find out where the urn is, you'll text me,' Ray continued in a petulant tone. 'I'll come and knock on the door saying I'm working in the area improving people's soffits and I noticed hers could do with replacing. Whilst I'm distracting her you can grab the urn and slip out the back.'

'That's right,' Ray cut in. 'It'll be quicker and easier than upsetting her with the story of the wrong urn. Continue.'

'Once you're at a safe distance you'll call me so I can stop the doorstep bullshit. I'll walk around the corner and wait for you there.'

'Good.'

'Though I don't understand why you can't just keep it simple like last time and convince her there's been a mix-up,' Kevin complained.

'This is better, trust me.' Ray was impressed that Kevin had remembered the plan. Or a version of it.

Ray's actual plan involved a second urn that Kevin didn't know about, which Ray would swap with Bernard Wyles's urn whilst Kevin was busy running interference. It was perfect. Kevin would never know. They would have to go through with trying to acquire the final urn on the list though, so that Ray could maintain the pretence that this one had no jewels. At the point of discovering no jewels in the final urn, Ray would pretend he'd had enough of the wild goose chase and give up.

They both agreed they were ready. Ray tightened his tie, checked his appearance and stepped out into the road. In minutes this would all be over, and he would be rich, or at least financially comfortable depending on his future choice of lifestyle.

He knocked at the door. The knocker was a large brass ring upon which perched what looked like a robin or it could have been a sparrow. Ray didn't really care. After what seemed like an eternity, he could hear someone on the other side of the door. Good, she was clearly not a fast mover, and he would have no problem escaping from her once he had the urn.

The door opened a few inches until the security chain prevented it from opening any further.

'Good morning Mrs Wyles,' said Ray in a sombre manner, which is how he perceived an undertaker should speak, but not knowing many, he wasn't sure of its accuracy.

'Who are you?' demanded Mrs Wyles in a hostile tone. 'What do you want?'

Ray had anticipated questions but not the unfavourable reception he was now getting. 'I'm from Kerton's undertakers.'

'Are you? What's their motto, then?' she asked, a beady eye staring through the narrowing gap in the door.

Ray had done his homework and answered a little too gleefully. 'Traditions here will never cease, leave it to us and rest in peace.' He felt himself smiling at the end of the sentence and checked himself.

'What's your name then?'

This wasn't going to be as easy as he'd hoped. 'I'm Edward Kerton.'

'Never heard of you. And I've definitely never seen you before either, I'd remember those eyes. You don't look old enough to be one of the Kertons. They're all old.'

'That's right, they are,' he agreed. 'I've not been working in the family business for long. I'm the youngest member of the family.'

'Oh.' She started to giggle. 'You must be the final Kerton.' With this she erupted into laughter. 'I always thought your family business motto should be "Need an undertaker? Then it's Kerton's for you!"'

Ray had to admit it was amusing, but his annoyance stopped him from joining in and his face maintained its solemn demeanour.

'Why the long face?' said Mrs Wyles. 'Has someone died?' Her laughter spilled out into the street as she slipped the chain back and welcomed him in with a gesture of her hand. 'Don't look so worried, Edward. I like a good laugh. I'm ninety-six years old, you know, and still on my pegs. It's my sense of humour what's kept me going. That, twenty a day, a gin at midday, a bottle of wine every evening and a thoroughly active sex life. I'm only joking … I only have half a bottle of wine.' She carried on laughing as she led him through to her tiny sitting room at the back of her house and invited him to sit in one of two high-backed chairs, in front of a large French window with a clear view of her garden.

Looking out, Ray had never seen so many bird feeders, or come to that, birds. They were all hopping around the smorgasbord of nuts and seeds that had been laid out for them around what look like a brand new moulded concrete bird bath on a pedestal, in which a number of smaller birds frolicked like toddlers at a splash park.

'Don't get too excited, Edward.' His hostess chuckled. 'I bet you've never seen so many tits before, have you?' She was on fire and obviously hadn't had any company for a while. 'Those over there are Blue Tits. If you hang around a little while you might be lucky enough to discover that I have Great Tits. I was just about to have my mid-afternoon gin. Will you join me?'

Looking around her living room and into her small adjoining sitting room, he couldn't see the urn anywhere. If he joined her for a drink, he might be able to question her as to the urn's whereabouts, but he was beginning to formulate a horrific fantasy about the lengths he might have to go to in order to acquire it. On balance he accepted her offer. He could text Kevin if things got out of hand.

'Just a small one, please.'

'Really, love?' She stopped to laugh again.

'I'm driving.'

'Oh, I see. Just a small one then,' said Mrs Wyles, pouring at least a triple measure of gin into a tall glass. 'Ice and a slice?'

'Yes please, Mrs Wyles.'

'Call me Margaret.'

'Yes please, Margaret.'

'So, what can I do for you, young man?' Margaret passed Ray a gin and eased herself into her chair by the window. 'I've paid up. I don't owe you any more money, do I?'

'No, not at all. It's part of the service. We just wanted to follow up and check you were happy with everything.'

'You weren't at the funeral yourself, were you?' Margaret eyed him suspiciously, her joviality temporarily slipping away. An uncomfortable silence followed.

'No,' said Ray, thinking quickly. 'I was on another job, we had a busy day.'

'They dropped the coffin and he fell out! Right there in front of everyone.'

A look of horror crossed Ray's face. He would have known this if he was a real undertaker. He felt his face flush.

'It was fine, Edward. I'm just pulling your leg. I was happy with the service, and I think Bernard would have been too. You can ask him, if you like. He's just over there.' Mrs Wyles pointed out into the garden.

'Have you buried his ashes under the lawn?'

'No, the birdbath.'

'Under the birdbath?'

'No, in it. My neighbour Albert made it. He's done well, don't you think? Considering he's as blind as a bat and has terrible arthritis. Doesn't stop those roving hands of his, though. He mixed the ashes in with some quick-setting concrete and moulded it in an old dustbin lid. Looks pretty good, doesn't it?'

'Yes, it does. So, Bernard's in the birdbath. He's part of it? Mixed in with the concrete?'

'Yes, dear. That's what I said, keep up! He's just in the bath part, not the pedestal. There wasn't enough of him to go that far. But he'll be happy for eternity now. He loved his birds.'

Ray stayed for a couple more gins before excusing himself, trusting that if Mrs Wyles drank a few more she would sleep soundly that night.

Which she did.

45

NICK HAD SPENT AN annoying amount of time sat at his breakfast bar with his coffee going cold. He was on a video call with Shirley Hopkins after his return from the soup kitchen, where someone had thought his dad's urn was a pot of herbs and had attempted to prise the lid off, unsuccessfully, thank goodness. His dad could have ended up in a large vat of soup and consequently in the stomachs of the many people they had catered for that day; not the bucket trip his father had planned.

Shirley insisted on displaying her superior Zoom skills by changing her backdrop a multitude of times from deep space to the Golden Gate Bridge. She'd appeared on their call using a talking cat filter and had, as yet, and unlike Nick, not become tired of it .

'I've been happy to give up my time for you today, Nick, and my research, which I started in the office yesterday, has come to fruition,' Shirley announced triumphantly. 'I've contacted the circus skills company and have booked a tightrope – or tight-wire as it's now called – workshop.' Shirley's background changed to an exotic beach.

'Where are you now, Shirley?' Nick humoured her.

'Oh,' she said, smiling, 'this is the Maldives. Where I went last year.' The background looked very inviting.

'You'd be a bit hot in the Maldives with so much fur.' Nick was referring to the fact she was still a talking cat.

'Yes, indeed I would,' she agreed and switched off the cat filter.

Nick started laughing at seeing another change to Shirley's appearance. 'That's hilarious,' he said. 'That is an extraordinarily comic bouffant purple wig filter you have found. I've not seen that one before.'

'I'm not using a filter at that moment,' came the curt response. 'This is the new hairstyle I had done at great expense this morning.'

Nick was unable to backtrack quickly enough, and she seemed upset, but he couldn't really tell as she immediately morphed into a clown.

The morning's soup kitchen experience had both humbled and inspired Nick greatly. The tales he had heard that day, especially the story of one young pregnant woman who faced giving birth on the streets and probably losing her child to the care system, had made him reconsider his privilege. Nick had always assumed it was alcoholics and addicts that ended up homeless; now he learnt that anyone could, even someone like him. You might not arrive on the streets as an addict, but the chances were that you would become one.

Nick sighed, thinking of his own financial situation and what he'd risked, imagining his own family destitute. His stomach swam, and once again he felt a wash of bile at the back of his throat. But then he thought back to Uncle Keith's unstoppable optimism and laughter at the shelter, and it snapped him out of his downward spiral.

Uncle Keith had attracted considerable attention at the kitchen, both in person and online, and had called on his followers to donate their time or money to homeless charities. He appealed for volunteers and the response had been overwhelming. Marnie had accompanied him again. Nick hadn't asked any questions.

A talking Mona Lisa now appeared on the screen, commenting how nice the people at the circus skills workshop company had been and how they offered corporate days as well as drop-in workshops. 'Did you know that, as well as the tightrope you could learn stilt walking, diablo spinning, juggling, plate spinning, unicycle riding and aerial skills?'

'I didn't know that, no,' Nick admitted.

'It would be great to have a day out for the office before the autumn, when I'm due to retire.' Shirley paused, as if unable to continue.

Although Shirley's retirement was a day which Nick was increasingly looking forward to, he spoke the words she wanted to hear. 'You'll be greatly missed. I don't know how the office will run without you.' He took solace in the fact that she would be gone from his life one way or another, sooner or later with her retirement or the company sale.

The Mona Lisa nodded. 'I've booked the company to come to your mother's house tomorrow and set up there. Barbara said she has plenty of space and a number of trees the company could use to attach the tight-wire to.'

Nick was annoyed that she had contacted his mother without his consent but let it go, reminding himself again that Shirley was not going to be in his life for too much longer.

The Mona Lisa offered a wry smile. 'Your mother is looking forward to being present at one of the bucket-list activities. In fact, she's decided to make it a social event and has planned a barbecue for some of her new friends from the wake: Terry, Ken and Nigel. She has also invited me and I've accepted her invitation.'

46

Sunday 3rd July

'WELL, THAT'S IT,' SAID Ray, re-examining the last pieces of smashed birdbath, spread across the floor of his rented garage. 'No fuckin' jewels here.'

Kevin limped over to the garage door and pulled it up and over to open it, to let more light in.

'Don't do that,' barked Ray.

Kevin pulled the garage door shut again.

'You really should get your foot X-rayed. I'm pretty sure you broke something dropping the birdbath on it. I told you to wait for me.'

'It's fine, I've had worse. I can't believe the sound didn't wake the old dear up.' Kevin opened a grab-bag of rank-smelling pickled onion-flavoured crisps. 'Want one?' he said, offering them to Ray, who waved away his offer with a look of disgust.

'Nothing was going to wake her up after the amount of gin she had. Not even your screaming.' Ray's head was still splitting open from the inside out and smashing up the concrete birdbath with a sledgehammer hadn't helped. 'We've been through these fuckin' fragments thousands of times now. They ain't here.' His frustration was evident.

'Well, at least we know where they are now. They are with Mrs Barbara Swift,' Kevin said, reading from his list and crossing the previous name off. 'The last one on the list is Charles Swift. How are we going to play this one, Ray?'

'We'll use the tried and tested method. But we'll have to act quick before word gets around about two dodgy geezers posing as undertakers. We'll have to go first thing Monday. We can't go today 'cos it's Sunday.'

'Why not? People die every day of the week. If we don't go today, we might be too late.'

'Where is the spare urn, Kevin?'

'It's in the van. It's been there a few days.'

'Good. Make sure it's filled with something ash-like and that the lid is tightly sealed.'

They were both formulating slightly different plans. Ray's last plan had been scuppered by the surprise that Mr Wyles had become a birdbath. His new plan had just been scuppered by Kevin's suggestion that they go to see Mrs Swift today and not wait until tomorrow. He had planned to go alone that afternoon.

Meanwhile, Kevin hadn't quite worked out how he would acquire Ray's share of the jewels, but his sheer physical size and propensity for violence always provided him with a ready-made plan.

'On second thoughts, open the garage now please. Your fuckin' crisps are making me gag.'

47

'DON'T LOOK DOWN, LOOK straight ahead. Focus on where you are going and not where you are,' said Gunter, the extraordinarily chiselled instructor from The Funky Funambulists. They were *Putting the FUN in Funambulism*, according to his extra-tight T-shirt.

'It's a good thing he isn't an undertaker,' joked Terry inappropriately and was obliged to explain to Ken and Nigel that you didn't need to look very hard to find the *fun* in a funeral. He seemed to be the only one able to discover that particular holy grail.

Nick was now on his fourth attempt to cross the distance between the two trees. A queue of people stood behind him, all waiting to have a go. The audience added extra pressure and their constant laughing and jeering put him off. He was the only person so far that had failed to get across. Louise, Charlotte, Harry and even Keith had managed it. Yet Nick just couldn't get it and was becoming increasingly frustrated.

'Okay,' said Gunter, 'I think a little break for you, yes?'

'No, no. I can do this,' said Nick. After one more step, the trembling in his legs transferred itself to the wire below his feet and he was thrown from the rope like a drunken office party reveller trying to master a bucking bronco machine whilst clutching a cocktail. He landed in a heap in front of Louise, only his ego bruised as the wire was only one metre off the ground. Luckily, they'd agreed it wasn't necessary for him to carry his dad's urn across the wire. In hindsight, that had been a wise decision.

'You need to find the sweet spot, Nick,' said Gunter, addressing Nick but taking everyone present in. 'You are trying too hard. You need to find a rhythm. Minimal effort is needed to cross the wire. It is your movement that is the destabilising element. Your small errors are amplified and before you know it, you have failed.'

Nick suggested that Gunter should consider a career as a life coach. Gunter did not understand. Nick started to explain when he was interrupted by cheers and whoops from behind him.

'Woo-hoo! This is so easy. I've certainly found the sweet spot.' Shirley squealed with delight as she effortlessly strode across the tightrope to great applause.

'Maybe you could help me find the sweet spot, Shirley,' cried Terry. This time he wasn't the only one to laugh at his humour. The laugh spread around the group like a Mexican wave, missing only Nick in its wake.

* * *

'This is the place, Kevin. Let's leave the van around the corner and walk in. There's nowhere to park anyway.'

'Look at all those cars and motorbikes. They must be having a party.' Kevin dug into another bag of stinking pickled onion-flavoured crisps, the urn gripped between his knees. 'Perhaps we should come back tomorrow.'

'No, today is good. They'll all be distracted. Unless…'

'What?' asked Kevin through a mouthful of half-chewed crisps.

'Unless this is some sort of urn-related gathering. In which case we may be too late. We need to get a move on. And get rid of that crisp packet, for fuck's sake.'

Ray drove the van around the corner and parked in a lay-by behind a large hedge. The van was reasonably well concealed. Kevin emptied the rest of the contents of the crisp packet into his mouth and scrunched it up.

'And don't litter my van with that. I'm sick of clearing up your rubbish,' said Ray. 'Throw it away properly.'

Kevin went to unwind the window.

'And not out of the window – you'll draw attention to us.'

Kevin wound up the window and opened the glove box.

'Don't open that,' shouted Ray.

'For fuck's sake,' said Kevin. 'Where am I going to…' The glove box door swung open, revealing something that stopped Kevin in his tracks. He recognised it as a Glock 17 Gen 4 pistol. A gun exactly like one he'd had in the army. 'What the fuck?'

'Just put it back, will you.'

'You're not thinking of using this, are you?'

'Put it away, Kevin.'

'Jesus, Ray. It's fucking loaded,' said Kevin, inspecting the gun more closely.

'Just put it back before anyone sees it, you twat. And get rid of that fuckin' crisp packet.'

Kevin put the gun back in the glove box and closed it firmly.

* * *

Uncle Keith could see Nick was struggling and offered to get him a drink. Nick gratefully accepted and Keith set off for the house. As he walked back towards it, he saw two men in black walking up the long drive approaching the front door. One of them, a shorter, heavily set man, was carrying a small container and limping quite badly. The much taller man with him saw Keith and raised his hand in a half wave and then called out.

'Is Mrs Swift at home, please?'

'Yes, she is,' Keith replied. 'Can I ask what this is about?'

'It's rather delicate. I'd rather speak with her directly,' said the tall man in an overly friendly tone that didn't sit well with his appearance.

Keith frowned. There was something not quite right about the men. The tall man had extraordinary eyes: one eye was a piercing blue, the other looked black.

'I'm sorry,' said Keith, 'I'm her brother-in-law. I'd like to know the nature of your business and why you are here on a Sunday. We're having a family gathering at the moment. So, with respect, before I interrupt her, I'd like to know who you are and what you want.' Keith could now see that the shorter man was holding a plastic urn similar to the urn that Nick carried around containing Charlie's ashes.

'We're from the undertaker's,' said the shorter man in a clipped voice. 'We need to speak with Mrs Swift. Would you go and get her, please?'

Keith decided to push the men a little further. 'Okay, which undertaker's and what are your names?'

'Just get Mrs Swift, please. We'd like to speak with *her*.'
The short man's tone was becoming increasingly impatient.

'We're from Kerton's. I'm Edward Kerton,' said the taller man, stepping forward. 'I must apologise for my colleague here. He's in rather a lot of pain since he dropped a memorial stone on his foot.'

'That doesn't excuse his rudeness,' said Keith. 'What is it you want?'

'Well, it's rather embarrassing,' said the taller man. 'You see, there has been a mix-up and we need to give these ashes to Mrs Swift and take Mrs Swift's ashes back to someone else.'

Keith could see he was flustered now; this was utter nonsense.

'Yes, these ashes,' said the short man, thrusting the ashes forwards. Keith instinctively went to take the urn from him. As he did so the taller man stepped forward in an attempt to intercept the urn.

'Fetch the other ashes first, please,' said the tall man in a now desperate tone, trying to lift the urn from Keith's hands.

The short man finally caught on to what was happening and stepped forward to grab the urn. All hands were now on the urn like a game of pat-a-cake.

'What on earth?' said Keith, stepping forward to get a better grip on the urn and accidentally standing on one of the feet of the short man. As he did so the man let out a deafening scream of pain and pulled at the urn, separating the lid from the container. Ash flew from the container, along with what looked like an empty crisp packet. The ash went into Keith's eyes, temporarily blinding him. The two men, fortuitously unaffected by the spray of ash and realising their charade was at an end, pushed Keith to the ground and ran and hopped wildly back up the path. By the time Keith had wiped the dirt from his eyes they were nowhere to be seen.

Terry, Ken and Nigel appeared, wondering where Keith had disappeared to. Keith briefly explained what had happened and asked them not to mention it to Barbara, as it would upset her, and not to mention it to Nick, as he had plenty on his plate and appeared to be deeply stressed, although Nick was unaware of this himself. Terry, Ken and Nigel complimented Keith on his appraisal of the situation and Nick's state of mental health. They agreed to support Keith and keep it quiet.

He would talk to his motorcycle policeman friend and see if he could get this reported quietly. It was clearly an attempted 'distraction' robbery gone wrong. They all knew Sergeant Reggie Hardy and agreed he would be discreet. In the past he had overlooked a few things, including a few plants that Ken had grown that didn't really do anyone any harm assuming they were for personal use only and he didn't ride his bike or operate heavy machinery after smoking their leaves and buds.

They decided that they would sweep up the ashes and give the pickled onion crisps wrapper to Sergeant Reggie. When sweeping up the spilled ashes, Ken noticed that they weren't ash at all but appeared to be some sort of compost.

Nigel held a palmful to his nose and inhaled deeply. 'This is worse than we thought, lads. These are bad men, bad, bad men we are dealing with,' said Nigel. 'This compost is a peat-mix.' He offered it up to Ken and Terry who agreed and said there seemed to be a hint of quality manure in the mix too.

Terry took several more deep sniffs. 'Oh, yeah. That's some good shit.'

Back down by the tightrope, a crowd had gathered and were encouraging Nick as he attempted his fifth crossing.

'Just keep your focus ten feet ahead and balance one leg at a time,' said Gunter, as if he were talking a rookie through bomb defusing.

'One step…' said Nick.

'At … a … time,' whispered Gunter.

Keith, Terry, Nigel and Ken all arrived to see Nick make his way onto the last metre of the wire. Moments later the air resounded with a roar of joyous applause.

48

Monday 4th July

'SO, THIS IS GOING to teach us the difference between a tap and a step,' said Reinaldo, his long curly black hair doing its own dance around his shoulders with every utterance.

'I just can't get this,' said Nick. He was having difficulty focussing as he'd earlier intercepted another letter from the mortgage company about late payments. He would deal with it later.

'Don't give up, handsome man. For a tap, you just put your foot down, there is no weight transfer.' Reinaldo's brown eyes earnestly examined Nick as he stepped deep inside Nick's physical comfort zone, spinning around once more as he demonstrated the difference between a step and a tap.

'No weight transfer ... oh, okay,' said Nick, trying to put a little distance between himself and Reinaldo.

'You got it?' Reinaldo asked in a gritty, resonant voice with an American-cum-Spanish melodious lilt as he moved even closer to Nick.

'I think I need some help here,' said Sunflower, who was standing next to Keith in front of the wall of mirrors.

Yes, please go and help Sunflower, thought Nick.

Keith was embracing the steps with glee. 'Watch me, Sunflower,' he said. 'I'll show you how it's done. I learned how to do this in Cuba.'

'Was that a long time ago, Keith?' asked Reinaldo.

Sunflower laughed at Reinaldo's comment and thanked Keith for his kind offer but said she thought that the expert should show her. Reinaldo delighted her by saying that he would be over to see to her after he had finished off with the handsome boy. Nick was beginning to feel slightly uncomfortable but strangely flattered by Reinaldo's attention.

Keith was delighted that Sunflower had agreed to come with him today, but she had insisted on bringing Marnie with her, to cheer her up. Keith suggested that Nick invite Louise, which he wished he'd thought of doing. He did. She refused to come.

Marnie stood to Reinaldo's right and had already mastered the basic steps. Nick's dad's urn sat on top of the old piano and watched them all non-judgmentally, though his proximity to Marnie might have meant his attention would no doubt have been fixed on her. Nick was grateful that the level of attention required to master the Cuban Salsa meant his own focus was entirely on his feet with a little left, trying to avoid Reinaldo's radiating aura. The heat in the basement of the Duke of York, a North London pub-cum-club, didn't help. There were definitely pheromones flying around, but Nick wasn't sure where they were coming from. Were they his? He hadn't felt this confused since watching John and Johannes dance the Argentine Tango on *Strictly Come Dancing*.

'So, tap with the right, step with the right and the weight transfers.' Reinaldo almost sang the instructions. 'Tap with the left, step with the left and the weight transfers…'

Reinaldo clearly spent a lot of time exercising and

dancing off his calories and had the kind of body that Nick could only dream of. The kind of lithe, muscular but not bulky physique that he felt was now beyond his age to attain. No matter how many times he attempted to follow an exercise programme, most recently one by Joe Wicks, he could never achieve such a physique. His love of food and wine meant he would always be five short of a six pack.

Reinaldo never stopped moving, as if he had a Cuban rhythm constantly playing in his head and beating in his heart. He circled Nick and Nick started to become infected by the rhythm; he started to pick up the beat by osmosis; he was getting it and felt good.

'Bueno Nick, I think you are now ready for the *Paso de Son*. This cadence introduces the idea of quick, quick, slow … quick, quick slow.'

'I like a bit of quick, quick, slow,' cried Keith.

'More like slow, slow, slow,' said Sunflower, and they both collapsed laughing.

'Quick, quick, slow … quick, quick, slow,' said Marnie, immersed in the moment as she mastered the *Paso de Son*.

'That's really good, Marnie,' said Reinaldo, moving his focus for the first time in a while away from Nick. 'You'll hear a lot of Salsa teachers saying "hold the pause" instead of "quick, quick, slow", but I don't like that as it stops your flow. You've got to keep moving. Continue your journey – isn't that right, Karmic Keith?'

'That's right, Reinaldo,' agreed Keith. 'It's all about the ride, not the destination.'

This wisdom was relayed to all his followers on his live podcast. His phone was connected to the pub's superfast fibre connection and was positioned next to the urn on top of the piano, with Marnie's *Paso de Son* filling most of the frame. Since she'd started dancing the number of live views had increased exponentially. Keith couldn't see the live comments but news of Marnie's talent was spreading faster than a pandemic.

Keith's funeral director friend, Graham Kerton, was watching and commented that Keith's dancing looked like someone desperate for the toilet standing at the back of a Portaloo queue at a music festival. Sergeant Reggie Hardy gave the comment a like.

Amongst the new followers to the channel, sitting in a white van watching the feed, were two men in dark suits, one tall and the other squat and built like a rhinoceros. Their van had a strong odour of pickled onion crisps.

Back in the basement it was getting hot, so Reinaldo called a break and they all went upstairs for some air and some refreshments. Nick, not having a phone signal in the basement and not having bothered to connect to the free Wi-Fi, was alerted to a number of messages as he stepped outside of the pub with a warm, flat Coke and sat in the shade of a London plane tree. Several missed calls originated from the office and then Brian's mobile.

Oh shit, what now? Nick pressed the return call button and waited for Brian's dull tone to depress him.

Brian picked up immediately. 'Nick, great news.' Not words Brian usually employed. 'Whilst I've been burning the midnight oil preparing the presentation, another offer has come in.'

'But how?' queried Nick. 'It's not public knowledge that

we're preparing a sale. If the staff hear about this—'

'I don't know, but it doesn't really matter, does it? It may just be a coincidence. If we are looking at selling to two buyers, we could play them off against each other. This could save us!' Was this what Brian would sound like if he won the lottery? 'It's a guy called Simon Myers from SM Enterprise Solutions.'

'Doesn't ring a bell,' said Nick.

'I thought I'd come across them before, but they've not been a competitor or interested in our specific marketplace, which is probably why they've not been on our radar. I've checked them out and they are legit. They now offer web services to clients, platform integration and online small business services. They have been trading for a few years now. They turn over £25 million.' Brian was on a roll. 'They're going into business with a French firm who want to bankroll their rapid expansion in the UK, so they're looking to acquire a number of businesses to increase their offerings here, especially in project and time-management. They've had their eye on us for some time, apparently, and could move quickly. We would be a perfect acquisition for them.'

It felt too good to be true, but Nick couldn't help feeling excited by the prospect. PlanIT-UK was proving to be a headache. This could give him the leverage he needed. A feeling of euphoria rose from the pit of his stomach to the crown of his head, and he became giddy with excitement. He took a swig of his Coke to bring him to his senses.

'What do they want?'

'They're keen to arrange a meeting tomorrow. They want a buyers' pack. It's just as well I have one ready to go. It doesn't have everything they'll need yet, but it'll give them a good idea. I could send it now. My finger is, at this very moment, hovering over the send button.'

Nick stopped for a moment. Sitting in the cool shade, he looked around him to see a picture of life passing by. Delivery vans and scooters zipping past; mothers with pushchairs; a jogger plugged into her iPods, oblivious to the dangers around; businesspeople chatting at the deli next to the pub waiting for their sandwich orders; Keith and Sunflower standing by their bikes, laughing in the sunshine; and Reinaldo introducing Marnie to a new and very challenging stretch. Maybe Nick didn't need to worry too much about Reinaldo's proximity to him when teaching.

'Nick? Are you there?' Brian interrupted Nick's reverie.

'Yes … Yes, I am, sorry.'

'Shall I press send?'

'Yes. Go ahead and send the pack and then arrange a meeting for tomorrow afternoon.'

*   *   *

Reinaldo was delighted with the group's progress and the rest of the afternoon was spent mastering the five basic steps for the Casino, or Cuban Salsa, with an extra step thrown in for luck. Reinaldo was joined in the afternoon by his partner, Yaritza. He explained that her name meant a tiny butterfly and she certainly moved like one, flitting around the dancefloor.

Nick couldn't get the news of the new buyer out of his head and spent his afternoon checking in with Brian to see if they'd heard anything back from them yet. Not that he was expecting anything, but SM Enterprise Solutions had acknowledged receipt of the pack and would be in touch soon to confirm the meeting time.

Yaritza joined Nick and Keith as their dance instructor for most of the afternoon and Reinaldo alternated between Marnie and Sunflower. Once all the students had mastered the basic steps, all couples rotated for the remainder of the session. The air conditioning finally kicked in as the staff started to arrive to ready the bar for the evening. As the session came to an end, Reinaldo congratulated everyone on their dancing and produced a tray of daiquiris to celebrate the fact that it was his birthday. He was having a Cuban salsa party in the basement that evening and invited them all to join him. Several of his dancer friends would be joining them as well as quite a few of his pupils.

After a brief discussion it was decided that it would be the perfect way to spend the evening and Nick agreed. After all, he felt he had something to celebrate too. Reinaldo joined Keith in signing off the live podcast and put in a plug for his regular classes and sessions not only at the Duke of York but in the many other pubs and clubs that he and Yaritza taught at.

Nick returned above ground for a while to check in with Brian and was delighted to hear that they had confirmed the meeting time. Brian reminded Nick that they needed to continue preparing for the presentation to PlanIT-UK and that he needed to keep quiet about it and not unwittingly mention anything during his uncle's webcasts, as he too seemed to be growing quite a following. His LinkedIn profile featured the story of the bucket list and was directing a lot of traffic to their website.

Despite Brian's now less excited tone and more cautious approach, Nick still felt a huge sense of excitement. Deep in his bones he knew this was the deal. It was going to work. Everything he'd worked for was about to pay off. He'd been right to put everything on the line and tonight he'd allow himself to let his hair down, have a few drinks and dance as if no one was watching, although knowing Keith, there could be twenty thousand odd live views.

Sadly, Louise couldn't be persuaded to come and join Nick at the Duke of York that evening despite his best efforts. He felt able to share with her that there had been a development and that, once again, she shouldn't worry as everything was going to turn out fine. Her perfunctory response revealed her ongoing disbelief in his confidence, and she said he should wait to celebrate if there indeed was anything to celebrate. Nick sighed. He'd have liked to have shared the moment with her. He became aware that he'd been gently stroking his father's urn during the conversation; he would have to share the moment with him instead.

And so Nick sat with his father's remains next to his third daiquiri and reflected on the fact that he'd never shared a moment like this with his father. Those formative moments in a boy's life that should have involved his father were mostly spent alone or with his mum. He struggled to recall any time when his father had been there, but as he looked over at Uncle Keith, Sunflower and Marnie all standing over by their motorbikes, he saw a vision of himself as a small boy on his first two-wheeled bicycle, being supported by his father as he tried to balance without stabilisers. Then came the rush when he felt a great change as he rode unknowingly solo, looking back to see his father behind him, disappearing into the distance and triumphantly applauding his success.

Hot salty tears ran down Nick's cheeks. He allowed them to rest upon his chin before wiping them away and draining his drink. Picking up the urn, he returned to the basement bar, which was much darker than it had been earlier, with the lighting now atmospherically low. Salsa music quickened the pulses of those itching to take to the floor. Nick joined the queue at the bar behind a very tall guy chatting to his short stocky friend.

49

NICK WAS RUDELY AWOKEN by what felt like a samba band marching through his skull. His arid mouth threatened to crack at the corners and his heartbeat throbbed in his face just above and behind his eyes. As he tried to move his limbs, the bang of the cranial drum intensified, regulating his movement to a legato crawl. The banging increased with every attempt to increase tempo, like a galley-slave drumbeater.

'Drink this. It will help,' said the deep voice of a bleary image though his crusty-eyed, swimming vision.

'What, who?' Nick could barely focus on the entity before him. He could feel the countless daiquiris rushing through his veins: the strawberry daiquiris, the Hemingway Papa Doble and the house special, La Terraza's blue daiquiri. His blood must be forty per cent proof.

'Trust me, Nick, this concoction will help. It's the perfect hangover cure.' The voice did not belong to Louise.

Nick was on a leather sofa, lying on a thin blanket which had moved, meaning that he slid around sweatily as he tried to sit up. He was wearing only his underwear.

'Oh God, my head,' he moaned. He raised the concoction to his lips and began to sip. Although it looked like Shrek had sneezed into a glass, the thick liquid tasted like it was going to help. If he could keep it down.

'It's a blueberry and spinach superfood green smoothie,' said the voice, which he now recognised as Uncle Keith's. 'It's full of good things. Potassium in the banana to help your liver, hemp protein powder; it's full of antioxidants and is naturally sweet. Get it down you now, and you'll feel better. Along with these.' Keith dropped a number of painkillers onto the coffee table. 'Not sure we can avoid lining the pockets of Big Pharma today,' he continued in an avuncular fashion. 'You're gonna need to keep dosing up. You'll need to get some milk thistle and dandelion to help your liver after the night you had.'

'Oh God, I feel awful. Where am I? What time is it?'

'Time you took a cold shower to fire up your immune system. Don't worry – I called Louise last night to let her know you were staying with me at Sunflower's flat, as you'd partied so hard. You don't need to worry, she was pleased.'

'That's a relief.'

'Yeah. She didn't want you at home in the state you were in. But she said she'd see you later.'

∗   ∗   ∗

'Jesus, that's freezing!'

Keith hadn't been joking. There was no hot water but after ten minutes acclimatising to the shower's Antarctic water temperature, Nick started to feel vaguely human again.

Snippets of the previous evening's events began to emerge. The party had gone on until the early hours when they had all taken a cab back from the club, apart from Keith who didn't drink much and had ridden back. Sunflower and Marnie had gone back to Sunflower's Camden flat in an Uber and looked after Nick on the way home. With each new flashback Nick felt embarrassed and ashamed, but those feelings were offset by the underlying sense of optimism that all his problems could soon be solved. Thank God he didn't have to meet with the client in his current state this morning. He'd have time to recover and get cleaned up before the meeting this afternoon.

After his shower he dressed and sat down to a fruit salad with Greek yoghurt and oats prepared by Sunflower. Keith had just left to ride Marnie back to York Way to pick up her own bike. Nick checked his pockets for the usual items he mislaid after a big night out. Not that he'd had one like this in years. Phone, check. Wallet, check. Keys, check. But something wasn't right.

Something was missing.

Oh fuck.

There was no urn to be seen.

Nick had lost his father. For the second time.

His pulse started to race, which made his head start to throb with renewed energy. He wanted to push his worry to one side but the hangover wouldn't let him. The fruit salad and Greek yoghurt threatened to make a reappearance. How could he lose the urn? Where could it be? The whole point of the night was to 'experience something' with his father, yet he'd completely forgotten about that and consequently had taken no care of the urn as he'd been having too much of a good time. He'd forgotten all his worries for one glorious and all-too-brief evening. Was that his father's intention? Moments later, Sunflower radiated back into the sitting room to find a very worried-looking Nick. Nick explained the situation to her as she passed him an organic decaf coffee with oat milk. She slumped down on the sofa opposite him, scanned her phone and started to giggle.

Nick didn't feel much like laughing.

'You don't remember much of last night, do you?' she said. 'You've become an internet sensation in your own right.'

Nick's stomach sank. He didn't want any adverse publicity at the moment. Would a potential buyer want a crazed party animal at the helm of a tech company? Perhaps it would.

More memes were spreading around Nick's followers, including one developed from an earlier meme 'Sick Nick blizted', and one Louise wouldn't enjoy too much of Nick dancing with Sunflower and Marnie with the caption 'Slick Nick'. There were a few videos of him performing the Casino, which had already started to go viral on TikTok with lots of much, much younger people perfecting his moves. There was a picture of him dancing with his father's urn and captions saying 'Nick and Urnie'.

'Oh God, what's Louise going to think when she sees this? And I've lost the urn. You don't know where it is, do you, Sunflower?' He really hoped this would be one of those moments when a simple solution presented itself with an affirmative response.

'I'm afraid not. But don't worry, I'm sure it's safe.' Sunflower said it in such a way that Nick was almost able to deceive himself into believing her. 'You could wait for Keith to get back or I'll check with him once he's dropped Marnie off. Hopefully, I'll catch him before he disappears to pick up the new bike he's reviewing.' Sunflower made it all sound like everything would be fine.

He tried to believe it again and failed, again. 'Thanks so much, Sunflower. I'll book an Uber.' His voice cracked. 'I can't wait for Uncle Keith to come back. I've got a meeting I can't miss. Please let me know about the ashes as soon as you hear anything.'

She promised she would.

*   *   *

By the time Nick arrived home he'd arranged a few things with Brian. They would meet at the hotel in Royal Tunbridge Wells at 1 p.m. to quickly look over the presentation Brian had adapted from the PlanIT-UK presentation and customised for SM Enterprise Solutions before their lunch meeting at 2 p.m. Once home he would have forty minutes to get himself turned around, in time to leave for the meeting.

This was it. This was the one. He could feel it in his bones. Finally, all his blood, sweat and tears would pay off.

The Uber driver dropped him off in the road as there wasn't room on his drive. He could see that Louise's car, Charlotte's car and Louise's parents' car were all being loaded with boxes.

As he walked through the utility room into the kitchen, he noticed something strange. The house was a hive of activity, but no one was speaking. It was as if someone had died. No one noticed Nick enter, as they were all busy helping carry boxes out to the cars. Louise's parents, Paul and Judi, were helping Louise tape up boxes in the kitchen, Godzilla could barely be seen behind the three enormous boxes he was managing to carry at once, whilst Charlotte packed more things into a box on the kitchen worktop. Barry stood amongst the bustle, sniffing the air, no doubt waiting for something edible to fall from one of the boxes. Where was Harry?

'Dad!' Harry appeared from nowhere, shattering the silence. 'You came to help! I said he'd come, everyone.' He crashed into Nick at speed, giving him a massive hug and nearly knocking the wind out of him.

Oh fuck. Oh no. He'd promised to help with the fundraiser preparation, and he'd forgotten all about it. Nick felt his familiar symptoms of anxiety appear simultaneously and fight for his attention.

'Oh wow, everyone. This looks ... amazing. You've got so much stuff,' Nick said in a loud and falsely encouraging voice. How the hell was he going to phrase his next sentence?

'It's going to be a great day tomorrow,' said Harry. 'We've got so much stuff to sell. I'm so pleased you're here, Dad. Mum, Charlotte, Grandpa and Grandma said you wouldn't be.' Harry seemed to be trying to inject some happiness into the air, which was distinctly lacking from all others present.

Best cut straight to the point.

'I'm really sorry, Harry,' said Nick. 'I can help with a couple of boxes but then I need to get changed and go to a meeting.' He tried to make it sound positive, like a children's TV presenter telling a child that their dog had been run over, but the viewers had clubbed together and bought them a new cat.

Silence.

Harry took a step away from his father. Everyone stopped what they were doing and looked over at Nick. It was as if they'd all suddenly been able to see him at once.

Harry's eyes started to fill up and he turned and stumbled out of the room, heading for his bedroom. Nick called after him, asking him to come back, but Harry ignored him.

'I wouldn't worry, Dad,' said Charlotte. 'I don't think he really expected you to be here, especially under the current circumstances.'

'Oh come on, that's not fair … and what do you mean?' Nick said defensively.

'What do you mean, not fair?' Louise turned to Nick and looked at him for the first time since he'd arrived home. 'I'll tell you what's not fair.' She crossed to the kitchen island, picked a letter up and brandished it in the air.

'Not now, Louise, please,' Paul said in a gentle, calming tone, to try to diffuse what he, and everyone else knew, was about to erupt.

'No, Grandpa, Dad needs to hear this too,' said Charlotte.

'This, Nick. *This* is not fair.' Louise threw the letter at Nick.

He knew what it was. It was a letter from the mortgage company saying that he was overdue with payments.

'Louise, it's all going to be fine. It's a formality,' he said dismissively.

'It is not going to be fine! You've risked our home. You've remortgaged our house without discussing it with me. Did you think I wouldn't find out, or that my opinion wasn't important?'

'Let's not discuss this now. Of course I was going to tell you.'

'Were you? Were you? When? When were you going to tell me, Nick?'

'When it was all settled. There was no need for you to know. No need for you to worry.'

'That's utter fucking shit,' shouted Louise.

'I'll just put these boxes in the car,' said Godzilla, slipping out of the room.

'Louise, please. Not in front of everyone. Not in front of the kids, for God's sake,' pleaded Nick.

'Do you know what is more upsetting than the fact you've remortgaged our home, Nick? It's your lack of trust and your dishonesty. You've not been honest with me, or the kids. You've put no trust in me and obviously don't care about my opinion.'

'I'll help you with those boxes.' Paul grabbed a large box and followed Godzilla out of the combat zone.

Judi didn't budge. She stood transfixed by the drama, clearly trying to engage Nick with her laser-lock stare of deep disappointment.

'I haven't been dishonest,' said Nick looking at his watch and immediately regretting doing so.

'Got to go have you, Nick? Have you got to go off galivanting and having a good time whilst we all wait for you to put in an appearance?'

'My cab will be here in ten minutes. Look, you know how hard I've been working, and I have had to do the bucket list. I had no choice.'

'We all have a fucking choice, Nick.'

'There's no need for such language,' Judi quietly offered.

'Shut up, Mum!' Louise never shouted at her parents.

Charlotte left the room, without any boxes and trying to hide her tears. Barry hung his head and tail and followed her out of the room.

'I'm doing all this for us, you know. For our family.'

'What's the point when you are never here?'

'Look, I have to go, I have an important meeting.' It sounded ludicrous as he said it.

'Of course you do. Off you go. Go on, fuck off again.'

Louise took a box and carried it outside, followed by Judi, still staring at Nick until she bumped into Louise and had to turn her attention to where she was going. She came back and slammed the door behind her.

Nick picked up the letter from the floor. It wasn't a statement of account, saying he'd missed payments. It was a letter of notice to start repossession proceedings unless he settled all outstanding payments to date before Friday 8th July, which also happened to be his father's birthday and the day he was due to meet with Jeff Silverman.

50

DESPITE THE AMOUNT OF pain medication Nick had consumed, he still had a headache and was feeling well below par. He'd not been able to convince anyone at home that he was doing all of this for them. A strong sense of righteous anger rose up within him. He was right! How could they not see? How could Louise be so unreasonable?

He thought back to the evening before and the fun he'd had dancing and drinking the night away. But he'd not done that for himself. He had done it to please everyone else. Selflessly. For his mother, for his family and the kids and those followers, those disciples of Karmic Keith. The fun he'd had was incidental. He thought of his father's urn and then of his father. What would he have done in this situation? Probably the same; he was always working, never around. Now Nick had managed to lose his urn. How was that going to look on social media?

Nick called the pub but there was no one there yet and so he left a message. He tried to call Keith again but couldn't get through, so left him a message too, asking him not to call back but to text him with news of the urn, if any. He didn't want to be disturbed by a call during the meeting.

The pressure he was feeling was intense but it was eclipsed by the rush of adrenaline through his veins the closer he got to the hotel. This was it. This was the one, and this evening he would be celebrating. Again. They were all wrong about him; he had been right to take risks. Comfort is overrated; no one achieved anything inside of their comfort zone, that's something he could teach Uncle Keith. His whole family would benefit. They would all see. He was in the middle of the biggest gamble of his life. He felt equally terrified and thrilled. This was why he did what he did.

Brian was waiting for Nick in reception. He'd been pacing backwards and forwards and couldn't settle. He had just sat down again when Nick appeared. He immediately leapt up to greet him.

'Get checked in and then we can go to the meeting room,' said Brian excitedly.

'Why do I need to check in?'

'We're staying late and they've laid on quite an evening for us.' Brian looked irritated that this news had not reached Nick. 'It would be rude to refuse their hospitality.'

Nick frowned in confusion. At least he wouldn't have to foot the bill. 'Where are they now?' he asked.

'They are enjoying the spa facilities. We've got a bit more time to go over the presentation. Simon Myers has told us to relax and enjoy whatever we want before we meet at 5 p.m.'

'I thought they were in a hurry to meet. This isn't a corporate jolly, it's a business meeting.'

'They have a new incoming CEO. He wants to be here and can only get here by eight at the earliest,' Brian explained.

'Eight o'clock? For God's sake. That's seven hours away.'

'I know. We will still be meeting Simon Myers and his team at five. I'm guessing the new CEO will just be coming in to introduce himself. Myers will be the one doing the deal.'

'Who is the new CEO?' Nick wanted to know.

'Who is it?' said Brian uneasily after a brief hiatus, as if he knew or suspected but didn't want to say.

'That's what I asked, yes.'

'I don't actually know. It's a surprise. Apparently.' Brian shrugged his shoulders.

'I don't like surprises. I like to know who I'm dealing with.'

Nick now had hours to wait and he didn't want to stay over. A pang of discomfort settled in his stomach. Four hours until the first meeting. He could've helped at home after all. He might have been able to mitigate some of the carnage, but considering the mood Louise had been in, probably not. They would have to use the time well.

The afternoon's preparations and rehearsals flew by. Their tech was all working, and they had a killer presentation, which Brian and Nick would be sharing. Then there would be a Q&A session. Nick would answer any operational and development questions and Brian would deal with financial matters. They'd worked out a timeline for handover and a period of consultation following that.

At five on the dot the hotel staff entered the meeting room with trays of food and drinks. Simon Myers and his team of three followed. Nick felt uncomfortable that he wasn't in control of the hospitality, but let it go. After all introductions had been made, Myers insisted they all have a drink to celebrate the occasion. Nick suggested they might want to wait until after the presentation and discussion and the meeting with the new CEO, but Myers insisted. He explained that they liked to do business in a relaxed fashion and he was confident that they would all soon have something to celebrate.

'Just one wouldn't hurt, I suppose,' said Brian, looking to Nick for agreement.

Nick didn't mind Brian having one but couldn't touch a drop himself. He politely refused and discretely took more painkillers.

*　*　*

The meeting with Simon Myers and his team went well. They had done an incredible job with their due diligence. They knew exactly what state the company was in and its prospects. There was no corner they hadn't covered, and they seemed satisfied with all the answers Nick and Brian had given them. They questioned the large cash injection of nearly £1 million six months earlier and wanted to know how Nick had raised that money. He candidly told them that he had mortgaged his home. They were impressed with his commitment to the business, but Nick could see by the look in Simon Myers's Financial Director's eyes that he subscribed to the old adage: always risk other people's money, never your own. Whether this would affect their offer price was yet to be seen.

As eight o'clock came and went it was clear that the mystery CEO was delayed. Simon Myers took a call at 8.20 p.m. to say that the CEO's flight from Paris was delayed and he would be with them as soon as possible. They decided at that point to adjourn the meeting and resume once the new CEO arrived. Nick was relieved to have a break from proceedings but couldn't help feeling a creeping sense of apprehension about the arrival of the new CEO. Something wasn't quite right, yet he couldn't put his finger on what it was.

*   *   *

The phone in Nick's hotel room rudely awoke him from his nap, going off like a hand grenade to shatter his peace. He had returned to his room and suggested that Brian do the same to get some rest before meeting the CEO. He had drunk a large glass of water and lain down on the bed to rest. He had tried to call both Louise and Keith but neither picked up. He'd then tried to call home, but no one ever answered the home phone, even if they were able to find it.

Nick glanced at the time before picking up the phone. It was just before midnight. Simon Myers apologised for the lateness of the call and the inconvenience and said that the CEO had arrived from Paris and would be at the hotel at twelve-thirty and was Nick happy to meet then?

Nick confirmed that he was. He got off the bed, stretched and went and freshened up before leaving his room to collect Brian for their final meeting.

Moments after twelve-thirty, Simon Myers entered the meeting room to greet Nick and introduce the new CEO of SM Enterprise Solutions. The door swung back energetically and before the new CEO's unmistakable physique entered the room, his energy and voice beat him to it.

'Swifty boy! So good of you to stay up late for me.'

51

THE MEETING WITH DAVE Dolon didn't go well. Dolon's
arrival and his new role within SM Enterprise Solutions
was a crushing blow. Nick did well to hide his shock.
Brian, who'd had a couple of drinks, had not covered up his
disapproval of the appointment. Dolon laughed it off, his
presence filling and controlling the room as he sat down
at the head of the table. Everyone else had taken care not
to sit there so as not to exhibit any aggressive assertion of
position.

The meeting started off badly and soon got worse.
Dolon had obviously been briefed on the way to the hotel
and, having learnt that Nick had mortgaged his home,
arrogantly expected SwifTech to accept an offer there and
then. He'd even had a head of terms contract drawn up
and a large bottle of champagne on ice brought into the
room. Indeed, the offer came close to settling all of Nick's
immediate financial problems but didn't reflect the years
of struggle and investment he had given the company. It
certainly wouldn't leave room for the plans he'd made for
the years ahead. The last fifteen years of his life would have
been wasted, but he was desperate. This was now a matter of
principle. Take the money and solve his immediate issues,
or risk waiting for a better offer.

Dolon reiterated that the deal was a one-time
opportunity and wasn't up for negotiation. 'Under the

circumstances, you're not gonna get a better offer, Swifty boy!'

Nick didn't need to leave the room to consult with Brian, although he could see that Brian wanted to. Stealing himself, Nick thanked Simon Myers and his team for their time and hospitality and left, saying he was not in a position to accept their offer. It was the second time only that Nick had known Dave Dolon to be speechless. The other time was when he asked him to leave their business.

It was nearly 4 a.m. by the time Nick arrived back at home. He could see no point in staying at the hotel and checked out as soon as he was able. Brian wasn't able to and decided it best to stay the night. He'd see Nick at the office in the morning. Nick could see how disappointed Brian was with his decision. Brian would have done well out of the deal, certainly a great deal better than Nick would have, and Brian, although he disliked Dolon, didn't feel quite the same way as Nick did about him. Nick's feelings had turned from deep dislike and distrust to hatred. Nick wanted revenge on Dolon for leaving his business with the contact book. He wanted to see him suffer. The best way he could do that would be by making a success of the sale at which he now had only one chance left.

At home there were no cars parked on the drive, alerting Nick to the fact that something wasn't right. No one was there. Nick let himself in through the front door and checked downstairs. Barry's basket was empty; his cushion, food and water bowls had gone too. Nick checked the rest of the house. As Harry would say he was 'all Macaulay Culkin' – he was home alone.

Back in the kitchen Nick checked his phone for any messages and, finding none, looked around for a note. Nothing. It was too late to call anyone now, so he checked Louise's and the kids' location on Life360. They were all at Louise's parents' house. It was too late and too early to call.

What a fucking awful day, Nick thought, as he helped himself to a beer from the fridge. He sat on one of the bar stools and leant on the worktop, his head in his hands.

52

NICK HAD BARELY SLEPT. He was the first to arrive at the office and had fired up the coffee machine. He'd tried again with no success to call Louise and Keith. He was just finishing his second coffee when Shirley came in with a third for him.

'You look like you need this,' she said softly. 'I saw you were out partying on Monday night. You've got some moves, haven't you. Did you have something to celebrate?'

'I thought so then,' Nick admitted.

Shirley tilted her head. 'I understand you met with a potential new client yesterday. Did that go well?'

'A potential client, yes, but it wasn't the outcome I'd hoped for.'

She nodded thoughtfully. 'Brian is running late today but called to say he'll be in soon to go through the presentation for Friday. Is that the same client as yesterday?'

So many questions. 'No, a different one.'

Mercifully, Shirley left him alone to continue going through the presentation for Friday's meeting with PlanIT-UK. He'd hoped to be able to negotiate with them over the price with a strong hand, but after the nightmare with Dave Dolon, he now only had one chance left. He had to get this right.

Brian arrived looking a little weather beaten, closed the office door so no one would hear them and rolled his sleeves up. 'Well, at least we've had a dress rehearsal for Friday. I'm still wondering how they knew we were considering selling. They must have known that we'd have everything ready for them to call a meeting at such short notice and have an offer ready. Is our network security up to spec, Nick?'

'Totally. They couldn't have accessed our files without encrypted passwords. Everything on the network has been changed many times since Dolon left.'

'Is it possible he had access to our files?'

'Nothing is impossible, but it's highly unlikely.' He gave an involuntary shudder. 'Anyway, we need to put yesterday behind us and look forward to Friday. We have to make it work.'

At that moment Shirley appeared again at the door. Nick took a deep breath.

'Your wife called.'

Nick looked at his mobile; Louise hadn't tried to call him directly.

'She didn't want to be put through. She told me to say...' Shirley then took her notebook and repeated exactly what Louise had said to her. 'Please tell Nick that the children, Barry and I will be staying with my parents for a few days. It's the children's bring-and-buy fundraiser today but no one expects you to come.' Shirley closed her notebook and turned to leave the room.

As she did, Nick's mobile phone rang. The number was withheld, but he answered it immediately, thinking it was Louise at her parents' house.

'Why on earth have you moved out and taken the kids?' he said, losing his composure.

'I haven't,' said Keith on the other end of the line, 'but I have heard what happened.'

'I'm sorry. I thought you were Louise.'

'I'm calling from Sunflower's phone as my mobile is on charge. It withholds the number. Are you okay?'

'Not really,' said Nick, calming down a little.

Shirley was still staring at him from the doorway.

'Thanks Shirley.'

She registered Nick's look and left, closing the door behind her.

'What can I do for you, Keith?' Nick wasn't in the mood for pleasantries.

'I was wondering where you were. We're meant to be doing a skydive today.'

'What? Oh, no. I can't. I really have to work. I have a presentation on Friday, and it must come first. Keith, have you got the—'

'Well, that's a bit of a problem, Nick,' interrupted Keith. 'You see, you announced to everyone on Monday night that you would be doing the jump at noon today. I've set up a live webcast and it's gained loads of traction. I've asked people not to come to the airfield as it's tiny. But they will all be watching online.'

Nick exhaled with a whistle. 'Why can't it wait?'

'You said you'd do it for the kids' animal shelter and people have made pledges. It will also raise awareness for today's bring-and-buy, which I've promised to help out at later. If you don't do it, a lot of money will be lost for the shelter. It's still facing closure. I'll text you the venue postcode. It's your chance to be a hero, Nick.'

'Oh, um, Keith, have you got the urn?' Nick asked, remembering he hadn't asked him yet.

Keith didn't answer.

'Keith, I couldn't find the urn. Have you got it?'

Still no answer.

Nick checked his phone's display. Keith had hung up. Not knowing Sunflower's number Nick tried Keith's phone, but it went straight to voicemail.

Nick realised he had no choice but to do the jump. With the loss of SM Enterprise Solutions as a buyer or for leverage, he still had the chance of selling to PlanIT-UK on Friday. All was not yet lost, but he couldn't believe he'd managed to lose his father's urn. A huge knot appeared in his stomach and a lurching emptiness took possession of him at the thought that his dad's ashes may have been cast aside in a filthy alleyway by a drunken reveller.

He thought of his father in his hospital bed. The grey image of his dad with a look of sad resignation on his face. Charlie had known that he couldn't make up for the lost years. The bucket list had been his last hope at some sort of redemption, and now Nick had lost the urn and taken that chance away from him. The knot twisted in his stomach. Did he really love his father enough to care this much? Had Charlie cared for him all along in the same way Nick cared for Harry?

At that moment a deeply buried memory surfaced, and he was reminded of the feeling of comfort and love he'd enjoyed as a little boy, when his father embraced him in his warm arms after a bad dream. As Nick fought to suppress his emotions once more, a lump rose up in his throat as hot tears welled up in his eyes and began to stream down his cheeks. After a moment he wiped them away and stood up. 'Brian. I have to go and do the jump. I'll be back later.'

*   *   *

Amira had rigged up her laptop so she could live-stream Karmic Keith's channel. She'd been following Nick's story ever since Giuseppe taught them the Krav Maga techniques. Giuseppe hadn't stopped going on about it and the attention had brought him a lot more business, for which he was grateful.

'So here we are,' Keith announced. 'I'm just pulling into the small private airfield in Buckinghamshire where we will be doing today's jump, once Nick arrives. You'll see a sign that says the airfield is closed today. That's because my friend and expert skydiving instructor, Harald Haraldsen, has closed the airfield for us specially. It will just be him, another instructor and his pilot taking us up today. You can see it is a beautiful day to leap out of a plane and plunge back to earth with just a bit of silk to stop you from going splat.'

Keith pulled into the small turning between some trees where he, and the six thousand or so live-streamers could see a clear image of a number of old barn buildings and a small aircraft hangar.

Amira had been chatting to Graham Kerton, the undertaker, earlier in the day. He was going to watch as well. He was concerned as he'd been to the airfield a year ago when a jumper hadn't opened his chute. What a way to go. It was a suicide and not anything negligent, but Graham didn't have a good feeling about anyone doing anything quite so dangerous.

There was a great deal of chat in the comments on the channel; some people saying that they couldn't do it while others congratulated Keith and Nick for being so bold.

Keith continued to chat as he got off his bike. 'Looking around, I can't see anyone here. I hope I've got the right day!' He took off his helmet and hung it over his handlebars, detaching the camera and holding it in his hand. He commented on what a beautiful scene it was: the lovely ancient buildings; the trees in full bloom; the birds singing; the light, cooling summer breeze; and the sun beaming upon him, warming his face. He walked over to a small container office and knocked on the door, his camera feed now a little shaky and the view at waist height. 'Let's see where Harald is. No answer here … this is pretty strange.'

Keith pulled the door, which opened outwards, and entered the darkened room. His camera took a moment to adjust to the new light levels and for a moment the screen went dark.

'Hello … is anyone there?'

At that moment Keith saw the shadowy outlines of Harald and his colleagues, all tied and gagged, and sitting in the corner of the room. He turned to look around the rest of the room just as his camera adjusted to the low light and began to focus again.

'What the hell is—'

Keith's feed was rudely interrupted with a loud crack and

a thud, and the video feed blurred as the camera seemed to fall to the ground before the link cut out. Amira checked her laptop to see if it was still connected to the internet; it was. After about thirty seconds of silence the online chat went mad.

ChopR-Mick: Woz goin on
Kertons4U: R U there Keith
SuziSuki750: それは私ですか、それともキースは消えましたか
CHiPs1969: Must have lost his signal
Dir-T-Rhydr: I hope he can still do the jump
Mthrfkr77: Lost his bottle LOL
HelzNGeL: @Mthrfkr77 Shut up u couldnt do it u coward
Mthrfkr77: Could
HelzNGeL: Put ur money where ur mouth is then loser
Mthrfkr77: U is the loser
YuriVolt1n: Будете ли вы оба, пожалуйста, заткнись!
HelzNGeL: Breakfast is ready btw
Mthrfkr77: Down in a minute
SuziSuki750: みんな黙れ！

53

NICK MADE PRETTY GOOD time and arrived at the airfield just after 11 a.m. He wondered why there was a sign saying it was closed for the day. He could see a couple of cars and a white, tatty-looking van parked up by the buildings. He was beginning to wonder if he was in the right place when he saw a bright orange-and-black sparkling beast of a motorcycle and realised that Keith must be there.

Nick called out, but all he received was silence, so he decided to call Keith's mobile phone again. It went straight to voicemail.

'I can't take your call at the moment because I'm busy enjoying the ride. Leave me a message if you must, or go and do something that makes you feel alive and present right now.'

Nick didn't bother leaving a message. He looked around for a moment and then went back and left his phone in the glovebox of his car. He didn't fancy dropping it from thirteen thousand feet up; even if his armoured case could save the phone. If it could, he'd like a jumpsuit made out of the same material.

Nick hadn't thought about the danger element until this moment as he'd had so much on his mind, but he now realised he was terrified. What a ridiculous thing to agree to do. He scolded himself for allowing skydiving to get on the bucket list in the first place, and then for drunkenly promising to do the jump live for the kids' charity. Yet he felt compelled to be here despite the fact he had preparation to do at work. He still didn't have the urn and had not heard from Keith as to its whereabouts. Surely Keith must have it, otherwise there wouldn't be any point in being here today. He walked over to the office and went inside. Under the shade of a couple of large sycamore trees the office was quite dark. He called out. No answer. He looked around for a light switch and, finding one, he switched it on. As he turned back into the room he nearly jumped out of his skin.

A man was sitting in a chair in the corner of the room, some distance from him. The man wore a thin black balaclava and army fatigues. He was holding a pistol and had it aimed at Nick. He stood up slowly, revealing long legs and considerable height while keeping the gun trained on Nick.

Nick saw that there were three frightened-looking men bound and gagged in the opposite corner of the office. Fortunately none of them was Uncle Keith.

'Do exactly as I say, and you won't get hurt,' the gunman said.

Although the gunman had a balaclava on, Nick was hypnotised by his piercing eyes, which were different colours. He felt a shiver of terror run down his spine and for a moment he thought he was going to lose control of his bladder and bowels. He'd always wondered what he'd be like in a situation like this.

Should he try and run? There was no question he could fight right now as he wouldn't stand a chance. Flight was out of the question as, should the gunman wish to, he'd have plenty of time to put a bullet in Nick's back. The Krav Maga session they'd had had not given him any idea of how to deal with the fear he now felt. It was fine for commandos to learn those techniques but not for directors of small-to-medium technology solution companies.

If Nick could get close enough to his assailant to try to take his gun, he was not sure that his muscles would stop spasming enough to be of any use. The question of Keith's whereabouts also came into his mind. Hopefully he had eluded the gunman. The situation was not looking good from any angle.

'What do you want?' Nick managed to say, his voice breaking and betraying his fear.

'I'll ask the fuckin' questions!' shouted the man in estuary English. 'Just keep your fuckin' mouth shut for now and do what I say, and no one needs to get hurt.'

Nick wondered if thugs or gangsters went to a special school to learn their stock phrases. This gangster, for that's what he was, was a crook who wanted something. Maybe it was a ransom situation. Keith had loads of followers who could probably raise thousands to deliver him safely back to them, but no. It must be something else, otherwise he would not need to be involved.

'Just turn around and start walking,' said the thug.

Nick did as he was told but his legs suddenly had the skeletal strength of octopus tentacles and he thought he was going to fall over. He couldn't feel them and he barely managed to put one in front of the other and leave the office. He stumbled out into the farmyard area.

'Where are we going?' asked Nick. A second later he was struck in the back of the head and fell to the ground. The blow jarred his neck and sent flashes of light through his vision.

'Shut the fuck up! I'll tell you when to speak. Now get the fuck up and walk to that barn over there. You do the walking and I'll do the talking.'

Nick rubbed his head and slowly raised himself up. He was beginning to feel a rage rise within him above his fear. He took a few deep breaths; he knew he would have to be careful and wait for the right moment. It would be foolish to try to fight back now. He could easily get killed.

Nick headed towards the large barn ahead of him and kept walking, knowing that to assume what the thug's intentions were by stopping or changing direction might earn him another blow to the back of the head.

'That's it, in there.'

Nick stepped inside the barn and after a moment his eyes adjusted to the change in light. To his left he could see a long ladder leading up to a hayloft. There was a long central beam leading to another hayloft at the opposite end of the barn, which had fixed steps up to it.

It was then that he heard the muffled cries of Uncle Keith. Up in the hayloft he could see Keith gagged and tied to a post, his hands bound together in front of him and resting on his stretched-out legs. Next to him was a stocky man in a balaclava. He backhanded Keith around the face to silence him. Keith continued to call out until the man punched him in the stomach.

'Climb the ladder,' said the thug behind Nick.

Nick struggled up the ladder, hoping that some great plan would spring into his mind. This couldn't be happening. At least his legs had stopped shaking now. He reached the top and stood a few feet from the open edge of the hayloft. The tall thug raised his pistol at Nick. As he did so a barn owl flew out from behind him, startling him for a moment, before it came to rest higher up in the eaves.

'Get on your knees,' the thug said.

Nick did as he was told. He wasn't in a position to argue. This really wasn't turning out to be a good day.

The stocky thug came over and tied Nick's hands behind his back with baling twine. He then told him to move over to a post and sit down with his back to it. Nick obliged and was tied to the post with some thin rope. The taller man, who was clearly in charge, stepped forward and knelt down, right next to Nick.

'Where is it?' he demanded.

'Where's what?' The confusion on Nick's face was clear to see.

'The urn, you twat. Where's the fuckin' urn?'

'The urn? I don't have it.'

The tall thug slapped Nick across the face. 'I can fuckin' see that. Where is it?'

'I don't know where it is!' This wasn't going to end well.

'Don't fuckin' lie to me.' The tall thug then delivered another stunning blow across Nick's face and he felt blood stream from his nose. 'Don't give me that, you twat.'

'Let me get it out of him,' said the stocky thug gleefully.

'No. Leave it,' said the tall thug, standing up and taking a step back. 'You couple of tossers have got an hour to think about where the urn is or things are going to get a whole lot worse for you.'

'Why don't we just get it out of them now?' pressed the stocky thug.

'Because I want them to have a think about what is going to happen to them if they don't tell us. They can discuss it between themselves.' He roughly pulled Keith's gag from his mouth. 'This could be your last hour, boys. Think about that. We've got plenty of rope here and there's quite a drop in front of you.'

54

'ARE YOU OKAY?' WHISPERED Nick, just loudly enough for Keith to hear but hopefully no one else.

Nick and Keith were both tied to posts on opposite sides of the barn with four or five metres between them. The thugs had left five minutes previously, removing the ladder after their climb down. Nick had waited until he was sure they'd gone before starting to speak.

'They didn't give me a chance to defend myself. The cowards hit me from behind. I should've left my helmet on,' Keith said in a hoarse whisper.

Keith didn't look fine; he looked battered and had marks on his face where he'd been punched. His lip was split and he was struggling to breathe, the air having been knocked out of him. For the first time since Nick had got to know him better, Keith looked every bit his age.

'I'm fine, really, just my pride is hurt. That's all,' Keith rasped.

'I thought you Buddhist types didn't have any pride?'

'Everyone has a little. You just need to observe it yourself and then it won't control you. Are you okay, Nick?'

'To be honest I'm terrified but I'm also really angry. What the fuck do they want with my father's urn?'

'I've no idea. It's just an urn as far as I can see.'

Nick lowered his gaze. 'I'm so sorry to tell you this, Uncle Keith, but I've lost it. I haven't seen it since the salsa session.'

'Don't worry, I've got it.'

Nick's eyes snapped up to meet his uncle's.

'I asked the manager of the salsa pub to lock it in his safe to keep it out of harm's way after you'd danced with it. People were taking selfies with it. I was worried it might get damaged.' Keith took a couple more laboured breaths. 'I collected it at the end of the night and took it home. I put it in the cupboard under the sink in case Sunflower tried to put any flowers in it. It's now in one of the panniers of my KTM 1290 Super Duke GT, which is powered by a 175 horsepower V-twin cranking out 141 Nm of torque.'

'It's in a bag on my bike would have sufficed, Uncle Keith,' said Nick, smiling.

'Don't make me laugh,' said Keith. 'It hurts.'

'I'm sorry.'

'I've seen those two before. The tall one has very distinctive eyes. I don't know why they are trying to hide their identities now. They must both be pretty dumb,' said Keith.

'Where have you seen them then? Why haven't you mentioned this before?'

'I didn't want to worry you or your mum, but a couple of thugs turned up on the day we did the tightrope walking. I didn't think much of it at the time and dismissed them as a couple of chancers. But I'm sure I saw the same two in the crowd at the salsa evening, which is also why I kept the urn safe. They didn't stay that long and it was so busy I didn't get a good look at them.'

'Why do they want the urn, though? What could they possibly want with my father's ashes?' Nick wondered.

'We should just give them the urn and be done with. Then maybe they'll let us go.' Keith sounded deflated.

'No, we can't do that.' Nick frowned. 'There must be something valuable in Dad's urn. Which, come to think of it, there is. My dad. His remains are in there, and I've promised I'll finish his list and scatter him on Frinton Beach on his birthday. At least I can do that for him.'

'But they are just ashes, Nick.' Keith closed his eyes. 'Your dad isn't in there, he's gone. He's somewhere else. Maybe you should just let them have the urn.'

'No, I'm not letting those fuckers have the urn. I haven't finished the list. We still haven't done the skydive. I can't believe they'll kill us. If they kill us, they won't get anything. They aren't going to shoot us. Are they?'

Keith's eyes opened and they looked wary. 'They seem mad enough, and they've got a gun, which isn't a great sign. But it takes a lot to pull a trigger.'

'If I just let them have the urn, then what kind of son am I? What kind of man would allow a couple of bullies to take his dad's remains away? A father-son relationship is a two-way street. My dad regrets not having done his part properly, but I have the chance to do mine now.'

'I admire your resolve.'

'So, when they come and ask where the urn is, we won't give Dad up. To hell with the consequences! We'll tell them they can go fuck themselves.'

'Yes,' Keith agreed, after a pause. 'They can go to hell and fuck themselves when they get there.'

Uncle and nephew fell silent for a moment.

'How the hell are we going to get out of here?' Nick said.

'I don't know. We're going to need a bit of a miracle.'

'I've been such a dick, Uncle Keith. I can't believe I'm tied up in a barn with you, no offence, waiting for a couple of fucking nutters to come back and possibly overcome the statistical barrier of not being able to pull a trigger when faced with the ethical challenge of taking a life. Fuck, fuck, fuck, fuck, fuck! I won't get to see Louise and the kids again, or Barry. I'll be the next one in an urn. How has everything come to this? At least you've had a good innings.'

'Gee, thanks. I'm only sixty-nine.'

'But look at your life, Keith. Your freedom, your bikes, your girlfriend, your friends and followers. You've been living the life of Riley.'

'But I've got nothing to show for it, Nick.'

'What do you mean? You've got fans all over the world. Your channel must be raking it in.'

'I've got no kids, no family life,' admitted Keith, as much to himself as to Nick.

'What do you mean?' Nick was surprised.

'Well, look at you. You've got a lovely wife and kids. I've got none of that. I wanted to be a father. I'd have loved to have had a son and a daughter like your dad did. But it's too late for me now. I haven't got the energy to chase around after a toddler in the park.'

'You'd be arrested,' joked Nick.

'I'm being serious.'

'I know, I'm sorry.' Nick felt foolish and regretted his comment.

'I actually didn't get on with your dad that well. He was such a workaholic. He was quite a bit older than me too, which didn't help. I wasn't planned, apparently. Charlie was, of course. Then he went on to plan every moment of his time, except that in that schedule he had no time for anyone else. It's only his death that has brought me back to the family. To see you and Barbara again has been lovely, and Tracey and your family. You are a lucky man, Nick.'

Nick thought about everything that had led him to this moment and all the fun he'd had during the last couple of weeks despite the financial Sword of Damocles hanging over his head. Who knew what awaited him and Keith right now. 'I've really enjoyed getting to know you too this last couple of weeks. Although I really didn't need to know what you look like naked, wearing a wig.'

'Yes, sorry about that. That was a bit embarrassing. It was cold in that room.'

To their astonishment they both started laughing, though not loudly.

'I realise now how wrong I've got things,' Nick continued. 'I've been trying to do the right thing all along. To work hard for my family, to give them everything they need...'

'That's admirable.'

'Maybe, but at what cost? I've been so focussed on selling my business and making a success of my life to prove myself, to achieve a goal, that I've missed the very reward that's been at my feet the whole time: my family. My wife, my son and daughter. I've missed birthdays, sports fixtures, days out ... Time has run away from me. Where has it all gone? My kids didn't want money, they wanted my time. Time is the most precious currency. Not how we spend it but who we spend it with. I could have sold my business this week, but my pride stopped me doing it and I stand to lose everything now.'

Nick looked over at Keith and saw that tears were streaming down his cheeks.

'I think you're doing exactly the right thing. You didn't sell the business because it wasn't the right price, and you want the best deal for you and your family.'

Nick felt encouraged by Keith's words, delivered in the most authentic way, with no hint of a live-stream.

'And I'm sorry I've pulled your leg a bit. I've let those memes and videos get posted on my channels, but I thought it would help you discover your true self and not turn into the worst version of your father. It was done with love, Nick. I hope you can see that?'

'I can, yes. I understand. I've been spending time with you and my dad's remains doing things that Dad and I should have done together as father and son during his lifetime, to reflect on what it is to be a father myself,' said Nick. 'I don't believe I'm being judged or that Dad's looking down on me now.'

'No, he's not,' said Keith, 'but he is.'

Nick followed Keith's gaze up into the eaves, where the barn owl was showing a great deal of interest in their conversation.

'I think he's looking for mice now we've disturbed his sleep,' said Nick. 'I just saw one running around your feet.'

'Oh great, I hate rodents,' said Keith.

'If I get out of here, I'm going to put things right, Uncle Keith. I will spend more time with my family. I have everything I need. I don't need to work towards some magical goal at which point I'll be able to start living. I'll start living the moment we get out of this fucking mess, provided I don't get shot along the way.'

Surprisingly, Keith didn't answer. Nick looked over and could see that he had closed his eyes and was resting, or meditating, hopefully not passed out. How could he be so calm?

Nick closed his eyes and tried to be more like Keith. The moment he started to notice his breath he was reminded of Toshin and the Buddhist temple. Immediately, he started to feel calmer. The faces of Louise, Charlotte, Harry and even Barry appeared against his closed eyelids. His eyes filled with warm tears and his heart overflowed with love. Thank God it was him here and not them in danger. Everything else in his life seemed not to matter; all that mattered now was getting out of here alive so that that he could see them all again. At that moment he heard the barn door below swing open.

Their time was up.

55

'RIGHT, YOU COUPLE OF bell ends. Time to tell us where the urn is,' the stocky thug said in an almost jovial tone.

So, this was the moment. They would never get the ashes. Nick and Keith had agreed that they could go to hell. It was the principle of the thing.

'It's in one of the panniers on my motorbike,' Keith called out without hesitation, earning himself a look of confusion and then disapproval from Nick. But Nick felt instant relief and gratitude, which he could worry about processing later.

'Throw me the keys,' said the stocky thug.

'That's a bit difficult,' called Keith.

'Don't try and be funny, old man.'

'He's tied up, you muppet,' said the tall thug. 'Go and get the keys from him.'

The stocky thug raised the tall ladder up onto the hayloft edge and climbed up, the ladder protesting creakily at his weight. Once at the top, he hauled himself onto the ledge and crossed over to Keith. 'Right. Give me the keys.'

'I told you, that's a bit difficult,' said Keith.

Oh God, what's he doing? Don't try to be a hero, Uncle Keith!

'Where the fuck are they, old man?'

'Here is the key,' said Keith, awkwardly giving him the middle finger from his tied-up hands.

From the livid look on the stocky thug's face, Nick could tell he was about to go and give Uncle Keith a slap.

'This *is* the key,' shouted Keith. 'My middle finger is the key. The lock on the pannier opens with fingerprint recognition. It's the only way in.'

The thug stood before Uncle Keith, reached down to his side and pulled out a large knife.

'Oh fuck,' said Uncle Keith. 'I did wonder if there might be a downside to this new system.'

'I'm not gonna cut your finger off, old man. I'm not a barbarian.'

The thug knelt down next to Keith to cut the knot at the back of his bonds and Keith shook himself off with audible relief. As he did so, Nick saw the mouse scampering back to the shadows.

'Urgh! What the fuck was that?' said the thug, leaping back out of the way.

'Just a mouse,' said Keith, trying not to laugh at the absurdity of his reaction.

'I fuckin' hate mice. I'll kill it if I see it again!' He took a moment to calm down. 'Right, easy does it. Now, down the ladder you go.'

'I'm not climbing down the ladder with my hands tied,' Keith protested.

The thug asked Keith to hold his hands out and then he cut the ties. Keith shook his hands to get the blood back into them, then descended the ladder, followed by the stocky thug. The ladder screamed at the weight of them both.

'I'm watching you,' warned the tall thug from down below, his gun trained on Keith.

They reached the ground and all three went out into the bright sunlight, Keith leading.

Nick started to feel a panic rising within. Whilst he'd had Keith in his vision, he'd felt a degree of comfort, that everything was going to be okay. Now, with Keith gone from his sight he felt sick and worried. Most of all he felt helpless. His mind filled with a battering of imagined outcomes, and he tried to rationalise the situation. They were wearing balaclavas, which meant they couldn't be identified if Nick or Keith saw them again. He'd seen that in films. If they had no balaclavas on, it would mean they didn't care about being identified, which would suggest they probably intended on killing them when this was all over. So, balaclavas were a good sign, Nick decided. All things considered, it still didn't make him feel any more comfortable.

He tried to drive the thoughts away but couldn't. He remembered again what Toshin had said: to focus only on his breath. As he did this, visions of his family entered his mind once more. He had to get out of this safely and prayed that Uncle Keith would too.

56

NICK DIDN'T HAVE LONG to wait as Keith and the two men soon returned. The tall thug ordered the stocky thug to take the old man back up to the hayloft and to tie him up again whilst he inspected the urn. The stocky thug did as he was told and followed Keith up the ladder.

Once back in the hayloft, he had just started to secure Keith to the beam, tying his hands behind his back, when they heard a scraping and looked behind them to see that the tall thug had pulled the ladder away. It crashed to the ground below, leaving all three of them trapped.

'What the fuck are you doing, Ray?' cried the stocky thug.

Ray. We know his first name now. That doesn't bode well, thought Nick.

'Oh dear, Kevin. Oh dear. You've given away my name. Why don't you just use my surname while you're at it?'

'What, Dyema?'

'You fuckin' half-wit!' The tall thug aka Ray Dyema pulled off his balaclava and looked up at them all. 'I'm keeping this urn for myself, Kevin. There is no need for us to share it.'

'You fucker. I'll kill you!' cried Kevin.

'This wasn't exactly what I had planned, gents,' said Ray. 'I'm sorry but thanks to that muppet, you are all fucked. Please don't take it personally.'

Kevin drew his knife from its scabbard and started to wave it around, promising that once he got near Ray he'd slit his throat from ear to ear. Being in the proximity of such a dangerous and livid berserker, Nick felt panic setting in. Clearly, Kevin wanted to hurt someone to alleviate his anger. It seemed that either he or Keith would do for starters.

It was at that moment that he started to smell smoke rising from beneath them. Ray had started a fire before disappearing.

Kevin whirled towards Nick and roared. Behind him Keith called out to get Kevin's attention.

'Shut the fuck up old man,' screamed Kevin, turning back towards Keith, who'd miraculously managed to free himself from the beam but had not yet managed to untie his hands.

Keith looked around for something, anything to defend himself. It was a little difficult with his hands behind his back. Kevin had not finished the job of tying Keith to the beam properly, but Keith was still at a disadvantage. Keith then demonstrated his extraordinary flexibility by stepping through his hands, so that they were in front of him. It was then that he spotted the mouse. With lightning speed he bent down, grabbed it and threw it at Kevin's head.

Kevin froze. The mouse landed on his balaclava and clung on. It then decided that, given the intensifying smoke, the inside of Kevin's balaclava was the safest place to be and it scurried inside. Kevin went apoplectic with fear and commenced a screaming frenzy.

A silent shadow swiftly swept across the space between Nick and Kevin. The barn owl had seen the mouse and wanted it. The owl landed on Kevin's balaclava and its talons tore into his head. Kevin dropped his heavy combat knife, which fell and sliced open his right trainer, easily piercing the fabric and severing two of his toes. Blinded by the owl and in excruciating pain from the cuts, he reached down and pulled the knife from his foot, but lost his balance. He toppled backwards over the edge of the hayloft and disappeared in a cloud of pure white feathers. Emitting an unholy wail, he fell from the hayloft to the ground below, landing with a sickening crack. His screaming abruptly stopped.

Without a moment's hesitation Keith was on his feet. He grabbed the bloody knife from the floor and cut Nick free. Then Nick cut Keith's bonds. The smoke was beginning to thicken, causing them both to cough.

The fire had not yet spread to the other side of the barn. Keith pulled Nick to his feet and dragged him to the middle of the hayloft, where the narrow beam led across to the temporarily safe side of the barn. 'You first, Nick. You'll easily manage this. It's much wider and steadier than the tightrope you conquered on Sunday.'

Nick looked at the beam and the long drop below, where he could see the body of Kevin lying motionless.

'No, Uncle Keith, you go first. I'll be fine.'

'No, after you—'

'Just fucking go!'

'Okay, okay,' said Keith, stepping forward and taking a deep breath.

'Remember what Gunter said: "Keep your focus ten feet ahead and balance one leg at a time,"' said Nick, grateful for their recently acquired skill.

Keith made his way steadily across the beam, soon reaching safety. Nick was more cautious but soon made his way clear of the worst of the smoke. At this point he became aware of a distant rumble coming from outside and the surreal sound of 'A Bat Out of Hell' being played on some sort of tannoy system. The rumble and the music were getting louder, audible even over the growing roar of the flames.

When Nick was no more than two metres from the end of the beam, the barn door below swung open and Ray Dyema ran in, brandishing his pistol and screaming. He looked up and saw Nick on the beam.

'Where the fuck are they? What the fuck have you done with them?'

The roar outside became deafening as countless motorcycles pulled into the farmyard, a police motorbike blaring out Meatloaf's epic singing through its loud hailer. Ray became increasingly panicked, he had clearly lost control. Nick kept walking forwards slowly. Ray continued to scream up at him, now barely audible over the fire.

The heat and the smoke were getting more intense when Nick became aware of the presence of at least a dozen leather-clad, slightly overweight, late middle-aged men entering the barn. They advanced towards Ray.

Ray pointed the gun at each of them in succession. 'Get back or I'll shoot!'

They all kept walking as one, slowly forward.

Ray screamed again and then fired the gun several times into the air above his head. The bikers ducked and scattered to avoid the bullets.

Nigel, the biker from Milton Keynes with an aversion to peat-based compost, looked up to see Ray Dyema running towards the door at the far end of the barn, dodging falling and flaming debris as he went. As Ray approached the door, a huge section of the hayloft gave way above him and fell down, throwing up a great cloud of smoke. That was the last Nigel saw of Ray.

Meanwhile, at the end of the beam Nick reached Uncle Keith's outstretched arms and stepped to safety. As they quickly descended the stairs, Nick became aware of a searing, burning pain in his right arm.

57

WHEN THE LIVE-STREAM had unexpectedly gone dark, word had gone out amongst Keith's many disciples. Graham the undertaker had called Nick's mum, Barbara, who had tried to call Louise but was unable to get in touch. It was her grandchildren's bring-and-buy sale and she guessed they were busy. Instead, Graham decided to put out a call on the channel to see who was in the area and who could investigate. It just so happened that Sergeant Reggie Hardy was nearby and, if Ken, Terry and Nigel rode fast enough from slightly different directions for about thirty minutes, they too could be in the right area. Graham carefully finished what he was doing and raced to the aerodrome in his favourite hearse.

By the time that the self-named Karmic Cavalry had arrived. Sergeant Reggie had called for more police backup, including an armed response unit, which all the bikers found very exciting, a couple of fire engines and an ambulance in case they needed one. He noted that someone had been premature in ordering a hearse, but you never knew. As it turned out one wasn't needed, but the ambulance was. A stocky man with a record number of broken bones and two severed toes had been dragged unconscious from the barn before the inferno became too great. He was immediately rushed to hospital and would remain there for a very long time.

This whole drama was now being watched by tens of thousands on Keith's channel. Keith was back online, explaining to his followers that quite an adventure had occurred but that he and his favourite and only nephew were fine. He couldn't give full details now as he didn't want to worry anyone – all would be revealed later.

Before the ambulance left, the paramedic patched up Nick's arm. The wound was minor, a mere graze, and the pain he felt came mainly from the burning effect of the heat of the bullet. He cleaned up the wound and dressed it, explaining how lucky Nick had been and that it wouldn't need stitches. But, he suggested, to be on the safe side, Nick and Keith should take themselves to the hospital for a onceover, given the trauma they'd been through and the smoke they'd inhaled.

Police dogs and armed police were scanning the area and questioning people, in case the armed man had survived and was on the loose. No one had seen the tall thug, now known to be Ray Dyema. It was believed that he had perished in the fire but notification was still sent out to all units that an armed man could be on the run and was not to be approached, other than by armed units. This notification accidentally and unofficially found its way onto social media, which created a great deal of excitement. Within ten minutes hundreds of motorcycle scouts were scanning the roads of the immediate area and the surrounding counties, looking for a tall, wiry, angry man with funny eyes dressed in black, but most definitely not wearing a balaclava.

Nick had picked up his phone from the car as soon as

he had the chance and tried to call Louise, Charlotte and Harry, but with no luck. They were either busy with the bring-and-buy or were refusing to pick up. He noticed he had a number of missed calls from the office and from an unknown number. The business sale and the hospital check-up could wait. They were not his priority now. His priorities were his family and the charity fundraiser.

'Keith, we need to get back for the bring-and-buy, but my satnav is showing it to be an hour and a half with heavy traffic.'

'Excuse me, Mr Swift.' One of the more senior police officers present interrupted Nick. 'We need you to come to the station to make a statement.'

Nick desperately tried to make the officer understand that he needed to go and couldn't he please wait to make a statement. Uncle Keith stepped forward to explain what Nick had to do and why it was so important. The senior officer remained insistent they go and make a full statement.

Their conversation was interrupted a second time when Sergeant Reggie Hardy stepped forward. 'Hello Inspector Daley, it's great to see you.'

'Reggie, can you please explain to the Inspector that we need to go,' said Keith.

'Reggie, I didn't know you were here! Good to see you too,' said Inspector Daley. 'You still riding the iron horses?'

'Yes indeed,' said Reggie proudly. 'I was first on the scene, but I'm afraid we have rather a pressing concern here. These two gents really need to get to Welwyn Garden City by 1 p.m., but their satnav is showing 2 p.m. or later due to a number of traffic incidents. If they go down to the station now, they are going to miss a very important event and this chap here may suffer dire domestic consequences as a result.'

Inspector Daley considered the situation for a moment and conceded that if Reggie would make sure they each gave a statement as soon as possible, they could go. 'Please take care, though,' he said. 'There may be a gunman on the loose, although it's looking unlikely. We won't know whether or not he survived until the fire is out and the forensic investigators have checked the site, and that won't be any time soon. So, off you go and don't forget to make your statements as soon as possible.'

'We won't, thanks so much,' said Nick.

Nick's phone ringing interrupted them once more. This time the number that came up on the caller display was the personal mobile number for Jeff Silverman, CEO of PlanIT-UK. Nick excused himself and stepped to one side.

'Hello, Nick Swift speaking.'

'Ah, Nick. Jeff Silverman here. I gather you've been a busy man today. Not even your office seemed to know where you were.'

'Yes, it's a long sto—'

Before Nick could finish his sentence Jeff cut in. 'The thing is, Nick, we need your proposal this afternoon. You need to get to Islington by two-thirty.'

'I thought we were meeting on Friday.' Nick felt sick with the turn of events. 'I'm afraid that's going to be really difficult. Can't it wait until Friday as we'd arranged?'

'Well, it could wait until Friday, but the goalposts have moved and we're looking at another company in the same marketplace as yours. I believe you know the company. SM Enterprise Solutions?'

Dolon. The utter fucker. He was never interested in buying my company, he just wanted to play us.

'Oh, Dave Dolon? Yes, I know him well.' Nick paused, recalling his decision in the hayloft to make his family his priority from now on. 'I'm afraid that I can't possibly be there by two-thirty. I may manage five-thirty, but I'm afraid I have a prior family engagement I can't possibly miss.'

'So, you're saying you can't get here?'

'Not before five-thirty.' Nick didn't even know if he could make that with the roads as they were.

'Well, it's your choice. You either get here as soon as you can, or you miss out. You need to get your priorities straight, Nick,' and with that Silverman hung up.

Nick turned to see Keith walking purposefully towards him.

'Change of plan?'

'Absolutely not,' said Nick resolutely. 'Bring-and-buy, here we come. We just need to get there in time.'

'Leave that to me,' said Keith.

'And me,' said Sergeant Reggie.

'And me ... and me ... and me ...' came all the comments on Keith's feed now that they were live-streaming once more.

58

NICK HAD NEVER FELT a thrill like it whilst dressed in leather and in close proximity to another man, and that was how things should be, he reflected. Moments after their release from the crime scene, a set of armoured leathers, boots, gloves and a spare helmet had been cobbled together for Nick and he had climbed onto the back of Uncle Keith's orange motorcycle, which had far more power than any two-wheeled machine designed to transport human beings ought to have. One of Keith's friends leant Nick his motorcycle outfit. He'd arrived as a pillion passenger, and was volunteered by Keith to drive Nick's car, The Pineapple Express, back home for him. Nick would ride pillion to Welwyn Garden City.

'Check?' said Keith into the Bluetooth intercom.

'Check,' said Nick, feeling like a fighter pilot's wingman.

Sergeant Reggie gave the thumbs up and, turning on his lights, turned out of the farmyard and pulled away, throwing up a huge cloud of dry dust. Within seconds Keith had pulled in behind him and behind Keith, Ken, Terry, Nigel and a host of other followers. Riding in the middle of a motorcycle cavalcade, accompanied by a police motorcycle escort was a boyhood dream come true, and Nick was enjoying every second of it. If only he'd had a motorcycle of his own to ride it would have been perfect. Maybe another time.

Word had gone out and over two hundred motorcyclists

were waiting along the route, ready to block junctions to stop traffic and to occupy lanes where Keith needed to ride. Sergeant Reggie chose to turn a blind eye to this and so did all of his friends and colleagues in the traffic division who took the opportunity that afternoon, realising that it was probably better if they were in charge rather than a couple of hundred Buddhist Hell's Angels, to run an informal exercise in emergency logistics. Should the Secretary of State for Business, Energy and Industrial Strategy ever need to get to or from that particular private aerodrome to a small village hall on the outskirts of Welwyn Garden City, they would have already carried out an exercise to ensure the operation's smooth running.

They rode in silence for a while, with just the sound of the road filling their heads. Keith was filming their ride and shouted occasional callouts to all those bikers en route that he recognised. The turnout of support had been overwhelming and Nick and Keith's journey to the bring-and-buy was gaining increasing online traction the closer they got to their destination.

Nick was the first to break the radio silence. Riding on the back of Keith's bike evoked in him a memory of his father riding his bicycle down a country lane, a fleeting memory of a sepia moment, the accuracy of which had been lost with time. The ashes were lost now and his father, gone. He would not be able to complete the bucket list as his father had wished and would not be able to scatter his ashes for him on his birthday.

'Thanks for all your help and your time since the funeral, Uncle Keith,' Nick shouted through the motorcycle intercom. 'I'm sorry I've put you through so much. You've been there selflessly for me, sharing all the highs and lows.'

'You're welcome, Nick, it was a joy. And there's no need to shout. This intercom is a pretty good one,' said Keith in a crystal-clear low voice. Nick thought he was about to give him too much detail on the make and spec of the intercom but he didn't. He fell silent again, his voice replaced by the rushing wind.

'I really hope,' said Nick breaking the silence, 'that I can have as much of an adventure with my son as I've had with you.'

At that moment Nick and Keith had exactly the same realisation: they cared greatly for each other.

'I wish I'd had a son,' confessed Keith, 'and if I'd had one, I'd have been proud to have one like you, Nick.'

'I think you'd make an excellent father, Uncle Keith,' said Nick. 'From now on I am going to try to be the sort of father to my children that you would have been to yours, had you had any.'

Keith hoped that from now on he could practise being a father to Nick and Nick could practise being the sort of son that he'd liked to have been, if he'd had a father like the sort of father Keith would be. The level of candour they were able to share was made so much easier by the fact that neither of them could look into the eyes of the other, which might have made the situation awkward, irrespective of their leather-clad bodies and close proximity, as Nick clung tightly to Keith, hurtling along on two wheels at nearly ninety miles an hour. It was a beautifully intimate moment shared by just the two of them, or would have been if Keith hadn't forgotten that he was still live-streaming into his other mic. The entire motorcycle cavalcade had to stop by the side of the road temporarily, as they all seem to have got a fly in their eyes at the same time. After a moment, and with their vision no longer impaired, the Karmic Cavalry took off again, heading for the emerald-green city of Welwyn Garden.

As they approached their destination they were met with a long queue of traffic, which the motorbikes were easily able to filter through. At first, Nick and Keith were worried there had been a ghastly incident, but it turned out to be the queue to get into the carpark of Lemsford Village Hall, for the bring-and-buy. The publicity online had snowballed, and the hall was heaving, with buyers snapping up as much as they could and then hoping to get a glimpse of Uncle Keith and his nephew-cum-newly adopted son.

59

NICK TOOK OFF HIS helmet and handed it to Uncle Keith, who told him to go and find his family immediately. The entrance to the hall looked like the top of an hourglass after it has just been upturned, a mass of single-minded souls trying to get on the last remaining lifeboat on the *Titanic*. Nick couldn't see a way through. He was just about to see if he could find another way in when Uncle Keith appeared alongside him on his motorbike.

'Jump back on,' he said.

Nick climbed on and Uncle Keith's bike crept forward. He then pulled in the clutch and revved all 1290ccs of the engine in an explosive, attention-grabbing roar. The sea of people parted as the leather-clad Moses rode through on his iron horse. Uncle Keith rode slowly into the hall, focussing everyone's attention on him. Despite his constant journey towards the total annihilation of the ego through meditation and mindful awareness, Keith basked in the glow of the attention he attracted. At least he was aware of that fact, so he was heading in the right direction on his spiritual path.

Keith came to a stop just inside. Nick stood up on the foot pegs of the motorbike and, now being the tallest person in the hall, had an excellent vantage point. He spotted Charlotte and Louise straightaway but couldn't see Harry. He climbed down off the bike as Keith kicked out the stand, switched off the engine and dismounted. Nick was almost knocked off his feet as a crashing force, rivalling a tackle from Maro Itoje, hit him from the right-hand side.

It was Harry.

'Dad! You made it! You made it!' Harry screamed with delight, as if all his birthdays and Christmases had come at once.

Tears filled Nick's eyes and not just because Harry had crashed into the spot where he had been shot. His body flooded with joy, the endorphins almost entirely alleviating the pain in his arm.

'You are staying this time, right?'

'Yes, I'm here to help and I'm staying until everything is sold,' Nick promised, and he meant it.

* * *

The atmosphere in the room was buzzing. People were buying everything up and more items were being brought in to be sold. People had come from all over to help save the animal shelter. Surely they would raise a decent amount of money from this event? Uncle Keith had made his way to a books and stationery stand, where he proceeded to help out. His arrival on the stand was swamped with people wanting his autograph. He obliged, saying that he would sign whichever books people bought with a dedication of thanks for supporting the cause. Within thirty minutes the book stand was almost clear, with only *Call Me Charlie: The Autobiography of Lord Brocket*, *Budgie: The Little Helicopter* and a well-thumbed *Pop-Up Karma Sutra* left to sell. By the end of the afternoon only the sale of *Budgie: The Little Helicopter* had failed to take off.

Nick went to say hello to Charlotte. She was easy to spot as Nick could see Godzilla looming high above the heads of the shoppers. As Nick approached the table of assorted sports clothing he came almost face to face with Godzilla, or would have done if he'd been six inches taller.

'Hello Mr Swift,' said Godzilla, not sure if he was allowed to be pleased to see him or not.

'Hello … I'm so sorry, I don't think I actually know your name,' confessed Nick.

'It's Tom, Mr Swift. My name is Tom.' At this point Tom struggled even harder to hide his pleasure at finally being acknowledged as having a name.

Nick asked Tom how things were going, and was pleased to hear that they were going 'incredibly well'. However, even if they sold everything in the room they still wouldn't make enough money to save the shelter. The shelter needed an immediate cash injection of £345,231.09 to break even and service debts that had been called in. Ongoing monthly costs were £46,983.22 and the onsite development they needed to carry out meant that they needed to raise another £783,667.98.

Nick was taken aback with Tom's handle on the financial position of the shelter and hoped that it didn't show on his face. It did, but Tom forgave him for it. Charlotte came over to talk to her dad, unhappy to see him and her boyfriend getting along, which was deeply uncool. She played it rather cooler than Harry had but still could not disguise her pleasure at seeing him show up.

'The leather jacket quite suits you, Dad, but aren't you a bit hot in that?'

Nick could feel the sweat running down his back and his arm was throbbing from where Harry had grabbed him. 'I'm sweltering but I can't get the thing off.'

Charlotte offered to help by trying to pull on one sleeve, but it wasn't enough to do the trick.

Louise appeared. 'Oh, for heaven's sake, what are you dressed like that for?' she said. 'You look like one of the Village People.' Louise looked briefly into Nick's eyes and, having made an inkling of connection, looked away again.

'I had to get on Uncle Keith's bike to get here in time,' he started to explain.

As Louise and Charlotte peeled off Nick's jacket, like two squires de-robing their knight, Nick stifled a squeal of pain. The dressing that had been applied to his wound was soaked through with blood, which had started to run down his arm.

'What's happened to your arm, Dad?' asked Charlotte with grave concern.

'It's nothing to worry about. It's just a flesh wound. The dressing must have come loose on the ride,' Nick said through unnecessarily gritted teeth.

'It looks like it needs some attention. What happened?' asked Louise.

'He took a bullet,' said Keith, who'd appeared with a new entourage of followers.

'You were shot?' cried Harry, his eyes wide with wonder.

'Yes, son, but I'm okay, it's fine.'

'It's not fine, Dad. It's cool! I can't wait to tell my friends.'

'That's saved you having to shoot him, Mum,' said Charlotte, glancing at her mother who looked slightly embarrassed by the comment.

Louise insisted that Nick follow her into the kitchen where there was a first-aid box. The small kitchen seemed to be the only space in the hall not crammed like a sixth-formers' party with free booze and the parents out of town. Louise led Nick inside and closed the door. The incessant noise from the hall was further muted when she closed the hatch. Without speaking a word, Louise got Nick to sit down and take off his T-shirt, so she could clean and dress his wound. Nick sat in silence, enjoying her attention despite his pain. How often did he get to spend time with Louise alone? Like everyone else in his family he had neglected her too. She was so beautiful; more beautiful now than the day he'd met her. He couldn't imagine not having her in his life.

Nick's hayloft hostage epiphany had changed his outlook and he hoped it wasn't too late to salvage the situation. The kids seemed so pleased to see him; hopefully Louise would let him back in.

'Louise, I'm really sorry. I realise I haven't been completely honest with you lately. I've been doing all these things for—'

'Not now, Nick. I'm glad you're here today for the kids' sake, but I need some time.'

Nick's heart sank and his hope withered as Louise continued.

'It's not just recent events that have made me think about our life together. I'm too angry to describe how I feel about the repossession notice, but that was just another thing on a long list. I was thinking about a trial separation before that bombshell hit.'

'Is there someone else?' asked Nick pathetically.

'No, there bloody isn't. When the hell do you think I'd have been able to find time to meet someone else? And before you ask it's not about sex, Nick. It's about you being absent from our lives. It's about you not giving any thought to our needs or to mine. We have a family, they come first. You've given more thought to Barry than anyone else. I just need some time to think about it all and I can't do that whilst we're together. And it doesn't look like we'll have a home tomorrow, does it?'

Nick was about to try to explain, but realised that the time wasn't right. Louise didn't want excuses or explanations; she was way too clever to believe anything he might have to say at this moment, and he knew he'd had one too many last chances. Actions, not words were what was needed. So, he said nothing.

'There, that looks better,' she said, inspecting her work, 'but you must go and get it looked at properly.' She packed up the first-aid box in silence and put it back on the wall and then went back to the main hall. Before the door closed behind her, Keith and Sunflower came in.

'There you are,' said Keith. 'Sunflower has something for you.' It was an urn, looking remarkably like his father's.

'What's going on?' asked Nick, now completely perplexed.

'I have a confession to make,' said Keith. 'As you know, I've had my concerns about Charlie's urn for some time, since the time at your mum's and the salsa lesson. So, I decided to collect a duplicate urn from Graham Kerton, which I filled with cat litter – clean cat litter, I hasten to add. I have to confess it would have come skydiving with us, Nick, and Charlie would have missed out on that adventure.' Keith paused, waiting for a response.

Nick said nothing.

'I'm sorry, Nick, you would never have known it wasn't the real urn and neither would your dad. I had planned to simply switch the ashes back before your dad's birthday so that you could scatter him, and not a bag of Catsan, on the beach at Frinton, without you knowing. Sunflower convinced me I should come clean.'

Whilst Nick appreciated Uncle Keith's good intentions, he was unsettled by the fact that he had failed to carry out his father's final wishes. But he knew deep down that it wasn't his father he was letting down, it was himself. He was now no better than his father had been at fulfilling family promises. He realised he desperately wanted to be better than his father had been as it was unlikely now, bearing in mind his injury, that he would be able to complete the jump, the final item on the list before Friday.

Nick's phone rang. It was Brian saying that it was already four in the afternoon and hoping to God that Nick was at least going to try and make an appearance at the meeting in Islington with Jeff Silverman. He had the presentation with him, and all Nick needed to do was show up. Brian sounded wired.

Nick just wanted the whole thing to go away. He felt totally drained and he'd promised to stay until the end of the sale. Walking back into the main hall he saw that things were indeed coming to a close. Charlotte and Harry, seeing him back in the room, ran over.

'Daddy,' said Charlotte, not having called him that in at least three years, 'Sunflower explained to us that you have a really important meeting you need to be at. She explained that it's crucial that you go.'

'Yes, but I'd promised I'd stay here with you guys,' said Nick.

'You must go, Dad. It's fine. We're nearly finished and there are plenty of people here to help,' said Harry cheerfully.

'Yes Dad,' Charlotte agreed. 'You must go and do your deal.'

'Are you sure?'

'Absolutely,' said Charlotte, kissing him on the cheek. 'Go get 'em, Daddy.'

'Good luck, Mr Swift,' said Tom, offering his hand in a most grown-up manner.

Nick smiled as he shook it. 'Call me Nick.'

Tom beamed from ear to ear, which was quite a distance.

60

NICK CALLED BRIAN TO let him know that, according to Keith's estimation, they should arrive in Islington no later than 5.15 p.m. Brian's relief did little to temper his anxiety, however. He might not stand to lose quite as much as Nick if the company went under, but he had a significant amount to gain if this meeting went well. Brian had exacerbated his nervous energy by significantly helping to increase the daily profits of Pret-a-Manger on Islington High Street.

Nick had shared his phone's location with Brian so that his progress could be tracked. Once Brian knew Nick was in the vicinity, he would walk to the Angel Building on the corner of St John's Street and Pentonville Road, but for now he stayed in the coffee shop, his caffeine intake approaching toxic-shock levels. He had been in intermittent text contact with Jeff Silverman's assistant and was assured they were still in the building.

Brian was able to see that Keith and Nick had taken an unusual route down to Upper Street, avoiding the Holloway Road as much as he could. To his relief they had arrived sooner than expected and would be there in seven minutes. He took his sixth tall skinny latte to go, and left the coffee shop, pulse racing, heart bouncing around inside his rib cage like a kangaroo tripping its tits off at a rave. Not that Brian had even been to a rave or tripped his tits off. Okay, maybe once. Not at a rave. Unwittingly at an international convention of Finance Directors in Melbourne, at the Australian-themed fancy-dress night where he was dressed as a kangaroo.

As Brian waited impatiently to cross Pentonville Road, he saw Keith and Nick arrive and pull up onto the pavement. They dismounted and Nick reached for his phone to call him. Like an excited child spotting a Mr Whippy van in a 1970s public information safety film, Brian ran out into the road without looking.

*　　*　　*

Nick and Keith hastily dismounted the KTM motorbike on the corner of Pentonville Road and St John's Street, right in front of the Angel Building. Nick took his helmet off and grabbed his phone to call Brian. Keith had parked on the large section of pavement and said he would stay with the bike. They had difficulty hearing each other due to a sudden cacophony of screeching tyres and blasting horns in the road behind them. They looked round to see a man, clearly high on drugs, dancing in and out of lorries, cars, taxis, van, scooters, cycles and motorbikes as if he were an avatar in a live version of *Crossy Road*. The closer the lunatic got to their side of the road the more recognisable he became. By some miracle Brian appeared before them unscathed other than for the verbal and gesticulated insults of those drivers and riders that had narrowly managed to avoid killing him, though, judging by their reaction, some now wished they might get another chance.

'You made it,' gasped Brian triumphantly.

'You almost didn't. For Christ's sake, Brian, what's got into you?'

'About 1,000 mg of caffeine,' Brian confessed between heavy breaths.

'Have you got the presentation with you?' Nick asked, removing the backpack from his back. He took his father's urn out of the backpack to hand to Keith, to store in one of the panniers.

'Of course, it's right here in—' Brian stopped mid-sentence. He was no longer looking at Nick but now had his gaze focused behind Nick, the look of triumph disappearing as quickly as he had crossed the road.

Nick turned to see a group of suits exiting the Angel Building. At the centre of the group, Jeff Silverman chatted energetically with Dave Dolon.

Dolon looked over and spotted Nick. A hideous grin took possession of his face, morphing him into Batman's Joker.

On seeing Nick, Jeff Silverman stepped forward. 'Sorry, Nick, thanks for coming down but I'm afraid you've missed your chance. SM Enterprise Solutions' presentation was phenomenal. They knew exactly what we wanted and knew about their position in the marketplace. They had an extraordinary knowledge of your operations. Dave Dolon here was able to explain to us exactly what they could offer us over your business. It's a no-brainer for us. Maybe if you'd got here a little earlier as I'd asked, you'd have had a chance. Better luck next time.' He turned away to speak with one of his team.

Dave Dolon took the opportunity to step in. 'Swifty

boy! Nice of you to show up.' He turned and gave Keith, who was still wearing his helmet with a camera attached, a once-over. 'Who's this? Boba Fett?'

Keith was still waiting for Nick to pass him the urn he held in his hands.

'An urn? Is it someone's funeral? Of course it is. It's yours, Nick, or at least the death of SwifTech. Please accept my deepest condolences.' Dolon laughed like an evil madman and then turned on his heels and walked away.

Seconds later a tall skinny latte exploded on the back of his head.

* * *

Nick had no idea that Brian was such a good shot. He'd failed to hit a single clay pigeon on their corporate shooting day, yet his accuracy with the full cup of latte was extraordinary. The cup had been launched in a parabolic arc, with a perfect trajectory, maintaining all its coffee contents as it sailed, almost in slow motion through the air towards the back of the large, very smug head of Dave Dolon. The cup crumpled in on itself, blasting the lid into champagne cork orbit, as the contents burst into a supernova of frothy coffee, which hung in the air for a glorious moment before falling back to earth to shower Dolon in a two-shot, skimmed milk half-litre of warm stickiness. Dolon's shock at the violation immediately turned to anger and he was about to lose control when Jeff Silverman, wiping a little of the spray from his face, said, 'I think you may have asked for that.'

Dolon stopped and, attempting to regain his dignity

with a hard stare, stood for a moment, willing his fury to go off the boil, before turning on his heel.

Nick, Keith and Brian dissolved into uncontrollable hysterics.

It felt so good. As Nick watched Dolon, Silverman and their entourage walk away, he knew he was watching his last chance go with them, but he found himself laughing. Laughing at the absurdity of the situation. When the laughter finally bubbled away, no one said a word. An extraordinary sublime peace descended. The bustle around Nick became a blur and time stood still.

There was a strange comfort in the fact that things couldn't actually get any worse for him at this moment in time. All the anxiety he had felt leading up to this point had melted away. He didn't have to worry about failing because here he was: he had failed, and it didn't feel all that bad. He was with two people whom he respected greatly, who had helped him with every ounce of energy they possessed to make things right for him, but he had fallen at the last hurdle. Nick thought of his kids and felt incredibly grateful to have spent time with them today. He thought of Louise and felt a huge surge of love for her. He resolved to win her back, but first he had to tie up a couple of loose ends. He would take his father on the last bucket list experience, and on his father's birthday he would scatter his ashes on Frinton beach, and wait for the tide to come in and take him away.

Uncle Keith finally broke the peace by gently reminding Nick that he needed to get his arm patched up and then they would have to go and give a full statement at the police station. Brian offered to meet them at the hospital so he and Nick could begin to discuss next steps for the business.

It was at that moment that Brian spotted Josh Wedgwood rushing out of the Angel Building to join Jeff Silverman and Dave Dolon's party.

61

'WHAT ON EARTH HAVE you been up to?' asked Malika in her therapeutically velvet tone.

Nick had been delighted to see Malika in the A&E unit where she had just returned after completing her last rotation. She listened attentively as Nick explained everything that had happened since he'd last seen her.

'Your father would be so proud of you, Nick.'

Nick sighed. 'I'm not sure he'd be proud of my business achievements of late.'

'Oh, I don't think he would care about that now,' said Malika dismissively. 'You have turned a corner. You have committed to something that had nothing to do with proving yourself, or financial gain. You took a man's dying wishes and have honoured them—'

'Not quite, I still need—'

Malika rested a warm hand on his shoulder. 'You have awoken to the realisation that there are more important things in life than your work and the material things it can give you. These things are not precious. You now know what is precious,' she paused, gazing into his eyes. 'Don't you, Nick? Mmm?'

'Yes. Yes, I do,' said Nick sincerely.

Keith was entranced by Malika, and his synapses lit up as he made cognitive connections and stored Malika's words. This was gold dust!

'You know what it is to feel pain?' asked Malika.

Nick nodded, thinking more of Louise and his family than his sore arm.

'We shouldn't be afraid of suffering, Nick. We should be afraid of not knowing how to deal with our pain.' On that note she ripped the adhesive dressing from his arm in one violent motion.

Nick flinched, but decided to embrace the pain. Bizarrely, it worked.

'Do you know who said that, Nick?'

Nick didn't.

'It was Zen master Thich Nhat Hanh, may he rest in peace.'

Keith made another mental note to reread all of Thich Nhat Hanh's writings.

Malika explained that she was about to clean and re-dress Nick's wound. If he had sat still for a while and allowed the wound to heal for a couple of hours before getting on a motorbike, it would have helped. 'You may feel that you are at rock bottom now, Nick, but there is one good thing about being there,' she whispered.

'The only way is up,' said Keith.

'Keith, you are a wise man,' said Malika in a voice that inflated Keith's ego far more quickly than he was able to bring it back down to earth with mindful reflection.

'You're right,' said Nick. 'Although the only way is up from here, tomorrow we will be going up thirteen thousand feet before jumping back down again.'

Malika pursed her lips. 'I'm not sure that skydiving will do your wound any good, but I don't suppose there is much

I can do to stop you finishing the list, is there?'

'No,' said Keith, 'and we may have to come back to pay you another visit, Malika.' He showed no signs of embarrassment of his blatant flirting.

'There doesn't seem to be much wrong with you following your recent experience, does there, Mr Keith Swift?' said Malika jovially. 'All the same, I'll need to give you a once-over. I need to measure your lung function and check for signs of concussion. They should have done that before they let you ride away.'

'I'm fine,' said Keith, rubbing his hands together. 'All the same, where do you want me?'

Nick walked back to the hospital canteen to find Brian sat at a table in the corner. Brian had something to tell Nick about Josh Wedgwood that would come as no surprise.

62

NICK AWOKE TO AN empty house and a heavy silence. Despite the success of the previous day's bring-and-buy sale, the children and Louise were still at her parents' and so was Barry. Though by all accounts Barry wasn't welcome there, as he kept getting on Judi's sofa uninvited and waking Paul at 6 a.m. Louise had dropped Nick a text asking him to fetch Barry as soon as possible.

Nick lay on his enormous lonely bed, staring at the ceiling. He hadn't bothered to pull the blind down and the light had woken him. The early morning sun still had a glint of gold in it, and it highlighted the urn, which sat serenely on top of his chest of drawers. What was so special about it that someone had wanted to steal it?

He sat up and wiped the sleep from his eyes. He stood, stretched and then crossed the room to the urn. Upon inspection he realised he would need a sharp blade to get it open. He would have to take one with him, or open it before he went to the beach to scatter the ashes. He tried to prise the lid off anyway to take a peek inside but was distracted by a roar outside his bedroom window. It was Uncle Keith on a different coloured motorbike.

Nick quickly dressed, grabbed the urn and went downstairs. He let Keith in and went to make some coffee.

344

'So, this is it,' said Keith, 'the last task. After that, we can go and scatter Charlie's ashes on Frinton beach and we will be riding there in RST breathable summer clothing, upon a Suzuki V-STROM 1050XT TOUR.' Keith spoke using his YouTube voice and Nick realised he was being live-streamed or recorded.

'Yes, indeed. The last task on the bucket list. But if you and your viewers don't mind, Uncle Keith, I'd like to go to Frinton beach early tomorrow morning on my own, so that I can scatter the ashes, as my father wished. Just him and me. I hope that's okay. And please don't forget that we are doing the jump today for charity, for the St Francis Animal Sanctuary, which desperately needs your help,' Nick said for the benefit of Keith's viewers.

'I understand. My viewers have heard me speak about nothing else other than how they can donate to St Francis.' Keith turned off his live feed with a customary dismissal and offered to make them both a drink.

As Keith and Nick stood drinking coffee and chatting, Nick had received numerous messages from Brian, something to cheer him up after the news about Josh Wedgwood.

'Brian is asking me if I've looked at the TikTok links he sent,' he said.

'You mean you haven't seen them yet?' Keith was amazed.

'No, I haven't. I haven't had a chance. Brian seems obsessed that I look.'

'And indeed you should,' Keith insisted. 'Oh my God, have a look now. The traction those videos has generated has been exponential. It's amazing, truly phenomenal. The best generated from my channel.'

They spent a few minutes looking at Nick's phone and killing themselves laughing. Nick could not believe how creative people had been, and how many views each post and video had received. Snippets from the live-feed outside the Angel Building the previous day had gone viral. Dave Dolon's unpleasant gloating and evil madman laugh had been made into TikTok videos and memes within two minutes of the live-stream. They spread, first amongst Keith's followers and then spilled into general circulation, with thousands of people creating their own versions of the evil laugh. Photoshopped images of Dave Dolon's face stuck onto Agent Smith's evil laughing face from the *Matrix* films were trending within an hour, followed by TikTok videos comparing Dolon's and Smith's laughs. This soon led to videos with people adding their own laughs, each post tagged #DaveDolon and #SMEnterpriseSolutions.

'This is amazing,' cried Nick.

'Isn't it,' agreed Keith with a great belly laugh.

'Yes, it is. And it's really bad news for Dolon, Silverman and SM Enterprise Solutions. It will do their public image no good whatsoever and the fuckers deserve every bit of it.'

'Look at the time,' said Keith. 'We'd better get going or we'll miss our slot.'

Keith checked Nick's arm to ensure that the bandage was securely fastened. Nick said it felt fine, and he was sure it would be okay. Keith reminded him that he could always pop back with him and get Malika to have a look at it. Both satisfied that it looked good, Nick suited up, put his father's ashes in a small backpack and followed Keith out to his shiny new red-and-grey motorcycle.

*   *   *

The rest of the day passed without event, other than Nick and Keith leaping out of an aeroplane at 13,000 feet and plummeting at 120 miles an hour towards the earth whilst strapped to an instructor, in whom they'd put their absolute trust.

They were at a different airfield from the previous site, as it was now considered a crime scene. Harald, Keith's traumatised skydiving friend, had contacted another skydiving friend who had managed to find them a spare jumping slot at another skydiving friend's nearby airfield and, given that the weather was perfect, and the Vale Skydiving School would receive a lot of free publicity, a deal was struck for two free tandem jumps.

They had both been absolutely silent on the climb up to 13,000 feet in the small aircraft. Nick felt the adrenaline building the higher they got. There was no way on earth that he would ever have contemplated doing a sky dive had it not been for his dad's list. He patted the urn, which was secured to his front in a tiny knapsack. His tandem partner had taken some convincing that it was a good idea, but Keith had used his charm to change his mind. Nick looked out of the window at the clear blue sky and had an image of his father flying past in a skydiving pose, waving, smiling and giving Nick the 'okay' signal.

As the plane reached its apogee so did Nick's

anticipation. Within moments he and his instructor were getting set by the door and, with an enormous rush of air, they were in freefall.

'Woooooooohoooooooo!' cried Nick to the rushing wind. His pulse raced as he looked at the world below him, exhilarated. He couldn't believe he was doing this. In no time at all his tandem partner pulled the cord, the parachute canopy opened and they were floating through the air with a sense of serene calm. Nick looked to his left and saw that Uncle Keith and his partner were floating down too. He expected that Keith would be enjoying this moment immensely. Nick wished he could be suspended there for ever, with the view of the world he currently had, which put everything in his life into perspective.

'Well, that was bloody awesome,' said Keith once they'd landed. 'Of all the experiences we've had in the last week, I think that was probably the biggest rush.'

'So, you think you'll take the sport up now, Keith?' asked his tandem partner.

'In the last week,' said Keith, 'we've been taken hostage at gunpoint, beaten, had someone threaten to hang us and stab us and Nick here has a minor flesh wound from a bullet that might have killed him. So, if you think I'm going to willingly put my life in danger for a bit of a thrill … you'd be absolutely right.'

The best thing about the day was the phenomenal amount of money that had been raised for the animal sanctuary. Nick and Uncle Keith were beside themselves. Nick knew that Charlotte and Harry would be too, and he tried to call them, but they didn't pick up and neither did

Louise when he tried her. Keith took the opportunity to thank his viewers and Nick jumped in and thanked them too.

Keith and Nick thanked the instructors, got suited and booted and then rode back along the A41, up the M1 to Junction 10 and then headed cross-country, skirting Luton, then Harpenden and back to Nick's along the B653. The ride was pleasant, with some enjoyable twisty roads on which Keith could try out his new bike. With the heat from the summer sun beating down from a cloudless sky being offset by a cool, caressing wind, they both felt a sense of calm and stillness despite reaching speeds of nearly 95 miles an hour, though not whilst Keith's camera was in view of his odometer. They soon arrived back in Attimore Road.

'Well, goodbye Nick,' said Keith, giving Nick a great big bear hug. Nick returned the sentiment and gave his uncle a great big squeeze. They then broke away and finished their embrace with strong back slaps.

'Thanks again, Uncle Keith.'

'Good luck tomorrow. I'd love to come with you but I appreciate it's something Charlie wanted you to do alone.'

'Yes. And I need to do it alone.'

'I understand,' said Keith. 'Give me a call after you've scattered the ashes. I'd like to know how it all goes.'

'Yes, of course. And this isn't goodbye. I'm looking forward to seeing a lot more of you from now on.'

'Agreed. And I promise when you see a lot more of me in future, there will be clothes and no wigs,' laughed Keith. 'See you, then.'

'Yeah, see you soon, Uncle Keith.'

Nick watched as Uncle Keith rode off, turning right and

disappearing down Handside Lane. He then went inside to prepare for the following day's event. He needed to get an early night for his early start. He turned towards the house and, for the first time, was glad to see the Pineapple Express sitting on his drive, having been safely delivered by Keith's friend.

Inside his house felt desperately bare and empty. He missed the buzz of his family's energy. He missed their noise and would have been happy to have had clutter to negotiate. Then he heard the click-clack of claws on the hard floor as Barry rushed to greet him as quickly as he could, which wasn't very quick. Barry must have been evicted from Judi and Paul's house and dropped here before Nick had a chance to fetch him.

'Hello old boy,' said Nick, ruffling Barry's head. 'Looks like it's just you and me now. You'll have to come with me to the beach tomorrow.'

Barry didn't look as excited by the prospect as Nick was trying to sound.

Nick wondered how long it would be before the repossession process started in earnest. His house was just a building now, an empty shell. Someone had been busy packing boxes; Louise had wasted no time in getting a company in to prepare for their departure. He came to understand then more than ever, that a home is not a building, but the place where all your loved ones are.

Sighing, he threw a frozen pizza into the oven, took the last beer from the fridge and sat at the kitchen island, next to Charlie's urn. Despite everything facing him, he felt a quiet sense of satisfaction possess him: he had finished the bucket list. There was only one remaining duty to perform. When that was over, he would start to pick up the pieces of his life and this time he would get his priorities right.

Tomorrow was his father's birthday when he would properly and finally say goodbye. Tonight, with the exception of Barry, he would be alone again. He still had his father's ashes and the amazing memories of recent events to keep him company, most of which he would cherish forever.

63

Friday 8th July

NICK HAD SET HIS alarm for 3 a.m. but woke before, worried that he would sleep through it. He wasn't sure if he'd slept at all or if he'd spent the whole night dreaming about being awake and waiting for his alarm to go off. Barry's usual alarm call would have been too late.

It was still dark as he and Barry drove through Coggeshall on the B1024 before re-joining the A120 in the direction of Colchester, where he would turn off onto the B1033 and arrive at Frinton within an hour, according to Google Maps. Slower than a ride with Uncle Keith, but there was no mad rush today.

The air was already warm when he had climbed into the Pineapple Express, and he was looking forward to arriving at the beach and watching the sun rise over the sea. He'd made a flask of strong coffee for the journey and had ransacked the garage, hoping to find the children's old buckets and spades, but they had either packed up or sold everything they could get their hands on to save the animal sanctuary. He'd been up into the loft and managed to find an old box buried deep in the eaves, containing a Peppa Pig bucket and spade set. It wouldn't create a great sandcastle but was better than nothing.

A warm glow flooded his body as he thought of the selfless fundraising Charlotte and Harry had done for the animal shelter. He was glad to have been of assistance, not only on the day itself but by committing to and carrying out the jump. According to Tom, who seemed to have a head for figures, St Francis was going to be fine for a few months more, giving them time to work out a plan. If only he'd been able to say the same for his business, but he'd worry about that after today.

Arriving in Frinton, Nick parked his car on the Esplanade at the junction with Pole Barn Lane. He fetched Barry from the back seat of the car and, armed with the Peppa Pig bucket and spade and his dad's urn, together they made their way across the greensward and down to the beach, dealing with Barry's needs along the way. Although it had still been dark when he arrived, the light was increasing now that the sun was on its way up.

He hadn't been to Frinton since he was a boy, and it didn't look like it had changed at all. The mixture of social and private houses built in the 1930s still stood, and had been beautifully maintained and probably improved. Uninspired but not altogether ugly 1950s constructions stood side by side with the most sublime 1930s Art Deco apartment blocks. The memories of his childhood holidays started to flood back. They came here every year and every time they drove along the Esplanade in his dad's old Morris Traveller, Charlie would remind them that Frinton had been the last target in England attacked by the Luftwaffe in 1944. He always followed this with a joke that they had mistaken it for Canvey Island, even though it was nowhere near and looked nothing like Frinton.

Not surprisingly there were very few people about. Passing a little old lady sitting alone on a bench, Nick gazed out to sea, where he could make out a number of boats and one cruiser drifting not too far away, possibly anchored to a buoy. Much closer and motoring backwards and forwards up and down the coastline was a substantial-looking inflatable dinghy. Its pilot seemed to be looking for something, occasionally stopping and scanning the shore with his binoculars. In the distance were a jogger and a dog-walker. Nearer by, two families had settled themselves by one of the breakwaters and were cooking bacon, the smell of which made him feel instantly hungry. They were here to watch the sunrise, no doubt. The children were mostly teenagers, and they all ran in and out of the water, protected from the cold by their cut-off wetsuits. Nick walked on a bit further until the sound of their excited chatter faded away.

Finding a quieter section of beach, Nick took off his shoes and rolled up his trousers. He felt the cool wet sand under his feet and between his toes. Instantaneously he was transported back to his childhood. Before him, superimposed into his vision, he saw memories of his parents and Tracey. He saw the sandcastles and their old golden Labrador, Fudge, bouncing across the beach.

The tide was quite a long way out, but would be coming in soon. The sky was growing brighter by the moment, even though the sun had still not yet risen above the horizon. Nick took the Peppa Pig bucket and spade and knelt down on the sand. He did his best to build a sandcastle the way he had done as a child and on the few occasions that he had made them for a delighted Charlotte and Harry. Barry watched with interest, occasionally wandering off for a quick sniff, but soon returning again.

He made the keep of the castle quite large and dug as substantial a trench as the tiny pink spade would allow. Once the castle was built, he would scatter the ashes on and around it, and wait for the tide to come in and take it all away. After filling the bucket a few more times, compacting its contents and then upending it onto the sand, Nick was satisfied he had a castle that, although it wouldn't win any prizes, was probably the best he was going to manage with the tools and limited skills he possessed. Barry inspected his work and seemed to approve.

Nick became aware of the change in the intensity of the light. The sun would crown over the horizon soon and would rise up quickly after that. He reached into his backpack and took out a sturdy plastic bag which contained the urn. He rooted around in one of the compartments of the bag to find a Stanley knife, which he used to cut the Gaffa tape securing the lid of the urn. After a short struggle, delicately wrestling with the lid, it came free, and Nick put it down next to his backpack. What was inside that had been so important? He looked, but could see nothing but ash. He approached the sandcastle and began scattering the ashes on and around it.

'I'm sorry that I haven't prepared a speech for this, Dad. I don't want this moment to be all about apologies and regrets. Neither of us can change the past, we only ever have this moment, and in this moment all we can do is sow the seeds of our good intentions for the future and hope that in the infinite moments to come, we will honour them.' He had spent way too much time with Uncle Keith.

The sun was coming up now and with it the deepest, richest orange glow, which lit up the horizon. It added to the warmth on Nick's cheeks, which had started with the tears that now ran down unchecked.

'Thanks for the adventure, Dad. Sorry you weren't here

with me to share it properly. It's time to say goodbye now.' He finished gently scattering the ashes around the castle's edges, upending the urn to make sure every last fragment of ash left it. Barry sniffed the air as he did so.

The tide had turned and was already making its way back towards him. He looked again across the horizon and saw the man in the boat had stopped and was looking at him. Were no moments private these days?

Further away, the other sections of beach were becoming busier as a number of people had come to witness the sunrise. He heard happy shrieks as children ran into the sea, he saw hardened Wim Hof wannabes swimming out and following the coastline, and a brightly dressed jogger in the distance who was running towards him and vaulting the breakwaters in his path.

Nick returned to his backpack to collect his phone, as he'd promised to take a photograph of the castle for his mum, Tracey and Keith, once he had scattered Dad. He put the lid back on the urn and put it inside the plastic bag, inside his backpack. He took his phone and turned to take a photo of the sandcastle. The sun was almost halfway up now and rising fast. Nick walked backwards far enough to get all of the castle in his shot. He had to admit that it looked pretty good. He took a number of shots to be on the safe side and then checked the photos to make sure they weren't blurred and that the quality was decent, knowing that Mum and Tracey would no doubt blow up the photo and hang it somewhere next to other pictures of his dad.

Nick frowned and peered closer at the screen. There was something funny about the castle in the photos. A trick of the light? He shook his head and looked again.

The sandcastle was sparkling.

Amongst the grains of sand, what looked like hundreds of tiny points of bluish and red light twinkled, illuminated by the rising sun. It was as if someone had laid a huge string of fairy lights on and around the castle. He scrolled back to the previous photos. No lights. He scrolled forwards to the sandcastle shot. There they were again.

Nick looked up from his phone in confusion. As soon as his gaze fell on the sandcastle, the lights twinkled before him as if some mystical event was occurring. He looked around to see if any other part of the beach was sparkling in the same way.

It wasn't.

The lights twinkled only where he had scattered his father's ashes, and it was the most beautiful sight he had ever seen.

64

NICK APPROACHED THE SANDCASTLE, intrigued by the heavenly light display. Was he experiencing some sort of spiritual phenomenon linked to his dad's soul? Was this one of those moments – his road to Emmaus? An event no one would believe him when he told them what he thought he had witnessed. But he had it on camera. He bent down to inspect one of the sparkling entities that glittered before him. He picked up the small shining stone.

No. It can't be.

He looked closer, brushing away a few tiny grains of sand. The light danced before his eyes, its character changing as he rolled it around between his fingers, holding it up for the light of the sun to catch its multiple facets. Its beauty almost blinded him.

It was a sapphire! A perfectly cut sapphire! And there were rubies too, hundreds of them, glimmering enticingly in the light.

The tide was further in now and advancing fast. Nick had very little time to collect as many of the precious stones as he could. He ran to his backpack and grabbed the carrier bag. Casting the urn to one side he returned to the sandcastle, Barry following, wagging his tail.

65

FLORA BRUFF SAT ON the same bench overlooking the sea that she sat on every morning. She'd had trouble sleeping ever since her husband passed away three months ago. Derek had loved the beach and had wanted his ashes scattered here, and so she had obliged.

Flora had read somewhere that it was better to get out of bed and do something, rather than lie in bed and ruminate. So, every morning that she woke up just after three, which was most mornings, she would get up and walk down to the beach to be closer to Derek. She loved her hometown of Frinton and had gotten into the habit of clearing up at least one piece of litter or discarded item each day that she came to the beach, to help keep the beach beautiful, clean and tidy.

Today she had picked up a cricket bat, which she would give to her great grandson. With the help of her husband's old pair of binoculars, she saw everything that went on here, which was pretty much the same every day. The same dog walkers, joggers and early morning swimmers. This morning was unusually busy with two families turning up for a picnic breakfast, a tall man in an inflatable dinghy motoring up and down and observing the coastline through some binoculars, and a middle-aged, slightly overweight man who'd built a sandcastle, accompanied by his elderly Labrador.

From Flora's experience, this was all a perfectly normal course of events and no cause for concern. But then things started to get weird.

Having finished quite an elaborate sandcastle, the middle-aged man appeared to scatter some ashes on and around it.

Ah, that's sad, Flora thought, recalling her own private ceremony of three months before.

Next the man had taken a photograph on his phone as the tide started to come in, again fairly normal. Suddenly, he ran over to his backpack and took a plastic bag out of it and, returning to the castle, frantically began scrabbling around on his hands and knees, desperately trying to put the ashes back into his plastic bag. In doing so he completely destroyed the sandcastle he had taken so long to lovingly construct. At the same time, the tall man in the boat watching through his binoculars had started to become very animated.

None of this made any sense but it looked so absurd that Flora couldn't help but laugh. A luridly dressed jogger, who'd deftly vaulted a number of breakwaters and did so every morning, also took great interest in the proceedings.

All this drama was interrupted by a muffled popping sound, which emanated from out at sea and must have come from the small dinghy in which the tall man sat. This caught the attention of everyone on the beach and, moments later, the dinghy deflated and capsized, catapulting the tall man into the water. He began at once to scream for help. It was clear to everyone watching that the tall man couldn't swim and, not wearing a life jacket, would soon drown.

The middle-aged man collecting up the remains of his dead relative was the only person near enough to do anything to help. He quickly tied up the top of his plastic bag and ran a few metres towards the shore, away from the advancing tide. There, he dropped the bag, pulled off his shoes, jacket and trousers, and ran immediately, without any regard for his own safety, into the sea. After acclimatising himself for a few seconds in the cold water, he swam directly towards the drowning man. His dog watched from the shore, barking encouragement.

The tall drowning man soon ran out of energy and surrendered himself to the sea and consequently to his rescuer, who was clearly trained in life-saving techniques.

Flora couldn't believe what she was seeing and after a quick call to 999, she started to video the whole episode on her new smartphone so that people would believe what she'd witnessed, including herself.

Having vaulted the last breakwater into the same section of beach, the brightly dressed jogger decided to find out why a sturdy plastic bag had been left on the beach and what was inside it.

The hero, in just his underpants and a T-shirt, dragged the tall man from the sea and into the shallows, then onto the sand, where he started to give him CPR.

What happened next was most unexpected.

Flora filmed it all on her smartphone.

66

NICK WAS COLD AND exhausted. His T-shirt clung to his skin and his sopping wet pants hung off him like a toddler's full nappy. With Barry shuffling around him in circles, not knowing what to do, Nick used nearly his last ounce of energy pulling the drowning man from the water and onto the shore.

The man was unconscious, and Nick wasn't sure if he was dead or alive. Digging deep, Nick forced himself to remember everything Marnie had taught him that day at the pool. He laid the man on his back and tilted his head back to open his airway. He wasn't breathing and Nick couldn't feel a pulse. Without a second thought, he gave the man five rescue breaths.

Nothing.

Nick started CPR. With both hands together, one on top of the other, he pushed down firmly in the centre of the man's chest, pushing down much further than felt natural or comfortable, but he knew it was the only way to get the heart pumping. He recalled what Marnie had said about the tempo of the pumping and he started to sing 'Stayin' Alive' in a screeching falsetto. But the more he sang about whether the man beneath him was a brother or a mother, it didn't look like he was doing much in the way of staying alive, despite Nick's meticulously regular and furious pumping.

Come on man! Wake up!

Nick continued the chest thrusts and simultaneously screamed the mostly wordless chorus, but the man remained unresponsive.

Until…

Whether it was the pumping or Nick's terrible Barry Gibb impersonation that did it, the man took a huge, gasping breath, and his eyes sprang wide open as he started coughing, vomiting up a great gush of sea water.

Nick ducked out of the way, staring in a mix of horror and elation. There was something familiar about this man. Was it …?

Those eyes.

In that instant the penny dropped. One of the man's eyes appeared to be a different colour from the other, the left eye staring at Nick with a fixed and dilated pupil.

Nick recoiled.

It was Ray Dyema, the thug who'd held him hostage at gunpoint, then tried to burn him to death and shoot him. Nick was possessed by a terror far worse than the one he'd experienced in the hayloft.

This was *Cape Fear*, Frinton-style.

67

RAY CAME TO WITH a start. Before that moment there had been only black. He had no recollection of what had happened or how he had got onto the beach. His senses were being assaulted from an infinite number of angles. His chest was bruised, his ribs felt broken, his lungs burned, his vision was blurred and he was freezing cold and soaked through. To add insult to injury, a smelly old dog with foul breath was sniffing him judgementally. He gasped desperately for air and instinctively lashed out at the person leaning down on him, the person who was pounding his sternum with all his weight. He rolled over to his left, out of the way of his attacker, and reached down to his belt, pulling out his British Army Survival Knife. He struggled to a kneeling position and then to his feet.

His assailant, about to run away, tripped on a Peppa Pig bucket and spade and stumbled over.

Ray leapt forward and grabbed him by his wet T-shirt, shoving the dog out of the way. The old dog snarled and, bearing its teeth, started barking furiously.

Ray's brain had rebooted, the blackout had cleared and he knew where he was and why he was there. This was definitely Plan B … but he didn't have a Plan B. He would have to improvise.

Today should have been straightforward, but just like every other episode so far in this fucked-up saga, something had gone wrong. He had planned to take out Nick Swift just before he scattered the ashes, but a wave had hit his dinghy as he'd pulled out his gun ready for his assault and he'd put a bullet in the boat, sinking it.

He'd had to overcome his crippling fear of water just to get in the dinghy in the first place. Ray's lust for the jewels and the wealth they would bring had buoyed him up just enough to overcome the paralysing effect that water usually had over him. Going on the water was a risk worth taking. He had stepped outside of his comfort zone and conquered his fear. The rest shouldn't have been so complicated. He'd planned to come to shore, take the urn with the jewels in it and return to the larger cruiser, anchored just out to sea, in which he was going to escape across the channel, never to be seen again. With everyone thinking he was dead, it had been the perfect plan.

But now he had no gun and no escape craft. He did have a very nasty knife, which he knew how to use, and the man with the jewels and his fortune was, quite literally, within his grasp.

68

'WHERE THE FUCK ARE my jewels?' Ray Dyema screamed. 'And shut your fuckin' dog up!'

Nick was too cold and exhausted to struggle any more. Saving his attacker had taken all his strength. He began to feel the last of it drain away. His instinct to survive for the sake of his family was greater than his desire to hold on to the rubies and sapphires. Dyema could have them and be damned, so he chose not to fight but it appeared Barry had not understood this and stood his ground, barking ferociously at Nick's attacker. Dyema waved the knife in Barry's face and Barry snapped, showing a terrifying set of teeth, and managed to evade the attack, backing off momentarily out of Nick's sight. Dyema slashed at Barry again, finding only empty air.

'Leave my dog alone,' cried Nick.

'Where are they?' Dyema screamed again. 'Where the fuck are they?'

'They're in the bag, they're in the fucking bag, over there.' Nick turned and pointed towards the place where he'd left the bag only to see a man, dressed in bright running clothes, jogging up the beach towards the walkway with the bag in his hand.

Ray looked on in horror as the jogger progressed up the steps towards the beach huts and let out another cry of rage. He raised his knife high into the air.

This is it, thought Nick. *This is the end.*

But it wasn't.

The cry of rage Dyema let out was actually a cry of pain. Nick turned to see Barry snarling furiously, having attached himself to Dyema's rear end. Galvanized by Barry's heroic loyalty and using energy he didn't know he had left in him, Nick pulled himself towards Dyema and headbutted him in the nose, hearing a sickly crack as he did so. Dyema fell away to Nick's left and, now released by Barry, got to his feet.

'I'll fuckin' deal with you two later,' Dyema growled through a bloodied mouth. He sprinted off after the jogger, his progress hindered not only by a sore buttock and a smashed nose but greatly weighed down by his wet clothes.

Nick lay where he was, relieved to be free of Ray and too exhausted to move. An extremely excited Barry came and gave his face a tongue-bath. Nick turned to see Dyema gain some ground on the jogger. A little old lady on a park bench was capturing events on her smartphone.

As the highly visible jogging jewel thief drew parallel with the last beach hut before the path back to the esplanade, a stranger stepped out of the shadows and stood in his path. The stranger was dressed in motorcycle clothing and wore heavy boots, one of which was plenty good enough to trip the thief over and send him careering to the ground, dropping the bag, which the biker from the shadows deftly retrieved to the applause of the old lady with the smartphone. The jogger picked himself up, brushed himself off and ran on, not feeling so bright now, despite his appearance. His running jacket shone with reflected blue and red light as he disappeared across the greensward. The biker watched him run away and let him go.

Nick looked on in amazement. There was no mistaking it: the biker was Uncle Keith and now Dyema was closing in on him. Feeling newly invigorated, Nick heaved himself up and sprinted towards the walkway, Barry at his heels.

As Keith turned back towards the beach, he was confronted with the sight of a soaking-wet Ray Dyema brandishing a large and lethal-looking knife.

'Just give me the fuckin' bag and you can go.'

Keith froze, staring into the face of his assailant with defiance. He clearly recognised him.

Oh no, thought Nick, *don't be a hero. Remember what Giuseppe said. A knife means that you run.* 'For fuck's sake run, Uncle Keith!' Nick screamed at the top of his voice. 'Run, Uncle Keith, run!'

Uncle Keith did not run. He stood his ground as Dyema crept towards him like a lion approaching his prey.

69

NICK LOOKED ON IN horror, helpless as Dyema came within striking distance of Uncle Keith. He raised his dagger high above his head, preparing to slash Uncle Keith across the body. Nick knew that although Keith's jacket would afford some protection, it wouldn't stop Ray's blade from causing grievous if not fatal, injury.

At the same moment two policemen emerged from a patrol car that had driven across the greensward, in blatant disregard of local by-laws, and sprinted down the path to the walkway. They shouted out to Ray to put down his knife; one was brandishing a Taser.

Ray didn't get a chance to comply, even if he'd wished to as, at that exact instant, from behind, a cricket bat smacked him hard across the side of his head, sending him spinning into the side of a beach hut. The force of his own weight bent his knife hand back against himself and he fell upon the blade, piercing his side, and sending him to the ground in intense agony.

Astonished by her actions, Flora dropped the cricket bat and took a few steps backwards. The two policemen attended to Ray, restraining him and telling him not to move or try pulling the knife out, as it could make things a lot worse. One officer radioed for an ambulance and applied pressure around the wound. The other asked Keith if he could go and retrieve a first-aid kit from the back of their car. Keith did so and was back within a few minutes.

Drained and relieved, Nick made it to the top of the steps to be greeted by Keith, who embraced him in a great bear hug before patting Barry, and then turning to see if the little old super-lady was okay.

Twenty minutes later, Ray Dyema was being blue-lighted to A&E and Nick, Keith and Flora were all sitting peacefully on Flora's bench, all except for Keith, wrapped warmly in blankets from the ambulance. Even Barry, who had curled up at Nick's feet, had been given one. They were all drinking coffee, generously donated by the two picnicking families, but had turned down a polite offer of a bacon sandwich. Keith was now beginning to regret this decision as he watched Barry gobble up a sandwich given to him by a blond-haired boy.

They sat for some time explaining to Flora just how events had led to this point and how important her role in bringing the saga to a conclusion had been. Flora wished them well, especially Nick and his family. She hoped that he could repair his relationship with his wife and suggested she might appreciate a pair of sapphire or ruby earrings now that he could afford them. She would look forward to giving the cricket bat to her grandson, once it had been returned from police evidence, as it had quite a story attached to it now, and objects only had value if they had a use, or a story attached to them. Keith made a mental note of this pearl of wisdom.

Flora agreed that she would meet Keith another time to discuss the merits of Frinton-on-Sea, as it would make a great day-tripping destination for all his biker friends.

Frinton had a lot of history, she said.

'Did you know that it was the last place in England to be bombed by the Nazis?'

70

ESCAPADE ON THE ESPLANADE

--- Clacton and Frinton Gazette Online ---

This morning, local hero Mrs Flora Bruff, 84, foiled a robbery on Frinton beach, in front of the Esplanade.

The great-grandmother of three and lifetime resident of Frinton-on-Sea saved a man from attack and foiled a jewel theft. Who'd have believed it could happen in Frinton?

Picking up a discarded cricket bat, five-foot-one Flora singlehandedly disarmed Ray Dyema, 32, a six-foot-two bailiff and ex-soldier from Hertfordshire, with a striking blow across the side of his head.

'I knocked him for six!' she triumphantly declared.

The England cricket team could certainly learn a thing or two from Flora!

The rubies and sapphires, said to be worth millions, originally belonged to deceased jeweller Anthony Dyema, a relative of Ray Dyema, who is now in police custody in a secure hospital ward where he is recovering from an allegedly self-inflicted knife wound. Ray Dyema had planned to escape with the jewels on a motor cruiser to Holland. He claims he has no memory of recent events.

In his will, Ray Dyema's uncle, Anthony Dyema, stated that whoever found the jewels could keep them. Anthony Dyema was survived by his wife Valerie, who tragically died shortly after his funeral in a domestic accident.

Nick Swift, who was also attacked by Dyema, discovered the jewels in his father's urn whilst scattering his ashes at his family's favourite holiday destination and is now their legal owner. Asked what he would do with his newfound fortune he politely refused to comment, saying that all he wanted to do was go home to his wife and family with his dog Barry, who had also helped fight off Dyema.

Keith Swift, Nick's uncle, who hosts the popular blog *Karmic Keith's Motorcycle Mantras* and was with him that day, said that it had been a very stressful time for the family, and everyone was glad that it had come to an end. The Swift family were eternally grateful to Flora for her courage and selflessness, commenting that she deserves a medal.

If only she'd been standing on the beach with her cricket bat in 1944, the Nazis might have thought twice about coming to Frinton.

EPILOGUE

NICK LOOKED OUT ACROSS the infinite calmness of the beach. This was truly the happiest he had ever felt. It wasn't a feeling of euphoria or a sugar-rush high, but a complete absence of worry accompanied by a feeling of immense contentment, acceptance and unconditional love for those around him. The feeling you get when something has an ending and a beginning, all rolled into one. A realm of infinite possibilities.

The summer sun gently warmed his face, and he closed his eyes and turned his head to fully embrace its rays. He took a deep breath in through his nose, filling his head with saltiness, whilst a gentle whispering wind quietly teased his ears.

It had been just over a month since he'd last been in Frinton. The party just a week ago had taken most people a week to recover from. Everyone from Sergeant Reggie to Giuseppe had attended, Salsa-dancing the night away in Barbara's garden under the close guardianship of an eclectic mix of at least eighty motorcyclists. Undertakers had danced with skydivers; motorcycle policemen had danced with art teachers and a diminutive Buddhist monk had learned how to disable someone pointing a Glock 17 Gen 4 pistol at him; you never knew what could happen in a Hemel Hempstead monastery, after all. The master of disguise and deception, the Magnificent Mysterioso, had promised to come but had failed to make an appearance. He may have been there, but no one knew for sure.

To everyone's delight the animal shelter had been saved, and one ecstatic crematorium technician had found a rare breed of cat she'd immediately given a home to. Her boss from work, Ms Perkins, had generously offered to buy it for her at the same time as giving her a gift of a portrait of Amira as Venus, which she'd painted. Amira pretended she liked it and it now hung above Giuseppe's bed.

Uncle Keith had increased his following exponentially and was delighted to now have over one and a half million fans. That evening Keith got even more attention than usual, especially from Lillian Anderson, who'd been invited along from Lido Mansion. With Sunflower following her free spirit to India, Uncle Keith now had a new girlfriend, but it wasn't Lillian. Much to Lillian's disappointment Keith proudly introduced his new soulmate, 'spiritual guide and goddess of great wisdom', Malika.

For now, Nick's future was financially secure. He'd kept some of the jewels, but had given quite a few away, not only to support the animal shelter but the homeless charity too.

Following a PR nightmare with Dave Dolon's SM Enterprise Solutions, Jeff Silverman had made Nick a generous offer for his business. After a brief negotiation swinging in Nick's favour, an agreement had been reached, Nick selling a sizeable portion of his stock, but retaining some. Nick would work for the next twelve months providing business continuity through an earn-out before taking a year's sabbatical, during which he intended to spoil his family rotten and spend all his time with them. The business would then be safe in the hands of PlanIT-UK's new Chief Financial Officer, Brian, who had decided not to retire, saying he still had many more spreadsheets in him and that he had found new purpose in his role as mentor to PlanIT-UK's new apprentice accountant, Tom, Charlotte's boyfriend.

Nick opened his eyes to inspect the magnificent sandcastle before him. It was, without doubt, the best sandcastle he'd ever had a hand in creating. Next to Barry, who appeared to be on guard should any criminals appear from the sea, Harry was crouching in the sand, further deepening the trenches before the tide came in, whilst Charlotte added fine detail to the main tower. Behind them Tom deftly calculated how many more buckets he needed to load with sand to complete the line of fortified towers along the trench to the sea.

Louise turned to Nick and smiled, the wind gently blowing back her hair to allow her beautiful sapphire earrings to sparkle in the sunlight. While the jewellery had sweetened the events of the past months, it was Nick's devotion to completing his father's list and promise of undivided attention for his family from now on that had convinced her to stay. They held each other's gaze for a while before Nick turned to look back out to the horizon.

He thought of his dad and the adventure they'd shared. He had no idea what had happened to Charlie's actual ashes, but it didn't matter. Keith had been right about that. It was the sentiment that mattered.

'Goodbye Dad,' Nick murmured to the sea. 'Wherever you are.'

He turned and took Louise's hand. Together they made their way back towards the walkway, where a little old lady, sitting on a bench and holding a pair of binoculars, waved at them.

ACKNOWLEDGMENTS

In the first instance I'd like to thank Bryony Sutherland, my editor, for believing that I could do this and helping me to produce the book I hope you will have just finished reading. Her attention to detail, skill and creative input have been invaluable. Above all else she was a joy to work with, she held my hand when I 'killed my darlings' and when it looked like some research I should have done more thoroughly before I wrote the book threatened to end its life there and then, she saved the day with a solution I hadn't seen. Without her calm advice in my personal 'all is lost' moment there may well not have been a book at all. Thanks so much B, I'm really looking forward to the next book. I promise to do most of my research before I start writing 94,000 words.

I'd like to thank award-winning cover designer Jamie Keenan, for agreeing to do the design work, for his unbridled enthusiasm for the project and for his phenomenal design, making my novel look like a proper book.

Before I thank my beta readers I'd like to thank those professional organisations who helped me with my research: Kelly Starling, David Fisher at De Beers Group R&D, Aurore Mathys, FGA, EG, of the Gemmological Association of Great Britain, The Cremation Society of Great Britain and Tim Jones, of Bradley & Jones Funeral Directors of Pinner. Tim was kind enough to treat me to lunch on my birthday, and he answered all my questions with great humour. If he is still around when I pop off into the great unknown, he'll get the gig.

The financial jeopardy Nick faces in the book didn't quite work in the first draft. I'm extremely grateful to two of my mates, Tim Parfitt and Jim Keddy, for spotting it. I am grateful to Ian Mitchell for his help and to Paul Jesson for his time and expert advice in helping me make the jeopardy credible.

I want to thank all those people that took the trouble to read the first couple of drafts and for feeding back, especially my wife Kate, who was greatly relieved that it wasn't awful. My thanks also to Poppy, my daughter and to Anita Parfitt and Fiona Martindale, not my daughters.

Special thanks goes to my friend Simon Thompson, who read and loved the book so much that he introduced me to a potential agent.

Thanks to Sally McFall for introducing me to Peter Darman, author of historical fiction, and to Peter himself for pointing me in the right direction to self-publish.

Thanks to one of my environmental activist buddies David Woodcock, who set up and designed my website so quickly for me.

Finally, thanks to my friend and polymath Andrew Rajan, who shared his experience of self-publishing with me. His enthusiasm for his art and life has always been an inspiration to me. If I've missed anyone out I apologise, and promise to include you in the next book's acknowledgements. Provided you read that one.

About the Author, me, TIM ARMSTRONG-TAYLOR

This is my first novel. The first one I have finished, that is. I started one about thirty years ago but never finished it. I think we can all be glad about that. It wasn't very good.

When I'm not writing I am immersed in music as a teacher, conductor and listener, who occasionally dances when no one is watching. I love walking, my Royal Enfield Himalayan and nature. I am a passionate environmentalist. My greatest joy in life is my family, including my dog Reggie, a black Labrador. The dog in *An Urn for the Worse* is dedicated to the memory of another black Labrador, Bramble, who brought so much love and entertainment to us all.

I hope this book will be the first of many. I would love to hear your thoughts on it, and would be grateful if you would sign up to my mailing list on my website (armstrong-taylor.co.uk) for more details of my future writing. Please, please, please leave me a review on Amazon so that lots of people can see how much you liked the book (hopefully) and buy one themselves or for a friend, or an enemy if you didn't like it – in which case, I apologise. Thank you for reading *An Urn for the Worse* and for taking the time to read this bit too. It will be different in my next book, as I'll be able to say that I've written one book already.

Printed in Great Britain
by Amazon